A MUSE OF FIRE

O, for a Muse of fire, that would ascend
The brightest heaven of invention!

Shakespeare, *Henry V*

A Muse of Fire

LITERATURE, ART AND WAR

A.D. Harvey

THE HAMBLEDON PRESS

London and Rio Grande

Published by The Hambledon Press, 1998

102 Gloucester Avenue, London NW1 8HX (UK)
PO Box 162, Rio Grande, Ohio 45674 (USA)

ISBN 1 85285 168 6

A description of this book is available from
the British Library and from the Library of Congress

Typeset by The Midlands Book Typesetting Co., Loughborough

Printed on acid-free paper and bound in
Great Britain by Cambridge University Press

Contents

Acknowledgements

Part of Chapter 6 is a shorter version of an article entitled ' "Oh, What a Literary War!" An Alternative Version', published in the *London Magazine*, 33, no. 9/10. I am grateful to the following for permission to reproduce poems: 'Where Are the War Poets?', from *The Complete Poems* by C. Day Lewis, published by Sinclair-Stevenson (1992). Copyright © 1992 in this edition The Estate of C. Day Lewis; 'Landscape with Figures', from *The Complete Poems of Keith Douglas*, edited by Desmond Graham (Oxford University Press, 1978), by permission of Oxford University Press; 'An Inscription for Dog River' by Kenneth Slessor, by permission of the University of Queensland Press.

Introduction

This book is neither a bibliography nor a summary of existing scholarly literature. It is merely one individual's attempt to see some pattern in the responses of writers and artists to the phenomenon which, more than any other, has dominated the imagination of the twentieth century.

The story I have to tell is of how war, at first a surprisingly disregarded topic, became by degrees more acceptable as a theme for writers and artists till, with the outbreak of the First World War, it emerged as perhaps the greatest theme of all; of how this theme was handled by those who fought in the First World War, both with regard to what they tried to say and how they tried to say it; of how far writing about the First World War contributed to the renewal of war in 1939; and how it shaped, if not perceptions of the new war as such, at least the way those perceptions were written up. But this story is also the story of war itself, of its increasing scale, cost and horror, and of those who found other ways of responding to its challenges besides writing about it or painting it. I hope I will be forgiven if I have occasionally dwelt with excessive detail on some of the odd dark corners of war that have eluded the attention of military historians.

Birth, prejudice and want of opportunity have caused this survey to take on a predominantly British perspective but the account I have tried to give would have been meaningless without reference to the literature and art of other countries, and if at times I use foreign examples simply to back up my British material in other instances I have had to emphasize the independent trajectory of developments beyond the English Channel. Similarly I have tried to present developments in art as providing parallels with developments in literature, but on occasion have found them apparently moving in different directions.

I have generally made use of published translations of prose works originally written in other languages, when available, though a number of important texts have never been rendered into English, including F.T. Marinetti's gimmicky war sketches and Werner Beumelburg's *Die Gruppe Bosemüller* ('Bosemüller's Squad'), which sold a million copies in Germany during the Nazi period. The translations offered of poetry are my own, but as Robert Frost said, 'Poetry is what is lost in translation' and a number of passages have been printed in the original, in the belief that some readers will want to pause and read them out aloud.[1]

I have brought my account only down to 1945 – just over fifty years ago at the time of writing. Since 1945 wars have not ceased, but with the exception of the Arab-Israeli conflict and the internecine struggle in post-Communist Yugoslavia none have been fought by whole societies of people accustomed to the material and social conditions of western civilization, and the question of war's place in cultural development and the issue of comparison between different cultures involved in the same war have not had the same relevance as they had in the first half of this century. War has also, in a sense, been commercialized in this era of global media networks, and writing about war has been commercialized too. Before 1918 nobody ever thought of joining the army with the primary motive of being able to write a war book, and though it seems likely that the idea occurred to people between 1939 and 1945 they were subject to universal conscription in any case. Some of the finest writing ever published about war has come out of the Vietnam conflict of the 1960s and early 1970s (though nearly all of it from one – or part of one – side) but amongst the peculiarities of the Vietnam War was the way the Americans instantly identified it as something to be written up: of 429 novels dealing with the conflict published between 1964 and 1988, fourteen came out as early as 1966 and twenty-two in 1967. And most of the best of these books seem to have been written by men who went (or were sent) to Vietnam to write about it. Michael Herr, author of *Dispatches* (1977, perhaps the best of the lot, though it provoked an outrage reminiscent of that

[1] Louis Untermeyer, *Robert Frost* (1964), p. 18. (All books cited were published in London unless otherwise stated.)

provoked by Erich Maria Remarque's First World War classic *Im Westen Nichts Neues* forty-eight years earlier) was a newspaper correspondent, as was David Halberstam (*One Very Hot Day*, 1968) Robert Stone (*Dog Soldiers*, 1974) and William Eastlake (*The Bamboo Bed*, 1969). Robert Lowell Moore (*The Green Berets*, 1965 – not amongst the best Vietnam novels in quality but probably the best-known) was an advertising consultant. Philip Caputo (*A Rumor of War*, 1977) was in Vietnam as a lieutenant in the marines but returned as a correspondent. Gustav Hasford (*The Short Timers*, 1979, filmed as *Full Metal Jacket*, 1987) was a marine, but assigned as a 'combat correspondent'. John Del Vecchio (*The 13th Valley*, 1982) had a similar assignment in the US Army. David Rabe, author of the plays *Sticks and Bones*, 1971, and *Streamers*, 1976, was in a hospital support unit and, despite Vietcong guerilla activity, seems not to have come particularly close to the sharp edge of war: he claimed that a formative experience for him was seeing soldiers 'standing around some bar like teenagers at a soda fountain, talking coldly of how many of their guys got killed in the last battle'. The two most important books by people sent to Vietnam in order to blow away Vietnamese are *Born on the Fourth of July* (1976) by Ron Kovic, a prominent peace campaigner, and *Chickenhawk* (1983) by former helicopter-pilot Robert Mason, but they do not subtract from the impression that the best writing about the war was by onlookers.[2]

The author of the following pages has not even been an onlooker in war. If he had been he would have written a different book. The historian's understanding and personal framework of reference are as much a part of his working materials as his sources. No doubt personal experience of being shot at would have provided extra insight; but if the author had been a newspaper correspondent in Vietnam, or a soldier in the Falklands (let alone a cavalry trooper at Waterloo, an infantry subaltern at the Somme or a fighter pilot in the Battle of Britain) he would necessarily have written with a different perspective from the one adopted here. One can only do one's best with what

[2] John Newman with Ann Hilfinger, *Vietnam War Literature: An Annotated Bibliography of Imaginative Works about Americans Fighting in Vietnam* (New York, 1988 edn), passim; David Rabe, quoted in Francis Carol Locher, ed., *Contemporary Authors, 85–88* (Detroit 1980), p. 482.

A recent contribution from the North Vietnamese side is Bao Ninh's *Thân phân cua tình yêu* (1991; English translation published in 1993 as *The Sorrow of War*).

one has. We who were born after 1945 and whose wars either never quite broke out (like the Russo-American H-bomb war), or else occurred as edited television footage from another continent, have been shaped by defeats, disillusions and betrayals no less maiming, even if so much less picturesquely violent, than those experienced by our fathers and grandfathers; we are not unqualified to write about dark times. Paul Fussell dedicated his best-selling *The Great War and Modern Memory* to 'Technical Sergeant Edward Keith Hudson, Co. F 410th Infantry, killed beside me in France March 15, 1945'. I should like to dedicate this book to all those who, after their death, have been used as alibis.

Part One

Before 1914

O! for a Muse of fire, that would ascend the brightest heaven of invention;

Shakespeare, *Henry V*

CHAPTER 1

From Shakespeare to Goya

THE RENAISSANCE is sometimes described as representing the birth of the modern, but by no means all modern ways of perceiving and doing things can be traced back to the fifteenth and sixteenth centuries. For example, neither the poets nor the artists of the time seem to have had much interest in a topic which from about 1500 onwards was both a key preoccupation of governments and an immediate concern of growing numbers of individuals. Improvements in technology and communications meant that the scale, expense and destructiveness of war grew exponentially during this period – as Albrecht Dürer said in 1527 'the necessities of war weigh more heavily and in a new manner upon our age' – yet they seem to have had little impact on the imaginations of those not directly involved.[1]

The best-known of the battle paintings by Paolo Uccello in the fifteenth century were of imaginary contests, though in the late 1450s he executed a picture of a skirmish that had occurred in 1432, the Battle of San Romano. The National Gallery in Dublin has an almost contemporary painting, by an anonymous artist, of the Battle of Anghiari of 1440, a Florentine victory over Milanese troops which helped cement the dominance of the Medici family in Florence: this work is even more stagey and static than Uccello's, and shows remarkably few combatants. The same battle, sixty-three years later, was chosen by the government of Florence as the subject for the frescos they commissioned to decorate an extension of the Palazzo della Signoria. In

---

[1] J.R. Hale, *Artists and Warfare in the Renaissance* (New Haven, 1990), p. 169, for the quotation from Dürer.

the event the project was never completed, but Leonardo da Vinci's preparatory cartoons inspired generations of painters specializing in battle scenes, including Luca Giordano's *The Battle of Constantine* of 1523–24, which has been described as 'the greatest of all finished Italian battlepieces'. *The Battle of Constantine* showed, in modern dress, a battle that had occurred in AD 312. A similar transposition of the present into the past occurs in Albrecht Altdorfer's masterpiece *The Battle of Alexander*, but though prints and drawings of soldiers were popular, at least in Germany, of the great battles of the sixteenth century only Lepanto, western Europe's last anachronistic victory over the Turks, seems to have been commemorated in a contemporary painting. Even the defeat of the Spanish Armada, which instantly took a key position in England's national mythology, had to wait twenty years before being made the subject of a painting on the grand scale.[2]

Something similar occurred in literature. In England, Elizabethan and Jacobean playwrights steered clear of contemporary themes. The most up to date Shakespeare ever got was the reign of Henry VIII, which closed seventeen years before his birth, and though George Chapman, in his tragedy *Bussy D'Amboise*, ventured down to the 1580s, not much more than twenty years earlier than the time of writing, his subject was from the history of a foreign country, and he was in any case probably much more interested in his translations of Homer. It was not that writers were totally unresponsive to contemporary events: during the 1590s soldiers were frequently to be encountered in the streets and taverns of London, and in *Henry V* Shakespeare showed a convincing familiarity with their manners and habits:

> *Gower*:   Why, 'tis a gull, a fool, a rogue, that now and then goes to the wars, to grace himself, at his return into London, under the form of a soldier. And such fellows are perfect in the great commanders' names: and they will learn you by rote where services are done; – at such and such a sconce, at such a breach, at such a convoy; who came off bravely, who was shot, who disgraced, what terms the enemy stood on; and this

---

[2] Ibid., p. 154; ibid., p. 167. A painting conflating various incidents in the Armada campaign was executed early in the reign of James I, and is reproduced as plate 53 (between pp. 240 and 241) in Colin Martin and Geoffrey Parker, *The Spanish Armada* (1988).

they con perfectly in the phrase of war, which they trick up with new-tuned oaths: and what a beard of the general's cut, and a horrid suit of the camp, will do among foaming bottles and ale-washed wits, is wonderful to be thought on.

(*Henry V*, act III, scene 6, lines 66ff)

But *Henry V* deals with the early fifteenth century. The first attempt in England to write a serious work of literature about a contemporary war was probably Edmund Waller's poem 'Of a War with Spain, and a Fight at Sea', published as a broadsheet in 1658; and though Waller undoubtedly read the latest news of the fighting, he witnessed it from the safe distance of the Home Counties.

By 1658 of course England had experienced four years of Civil War and other crises. Neither during Cromwell's Protectorate nor during the Restoration era was there any official ban with regard to reminiscing about the Civil War. One can see that after 1660 former Parliamentarians now employed by the restored monarchy, from George Monk, Duke of Albemarle downward, might have a motive for avoiding potentially divisive topics; but not all Parliamentarians found agreeable employment either before or after 1660, and there was no shortage of disgruntled former Royalists who found little advantage in the eventual triumph of the cause they had fought for. Yet of the twenty-three personal accounts of the Civil War listed in William Matthews's *British Autobiographies* (Berkeley, 1955) only two were published before 1699: John Hinton's *Memoires* of 1679 and Joseph Bamfield's *Apologie* of 1685. People were evidently interested in setting down their version of the record – this was, after all, the era of Samuel Pepys – but were less certain that contemporaries wanted to read about it. At the same time there are indications of a new awareness that war was a phenomenon that might touch everyone in a society, and might therefore represent a kind of common ground, an instantly recognizable territory in which a writer could establish his identity and location. Dryden's *Essay of Dramatic Poesie* of 1668 begins:

It was that memorable day, in the first summer of the late war, when our navy engaged the Dutch; a day wherein the two most mighty and best appointed fleets which any age had ever seen, disputed the command of the greater half of the globe, the commerce of nations, and the riches of the universe: while these vast floating bodies, on either side, moved against

6

each other in parallel lines, and our countrymen, under the happy conduct of his royal highness, went breaking, by little and little, into the line of the enemies; the noise of the cannon from both navies reached our ears about the city, so that all men being alarmed with it, and in a dreadful suspense of the event, which they knew was then deciding, every one went following the sound as his fancy led him; and leaving the town almost empty, some took towards the park, some cross the river, others down it; all seeking the noise in the depth of silence.

Among the rest, it was the fortune of Eugenius, Crites, Lisideius, and Neander, to be in company together . . .

Taking then a barge, which a servant of Lisideius had provided for them, they made haste to shoot the bridge, and left behind them that great fall of waters which hindered them from hearing what they desired: after which, having disengaged themselves from many vessels which rode at anchor in the Thames, and almost blocked up the passage towards Greenwich, they ordered the watermen to let fall their oars more gently; and then, every one favouring his own curiosity with a strict silence, it was not long ere they perceived the air to break about them like the noise of distant thunder, or of swallows in a chimney: those little undulations of sound, though almost vanishing before they reached them, yet still seeming to retain somewhat of their first horrour, which they had betwixt the fleets. After they had attentively listened till such time as the sound by little and little went from them, Eugenius, lifting up his head, and taking notice of it, was the first who congratulated to the rest that happy omen of our nation's victory . . .

Dryden's main literary work however was a series of plays which were as detached from ostensibly contemporary concerns and themes as those of playwrights a couple of generations earlier, but he lived at a time when the adherents of the Royalist cause were one party in an evolving system of party conflict, as had not been acknowledged to be the case during the reigns of Elizabeth and James I, and his startlingly malicious poem 'Absalom and Achitophel' of 1681 treated contemporary politics with a relish for personal detail that would have been inconceivable at any earlier period. On the other hand his account of the war with the United Provinces in his 'Annus Mirabilis' of 1667 is as redolent of long hours spent over musty volumes as his heroic dramas:

Our dreaded Admiral from far they threat,
  Whose batter'd rigging their whole war receives.
All bare, like some old Oak which tempests beat,
  He stands, and sees below his scatter'd leaves.

Heroes of old, when wounded, shelter sought,
  But he, who meets all danger with disdain,
Ev'n in their face his ship to Anchor brought,
  And Steeple high stood propt upon the Main.

At this excess of courage, all amaz'd,
  The foremost of his foes a while withdraw.
With such respect in enter'd Rome they gaz'd,
  Who on high Chairs the God-like Fathers saw.

And now, as where Patroclus body lay,
  Here Trojan Chiefs advanc'd, and there the Greek:
Ours o'r the Duke their pious wings display,
  And theirs the noblest spoils of Britain seek.[3]

One wonders what Dryden would have made of Grimmelshausen's *Der abenteuerliche Simplicissimus,* which first appeared in German in 1669 but in English not till 1912. Hans Jacob Christoph von Grimmelshausen (1622–76) was carried off from his home at Gelnhausen, a small town in Hessen, by marauding troops when aged only thirteen and during the next dozen years served in various of the armies that marched back and forth across Germany in the course of the Thirty Years' War. *Simplicissimus* is a largely autobiographical work, the resemblances to Rabelais' *Gargantua and Pantagruel* (which he probably did not know), to Spanish picaresque fiction (with which he was probably familiar) and to the dream satires of Quevedo (which he probably also knew) being the result less of literary assimilation than of the objective conditions of what was, at that date, the most destructive and meaningless war ever fought. The reasonable-minded Dryden, whose whole career can be seen as an attempt to impose the order and balance and sanity of classical values on English literature, belonged to a very different seventeenth century from the German veteran recalling his battle against lice:

[3] John Dryden, *Annus Mirabilis: The Year of Wonders, MDCLXVI* (1667), stanzas 61–64 (lines 241–56).

At last I could bear my torment no longer, but when the troopers were busy – some feeding, some sleeping, and some keeping guard – I crept a little aside under a tree to wage war with mine enemies: to that end I took off mine armour (though others be wont to put it on when they fight) and began such a killing and murdering that my two swords, which were my thumbnails, dripped with blood and hung full of dead bodies, or rather empty skins: and all such as I could not slay I banished forthwith, and suffered them to take their walks under that same tree . . .

I went on so furiously in my tyrannical ways that I did not even mark how the Imperialists were at blows with my lieutenant-colonel, till at last they came to me, terrified my poor lice, and took me myself prisoner. Nor had they any respect for my manhood, by the power of which I had just before slain my thousands, and even surpassed the fame of the tailor that killed 'seven at a blow'. I fell to the share of a dragoon, and the best booty he got from me was my lieutenant-colonel's cuirass, and that he sold at a fair price to the commandant at Soest, where he was quartered. So he was in the course of this war my sixth master: for I must serve him as his foot-boy.[4]

Waller's 'Of a War with Spain, and a Fight at Sea' and the naval part of Dryden's 'Annus Mirabilis' established something of a tradition in England: the next generation's best-known contribution to the genre was Addison's 'The Campaign' of 1704:

> With floods of gore that from the vanquished fell
> The marshes stagnate and the rivers swell.
> Mountains of slain lie heaped upon the ground,
> Or 'midst the roarings of the Danube drowned . . .
>
> (lines 350–53)

The fact that the poets celebrating British victories had no direct knowledge of warfare was balanced by the fact that, in those days of small professional armed forces, their ignorance was shared by almost all their audience. At least contemporary war had become an acceptable literary subject, and one might therefore have expected that eventually a writer would turn up who was qualified by personal experience as well as literary talent to make something of it. But no: just as the wars began to be bigger and more important, they took a dive in fashionability. Samuel Johnson wrote in 1780:

---

[4] The 1912 translation, entitled *The Adventurous Simplicissimus*, was by A.T.S. Goodrich; the passage quoted is on p. 178.

Everything has its day. Through the reigns of William and Anne no prosperous event passed undignified by poetry. In the last war [1756–63], when France was disgraced and overpowered in every quarter of the globe, when Spain, coming to her assistance, only shared her calamities, and the name of an Englishman was reverenced through Europe, no poet was heard amidst the general acclamation; the fame of our counsellors and heroes was intrusted to the Gazetteer.

This was not precisely true. George Cockings's *War: An Heroic Poem, from the Taking of Minorca by the French; to the Reduction of Manilla . . .* was a considerable success. Initially published as a local bookseller's venture at Boston, Massachusetts, in 1762, it was reprinted three times by 1765. Thomas Penrose obtained even greater celebrity with a short but lurid poem entitled 'The Field of Battle':

> The field, so late the hero's pride,
>   Was now with various carnage spread;
> And floated with a crimson tide,
>   That drench'd the dying and the dead.

The anonymous author of *Quebec: A Poetical Essay in Imitation of the Miltonic Style* (1760) and James Ogden, with his *The British Lion Rous'd; or, Acts of the British Worthies, a Poem in Nine Books* (1762) also deserve mention, at least for trying. But Johnson's point was essentially valid, for Waller's 'Of a War with Spain, and a Fight at Sea' and Dryden's 'Annus Mirabilis' added to already considerable literary reputations, while 'The Campaign' made Addison famous. Cockings and Ogden, despite a fearsome assiduity in writing, were never taken seriously – perhaps not even noticed – by the literary establishment of their day, let alone by posterity, and Penrose, despite influential admirers, had only a minor vogue as a one-poem prodigy.[5]

It was perhaps not uncharacteristic that, having interrupted his studies at Oxford to go on an expedition to the River Plate, Penrose only

---

[5] Samuel Johnson, *Lives of the English Poets*, ed. George Birkbeck Hill (3 vols, Oxford, 1905), ii, pp. 186–87 (Life of Prior) A well-known newspaper of the period was the *Gazetteer and Daily Advertiser*, founded in 1756, but Johnson was probably using 'Gazetteer' as a generic term of abuse; cf. his *Dictionary of the English Language* (1755): 'Gazetteer. A writer of news. It was lately a term of the utmost infamy, being usually applied to wretches who were hired to vindicate the court.'

ever saw action on board his ship, but achieved his success with a poem about a battle fought on land. One recalls the story of how Major-General James Wolfe, hearing one of his officers recite Gray's 'Elegy, Written in a Country Churchyard' on the eve of his attack on Quebec in 1759, exclaimed, 'I would rather have been the author of that piece than beat the French tomorrow'. A few years later Lieutenant-General John Burgoyne, who had arrived in North America to help put down the rebel colonists shortly before his first play was staged by Garrick at Drury Lane, confined himself to writing comedies after his defeat at the Battle of Saratoga effectively terminated his military career. Clearly even those who were in a position to judge did not consider first-hand experience of war to be a valuable literary asset. The celebration of warfare in eighteenth-century English literature most read today, Laurence Sterne's satirical treatment of the rambling military reminiscences of Uncle Toby in Volume One of *The Life and Opinions of Tristram Shandy* (1760), may even have served to deter veterans from setting forth their recollections:

> I must remind the reader, in case he has read the history of King William's wars, – but if he has not, – I then inform him, that one of the most memorable attacks in that siege, was that which was made by the English and Dutch upon the point of the advanced counterscarp, between the gate of St Nicholas, which inclosed the great sluice or water-stop, where the English were terribly exposed to the shot of the counter-guard and demi-bastion of St Roch . . .
>
> As this was the principal attack of which my uncle Toby was an eye-witness at Namur, – the army of the besiegers being cut off, by the confluence of the Maes and Sambre, from seeing much of each other's operations, – my uncle Toby was generally more eloquent and particular in his account of it; and the many perplexities he was in, arose out of the almost insurmountable difficulties he found in telling his story intelligibly, and giving such clear ideas of the differences and distinctions between the scarp and counterscarp, – the glacis and covered-way, – the half-moon and ravelin, – as to make his company fully comprehend where and what he was about . . .
>
> What rendered the account of this affair the more intricate to my uncle Toby, was this, – that in the attack of the counterscarp, before the gate of St Nicolas, extending, itself from the bank of the Maes, quite up to the great water-stop, – the ground was cut & cross out with such a multitude of dykes, drains, rivulets, and sluices, on all sides, – and he would get so

sadly bewildered, and set fast amongst them, that frequently he could neither get backwards or forwards to save his life; and was oft-times obliged to give up the attack upon that very account only. These perplexing rebutts gave my uncle Toby Shandy more perturbations than you would imagine: and as my father's kindness to him was continually dragging up fresh friends and fresh enquirers, – hc had but a very uneasy talk of it.[6]

Paradoxically, the decline of interest in war as a literary theme coincided with an upsurge of interest in warfare as a subject for painters. During the later seventeenth century battle painting had established itself as a genre, but a distinctly minor one. The influence of Leonardo's *Battle of Anghiari* cartoons was still evident in the work of Philips Wouwerman, who died in 1668, but the growing preoccupation with accurate portrayal of the disposition of the troops in the battles which official patrons wished to commemorate, and the need to focus attention on commanders who no longer placed themselves at the forefront of the struggle, as in the sixteenth century, but loitered observantly in a safe area surrounded by their beribboned and bewigged entourage, resulted in paintings of remarkable uninterestingness. Analogous problems of grouping and focus were encountered in the portrayal of naval battles, a genre developed particularly by the Dutch. Though in marine painting it was impracticable to focus on individual commanders, it was still desirable to show as much of the battle as possible. Adriaen van Diest's *Action between French and British Ships during the War of the English Succession*, for example, is less a single unified composition than a panorama. In the left foreground survivors cling to half-submerged wreckage, suggesting the gigantic size of the warships and the human misery concealed behind the wooden bulwarks. At left-centre are clouds of smoke and muzzle flashes from one of the ships, the poop of which occupies the right-centre. Further to the right a ship in flames provides the picture's most striking patch of colour. Diest died in 1704, Abraham Storck, another notable practitioner of the

[6] For Wolfe and Gray's 'Elegy', see William Wallace Currie, ed., *Memoir of the Life, Writings and Correspondence of James Currie* (2 vols, 1831), ii, p. 248; W.W. Currie to James Currie, 10 February 1804, and Edward E. Morris, 'Wolfe and Gray's "Elegy"', *English Historical Review*, 15 (1900), pp. 125–29. The passage quoted from Laurence Sterne's *The Life and Opinions of Tristram Shandy* is from vol. i (1760), chapter 26.

genre, probably four years later. During the course of the next eighty
years little progress was made in solving the problems of pictorial
organization. This may partly have been due to the technical
knowledge of rigging and ship construction required for large-
format paintings of ships under sail: marine painters were often men
who became professional artists in middle life after a career at sea,
or as dockyard employees. Of eighteenth-century marine painters
working in England, Dominic Serres and Nicholas Pocock had been
merchant navy captains, Richard Paton an excise official, Charles
Brooking a dockyard artisan, perhaps responsible for decorating ships,
at Deptford. There was also the problem, when painting a battle
between fleets, of how to show all the ships. William Gilpin, the
theorist of the Picturesque, wrote, 'The *line of battle* is a miserable
arrangement on canvas; and it is an inhumanity in an admiral to
injoin it. If the line of battle must be introduced, it should be formed
at a distance; and the stress laid on some of the ships, at one end of
the line, brought into action, near the eye'. But this was only likely
to be done if marine painting were to be taken up by artists more
interested in painting than in ships.[7]

A movement in this direction is detectable from the 1760s. The
Seven Years' War (1756–63) turned out to be more ruinously expensive
than any previous war, and forced the governments of western Europe
not merely to reorganize their finances but to give thought to the
question of how, in future, they could more effectively mobilize the
human and monetary resources of the populations under their control.
It became fashionable to talk of the arts as a national resource, and
as a means of inculcating moral and patriotic virtues. Though High
Art continued to occupy itself with themes from classical literature,
their didactic aspect received a new emphasis, and it became less
unusual for artists to attempt subjects from the history of their own
country. In France the Comte d'Angiviller, Directeur Général des
Bâtiments du Roi, energetically sponsored this development; in Britain

[7] *Action between French and British Ships during the War of the English Succession*, by
Adriaen van Diest (1655–1704), is in the National Maritime Museum, London. The
War of the English Succession (1689–97) is more often in Britain called the War of
the League of Augsburg. The quotation is from William Gilpin, *Observations Relative
Chiefly to Picturesque Beauty, Made in the Year 1772, in Several Parts of England: Particularly
the Mountains of Cumberland and Westmoreland* (2 vols, 1786), i, p. 65.

King George III, acting in his private capacity, became the patron of Benjamin West, whose *The Death of Wolfe* (showing one of the rare instances in the eighteenth century when an army commander was killed in action) pioneered a new style of battle painting.[8]

The didactic intentions of West's generation of artists, together with a re-examination and revaluation of classical models, led to a speedy resolution of the problem of lay-out and organisation which had dogged battle painting during the period when it had been neglected by the more ambitious of the artistic fraternity. West in Britain, Louis David in France, Vincenzo Camuccini a little later, but still independently, in Italy, all realized the importance of focussing the attention of the viewer on the key motif in their pictures. They turned away from the exhilarated centrifugalism of Baroque art, and practised a simplicity of grouping that foreshadowed the twentieth-century advertising poster. Generally the focus of their paintings would be an individual of heroic moral stature, struck down, it might be, at the moment of his greatest triumph, as in John Singleton Copley's *The Death of Major Pierson* (1783) in the Tate Gallery or West's two pictures of the dying Nelson (1806 and 1808, in the Walker Art Gallery, Liverpool and in the National Maritime Museum respectively); or astride a rearing horse with troops toiling up a mountainside behind him, as in David's *Napoleon Crossing the Alps* (1800); or passing amongst the shattered ranks of the followers who have sacrificed themselves in his glorious cause, as in Jean-Antoine Gros's *Napoleon on the Battlefield of Eylau* (1808) in the Louvre.

Philip James de Loutherbourg, a native of Fulda in Germany, who made his career in England, attempted an interesting variation on this, in his *Lord Howe's Victory on the Glorious First of June* (now in the National Maritime Museum) which makes not Lord Howe but his flagship, the *Queen Charlotte*, the focus of his painting. *Lord Howe's Victory on the Glorious First of June* is full of dramatic contrasts: the contrast

---

[8] For Angiviller, see Jacques Silvestre de Sacy, *Le Comte d'Angiviller: dernier directeur-général des Bâtiments du Roi* (Paris, [1953]), pp. 100–101, 106–13. For West, see Robert C. Alberts, *Benjamin West: A Biography* (Boston, 1978), especially pp. 158–60, 179, 183; and Helmut von Erffa and Allen Staley, *The Paintings of Benjamin West* (New Haven, 1986), pp. 55–64 and 577. The 1776 engraving of *The Death of Wolfe* supposedly earnt the engraver £7000 and the print publisher £15,000; the amount of West's royalty is not known.

between the British boats humanely rescuing French survivors in the foreground and the two men-of-war firing furiously into each other just behind; the contrast between the relative orderliness on board the British man-of-war – despite the loss of her fore-topmast – and the disorder aboard the French *Montagne* alongside; the contrast between the massiveness of the ships' hulls and the flimsiness of their ragged sails and the broken stays which swirl madly across the upper part of the picture; even the contrast between the serenity of the *Queen Charlotte*'s figurehead and the rococo desperation of the *Montagne*'s figurehead just to the right. All these contrasts are triumphantly integrated into a single expressive pattern; and yet, perhaps, something is missing. Impressive as the works of de Loutherbourg, West and Gros are at one level, they exist only as public statements, in no way transfusions of the private into the public sphere. None of these artists had even *seen* a battle.

West was in his late sixties when he painted the death of Nelson; Loutherbourg, when he painted Howe's naval victory, and David, when he painted Napoleon crossing the Alps, were in their fifties. Perhaps nobody would really have expected them, at that age, to have been active participants in the scenes they depicted; but there were plenty of younger artists around in the 1790s and 1800s, some of whom did take part in battles. In fact the Napoleonic War was the first conflict in which artists regularly accompanied armies on campaign; yet a survey of which artists went to war and which ones stayed behind suggests that participating in battle was still seen as a fairly minor qualification for becoming a battle painter. The Bavarian painter and museum director Georg von Dillis stated, 'It is unavoidably necessary that such an artist should partake of the campaign, on the spot, and pick up the circumstances during the business, so as to stamp them with truth and individuality', but Dillis himself took care to keep out of the way of flying bullets. Théodore Géricault's switch from the antique to modern military subjects in his painting coincided with his father mortgaging family property to raise 4000 francs to pay someone to serve in the army in the artist's place.[9]

---

[9] *Bayerische Militärmaler: von Beich bis Thöny* (publications of the Bayerisches Armeemuseum, 5, Ingolstadt, 1982), p. 10; Lorenz E.A. Eitner, *Géricault: His Life and Work* (1983), p. 19; Germain Bazin, *Theodore Géricault: étude critique, documents et*

Occasionally artists had the benefit of sketches executed at the scene of action by serving officers or civilian members of a commander's entourage. Karl von Heideck, an officer in the Prussian artillery, provided sketches and advice for Wilhelm von Kobell; Gros's twenty-seven foot canvas *Napoleon on the Battlefield of Eylau* was partly based on a sketch done on the spot by Vivant Denon, Napoleon's director of museums, and himself an accomplished engraver of topographical and pornographic prints. Some serving officers were themselves artists: Louis Bacler d'Albe, director of the topographical section on Napoleon's staff in Italy, painted a view of the Battle of Arcola (incongruously reminiscent of Gainsborough in its emphasis on clouds and foliage) which was exhibited at the salon in 1804; Louis François Lejeune, *général de brigade* and baron under Napoleon, Director of l'École de Beaux Arts at Toulouse after the Restoration, exhibited paintings of the battles in which he had participated, even in London; James Pattison Cockburn, who had studied landscape drawing under Paul Sandby at Woolwich, made drawings, subsequently published as engravings, of the bombardment of Copenhagen, at which he had served as a captain in the Royal Artillery: after Waterloo he became a respected topographical illustrator.[10]

During the latter part of the Napoleonic War commanders even began to make a point of having an artist attached to the headquarters of their armies in the field. Lieutenant-General Sir John Moore invited Robert Ker Porter to accompany his expedition to Spain in 1808. The sketchbook Porter used during the expedition is in the Print Room of the British Museum, still in its original leather case. The sketches, delicate outlines in ink tinted in pale water-colours, mainly show church interiors, townscapes and bridges, though there are a few drawings of marching troops. The only drawing of a battle – the rearguard action at La Coruña covering the evacuation of the British troops – was

---

catalogue raisonné (5 vols, Paris, 1987–92), i, p. 29, prints text of the agreement between Géricault and his replacement, dated 30 April 1811.

[10] *Bayerische Militärmaler*, p. 10; Pierre Lelievre, *Vivant Denon, homme des lumières: 'Ministre des Arts' de Napoleon* (Paris, 1993), p. 168; C. de W. Crookshank, *Prints of British Military Operations: A Catalogue Raisonné* (1921), p. 43. James Pattison Cockburn (1779–1847) rose to the rank of major-general. His later drawings were used to illustrate such books as *Views to Illustrate the Route of the Simplon* (1822) and *Pompeii: Illustrated with Picturesque Views* (1827).

evidently executed on board a ship that was already well out to sea: as a noncombatant Porter had evidently been one of the first to be embarked. Later that same year Albrecht Adam accompanied the Bavarian Corps in the campaign which ended at the Battle of Wagram, and in 1812 he was with Eugène Beauharnais's headquarters during the invasion of Russia: the Stuttgart-born artist Christian Wilhelm Faber du Faur, who had obtained a commission in the Württemberg artillery, was in the same invading army, in the corps commanded by the Crown Prince of Württemberg; but the first German painter to be *officially* engaged as a war artist and to wear uniform as such was Peter von Hess, who accompanied the Bavarian army on campaign in 1814. Another Bavarian painter, Georg Scharf, joined the baggage train of the British army as a lieutenant in 1814. In 1811 Denis Dighton was appointed to an ensigncy in the 90th Foot, apparently so that he could paint – or at least sketch – the British army in action, though since the 90th Foot was stationed in the West Indies where there was no longer any fighting it is not clear how this arrangement was supposed to have worked. Dighton resigned his commission after a few months in order to marry but later, as Battle Painter to the Prince Regent, visited the battlefield of Waterloo five days after Wellington's victory and executed nine drawings showing scenes of combat he had not actually witnessed. Clearly the idea was developing that the war offered a professional opportunity for artists, but the only painter of the period of even the second rank – one cannot place Bacler d'Albe or Lejeune so high – who produced a painting of a battle in which he had participated seems to have been Horace Vernet, who fought at the Barrière Clichy in 1814 and exhibited a canvas depicting the action (or rather a lull in the action) at the salon in 1820.[11]

The truest war artist of the period was one who never witnessed or painted a battle as such, and, as a middle-aged (almost elderly) court painter at the fuddy-duddiest court in Europe, was very far from

[11] The call mark of Robert Ker Porter's sketch book in the Print Room of the British Museum is 198 a 17, and see Peter Harrington *British Artists and War: The Face of Battle in Paintings and Prints, 1700–1914* (1993), p. 90; Albrecht Adam, *Aus dem Leben eines Schlachtenmalers* (Stuttgart), pp. 46–101, 145–258; *Bayerische Militärmaler*, p. 12; Harrington, *British Artists and War*, p. 93, and Dennis Rose, *Life, Times and Recorded Works of Robert Dighton 1752–1814: Actor, Artist and Printseller and Three of his Artist Sons* (Salisbury, 1981), p. 28.

regarding war as an eligible professional opportunity. Goya's *The Disasters of War* etchings are amongst the most striking depictions ever executed of the awfulness of war, and leave no doubt at all that he knew what it *felt* like to be a citizen of a country overrun by invaders, though the fact that the preliminary drawings for these etchings were done two years or more after the events shown raises questions about his emotional state and motivation: perhaps, after all, they were as much propaganda, though for a different type of audience, as the work of West and David.[12]

But Goya was definitely a man who stood in an unusual relationship to his life and times, for during the whole twenty-three years of the French Revolutionary and Napoleonic Wars no one seems to have produced a literary counterpart to the *Disasters of War*. While leading artists simply dealt with the war from a distance, writers for the most part seem to have been reluctant to deal with it at all.

[12] The etchings of Goya's *The Disasters of War* were completed some time between 1810 and 1820 but not published till 1863.

CHAPTER 2

Writers and the Great War with France

At about the time Goya was preparing his war etchings Major Charles
Napier of the British Army's 50th Regiment of Foot wrote an account of the Battle of La Coruña which, in its patient transcription
of sensations and responses, its occasional striking images and its
deft sketching in of the horrors inseparable from violent death,
gives as powerful a sense of the author's individuality as anything
produced by the First World War more than a century later. Napier's
reminiscences of La Coruña, which are printed at the end of this
volume as an appendix, show that writers of the 1800s could have
written effectively about war if they had chosen to. The idea, popularized towards the end of the nineteenth century by Tolstoy and
Stephen Crane, that war was something experienced *subjectively*, and
that one might thereby learn some sort of fundamental truth about
oneself, seems already to have been familiar. The following was written by an MP during a visit to the front line in Flanders in 1793:

> July 17th. – Though I had thus seen the plan of the trenches, and the
> manner of their formation, more effectually than I could in any other
> way, yet I had not seen, or rather had not experienced, what was most
> the object of my curiosity, the situation of persons employed in doing
> duty there. I therefore accepted readily the offer of Major Crawford to
> accompany me thither the next morning. It was not without anxiety that
> I ventured into a situation so new and untried, as that in which I was
> about to enter. It was impossible to tell the effect of circumstances, which
> have been found occasionally to operate so strangely on minds not
> distinguishable beforehand from the rest of the world. How could I be
> certain, that the same might not happen to me, as happened to certain

persons, that one knows of? I did all that could be done in such a case,
'omnia praecepi atque animo mecum ante peregi'. How far I had succeeded could be known only by trial. The result of the trial answered, I
am happy to say, to my most sanguine expectations. I think, with
confidence, that during any part of the time, I could have multiplied, if
necessary, a sum in my head.

Just over a year later, having in the meantime become a cabinet minister,
the same man made another visit to the front, and was struck by how
little he responded to what was going on about him:

> It was a grand and (to me) a new situation; I am angry with myself that I
> did not seek to impress my mind with a fuller sense of the magnificence
> of it. The army of the enemy, of which we had heard so much, were advanc-
> ing upon us. The action was going on in the close country in front. An
> attack, it was likely, would be made upon us in the morning. The fate of
> the British army and with that of the whole cause, probably, depended
> upon the event. What a situation for the imagination of Burke or Dr
> Johnson! I am afraid I must say that I felt this hardly more than a grenadier;
> I hope only that I felt as much as a grenadier, at least, that if I felt it but
> little in one way I felt it but little also in another.

But these two passages were not intended for public consumption;
they are from a private diary published long after the author's death.
Similarly, Charles Napier's account of the Battle of La Coruña, apparently written for his mother and sisters, was only printed
posthumously.[1]

It was not that there was no widespread interest in the war. Apart
from a minuscule landing on the Pembrokeshire coast in February
1797, Britain escaped enemy invasion – the only European country
to do so – and consequently escaped the worst horrors of what was
afterwards described as 'the most extensive and expensive war that
ever raged', but even in Britain the struggle which began with the
French Republic's declaration of hostilities in February 1793, and
continued, with two short intervals, till Napoleon's final defeat at

---

[1] Mrs H. Baring, ed., *The Diary of the Right Hon. William Windham, 1784 to 1810*
(1866), p. 282, 17 July 1793, and p. 317, 3 September 1794. Windham was a close
friend of both Johnson and Burke. The Latin tag is from Virgil, *Aeneid*, vi, line 105,
and means 'I have already taken all advice and reflected with my mind'.

Waterloo in June 1815, was a constant factor in the lives of every man, woman and child in Britain for almost a generation. There were enormous numbers of troops stationed in different parts of the country; 'the whole Kingdom' was said to be 'one vast camp'. Most gentlemen were enrolled in the Yeomanry or the Volunteers – the period's counterpart of the Home Guard, except that their principal function was to reinforce aristocratic patronage networks and to overawe the poorer classes – and were obliged to use some of their endless leisure in drilling their tenants. Some smaller inland towns became depots for captured French officers on parole, and in many instances these unwilling guests were a valuable addition to the social life of stuffy little market communities, though they were also often the object of the wildest suspicion: in 1810, for example, it was reported that 'there is a general system of organisation, that each officer has his corps, that a correspondence is maintained between them and Napoleon's Government, and that it is his policy to keep them in this country so that they might assist him in the case of an invasion'. On the coast it was occasionally possible to see French privateers attacking British coastal vessels, and in many seaside areas the war years saw the building of Martello Towers and other fortifications. At Dover the beach was constantly under guard; a holiday-maker noted, 'I was only allowed to walk on the beach from sentry to sentry – and then not without every time I approached each being always challenged'. And of course the great seaports were in a constant bustle with troops departing overseas or returning home from foreign campaigns.[2]

There were also periodic fears of invasion, particularly in the years 1803 to 1805, and all along the south and east coast warning beacons were built and arrangements made to evacuate seaside and estuary towns at short notice, especially between Dorset and Essex. At Colchester, in 1803, a rumour of an imminent French landing caused many of the principal inhabitants to flee the town. Even in Cumberland and Westmorland 19,322 people signed a Declaration stating that,

[2] G.E. Bryant and G.P. Baker, *A Quaker Journal* (2 vols, 1934), i, p. 30; Elizabeth Lady Holland, *Journal* (2 vols, 1909), ii, p. 263, 21 July 1810; L.J. Jennings, ed., *The Croker Papers* (3 vols, 1884), i, p. 33, Barrow to Croker, 8 and 27 July 1810; W.B. Pope, ed., *The Diary of Benjamin Robert Haydon* (5 vols, Cambridge, Massachusetts, 1960–63), i, p. 9.

'trusting in the God of Battles, we boldly bid them [the French] try our strength'. Yet there were those who ridiculed the general fear of an invasion. For example the antiquary Charles Kirkpatrick Sharpe wrote in 1803:

> For my own part, I wish the French would come, and have done, for the people here keep such a devil of a drilling, that a sober-minded Christian can get no peace for them. Gentlemen and clowns are at it from morning till night: the butler drills the footman with a cudgel in the servants' hall, and the cook-maid instructs the flea-catchers with a ladle in the kitchen; nay, the very cows and hogs at the approach of a hostile cur draw up in battle array, in imitation of the two-legged bumpkins who are spoiling the exercise under every hedge in Annandale.

After a while of course the unending suspense generated a certain indifference; at one London dinner party for example, 'The invasion was talked of and it seemed to be thought an attempt would be made, but it seemed to make very little impression as a *subject* of conversation'.[3]

It is frequently pointed out that Jane Austen refers to the war in none of her novels, except *Persuasion* – and even in *Persuasion* it is not entirely clear that the war referred to was specifically the one she had just lived through – and the impression that the war was scarcely noticed by civilians is confirmed by, for example, the voluminous letters of the governess Ellen Weeton. Yet it is possible Jane Austen deliberately edited the war out of the social life she described; a case can be made for supposing that she preferred to portray the life of upper middle-class misses as it might have been in normal times rather than in a period of upheaval and emergency which she considered to be only temporary. She belonged to an era when writers were still less interested in the uniqueness of their own times than in aspects of social life they considered permanent and enduring: even novels like *Frankenstein* or, a generation later, *Jane Eyre*, that seemed to engage

[3] Jane Taylor, *Memoirs* (4th edn, 1841), p. 45; Public Record Office, HO 42/72/20, August 1803; Alexander Allardyce, ed., *Letters from and to Charles Kirkpatrick Sharpe, Esq.* (2 vols, 1888), i, p. 191–92, Sharpe to Newton, 5 December 1803; K. Garlick, A. Macintyre and Kathryn Cave, ed., *The Diary of Joseph Farington* (16 vols, New Haven, 1978–84), vi, p. 2254, 26 February 1804.

head on with contemporary issues, were set in a historical time prior to the authors' birth. In real life Jane Austen had two brothers who were in the Navy, one of whom, having served under Nelson, wrote of his bitter regret at not being present at the Battle of Trafalgar: 'to lose all share in the glory of a day which surpasses all which ever went before, is what I cannot think of with any degree of patience; but as I cannot write upon the subject without complaining, I will drop it for the present, till time and reflection reconcile me a little more to what I know is now inevitable'. Her circle of acquaintance must also have included many men who were in the Yeomanry; and the Knightleys and Darcys and Willoughbys of her novels were exactly the sort of men who would have been in the Yeomanry and who would at least occasionally have appeared in uniform and discussed training problems, for all that this might have made little difference to their womenfolk. Though there is no sign of this in Jane Austen's novels, the Yeomanry provided a major focus for the social life of the rich; such ceremonies as the presentation of regimental colours provided an opportunity for local gentry to turn out in force to demonstrate their patriotic solidarity. When Lady Clerke, wife of the local clergyman-baronet, presented the colours to the Bury Association, it was reported that:

> Mr Peel [the lieutenant-colonel commanding] received them with much agitation – paid her ladyship and the Ladies of Bury and its Neighourhood some very handsome compliments and then presented them to the offic- ers, addressed the Corps in a most Animated and Nervous Speech descrip- tive of the times, and encouraging Patriotism and Loyalty to our King and Country. He clearly felt what he uttered and spoke so home to the feelings of his hearers, that Tears filled many Eyes – more were certainly not dry . . . Ale, and Bread and Cheese were distributed, both to the Soldiers and Multitude, and a very Handsome Cold Collation prepared for the Officers and Friends of our liberal Host.

In the 1790s upper-class women also exerted themselves to collect flannel waistcoats for 'our gallant soldiers' in Flanders (just as their great-great-granddaughters knitted scarves and balaclava helmets for the boys in the trenches in 1915). The war even affected upper-class fashions in dress; hair-powder was banned (except for military person- nel) because of grain shortages, and short hair worn naturally replaced the silver-powdered hair worn in a queue which had been customary before 1793. Officers on active service began to wear trousers (originally known as overalls) to protect the upper parts of their boots, and to save time shaving they began to cultivate whiskers and moustaches; by 1815 whiskers and trousers were becoming fashionable for civilians.[4]

Even in families that were in no way directly affected by the wars, the world conflict was an enduring topic of interest. Harriet Martineau later recalled, 'I suppose most children were politicians during the war', yet her own family, that of a Norwich industrialist, 'never had a relative, nor, as far as I know, even an acquaintance, in either army or navy'. Similarly John Flint South remembered, 'We were great politicians in our way at school; but though at first we subscribed for a weekly newspaper, the *Observer*, and afterwards changed it for the *St James's Chronicle*, which came out thrice a week, I feel quite sure that we thought more about the warlike news than anything else, and were always looking for victories, illuminations and fireworks'. Victories were regularly celebrated with bonfires and illuminations and, in the country, 'by sheep-roasting and extraordinary rustic festivities'. Though the poorer classes suffered badly from war-induced hardships, this enthusiasm was to be found even amongst manual workers, such as the bricklayer of whom it was recalled, 'King-worship and war were his favourite topics – the absorbing one, battles! On his return from labour, he used to tell over to me the glories of war, and the amount killed, with a gusto equal to the mad boast of bacchanals, who swagger how the table was flooded with champagne at the midnight hour.'[5]

[4] E. Hall, ed., Miss Weeton: *Journal of a Governess, 1807–1811 . . . 1811–1825* (2 vols, 1936–39), ii, p. 108; A.D. Harvey, *Literature into History* (Harmondsworth, 1988), pp. 36–38; J.H. and Edith C. Hubback, *Jane Austen's Sailor Brothers: Being the Adventures of Sir Francis Austen, GCB, Admiral of the Fleet and Rear-Admiral Charles Austen* (1906), p. 156. Francis Austen to Mary Gibson, 27 October 1805; Staffordshire County Record Office, E. Hall, typescript, 'The "Hero of Badajoz": Diary of a Soldier's Wife, 1789–1814', MS F 920 7 W80, p. 92, 18 October 1798; *Factotum: Newsletter of the XVIIIth Century STC*, 36 (February 1993), p. 2.

[5] Harriet Martineau, *Autobiography* (3 vols, 1877), i, pp. 78, 80; C.L. Feltoe, ed., *Memorials of John Flint South* (1884), p. 20; Sir Archibald Alison, *Some Account of My Life and Writings* (2 vols, 1883), i, p. 14; Charles Thomson, *The Autobiography of an Artisan* (1847), p. 34.

The experience of the twentieth century has encouraged the assumption that a major event like a war, encroaching on millions of lives, will automatically generate a body of literature portraying it. The French Revolutionary and Napoleonic Wars show that this is not necessarily the case. Occasionally some incidental event might provide a poet in his study with a memorable theme, as in Charles Wolfe's 'The Burial of Sir John Moore at Corunna':

> Not a drum was heard, not a funeral note,
> As his corpse to the rampart we hurried;
> Not a soldier discharged his farewell shot
> O'er the grave where our hero we buried.
>
> We buried him darkly at dead of night,
> The sods with our bayonets turning;
> By the struggling moonbeam's misty light
> And the lantern dimly burning . . .
>
> But half of our heavy task was done
> When the clock struck the hour for retiring;
> And we heard the distant and random gun
> That the foe was sullenly firing.
>
> Slowly and sadly we laid him down,
> From the field of his fame fresh and gory;
> We carved not a line, and we raised not a stone,
> But we left him alone with his glory.

With its restraint and precision, and the dying fall of its feminine endings, its half-rhymes, and its anapaestic metre (at that period generally used only in comic verse), Wolfe's poem is the literary counterpart of West's *The Death of Wolfe*, and in its day was regarded as a masterpiece. On the other hand the hollow rhetoric of poets too distant from their subject might excite the mirth of their audience: Thomas Campbell's 'Hohenlinden', for example,

> Few, few shall part, where many meet!
> The snow shall be their winding-sheet,
> And every turf beneath their feet
> Shall be a soldier's sepulchre

caused readers to ask how a single turf could be the sepulchre of a full-grown soldier. (And it was later rumoured that the word had originally been not 'sepulchre' but 'cemetery'.) Though it cannot be said that the poets of the 1800s failed to recognize that war was a subject for lyric rather han epic poetry, they did tend to lack the one essential lyric ingredient: personal experience as an involved participant. Campbell in fact was one of the few professional poets of his generation who had actually witnessed a battle. Leigh Hunt recalled:

> We have had the pleasure of falling into Mr Campbell's company several times, and think we have heard him relate that he had the singular fortune of witnessing, from the top of a convent, the great battle of Hohenlinden, upon which he has written some stately verses. We think we remember also that he spoke of hearing the French army singing one of their national hymns before the engagement, and of seeing their cavalry enter the town, wiping their bloody swords on their horses' manes. But whether he related this of himself or others, or indeed whether others told it us of him, we must leave among those doubtful recollections which are apt, at a distance of time, to put one's veracity upon its candour.

Yet even if it was not the Battle of Hohenlinden that he witnessed (he was at Altona at the time) but a skirmish near Ratisbon earlier in the same year, it was characteristic of Campbell as a poet that the details he recalled at the dinner table were more interesting than those in his poem.[6]

It may be, too, that part of the appeal of Campbell's 'Hohenlinden' poem was that it referred to a battle in which no Britons took part. In 1809 Walter Scott wrote (anonymously)

> There is no point in which our age differs from those which preceded it, than in the apparent apathy of our poets and rhymers to the events which are passing over them . . . some of them roam back to distant and dark

[6] Charles Wolfe's poem first appeared in the *Newry Telegraph*, 19 April 1817; Campbell's 'Hohenlinden' was included in the 1803 edition of his poems; Thomas Moore, *Memoirs, Journal and Correspondence*, ed. Lord John Russell (8 vols, 1853–56), vii, p. 197, 10 August 1837, and footnote by Lord John Russell; Lawrence Huston Houtchens and Carolyn Washburn Houtchens, ed., *Leigh Hunt's Literary Criticism* (New York, 1956), p. 160 (item originally published in the *Examiner*, 21 August 1821), and cf. p. 643 note 5.

Walter Savage Landor, a poet today almost as forgoten as Campbell, served as a volunteer in the Spanish army in the autumn of 1808 but did not see a battle – or write about one.

ages; others wander to remote countries, instead of seeking a theme in
the exploits of a Nelson, an Abercromby, or a Wellesley; others amuse
themselves with luscious sonnets to Bessies and Jessies; and all seem so
littel to regard the crisis in which we are placed, that we cannot help thinking they would keep fiddling their allegros and adagios, even if London
was on fire, or Buonaparte landed at Dover.

These remarks are to some extent rebutted by their context: they appeared in the course of a review of John Wilson Croker's poem *The
Battle of Talavera*, which was about to become a best-seller:

> Now from the dark artillery broke
> Lightning flash and thunder stroke;
> And volumed clouds of fiery smoke
>   Roll in the darkened air.

But the attraction of Croker's verse for readers may have been due to
the novelty of a junior minister publishing a poem about the first British victory in years that hadn't been followed by an evacuation or a
truce; it certainly cannot be said that Croker (then Secretary to the
Admiralty) showed any specialist knowledge or even detailed interest in his subject:

> What English hearts the Frenchmen gor'd,
> What crests were cleft by British sword,
> When horse and foot infuriate met,
> And sabre clashed with bayonet,
> And how they fought and how they fell,
> And man and steed, 'midst shout and yell,
>   The field of carnage strewed:
> It were a tedious tale to tell
>   A tedious tale of blood.[7]

The eight printings of *The Battle of Talavera* in 1809 and 1810 were
a unique success in this period for a poem on a contemporary theme:
and Lord Byron was soon doing even better with escapist verse narratives set in a Levantine never-never land. It seemed that the sixteenth-
century assumption that the contemporary was not a literary domain

---

[7] *Quarterly Review*, 2 (1809), pp. 426–27; John Wilson Croker, *The Battle of Talavera*
(8th edn, 1810), pp. 15, 18.

still persisted. Scott himself, as the anonymous author of the best-selling verse romances *The Lay of the Last Minstrel* and *Marmion* – which, in his capacity as an anonymous reviewer, he said he was reminded of by Croker's poem – was himself foremost amongst those who 'roam back to distant and dark ages' for their themes. Later he would embark on a second career as a writer of historical novels. Apart from his insipid *The Field of Waterloo* and his later pot-boiling biography of Napoleon, his only treatment of the European-wide crisis that extended from his twenty-first to his forty-fourth year was at the end of *The Antiquary*, a novel published in 1816 but set in the 1790s with the Revolutionary War as a very distant background: a false alarm regarding a French invasion provides the setting for the denouement of the plot and the excuse for ending on a patriotic note, though the transfer of the timing, from February 1804 when a false alarm really did cause a reaction of the sort described, to the mid-1790s leads to a perhaps exaggerated idea of the national fervour at the earlier period:

> Those who have witnessed such a scene can alone conceive the state of bustle in Fairport. The windows were glancing with a hundred lights, which, appearing and disappearing rapidly, indicated the confusion within doors. The women of lower rank assembled and clamoured in the market-place. The yeomanry, pouring from their different glens, galloped through the streets, some individually, some in parties of five or six, as they had met on the road. The drums and fifes of the volunteers beating to arms, were blended with the voice of the officers, the sound of the bugles, and the tolling of the bells from the steeple. The ships in the harbour were lit up, and boats from the armed vessels added to the bustle, by landing men and guns, destined to assist in the defence of the place. This part of the preparations was superintended by Taffril with much activity. Two or three light vessels had already slipped their cables and stood out to sea, in order to discover the supposed enemy.[8]

The distance most writers maintained between themselves and the war suggests the explanation that books were written, and wars fought, by quite distinct social groups. There is something in this. As we have already seen, Harriet Martineau, whose father was a textile

---

[8] Walter Scott, *The Antiquary* (first published 1816, but quoting from 1939 Nelson edition, p. 504.) Scott himself had been Quartermaster in a Yeomanry formation, the Royal Edinburgh Light Dragoons.

manufacturer in Norwich, did not know anyone who was in the armed forces. The only forms of conscription in Britain were the press-gang for seamen – and, contrary to legend, very few people other than merchant navy deck-hands were ever press-ganged – and the militia ballot. One young man thought that to be balloted would mean 'the destruction of all my hopes and happiness both present and future . . . The ruinous neglect of business – the horrors of a military life – cut off from all enjoyment – and associating with the outcasts of society', but in practice one could always pay someone else to go as a substitute, if one had the money, or gain exemption by enlisting in the Volunteers. Edward Daniel Clarke the geologist was able to escape his obligation by the simple expedient of going into residence as a Fellow of Jesus College, Cambridge.[9]

The recollections of the few enthusiasts for the war probably exaggerate the degree to which opportunities for military adventure were welcomed. Someone who was a schoolboy in 1808 later recorded:

> Every boy at school was ardently looking forward to the time when he should be old enough to join either the Army or the Navy. The patriotic enthusiasm which had been excited throughout Great Britain by the threatened invasion of the French, under Bonaparte, was scarcely subsided, and was kept alive by the accounts which were constantly reaching England of fresh triumphs of our arms both by sea and land. In short, the profession of arms, both Naval and Military, was highly popular; and the sons of the noblemen and gentlemen of Great Britain were eagerly entering both services.

Yet other sources provide little confirmation of this. There do not seem to have been many men like George Robert Gleig, later famous as author of that dull novel *The Subaltern*, who at the age of fifteen interrupted his studies at Balliol to join the 85th Foot. It is noteworthy that, in contrast to the dreadful slaughter of graduates in the twentieth-century World Wars commemorated on memorial plaques in every

[9] British Library, Add. MS 32,558, fol. 41, diary of W. Upcott, August 1803; W. Otter *The Life and Remains of the Rev. Edward Daniel Clarke, Ll.D.* (1824), pp. 333–34.
  The militia was only available for home service though many of its rank and file, being men too poor to afford substitutes or actually substitutes themselves, individually volunteered for service in the regular army. In 1814 the Buckinghamshire militia joined Wellington's army in the south of France, but saw no action.

Oxford and Cambridge college, only *one* Oxbridge man died in bat-
tle during the entire 1792–1815 period: the Hon. Edward Meade of
Wadham, who was killed at the head of the flank company of the 40th
Foot at the Aboukir landing on 8 March 1801; another Oxford man,
W.G. Browne, and the Rev. Joseph Richard Turner of Gonville and
Caius College, Cambridge, were murdered by brigands on the
Continent during the war years, in separate incidents, which sug-
gests that a certain class of Briton found the war less dangerous than
foreign holidays.[10]

We unfortunately have no record of the private opinions of the
man who may well be the period's unique instance of someone sacrific-
ing a successful career in order to take part in the war. In 1804 the
Rev. George Grigby, Dean of Chapel at Caius and formerly headmaster
of the Perse School, bought a commission in the 1st Dragoons, despite
the prejudice against clergymen bearing arms. Later he transferred
to the 11th Foot as a captain, and was drowned with 233 others off
Falmouth when a Royal Navy frigate rammed the transport vessel carrying him and his troops towards the theatre of war in Spain.[11]

The problem with explaining writers' relative indifference to the
war simply in terms of their membership of a social class that was able
to avoid having anything to do with the fighting is that, though there
was no conscription in Britain, military service was obligatory for men
of all social classes in France and parts of Italy and Germany, and
substitutes willing to take one's place in the ranks were much harder
to find and thus relatively much more expensive than in Britain; yet
apart from a passage describing the Battle of Waterloo in Stendhal's
novel *La Chartreuse de Parme* one looks in vain for prose and poetry in
French or Italian that has anything to say about the war that is not
being said, and more frequently, in English. Stendhal, who saw action as a cavalry officer in Italy in 1800 and 1801, recalled thirty-six

[10] The quotation is from Charles Loftus, *My Youth by Sea and Land* (2 vols, 1876),
i, p. 4. The later careers of men who were undergraduates in this period can be traced
in the published registers of the different colleges.

[11] The only reference to Grigby's resignation in the records of his college is in
connection with the election of his replacement. Gonville and Caius College Archive,
Gesta, 30 October 1804 (GOV 03/07). I am grateful to Dr R.B. Outhwaite and to
Ellie Clewlow, archivist of Gonville and Caius, for supplying me with information on
this point.

years later that coming under fire for the first time was 'the *sublime*, yet a little too close to danger. Instead of pure enjoyment, the soul was still a little bit concerned with holding itself steady', but he hastened to point out 'all the fine reflections of this sort belong to 1836; I would have been greatly astonished by them in 1800'. The battle he chose to describe in *La Chartreuse de Parme* was in any case one that had taken place when he was hundreds of miles away, which suggests the same diffidence regarding the value of personal experience as that evinced by Thomas Penrose in 'The Field of Battle' and by Thomas Campbell in 'Hohenlinden'; nevertheless his account of his youthful protagonist's baptism of fire was one that was to influence even Tolstoy:

> Suddenly they all moved off at full gallop. A few minutes later Fabrizio saw, twenty paces ahead of him, a ploughed field the surface of which was moving in a singular fashion. The furrows were full of water and the soil, very damp, which formed the ridges between these furrows kept flying off in little black lumps three or four feet into the air. Fabrizio noticed as he passed this curious effect; then his thoughts turned to dreaming of the Marshal and his glory. He heard a sharp cry close to him; two hussars fell struck by shot; and, when he looked back at them, they were already twenty paces behind the escort. What seemed to him horrible was a horse streaming with blood that was struggling on the ploughed land, its hooves caught in its own entrails; it was trying to follow the others: its blood ran down into the mire.
>
> 'Ah! So I am under fire at last!' he said to himself. 'I have seen shots fired!' he repeated with a sense of satisfaction. 'Now I am a real soldier.' At that moment, the escort began to go hell for leather, and our hero realised that it was shot from the guns that was making the earth fly up all round him. He looked vainly in the direction from which the balls were coming, he saw the white smoke of the battery at an enormous distance, and, in the thick of the steady and continuous rumble produced by the artillery fire, he seemed to hear shots discharged much closer at hand: he could not understand in the least what was happening.

One notes however that this was not published till 1839, nearly four decades after Stendhal's own combat experience.[12]

---

[12] Stendhal, *The Life of Henry Brulard*, trans. John Sturrock (1995), p. 462 (originally written 1836); idem, *The Charterhouse of Palma* (Everyman 1992 edn), pp. 46–47.

Amongst German writers, Goethe was with the Imperial troops which invaded France in 1792 and which besieged Mainz in 1793. The narrative he wrote of the 1792 campaign is loftily detached to the point of abstractness. The female protagonist in his long poem *Hermann und Dorothea*, published in 1798, is a refugee from the left bank of the Rhine, which the French had occupied in 1796, but the political and military background is barely mentioned, and the story line was borrowed from an account of the expulsion of Lutherans from the territory of the archbishop of Salzburg during the 1730s. After *Hermann und Dorothea* Goethe turned his back on the wars – quite a feat considering his position as a senior official of one of the German princely governments caught up in the wars' successive crises. For reasons of age as well as expediency he kept aloof from the efflorescence of pan-Germanic feeling that developed after the astonishing defeat and subsequent occupation of Prussia in 1806, but Heinrich von Kleist, who as a sixteen-year-old in the Prussian Guards had also been present at the siege of Mainz in 1793 and in 1803 had attempted to join the French army that was preparing to invade England, was amongst those energized by the new nationalism. His verse drama *Die Hermannsschlacht*, written in 1808, commemorated the defeat of the Roman general Varus by German tribesmen in AD 9 but no one who read the manuscript – it was not printed till 1821 – could have had any doubts as to its modern application. When in 1809 Austria renewed the war with Napoleon it was seen through much of the German-speaking world – though not in the Danish dominions in the north or the French-controlled territories on the Rhine – as a Germanic Crusade. The first-ever war novel to be virtually contemporary with the fighting it describes – Julius von Voss's solemn and boring *Geschichte eines österreichischen Partheigängers* (The Story of an Austrian Partisan), about 'a young Austrian lieutenant of Uhlans' – belongs to this period: it was published in 1810 in Berlin, whither the focus of pan-Germanic sentiment had shifted after the defeat of Austria at Wagram. Both Prussia and Austria took a reluctant part in Napoleon's invasion of Russia in 1812, and turned on him when his great adventure ended in the retreat from Moscow. The campaigns in Germany in 1813 were seen as a War of Liberation – indeed were *called* a War of Liberation from at least as early as 1816 – and generated a substantial quantity of patriotic verse that was to be available to a new generation of patriots in 1914. Theodor Körner, a soldier poet who died of wounds in August 1813, prefigured Rupert Brooke as a cult-figure for martial-minded civilians, though his verse has worn even less well than Brooke's. The curious thing is that so much excitement was generated, not at the beginning of the war, but after it had been going on, with short intervals, for more than twenty years, and the explanation for this is to be found not in the war as such, but in the peculiar conditions of Germany in the 1800s. The patriotic ferment of Germany in 1813 and 1814 had no counterpart elsewhere in Europe (not even amongst Goya's fellow countrymen in Spain), and the stream of poetizing it generated clearly had more to do with propaganda than with the sort of literature that can be exported, or read with satisfaction a couple of centuries later. Nevertheless, by 1814 the *idea* of war literature – literature about, and celebrating, war – had clearly emerged in Germany, even if the practice still left a great deal of scope for improvement, whereas in Britain and France this development was still in the future. But even in Germany the best-known writer to see combat in 1813 and survive, Friedrich *Freiherr* de La Motte Fouqué (a Prussian officer of Huguenot descent), gave only the sketchiest account of his war experiences in his memoirs, and concentrated, both before and after the fighting, on churning out pseudo-medieval poems and stories analogous to the work of Walter Scott. Scott had complained primarily of non-combatant poets neglecting the war in favour of 'distant and dark ages'; La Motte Fouqué, still remembered as author of the fairy-tale *Undine*, had actually had a horse killed under him while charging a French square at Lützen.[13]

It might be useful to consider the whole issue of writing about war in terms of the larger issue of why authors write in any case. In Britain, because there was no conscription, the question of why and what one

[13] Ernst Beutler, ed., *Johann Wolfgang Goethe: Gedenkausgabe der Werke, Briefe und Gespräche* (24 vols, Zurich, 1948–54), xii (*Biographische Einzelschriften*), pp. 237–426, 'Kampagne in Frankreich 1792'; *Lebensgeschichte des Baron Friedrich de La Motte Fouqué* (Halle, 1840), p. 317.

Julius von Voss (1768–1832) had been in the Prussian army, 1782–98. A prolific writer, he also published, in 1810, a fantasy novel set in the twenty-first century entitled *Ini*, apparently the first work in German to refer to people living in underground bunkers in wartime.

A book entitled *Der Befreiungskrieg in Teutschland im Jahr 1813* ('The War of Liberation in Germany in the Year 1813') was published at Leipzig in 1816.

chose to write ties in suggestively with the question of why one might have chosen to take a personal part in the war.

At least half the novels published in English between 1760 and 1820 seem to have been by women, and most of the rest seem to have been by men of the commercial classes, without superior education; but the majority of authors who published two or more volumes of verse during the same period were university graduates – all of them male of course (and all of them people who kept out of the war). Perhaps the largest group of non-graduate poets were not men who had had a classical education at grammar schools but had then entered business or a profession instead of going to university – the counterpart, perhaps, of many male novelists – but men from the working classes with very poor formal education. The only one of this group to have sustained any considerable reputation is John Clare, but during Clare's lifetime there was a remarkable number of farmboy poets, or shoemaker poets, or poets like Robert Bloomfield who had been both a farmboy and then a shoemaker. As the careers of both Clare and Bloomfield showed, writing poems was a way – perhaps the only available way – for a poorly educated youth from an impoverished background to attract aristocratic patrons. Even without a calculation of this sort, the superior intellectual and social cachet of poetry – the literature of Oxbridge graduates rather than of middle-class females – meant that a working-class youth with an urge to write would naturally tend to gravitate to poetry rather than to the novel.[14]

The particular sociology of authorship at this period obviously affected the way people wrote, or failed to write, about the war. In Britain a military career was not something that attracted poets and intellectuals. *A Sketch of the Campaign of 1793*, a poem published in 1795 by 'An officer of the Guards . . . one of his Royal Highness the Commander in Chief's Aid-de-Camps on the Continent', was an almost unique instance of a man from a good family trying to turn his war experiences into

---

[14] For novelists see Andrew Block, *The English Novel, 1740–1850: A Catalogue Including Prose Romances, Short Stories, and Translations of Foreign Fiction* (1961); for working-class poets see A.D. Harvey, *English Poetry in a Changing Society, 1780–1825* (1980), pp. 84 and 135, and same author, 'The Cult of Chatterton amongst English Poets, *c.* 1770-*c.* 1820', *Zeitschrift für Anglistik und Amerikanistik*, 39 (1991), pp. 124–33, especially at p. 125.

literature, but it is difficult to avoid the impression that the reason why the author was in the army rather than at university was his backwardness as a pupil at school. The poem is mere doggerel:

> To the enemy now, we are fast drawing near,
> And should Williamstadt fall, they may shortly be here . . .
>
> (p.7)
>
> A battery op'ning, annoy'd us with grape
> And I verily thought not a man would escape.
>
> (p. 15)

And though French was a by no means unusual accomplishment amongst Guards officers, even in those days – and especially not amongst Guards officers assigned to a headquarters of an international army – he was apparently unable even to spell 'Aid-de-Camp' correctly.

A rather more interesting army poet, Robert Brown, a corporal in the Coldstream Guards, author of *The Campaign: A Poetical Essay* (1797) seems to fall into the category of the working-class poet who hoped to gain attention with his deftness as a versifier: it is dedicated to the Duke of York, and like so many of the poems of the period (especially those by working-class poets) takes Cowper's blank verse as its model:

> Now with sudden stroke
> The whizzing ball, from brazen cannon flung,
> Cuts off a file at once, or lops a limb,
> Tearing the ground in dreadful furrows long.

Though Brown had apparently been with the Duke of York's army in Flanders he was a poor hand at the personal, subjective point of view, and one is struck by how much more his battle conforms to the orderliness of text-book theory than the fighting described by Major Charles Napier:

> as for the rest,
> Whose duty is obedience, they employ'd
> In the fierce conflict, think of nothing more
> Than how defend themselves, or how destroy
> Their adversaries: and, like some complex,

> Complete machinery, they work, or stop,
> Or turn, as the high guiding hand directs.[15]

Thomas L. Morris, author of *The Daneid: An Epic Poem, in Four Books, Written on Board his Majesty's Ship La Desiree*, also seems to have been in a position to give eye-witness testimony, since he served on board a frigate that took part in the Battle of Copenhagen (the subject of his poem). According to the title page of his book – or rather pamphlet, as his epic is only twenty-eight pages long – it was 'sold by the widow of the author, Back-street, Tynemouth, and all the booksellers in Newcastle, Shields and Sunderland'. This was before the days of widows' pensions of course, and Morris, a 'Pilot' – i.e. helmsman – had probably had only his seaman's pay, which ceased with his death. He seems to have taken Oliver Goldsmith, rather than Cowper, as his model:

> The bullets whistle through the trembling sky,
> And show'rs of splinters round each vessel fly

> (p. 23)

The battle scene in George Woodley's *Britain's Bulwarks: or The British Seaman* was in a similar vein, though with more reliance on punctuation marks:

> Hark to the crashing of that dire broadside,
> Which sends a mass of ruins o'er the tide!
> So thick against the ship the bullets fall
> As rattling hailstones driven against a wall!
> Great God! how dread the scene! Where shall the muse
> Retire, the horrid sight of death to lose?

> (p. 162)

Woodley had begun versifying as a ship's boy on board a warship (imagine settling down to write a three-volume novel under those conditions) but left the sea about 1802, when aged sixteen. He does not seem to have put his time in the Royal Navy to particularly good account: the original owner of the British Library's copy of *Britain's Bulwarks* has written in pencil at the bottom of one page, 'George

[15] Pages 11–19 of Robert Brown's *The Campaign: A Poetical Essay* also appeared, as 'Description of a Battle', in *Poetry: Original and Selected* (Glasgow, 1797).

Woodley has made a mistake in placing the Purser next the Master –
the Gunner, Mates, Midshipmen, Boatswain, Carpenter, and Doctor
being his senior'. His relentless scribbling, which included two epic
poems, eventually paid off however: in 1820, after supporting himself
for nearly twenty years as a journalist, at that time one of the most
menial of professions, he was ordained and given one of the few jobs
in the Church of England where a plebeian background would not
be noticed: missionary in the Scilly Isles.[16]

Another poor man who may have been anxious for a comfortable
billet was Thomas Dermody, the one instance in this period of a
substantial poet – for so he was considered in his own lifetime – who
served in the British army in a theatre of war; but he may have had
personal reasons for writing almost nothing about his service experiences. In 1794 Dermody, then aged nineteen, enlisted in the army in
Ireland while drunk, was released at the request of officious friends,
but soon re-enlisted. As seems often to have been the case with soldiers
who could read and write fluently, he was quickly promoted to sergeant.
After his transfer to England he was commissioned second lieutenant in the Wagon Train and sailed with the Earl of Moira's expedition to Quiberon. His biographer later wrote, 'He was in almost every
considerable action, and received several dangerous wounds'. He
certainly appears on the half-pay list between 1796 and 1801, which
is consistent with his biographer's statement that he had lost the use
of his left hand as a result of a wound received at Quiberon; he had
also, it was claimed, sustained a disfiguring injury to his face. It is difficult to understand though how an officer serving in the Wagon Train
(i.e., in the rear lines) could be wounded by the short-range weapons
of the day, especially as the Quiberon expeditionary force never actually fought a battle. Dermody wrote a poem entitled 'The Invalid':

> Blest who in battle meets the friendly ball,
> While rattling guns proclaim his glorious fall;
> For honor's holiest tear has oft been shed
> On the cold sod, that wraps the soldier's head:
> What now, for me, condemn'd to peace, remains,
> But useless ardors, unavailing pains.

[16] There is a short biography of George Woodley in *The Dictionary of National Biography*, and see the British Library's copy of his *Britain's Bulwarks*, p. 31.

No doubt this was meant to be understood as referring to himself; but if so it seems odd that he wrote nothing else on the subject. It is more likely however that his injuries were the result of an accident, a not infrequent occurrence in armies, especially in those units responsible for heavy equipment; the fact that he drank himself to death by the time he was twenty-seven rather suggests Dermody may have been accident-prone in any case.[17]

It would seem fair to say that the work of Robert Brown, Thomas L. Morris, George Woodley and Thomas Dermody had less to do with what they had seen and felt as combatants than with their need to find a place for themselves in society, or at least raise some money. In this respect their verse provides a parallel with the much more proficient, but equally impersonal, battle paintings executed during the same period by professional artists looking for commissions. The poems just quoted, like the battle paintings of West, Loutherbourg and Gros (and even the patriotic effusions of Theodor Körner), seem to address themselves to the expectations of their audience much more than to the problems of expressing personal experience. The fact that the painters knew who their patrons were while the poets merely wrote in hope of finding readers was a difference of professional status rather than of intention.

Yet paradoxically the years of the French Revolutionary and Napoleonic Wars were the period during which a number of outstanding poets devoted themselves to giving the uniqueness of personal experience a literary form. When France declared war on Britain in February 1793 William Wordsworth and Samuel Taylor Coleridge were of much the same age as Wilfred Owen or Isaac Rosenberg were in 1914. Owen and Rosenberg were killed in action; Wordsworth and Coleridge kept well away from the shooting. It was not simply that in their day young men who had personal statements to make did not join the army; they both disapproved of the war intensely. It was in a fit of depression and certainly not because of any martial enthusiasm that Coleridge enlisted in the 15th Dragoons; he was rescued by his family before there was any chance of his being sent abroad; and unlike Dermody, he did not re-enlist. Coleridge's poem 'Fears in Solitude'

[17] James Grant Raymond *The Life of Thomas Dermody* (2 vols, 1806), ii, pp. 111, 115, 119–21; Thomas Dermody, *Poems, Moral and Descriptive* (1800), pp. 88–89.

of 1798 remains, *faute de mieux*, perhaps the most important literary response to the war, but his laudanum habit effectively prevented him from writing much poetry subsequent to the period in which he ceased to be hostile to Britain's participation in the war; and 'Fears in Solitude' is in many ways an old-fashioned poem, impersonal and too obviously addressed to a public audience:

> Boys and girls,
> and women, that would groan to see a child
> Pull off an insect's leg, all read of war,
> The best amusement for our morning-meal!
> The poor wretch, who has learnt his only prayers
> From curses, who knows scarcely words enough
> To ask a blessing from his Heavenly Father,
> Becomes a fluent phraseman, absolute
> And technical in victories and defeats,
> And all our dainty terms for fratricide;
> Terms which we trundle smoothly o'er our tongues
> Like mere abstractions, empty sounds to which
> We join no feeling and attach no form!
> As if the soldier died without a wound;
> As if the fibres of this godlike frame
> Were gored without a pang; as if the wretch,
> Who fell in battle, doing bloody deeds,
> Passed off to Heaven, translated and not killed;
> As though he had no wife to pine for him,
> No God to judge him!

Wordsworth expressed his disapproval of the war in more personal terms in *The Prelude*, though this was not published till 1850. In Book X of this poem he referred illuminatingly to the circumstances attending, and his own reactions to, Britain's entry into the war:

> I, who with the breeze
> Had play'd, a green leaf on the blessed tree
> Of my beloved country; nor had wish'd
> For happier fortune than to wither there,
> Now from my pleasant station was cut off,
> And toss'd about in whirlwinds. I rejoiced,
> Yea, afterwards, truth most painful to record!
> Exulted in the triumph of my soul

When Englishmen by thousands were o'erthrown,
Left without glory on the Field, or driven,
Brave hearts, to shameful flight. It was a grief,
Grief call it not, 'twas anything but that,
A conflict of sensations without name,
Of which he only who may love the sight
Of a Village Steeple as I do can judge
When in the Congregation, bending all
To their great Father, prayers were offer'd up,
Or praises for our Country's Victories,
And 'mid the simple worshippers, perchance,
I only, like an uninvited Guest
Whom no one own'd sate silent, shall I add,
Fed on the day of vengeance yet to come?

In *The Excursion* (1814) he described, less effectively, some of the changes which had been taking place in England since the war began; but except during brief phases – the invasion panic of 1803, the British intervention in Spain in 1808 – his attitude to the war remained embarrassed and equivocal: his *Tract on the Convention of Cintra*, which attempted to give a grand moral colouring to the first of the British expeditions to the Peninsula, offers itself in retrospect as an indication of why he did not write a major poem about the war, or at any rate gives a fair picture of what most of his contemporaries did *not* see as the war's objectives. A number of lesser poets who then enjoyed an exaggerated reputation seem to have shared his ambivalence: Thomas Campbell, Samuel Rogers, Anna Laetitia Barbauld. Byron and Shelley, whose childhood, adolescence and early manhood coincided with the war years, were frankly hostile to the British government's war policy. This self-distancing from the greatest events of their time was not unique to British writers: Schiller busied himself writing historical plays during Napoleon's rise to power and died before his part of the German world was sucked into the maelstrom, and Benjamin Constant and Chateaubriand spent most of the war years in exile or travelling. It does seem slightly strange that none of the young men conscripted into the French army wanted to write creatively about their experiences but they too would have been bred to a conception of authorship, analogous to that in Britain, which limited the appeal of the war as a literary theme. It may seem an odd coincidence that a war which touched so many people was held at bay by the writers of the time best qualified to write about it, but if it was a coincidence there were to be twentieth-century parallels: D.H. Lawrence spent the years 1914–18 in what might almost be termed internal exile; and in 1939 W.H. Auden fled beyond the Atlantic.[18]

After Napoleon's culminating defeat at Waterloo, at a not inconvenient distance for tourists from England, several poets rushed to the scene with the object of producing remunerative literary masterpieces. (One may see in this a belated rediscovery of the first, rather short-lived, emergence in Britain of the idea that war was at least a *marketable* literary subject.) Foremost amongst the poets who travelled to Belgium was Walter Scott, whose *The Field of Waterloo* was a reversion to his earlier *Marmion* style:

> In one dark torrent broad and strong,
> The advancing onset roll'd along,
> Forth harbinger'd by fierce acclaim,
> That from the shroud of smoke and flame,
> Peal'd wildly the imperial name.

Another poet who visited the site of the battle was Robert Southey, who in his earlier, francophil years had published an anti-war poem that is still anthologized today:

> It was a summer evening,
>   Old Kaspar's work was done,
> And he before his cottage door
>   Was sitting in the sun;
> And by him sported on the green
>   His little grandchild Wilhelmine.
>
> She saw her brother Peterkin
>   Roll something large and round
> Which he beside the rivulet
>   In playing there had found;

---

[18] Samuel Taylor Coleridge, 'Fears in Solitude', lines 104–23. William Wordsworth, *The Prelude* (1805–6 text), x, lines 254–75; the 1850 version, lines 278–99, is virtually identical, apart from punctuation, from line 283 onward. For the argument that Romanticism actually represented a retreat from the demands of the public realm see Harvey, *Literature into History*, pp. 160–66.

> He came to ask what he had found
> That was so large and smooth and round.
>
> Old Kaspar took it from the boy
>   Who stood expectant by;
> And then the old man shook his head,
>   And with a natural sigh
> 'Tis some poor fellow's skull', said he,
> 'Who fell in the great victory'.
>
> 'I find them in the garden,
>   For there's many here about;
> And often when I go to plough
>   The ploughshare turns them out.
> For many thousand men', said he,
> 'Were slain in that great victory.'

When, seventeen years after publishing these verses, he had his first experience of a recent battlefield, he must have been surprised by how reminiscent it was of the picture he had suggested.

> The ground is ploughed and sown, and grain and flowers and seeds already growing over the field of battle, which is still strewn with vestiges of the slaughter, caps, cartridges, boxes, hats, &c. We picked up some French cards and some bullets, and we purchased a French pistol and two of the eagles which the infantry wear upon their caps. What I felt upon this ground, it would be difficult to say; what I saw, and still more what I heard, there is no time at present for saying. In prose and in verse you shall some day hear the whole. At Les Quatre Bras, I saw two graves, which probably the dogs or the swine had opened. In the one were the ribs of a human body, projecting through the mould; in the other, the whole skeleton exposed. Some of our party told me of a third, on which the worms were at work, but I shrank from the sight.

In his *The Poet's Pilgrimage to Waterloo* it was the rubbish left behind by battle which inspired perhaps his most memorable stanza:

> Some marks of wreck were scattered all around,
>   As shoe, and belt, and broken bandoleer,
> And hats which bore the mark of mortal wound;
>   Gun-flints and balls for those who closelier peer;
> And sometimes did the breeze upon its breath
> Bear from ill covered graves a taint of death.

Viewing the scene three months after the battle, he found only one trace of blood, in a farm building, but that one trace was striking enough:

> One streak of blood upon the wall was traced,
>   In length a man's just stature from the head;
> There where it gushed you saw it uneffaced:
>   Of all the blood which on that day was shed
> This mortal stain alone remained impressed . . .
> The all-devouring earth had drunk the rest.

One almost wishes Wordsworth, who attended the same victory celebration as Southey on the summit of Skiddaw, could have seen it, and written about it: but he did not visit the battlefield till 1820 and his principal poetic achievement in 1815 was 'Artegal and Elidure', a poem based on a story in Geoffrey of Monmouth and composed 'as a token of affectionate respect for the memory of Milton'. Perhaps it was not entirely an accident that at the festivities on Skiddaw he knocked over the boiling water needed for the punch 'and thought to slink off undiscovered'.[19]

[19] The stanza by Scott is no. XI, on p. 22 of *The Field of Waterloo* (Edinburgh, 1815). Southey's 'The Battle of Blenheim' first appeared in the *Morning Post*, 9 August 1798. The prose quotation is from C.C. Southey, *The Life and Correspondence of Robert Southey* (6 vols, 1850), iv, pp. 134–35, Southey to John May, 6 October 1815, and the two stanzas from *The Poet's Pilgrimage to Waterloo* (1816) are nos. 39 and 48, on pp. 68 and 73 respectively. For the picnic on Skiddaw, see *Life and Correspondence of Southey*, iv, pp. 121–22, Robert Southey to Henry Southey, 23 August 1815.

Other Waterloo poems include *The Battle of Waterloo*, by George Walker (1815); *The Battle of Waterloo*, by C.F. Warden (1817); *Mont St Jean*, by William Liddiard (1816); and the anonymous *The Campaign of One Day* (1816) and *A Ballad of Waterloo* (1817). Byron went to Waterloo, in May 1816, and reported, 'The Plain of Waterloo is a fine one – but not much after Marathon & Troy': Leslie A. Marchand, ed., *Byron's Letters and Journals* (12 vols, 1973–82), v, p. 76. See also *Childe Harold's Pilgrimage*, canto III (1816) stanzas 17–30 and note to stanza 30.

CHAPTER 3

The Nineteenth Century

CHARLOTTE BRONTË was born the year after Waterloo. In 1848 she wrote to a friend:

> I remember well wishing my lot had been cast in the troubled times of the late war, and seeing in its exciting incidents a kind of stimulating charm, which it made my pulses beat fast to think of: I remember even, I think, being a little impatient, that you would not fully sympathise with my feelings on those subjects; that you heard my aspirations and speculations very tranquilly, and by no means seemed to think the flaming swords could be any pleasant addition to paradise.

It had not felt like that for most people who lived through the 1790s and 1800s, but the uninterrupted years of peace that followed Waterloo made the idea of a really big war seem more interesting than it had appeared at the time. One symptom of this was the stream of memoirs and reminiscences that began to issue from the presses, and continued, sons publishing their fathers' manuscripts, right up until the outbreak of the First World War, and beyond. William Matthews's *British Autobiographies* (Berkeley, 1955), under the index entry for the Napoleonic and Peninsular Wars, lists eighty-seven journals and memoirs by army personnel alone, including one by James Hope, *The Military Memoirs of an Infantry Officer*, that anticipates the title of Siegfried Sassoon's First World War classic. More have been published since the 1950s. There are also a number of unpublished items in the National Army Museum and other archive depositories which appear to have been written with eventual publication in mind. Although the population of Britain in 1810 was perhaps three times what it was in 1640 (though not proportionately much more literate), a larger percentage of the population saw action in the Civil War than in the campaigns against Napoleon, it being in the nature of civil war that the same society provides both armies, and also the audience: more Britons fought at Marston Moor than at Salamanca or Waterloo. The fact that the later conflict produced at least five times more personal memoirs reflects a change in sensibility, not in population statistics. This memoir-writing by other than generals, incidentally, was mainly a British phenomenon: eight of Napoleon's marshals died by violence, six wrote memoirs; of Britain's senior commanders only Sir John Moore even left a diary; but the French have little more than the *Mémoires de Robert Guillemard, sergent en retraite* (Paris, 1826) and Sergeant Bourgogne's *Mémoires de la campagne de Russie en 1812* (Valenciennes, 1856) to match the scores of memoirs written by men who served in the lower ranks of the British army.[1]

With the exception of Napier's account of the Battle of La Coruña, which is printed as an appendix to this book, none of these memoirs are of a literary quality to be compared with the best personal accounts of the 1914–18 war. Occasionally one comes across a bizarre or horrific detail that sticks in the memory:

> A tall athletic soldier of the 52d lay amongst the dead at the foot of the breach, on his back; his arms and legs being at their full extent. The top of his head, from the forehead to the back part of his skull, was split in twain, and the cavity of the head entirely emptied of brains, as if a hand-grenade had exploded within, and expanded the skull, till it had forced it into a separation with the parts rugged like a saw, leaving a gaping aperture nine inches in length, and four in breadth. For a considerable time I looked on this horrible fracture, to define, if possible, by what missile or instrument so wonderful a wound could have been made; but without being able to come to any conclusion as to the probable cause.

---

[1] Elizabeth Gaskell, *The Life of Charlotte Brontë* (Everyman edn, 1908), p. 244, Charlotte Brontë to Miss Wooler, 31 March 1848; see also Lascelles Wraxall, *Married in Haste: A Story of Every Day Life* (3 vols, 1863), i, p. 1.

The Diary of Sir John Moore, edited by Sir J.F. Maurice, was published in two volumes in 1904. The paucity – as it then seemed – of military memoirs and the predominance of those by 'persons in the *inferior ranks* of the army' was commented on by J.C. Mämpel in 1826, *The Young Rifleman's Comrade: A Narrative of his Military Adventures, Captivity, and Shipwreck* (1826), p. xiv.

Or, a little less gruesome, an artillery officer's account of his efforts to persuade his men to hold their fire while being shot at by cavalry skirmishers riding forty yards away:

> Seeing some exertion beyond words necessary for this purpose, I leaped my horse up the little bank, and began a promenade (by no means agreeable) up and down our front, without even drawing my sword, though these fellows were within speaking distance of me. This quieted my men; but the tall blue gentlemen, seeing me thus dare them, immediately made a target of me, and commenced a very deliberate practice, to show us what very bad shots they were and verify the old artillery proverb, 'The nearer the target, the safer you are'. One fellow certainly made me flinch, but it was a miss; so I shook my finger at him, and called him *coquin*, etc. The rogue grinned as he reloaded, and again took aim. I certainly felt rather foolish at that moment, but was ashamed, after such bravado, to let him see it, and therefore continued my promenade. As if to prolong my torment, he was a terrible time about it. To me it seemed an age. Whenever I turned, the muzzle of his infernal carbine still followed me. At length bang it went, and whiz came the ball close to the back of my neck, and at the same instant down dropped the leading driver of one of my guns (Miller), into whose forehead the cursed missile had penetrated.

At their best such accounts are examples of the painstaking fidelity to detail which was part of the nineteenth century's literary and artistic ideal: but fidelity to detail in itself does not constitute literature.[2]

The only known instance of a participant in the wars trying, long afterwards, to write a great work of art on the subject was an unfortunate Waterloo veteran who, out of admiration for Tennyson's ode on the death of Wellington, brought him 'twelve large cantos' on the Battle of Waterloo. 'The veteran had actually taught himself in his old age to read and write that he might thus commemorate Wellington's great victory', recorded the laureate's son. 'The epic lay for some time under the sofa in my father's study, and was a source of much anxiety to him.' Tennyson finally told the old soldier, when he called to collect

---

[2] *Memoirs of the Late War: Comprising the Personal Narrative of Captain Cooke . . .* (2 vols, 1831), i, p. 129; Cavalié Mercer, *Journal of the Waterloo Campaign* (2 vols, Edinburgh, 1870), i, pp. 318–19.

The wound described by Cooke was most probably caused by a small cannon ball or a grape-shot grazing the top of the soldier's skull. The passage of a musket ball would not have exerted sufficient suction to remove the brain tissue, and a large cannon ball would have taken away more of the skull.

his manuscript, 'Though great images loom here and there, your poem could not be published as a whole'.[3]

Perhaps the most popular – certainly the most widely disseminated – branch of writing to come out of the Napoleonic War was the swashbuckling tale of derring-do in the Royal Navy, in which authors like Frederick Chamier, Edward Howard and above all Frederick Marryat had served, in accordance with the conventions of the day, when little more than children. Judging by the results, spending one's teens on active service was probably not the best means of fostering a literary sensibility, especially when Smollett's *Roderick Random* and John Davis's *The Post-Captain* (a novel published in 1806 which chiefly deals with the flirtations of socially inept naval officers) provided the most obvious literary models. It may be no coincidence that Edward John Trelawny, the most talented of the striplings who served in the Royal Navy after Trafalgar and lived to write about it, took an early opportunity to desert and, according to his own account, become a pirate: amongst his later exploits were supervising the cremation of Shelley's body on an Italian beach and, two years later, arriving at Missolonghi too late to see Lord Byron die, but in time to sneak a look at his feet to check out the precise nature of their deformity. And one of the most popular of the naval adventure yarns, Michael Scott's *Tom Cringle's Log* (1834) was written by a man whose only experience of seafaring was the several Atlantic crossings he made between 1806 and 1822 in the course of pursuing his business interests in Jamaica.[4]

---

[3] Hallam Tennyson *Alfred Lord Tennyson: A Memoir* (1898–99 edn.), ii, p. 215–16. This occurred in the 1850s.

[4] The *Athenaeum*, for 9 December 1843 (p. 1092 b), described *The Post-Captain* as 'the parent of all our nautical novels', but this is too generous. There were seven editions between 1806 and 1815, the third and fourth of which attributed the authorship to Dr John Moore, the novelist father of Sir John Moore of La Coruña fame. Charles Laughton recorded in *Notes and Queries* (fifth series, 10, p. 239) that Davis was said to have been 'a purser in the navy' but, since he was only eighteen when he joined the Royal Navy in 1793 and twenty-three when he left the service to go to America, his position was probably one of less responsibility.

For Trelawny and the cremation of Shelley see E.J. Trelawny, *Recollections of the Last Days of Shelley and Byron* (1858), pp. 132–35; for his inspection of Byron's feet, ibid., p. 224.

For Michael Scott see Mowbray Morris's introduction to the 1895 edition of *Tom Cringle's Log*, pp. viii-xii.

At least Michael Scott had been on the high seas during the war. Charles Lever, who wrote the nineteenth-century's most popular novel of the army side of the struggle against Napoleon, *Charles O'Malley*, was aged nine at the time of Waterloo. James Grant, author of *The Romance of War: or The Highlanders in Spain*, though able to draw on the reminiscences of his father, who had served in the Peninsula as an officer in a Scottish regiment, was not born till a year after Napoleon's death; as was Emile Erckmann, the elder of the two co-authors of the most popular French novel about the Napoleonic War, *Histoire d'un conscrit de 1813* (1864).

Marryat's *Frank Mildmay* (1829), *Peter Simple* (1834) and *Mr Midshipman Easy* (1836), Frederick Chamier's *The Arethusa* (1837) and *Tom Bowling* (1841), and Edward Howard's *Rattlin the Reefer* (1836) present a curious literary irony. The post-war years coincided with the growing fame of Goethe's *Wilhelm Meister*, the archetypal *Bildungsroman*, that is to say a novel dealing (at a significantly more reflective level than, for example, works like *Tom Jones*) with the developing self-awareness and individuation of a young man at the outset of his career. From the time of Stephen Crane's *The Red Badge of Courage* onward the *Bildungsroman* was to be one of the most enduring influences on novels and memoirs dealing with war service. One can already see elements of the *Wilhelm Meister* tradition in an insipid novel of army life, *The Youth and Manhood of Cyril Thornton* by Thomas Hamilton, a Peninsular veteran, published in 1827, four years after the appearance of what is generally considered the first British *Bildungsroman*, John Gibson Lockhart's *Reginald Dalton*, which, not untypically, deals with the completely civilian preoccupations of an undergraduate at Oxford about the time of the Battle of Salamanca. But the war novels of Marryat, Chamier and Howard, in which young boys are sent to sea and in the course of a brutal introduction to the most horrific aspects of real life achieve such personal maturity as they are capable of, represent a kind of *Bildungsroman* without Goethe's intellectual and psychological pretensions, and without much sign of his influence. The following was written, more than a quarter of a century after the event, by a man who, as a fourteen-year-old midshipman, commanded more than forty men operating a battery of 32-pounders on the lower deck of HMS *Defence*, at the Battle of the First of June:

After the two or three first broadsides, I became anxious to have a good view of the ship we were engaging. To effect this object, I requested the men at the foremost gun to allow me a few seconds, when the port was hauled up, to look out from it. They complied with my wishes. The gun being loaded, I took my station in the centre of the port; which being held up, I beheld our antagonist firing away at us in quick succession. The ship was painted a dark red, as most of the enemy's Fleet were, to denote (as previously mentioned) their sanguinary feelings against their adversaries. I had not enjoyed the sight long – only a few seconds – when a rolling sea came in and completely covered me. The tars, noticing this, instantly let down the port, but I got a regular soaking for my curiosity. The men cheered me, and laughingly said, 'We hope, Sir, you will not receive further injury. It is rather warm work here below: the salt water will keep you cool'.

One of these, John Polly, of very short stature, remarked that he was so small the shot would all pass over him. The words had not been long out of his mouth when a shot cut his head right in two, leaving the tip of each ear remaining on the lower part of the cheek. His sudden death created a sensation among his comrades, but the excitement of the moment soon changed those impressions to others of exertion. There was no withdrawing from our situation, and the only alternative was to face the danger with becoming firmness. The head of this unfortunate seaman was cut so horizontally that anyone looking at it would have supposed it had been done by the blow of an axe. His body was committed to the deep.

'The only alternative was to face the danger with becoming firmness.' Indeed: and the midshipman, as the officer in charge of men twice or three times his age, had to set an example. He may even have given the order for committing John Polly's body to the deep, which presumably consisted of thrusting his corpse out through the gun port prior to running out the gun for another salvo: he was certainly standing there when it was done. The reason why he says nothing of his own feelings, other than his curiosity, was at least partly that he had had to learn not to have any: and Marryat and Chamier had been trained in the same school.[5]

---

[5] Andrew Lang, *The Life and Letters of John Gibson Lockhart* (2 vols, 1897), i, p. 219, ii, p. 273, for Lockhart's admiration for Goethe: Lockhart was also a friend of Thomas Hamilton and, as a young man, had visited Weimar with Hamilton's elder brother,

During the period of Marryat and Co's writing career the twenty-two-year struggle with France was normally referred to as 'the late war', as if merely one of a series (which in a sense it was). It was the American Civil War of 1861–65 that was the first conflict to be known during subsequent decades (even if only in America) simply as 'the war'. In one of Edith Wharton's short stories, for example, some of the characters discuss an acquaintance: 'of course he was in the war'. 'I don't think he was in the war at all . . .' 'Why shouldn't he have been in the war?' Besides being a major turning-point in American history, the War between the States was the first war to be fought on the twentieth-century pattern, with armies supported all through the year at the battlefront by railways and linked together by the power of electricity – the North alone brought into operation 15,000 miles of military telegraph lines. It was also the first war to produce a mass-selling (not merely best-selling) war book and an anthology of war poetry. Willard Glazier's woodenly-written account of his escape from a Confederate prison camp, *The Capture, the Prison-Pen and the Escape* (New York, 1865) eventually had a sale of over 400,000 'larger by many thousands than that most extensively circulated and deservedly popular book *Uncle Tom's Cabin*' had ever attained. Its readers' appetite would already have been whetted by vast numbers of 'war poems' which had been printed in both South and North: William Gilmore Simms's collection *War Poetry of the South* (New York, 1867), containing over 200 poems, was culled mainly from the newspapers of South Carolina, Virginia and Georgia.[6]

The poems in Simms's anthology, mainly by civilians, testified to the popularity of Macaulay's *Lays of Ancient Rome* rather than to the native literary genius of the American people. As in Germany in 1813, bulk did not create quality. Herman Melville, the outstanding American writer of the century, remained silent during the war, to which in

continued
Sir William Hamilton the metaphysician; William Henry Dillon, *A Narrative of My Professional Adventures* (1790–1839), ed. Michael A. Lewis (2 vols, 1953, 1956), i, p. 130.
[6] Edith Wharton, 'The Lamp of Psyche'; Robert Luther Thompson *Wiring a Continent: The History of the Telegraph Industry in the United States, 1832–1866* (Princeton, 1947), p. 394; John Algernon Owen, *Sword and Pen; or Ventures and Adventures of Willard Glazier (The Soldier Author) on War and Literature* (New York, 1880), p. 309–10.

all probability he felt unsympathetic: his 1866 collection of poems, *Battle Pieces and Aspects of the War*, lacked both originality and conviction. Walt Whitman's war poems were later to be extravagantly admired by Isaac Rosenberg, one of the greatest of First World War poets – he told a friend, 'Walt Whitman in "Beat, drums, beat", has said the noblest thing on war':

> Beat! beat! drums – blow! bugles! blow!
> Through the window – through the doors – burst like a ruthless force
> Into the solemn church, and scatter the congregation

But it is arguable that this poem and its companion pieces were not up to the standard of Whitman's original *Leaves of Grass* collection of 1855. Bret Harte stayed in California, well away from the war, and Mark Twain, having joined a volunteer company that almost immediately fell apart, beat a hasty retreat to Nevada. Ambrose Bierce was an officer in the Federal Army and eventually published a number of stories derived from his experiences, but the authentic voice of the young Bierce – still a teenager when the war began – seems to have become quite lost under what he felt proper to add in the years that intervened between soldiering and writing, as if the incidents of the war itself had been insufficiently striking. More typical than the works of Melville, Whitman and Bierce was the poem 'All Quiet Along the Potomac' which, though written by a woman named Ethel Lynn Beers, was chiefly memorable for the number of men who claimed to be its author:

> All quiet along the Potomac, they say,
>   Except here and there a stray picket
> Is shot, as he walks on his beat to and fro,
>   By a rifleman hid in the thicket.
> 'Tis nothing, a private or two now and then,
>   Will not count in the news of the battle.
> Not an officer lost, only one of the men
>   Moaning out all alone the death-rattle.
>
> All quiet along the Potomac to-night,
>   Where the soldiers lie peacefully dreaming;
> Their tents in the rays of the clear autumn moon

Or in the light of their camp-fires gleaming;
A tremulous sigh, as a gentle night wind,
   Through the forest-leaves softly is creeping,
While the stars up above, with their glittering eyes,
   Keep guard o'er the army while sleeping.

There's only the sound of the lone sentry's tread,
   As he tramps from the rock to the fountain,
And thinks of the two on the low trundle-bed,
   Far away in the cot on the mountain.
His musket falls slack, and his face dark and grim,
   Grows gentle with memories tender,
As he mutters a prayer for the children asleep;
   For their mother, – may heaven defend her!

The moon seems to shine as brightly as then, –
   That night when the love yet unspoken
Leaped up to his lips, and when low-murmured vows
   Were pledged to be ever unbroken.
Then drawing his sleeve roughly over his eyes,
   He dashes off tears that are welling,
And gathers his gun close up to its place,
   As if to keep down the heart-swelling.

He passes the fountain, the blasted pine-tree;
   The footsteps are lagging and weary;
Yet onward they go, through the broad belt of light,
   Toward the shade of the forest so dreary.
Hark! was it the night-wind rustled the leaves?
   Was it moonlight so wondrously flashing?
It looked life a rifle! 'Ha! Mary, good-by'.
   And the life-blood is ebbing and splashing.

All quiet along the Potomac to-night,
   No sound save the rush of the river;
Whilst soft falls the dew on the face of the dead, –
   The picket's *off duty*, forever![7]

---

[7] Ian Parsons, ed., *The Collected Works of Isaac Rosenberg* (1979), p. 237, Rosenberg
to Mrs Herbert Cohen [July 1916?]; John Wood Davidson, *The Living Writers of the
South* (New York, 1869), p. 194, states that 'All Quiet Along the Potomac', originally

The Franco-German War of 1870 produced not very much more, though Paul Deroulède, who had been captured by the Prussians but escaped, and was later wounded fighting against the Commune, enjoyed a huge popular success – forty-nine editions 1872–78 – with his *Chants du soldat.* The best of the writers to deal with the war either had been on the sidelines or else, like Maupassant (who had been in the fighting) took an onlooker's point of view, as in his short story 'Boule de Suïf', which deals with the aftermath of defeat and occupation. Zola's *Débâcle,* and *La bête humaine* with its unforgettable final image of the driverless troop train – 'a blind, deaf beast, unleashed amidst death, it rolled on and on, loaded with cannon fodder, with soldiers dazed with exhaustion, drink and singing' – dealt with the war as only a single part of the huge canvas of his twenty-volume Rougon-Macquart series. The best-known German novels about the war, published not long before the First World War, were by Walter Bloem, who was a toddler at the time of the events he described in *Das eiserne Jahr* and *Volk wider Volk*: in 1914 he served as a frontline officer in the invasion of Belgium and finally discovered what it was like to be shot at, noting ruefully: 'How many times had I not experienced all this in my imagination during the writing of those war-novels, and yet now, just this one time, I was asked to believe it to be solid fact'.[8]

continued

published in *Harper's Weekly,* 30 November 1861, was claimed by six poets, the most vociferous of whom, Major Lamar Fontaine, stated in 1868, 'I wrote it, and the world knows it; and they may howl over it and give it to as many authors as they please. I wrote it, and I am a Southern man, and am proud of the title' (ibid., p. 197). Ethel Lynn Beers does not appear in the authoritative 2241-page *American Women Writers: A Critical Reference Guide from Colonial Times to the Present* (4 vols, New York, 1979–82), edited by Lina Mainiero.

[8] Walter Bloem, *The Advance from Mons* (1930; originally published as *Vormarsch,* Leipzig, 1916), p. 68; other well-known German writers dealing with the 1870 war included Carl Bleibtreu and Detlev von Liliencron: the latter had fought as a Prussian officer against Austria in 1866, as well as against France in 1870, but his volume *Kriegsnovellen* (1895) seems to have been quickly outsold by Bloem's novels on their appearance: see Scott D. Denham, *Visions of War: Ideologies and Images of War in German Literature Before and After the Great War* (Bern, 1992), pp. 23–41. For the French poetry of the war of 1870 see *Times Literary Supplement,* 10 September 1914, p. 416 a-c.

Physically the most substantial artistic legacy of the 1870 war was the large number of war memorials, those in France, like those commemorating the battles of the Risorgimento in Italy, generally showing bronze soldiers with contemporary uniforms in strained postures, as do some of the German ones in Alsace-Lorraine: those in German civic cemeteries are generally more old-fashioned and restrained, obelisks decorated with military trophies and bronze wreaths. Earlier epochs had erected statues and columns to great military leaders (often though not invariably monarchs) but the communal war memorial seems to have been an invention of the nineteenth century. One of the first was the Husarentempel at Mödling near Vienna, erected by Prince Johann von Liechtenstein in 1810. It contained the remains of five representative members of the prince's own regiment who were killed at Aspern and Wagram: the inscription refers to 'the noble boncs of the brave warriors of Austria'. Following a Prussian royal edict of 5 May 1813 tablets listing local men who had fallen in the struggle against the French were placed in every church in Prussian territory. In Britain colonial wars gave increasing scope for group memorials, and an interesting development as the century progressed is that the common soldiers, initially left out or recorded in smaller lettering after the listing of officers, gain an equality in dying for one's country that superseded the distinction of ranks that had such importance in life.[9]

Yet even in Britain, whose army was engaged in fighting *somewhere* in the world during the course of every year of Queen Victoria's reign, the memorials of more recent wars were overshadowed by monuments to the victories of the 1793–1815 period. In central London the Guards' Crimean Monument by John Bell in Waterloo Place (formerly known as the 'Quoit Player' on account of the way Honour holds her wreath over the heads of the three guardsmen) is literally

---

[9] A possible reason for the difference in style of German and French memorials to the dead of the 1870 war is that the German monuments were erected soon afterwards whereas the French monuments generally date from the 1890s and 1900s: see Antoine Prost 'Les monuments aux morts', in Pierre Nora, ed., *Les lieux de mémoire* (7 vols, Paris, 1984–92), i, pp. 195–225, at p. 196.

For the Husarentempel at Mödling bei Wien see Joachim Giller, Hubert Mader, Christina Siedl, *Wo sind sie geblieben . . . ? Kriegerdenkmaler und Gefallenenehrung in Österreich* (Vienna, 1992), p. 30. In its present form the structure dates from 1813, the building erected in 1810 having been damaged in a storm.

dwarfed by Nelson's Column, Decimus Burton's triumphal arch on
Constitution Hill (formerly located nearer Apsley House, Wel-
lington's home, and surmounted by a statue of him), Richard
Westmacott's Achilles in Hyde Park, made from the metal of captured
French guns and dedicated to the duke, and John Nash's Marble Arch
(which was originally intended to have friezes showing British military
and naval triumphs). Perhaps one should also mention the Duke of
York's Column, which commemorates his administrative work as
Commander-in-Chief during most of the war period rather than the
feats of hill-marching immortalized in the nursery rhyme. In Paris
the Arc de Triomphe dominates the skyline while the battles of
Napoleon III's reign are most noticeably commemorated in street
names. In Leipzig, which has a fine monument commemorating the
victory of 1870–71 in the market place, and eight other monuments
to the same war in various suburbs, it is monuments to the Napoleonic
War which catch the eye at almost every turning.

Leipzig in fact possesses a unique assemblage of material illustrat-
ing the successive stages of the memorialization of Germany's so-
called War of Liberation. In May 1813 Napoleon's troops clashed with
Prussian forces to the east of the city, not far from the battlefield of
Lützen where Gustav II Adolf had been killed in 1632. Lützen was
part of the territory (now *Land* Sachsen-Anhalt) which Saxony ceded
to Prussia in 1815; soon afterwards the local council, no doubt anxious
to ingratiate itself with its new monarch, erected a monument to mark
the spot from where King Friedrich Wilhelm ('our good king') had
witnessed the battle. In 1817 the Prussian government itself erected
a monument nearby (known as *Das Monarchenhügel Denkmal*), with
the inscription 'King and Country thankfully honour the fallen heroes':
it is an early example of the use of neo-gothic by a regime which before
1800 had been one of the most frenchified in Germany. In the same
year a separate neo-gothic monument was erected to Prinz von
Hessen-Homburg who, the inscription stated, 'died the death of
honour for God and country'. A fourth monument on the battlefield, to Scharnhorst, was apparently erected in 1913 to mark
the centenary of his death. In the meantime the Swedes had erected
a monument not far off to Gustav Adolf in 1837, and dedicated a
memorial church to him in 1907; a few miles away at Breitenfeld a
local landowner had provided another Gustav Adolf memorial to

commemorate the 200th anniversary of the Swedish king's victory over Tilly in 1631.[10]

Five months after Lützen, on the other side of Leipzig, though with off-shoots as far west as the road leading to Lützen, a larger and more important battle was fought, known to posterity as the Battle of Leipzig or the Battle of the Nations. Some of the individual dead were honoured by memorials erected by their relatives almost immediately afterwards: for example John Motherby, son of a British-born merchant resident in Königsberg, and captain in the 3. *Ostpreussische Landwehr Bataillon*, was commemorated by a huge iron casting in the shape of an Iron Cross medal, which stands on the site of his death next to the Grassi Museum. Polish patriots erected two memorials to József Poniatowski, whom Napoleon created a marshal during the course of the battle and who died in its final stages: one of these monuments, the *Poniatowski-Sarkophag* is dated 1834; the other is undated and it is unclear which was erected first. The family of Prince Schwarzenberg, the Austrian commander, erected a monument to him in 1838, the twenty-fifth anniversary of the battle. The same year also saw the revival of the *Verein zur Feier des 19. Oktober* (Association for Celebrating the 19th of October), originally founded on the first anniversary of the battle, which had functioned – that is, perhaps organized an annual procession and a dinner, but it is not known what else – between 1814 and 1827. In 1843 the *Verein* was relaunched with the aim of erecting memorials to the battle. The first, the *Monarchenhügel Denkmal* at Meusdorf, where Friedrich Wilhelm of Prussia, Alexander of Russia and Francis of Austria had witnessed the battle, was much the most elaborate. It was inaugurated in 1847. A couple of years earlier another private initiative had led to the erection of the *Kugel-Denkmal*, decorated with fifty-seven cannon balls, (at the junction of what are now Chopinstrasse, Reudnitzerstrasse and Inselstrasse), to celebrate the thirtieth anniversary of the surrender of Paris following the Battle of Waterloo. The *Verein zur Feier des 19. Oktober*, erected a further six memorials, including another *Kugel-Denkmal* at Möcher,

---

[10] At 11 a.m. on 2 May 1813, when the nature of the Allied attack became evident, Napoleon was standing near a boulder known locally as the 'Gustav Stone' because it was close to the spot where Gustav Adolf had been killed. The Prussian headquarters were at Grossgörschen, about three miles away, and it is here that the German monuments are located. In Germany the action is usually called the Battle of Grossgörschen.

dedicated to the Silesian army commanded by Blücher and Yorck, and the *Elster-Brücken-Sprengung-Denkmal* commemorating the blowing up by the French of one of the principal bridges into the city. (This had occurred just before Poniatowski had been able to cross – covered with wounds, he threw himself into the River Elster and died in the water.) The Elster Bridge memorial, inaugurated in 1863, was the last one erected by the *Verein* but it carried on maintaining its monuments till 1908, when it transferred its funds and responsibilities to the Leipzig city authorities. Between 1861 and 1864 there were also erected forty-four modest stones (known as *Apelsteine*) marking key spots in the battle. The 1860s also saw the erection of three memorials to the patriotic poet Theodor Körner, one on the spot where he was wounded in June 1813 and two on houses where he was nursed: he recovered sufficiently to travel to northern Germany where he was killed in another skirmish on 26 August 1813. (The fiftieth anniversary of his death was commemorated all over Germany, and even in Budapest.) The war of 1870 naturally channelled monument-building into the commemoration of more recent events, but the approach of the centenary of the Battle of Leipzig spurred three national governments into action. The Austro-Hungarian army erected a fine double-headed eagle monument in Antonierstrasse, to the east of the city centre, the Russians opened a large memorial church to the west, and further out the Germans themselves erected the vast and hideous *Völkerschlachtdenkmal.* One is not quite sure whether this competitive monument-building augured badly for future events – within less than a year Europe would once again be at war – or demonstrated how remote such a contingency seemed in 1913.[11]

Such reminders of past military glories were backed up, in most European countries, by a system of obligatory military service. Public opinion generally acknowledged the necessity of such arrangements and it is one of the more striking achievements of European governments after 1815, in a period of what in retrospect seems a very unstable balance between provision of public services and the physical expectations of still largely agricultural populations, that

---

[11] Max Eschner, *Leipzigs Denkmaler: Denksteine und Gedenktafeln* (Leipzig, 1910), passim. See also *Erinnerungsblatt an die Körner-Feier in Pest* (Pest, 1863).

despite the unpopularity of conscription in France before 1815, during the rest of the century people were on the whole confident that
their young men would be well-treated and well-fed in the army. In
France, where after the war of 1870 every able-bodied male went to
the army, only candidates for university degrees enjoyed the comparative benefit of a reduced term of service, and that only between 1889
and 1904. In Germany, where about half of each age group was
inducted, the prestige of military service was such that those who
served had an advantage over those who did not; the army reserve
of former conscripts, which backed up the annual conscriptions,
providing the men who had done military service with a continuing social identity. To be an officer in the reserve involved considerable status within the community. Walter Bloem's book
Sommerleutnants: Die Geschichte einer achtwochigen Übung (1910: the title
means 'Summertime Lieutenants: The Story of an Eight-Week
Exercise') indicates both the author's pride and readers' interest
in what might seem the rather dull subject of peacetime training
manoeuvres.

Conscription and the maintenance of a reserve involved a certain
degree of visible militarism: not simply the constant sight of troops at
railway stations and in the streets, but also the provision of drill halls
in all the larger towns. The British did not have conscription (other
than the balloting for a home-service militia in times of war), but the
same effect was achieved by the Volunteer movement after 1859. The
emergence in France of Napoleon's nephew as head of government
worked on a kind of reflex appetite for military make-pretend in Britain
and produced vociferous calls for some sort of military training for
the population. From 1852 onwards rifle clubs began to be formed
on a semi-military basis: in 1853 the Royal Victoria Rifle Club was
permitted to assemble for military drilling. Then came the Crimean
War. New production techniques meant that the Battle of the Alma,
Balaclava and the Siege of Sevastopol could be reported in the periodical press in far more detail than had been possible in the Napoleonic
era, and with illustrations. The Indian Mutiny reminded Britons that
if ever they went abroad they might have to defend their women and
children at gunpoint. In 1859, when Napoleon III went to war with
Austria, the British middle classes' enthusiasm for the idea of military
training achieved critical mass. Training corps were founded at the

universities of Oxford, Cambridge, Edinburgh and Glasgow, and at
Rugby, Eton and Winchester. Propagandists seized their pens: though
there were only eleven books with the word 'Volunteers' in their title
published in 1859, there were thirty-four in 1860 and twenty-six in
1861. By 1861 there were 140,100 Volunteers classed as militarily efficient. Numbers continued to increase year by year thereafter, though
with the fall of Napoleon III in 1870 Germany replaced France as the
foreign foe most likely to violate Britain's imperial peace. In contrast
to the Volunteer movement of the 1790s there was absolutely no notion of organizing against the threat of domestic subversion, but the
Volunteers offered young men something to do with their spare time,
something to believe in, something to identify themselves by.[12]

In 1899 the outbreak of the Boer War gave the Volunteers a chance
of foreign service: of the 10,000 men enrolled in cavalry units (known
as Yeomanry) 3000 went to South Africa in specially organized battalions; and a further 32,000 recruited for such units by Yeomanry
organizations followed. A classic novel of schoolboy passion, *The Hill*,
published in 1905, ends with a letter from the loved one, who has
gone out to South Africa in one of the first Yeomanry units:

> Good night, Jonathan. I'm going to turn in; we shall be astir before
> daybreak. Over the veldt the stars are shining. It's so light, that I can just
> make out the hill upon which, I hope, our flag will be waving within a few
> hours. The sight of this hill brings back our Hill. If I shut my eyes, I can
> see it plainly, as we used to see it from the tower, with the Spire rising out
> of the heart of the old school. I have the absurd conviction strong in me
> that, tomorrow, I shall get up the hill here faster and easier than the other
> fellows because you and I have so often run up our Hill together – God
> bless it – and you! Good night.

The author of this, Horace Annesley Vachell, was already nearly forty
when the war began and was amongst the fascinated onlookers who
stayed at home; there was no real counterpart of the mad rush to
enlist that was to be seen in 1914; though 35,000 Yeomanry went out
to South Africa, this represents only an eighth of the 281,000 Volunteers
and Yeomanry classed as efficient in 1901. The best book about the

---

[12] Barrie Rose, 'The Volunteers of 1859', *Journal of the Society for Army Historical
Research*, 37 (1959), pp. 97–110, at pp. 99, 102–3.

war by a participant, Deneys Reitz's *Commando,* was actually written by a Boer, and was not published till 1929.[13]

At least the Boer War helped prepare little boys in Britain for what lay ahead of them in 1914: 'I had played at "fighting the Boers" in the nursery', recalled Charles Carrington in his First World War memoirs. But there was also a growing assumption that sooner or later there would be a great European war, and the sheer vigour of the organizational effort put into the conscription system abroad, and the Volunteer movement in Britain, must have encouraged some people to see war as something to hope for. In 1871, shortly after France's defeat by the German states, an Indian Army officer named G.T. Chesney published a story entitled 'The Battle of Dorking' in *Blackwood's Magazine.* As a sixpenny pamphlet it sold 80,000 copies in a month and set a fashion for novels like *The Invasion of 1883* (1876), *The Invasion of 1910* (1906), by William Le Queux, and *The Invasion That Did Not Come Off* (1909), by Napier Hawke. P.G. Wodehouse parodied the genre in *The Swoop! or How Clarence Saved England: A Tale of the Great Invasion* (1909). Military themes also found favour in the growing market for juvenile literature. George Alfred Henty, who had served in the hospital commissariat of the British army in the Crimea, and of the Sardinian army in the war of 1859, became almost a household name and made a better income than the Chief Paymaster and the Chief Accountants at the War Office with his adventure stories about the wars of previous centuries. He occasionally treated some comparatively recent British imperial triumph and as the years passed his novels followed closer on the heels of the mayhem they romanticized: *For Name and Fame: or Through the Afghan Passes* (1885) and *The Dash for Khartoum: A Tale of the Nile Expedition* (1891) both appeared half-a-dozen years after the events that inspired them, whereas *With Buller in Natal; or A Born Leader* (1900) and *With Roberts to Pretoria: A Tale of the South African War* (1901) were almost as up to date as the newspapers.[14]

[13] *Encyclopaedia Britannica,* 11th edn, xxviii, p. 209, for statistics for Volunteers and Yeomanry.

[14] Charles Carrington ('Charles Edmonds'), *A Subaltern's War* (1929), p. 63. I.F. Clarke, *Voices Prophesying War: Future Wars, 1763–3749* (Oxford, 1992), p. 333–36, for the success of *The Battle of Dorking;* Public Record Office, IR 59/207, note by J.E. Chapman, 5 May 1903, for Henty's income 'as Author and Journalist'.

Henty himself had seen a fair amount of action as a young man: following his official employment in the Crimea and in Italy, he had been with the Austrian fleet at the Battle of Lissa in 1866 as a newspaper correspondent and in the same capacity accompanied Sir Robert Napier's invasion of Abyssinia in 1867. (This, incidentally, was the first British campaign to be commemorated by a systematic Official History.) As the titles of so many of his books imply, he regarded it as a worthwhile object in a war simply to *be there* and see it for oneself. From the Crimean War onward newspapers began employing people like Henty to be on the spot to write up what they saw for the benefit of their steadily expanding readership. The idea of war as a unique personal experience was also to be found, in a more self-conscious form, in *The Red Badge of Courage* (1895) by the American novelist Stephen Crane (who did not himself experience action till two years after his book was written). The notion that personal experience was something inexpressibly important, the very essence of the uniqueness of one's individuality, derived of course from Romantic poetry, but the assumption that the more intense the experience, the more inexpressibly precious it would be took on a particular colouring from the Romantics' fascination with the exotic and the historically remote. As early as the 1850s Tennyson had hailed the outbreak of the Crimean War as an escape from the narrowness and moral abdications of a hum-drum present:

> many a darkness into the light shall leap
> And shine in the sudden making of splendid names,
> And noble thought be freer under the sun,
> And the heart of a people beat with one desire.

The growth of the Volunteer movement in Britain coincided with an extraordinary revival of interest in what was perhaps the most insubstantial and tantalizing aspect of medieval culture: chivalry. Knights in armour, whether or not tended by glamorous Burne-Jones maidens or bearing the tokens of latter-day Guineveres, provided much of the Volunteer movement's iconography. Military training was not merely fresh air and fun, it was fellowship with King Arthur and the Knights of the Round Table; both the militarism and the medieval trappings were a symptom of a revolt against being born in what William Morris called 'a dull time oppressed with bourgeoisdom and philistinism'. The Romance of War was to a large extent a late nineteenth-century discovery: which was to carry almost a whole generation through Gallipoli and the Battle of Loos, before withering under the machine-guns of the Somme:

> Here lies a clerk who half his life had spent
> Toiling at ledgers in a city grey,
> Thinking that so his days would drift away
> With no lance broken in life's tournament:
> Yet ever 'twixt the books and his bright eyes
> The gleaming eagles of the legions came,
> And horsemen, charging under phantom skies,
> Went thundering past beneath the oriflamme.
>
> And now those waiting dreams are satisfied;
> From twilight to the halls of dawn he went;
> His lance is broken; but he lies content
> With that high hour, in which he lived and died.
> And falling thus, he wants no recompense,
> Who found his battle in the last resort;
> Nor needs he any hearse to bear him hence,
> Who goes to join the men of Agincourt.[15]

Not everyone was taken in by these fantasies of course. Wilhelm Lamszus's *Der Menschenschlachthaus: Bilder vom kommenden Krieg* published in 1912 – the English edition of 1913 was entitled *The Human Slaughterhouse (Scenes from the War that is to Come)* – became an

---

[15] *Record of the Expedition to Abyssinia: Compiled by Order of the Secretary of State for War by Major Trevenen J. Holland . . . and Captain Henry M. Hozier . . . under the Direction of Colonel Sir Henry James . . . Director of the Topographical and Statistical Department* was issued by the War Office in two volumes in 1870. Separate accounts of the operations of the Royal Artillery and of the Royal Engineers at the siege of Sevastopol had been published in 1859 but no official account was provided of the operations of the infantry and cavalry in the Crimea. Alfred Tennyson, *Maud* part III, stanza 4; Mark Girouard, *The Return to Camelot: Chivalry and the English Gentleman* (New Haven, 1981), especially pp. 220–30 and 275–93; there was a parallel development on the Continent, especially in Germany, but this still awaits its historian; William Morris to Fred Henderson, quoted in E.P. Thompson, *William Morris: Romantic to Revolutionary* (1977 edn), p. 14; see also Thompson's discussion of Keats's disgusted turning away from actuality, ibid., p. 10–21; Herbert Asquith, *The Volunteer and Other Poems* (1917), p. 9 – first published December 1915.

international best-seller. Though reminiscent of Crane's *The Red Badge of Courage*, with its naïve youth goggle-eyed at his first experience of battle, it gave more emphasis to the confusion and, especially, the horrors of modern warfare. It is in fact the first programmatic anti-war novel. The author, born in 1881, had no personal experience of warfare but his evocation of its darker side was so convincing that his book sold even better in Germany after the outbreak of war in 1914 than before it: 23,000 copies sold by 1913, 75,000 by 1923. (The British Library's 1913 paperback edition of the English translation announces on the cover '100,000 copies sold' but this seems to refer to world sales.) There seems to have been no French translation, the French apparently preferring a work in a quite contrary vein, Ernest Psichari's novel *L'appel des armes* (1913) in which a teacher's son revolts against the values of his anti-militarist father, joins a colonial regiment, and learns that the army is the incarnation of the eternal France, and that war is the most divine of the divine things left to us, the most clearly marked with the hall-mark of the divine ('*du sceau divin*'). Psichari, a professional officer in the artillery, was killed in the first month of the world war, before he had a chance to change his mind.

The works of Stephen Crane, Wilhelm Lamszus and Ernest Psichari are part of the reason why literary young men had different expectations of war in 1914 from those detectable amongst writers in 1793, but an even greater influence – one that in fact dated from the decade of the American Civil War, though it was still in the process of being assimilated by western literary culture at the end of the century – was that of Leo Tolstoy's 600,000 word novel *War and Peace*.[16]

As a young man Tolstoy had been an officer in the Russian army and during the Crimean War had been part of the garrison of Sevastapol during its siege by the French and British. The Crimean War gave the Charge of the Light Brigade, Florence Nightingale and 'the thin red line' to British folklore but seems to have had little significant impact on the literary imagination of anyone in the invading armies. For Tolstoy however the war was a major factor in his

---

[16] *War and Peace* appeared in French translation in 1879, in German translation in 1885–86 and in English translation (from a French version) in 1886. An English translation from the original Russian appeared in 1889, but Constance Garnett's classic rendering appeared only in 1904. The Louise and Aylmer Maude version was published in 1922–23.

development as a writer. Though a lover of books – he claimed Homer's poetry and Goethe's *Hermann und Dorothea* had had 'very great influence on him' – he also thoroughly enjoyed military life in wartime, noting in his diary during the twenty-seventh week of the siege of Sevastapol, 'The constant charm of danger and my observations of the soldiers I am living with, the sailors and the very methods of war are so pleasant that I don't want to leave here, especially as I would like to be present at the assault, if there is one'. One of his earliest stories, 'The Raid', describing a volunteer's first experience of war in the Caucasus, had also been one of the earliest *Bildungsroman*-type treatments of war. The sketches he wrote during the siege of Sevastapol show that he already had an eye for the disconcerting, and possibly symbolic, contrasts that war throws up, as in the conclusion of the first of these sketches: 'The sound of an old waltz played by a military band on the boulevard is borne along the water and seems, in some strange way, answered by the firing from the bastions.' This corresponds with a passage in his diary: 'the sun was already setting behind the English batteries, puffs of smoke were rising here and there and shots could be heard . . . on the Grafskaya pier music was playing and the sounds of trumpets and a familiar tune drifted across'. Some of the incidental details in *War and Peace* also seem to be transcriptions of actual experience: the 'strange acid smell of saltpetre and blood' on the battlefield, for example, or the army surgeon 'holding a cigar between thumb and little finger of one of his bloodstained hands so as not to smear it'.[17]

Tolstoy also learnt from others – notably Stendhal. In 1901 he told a French visitor:

> I am more indebted to him than to anyone else: I owe it to him that I have understood war. Reread the account of the Battle of Waterloo in *The Charterhouse of Parma*. Who before him had described war like that, that is to say, like it really it is? . . . Later, in the Caucasus my brother, an

---

[17] Romain Rolland, *Tolstoy* (1911), p. 85 n. 1; R.F. Christian, ed., *Tolstoy's Diaries* (1994 edn), p. 89, 13 April 1855, but cf. Rolland, *Tolstoy*, p. 57 n. 1, for the account of his feelings on the Crimean War which he gave after he had taken to religion. 'Sevastopol: In December 1854', dated 25 April 1855 (Old Style); *War and Peace*, x, ch. 39 (1933 World's Classics edn of Louise and Aylmer Maude's translation, ii, p. 543); ibid., x, ch. 37 (World's Classics, ii, p. 536); *Tolstoy's Diaries*, p. 85, 7 December 1854.

officer before I was, confirmed the accuracy of Stendhal's descriptions . . . A
little later, in the Crimea, I had only to look to see it with my own eyes.
But, I repeat, in everything I know of war, Stendhal was my first teacher.

Yet in spite of this compliment to Stendhal, *War and Peace* was an avow-
edly chauvinistic work, full of jibes at the French and the Germans.
Tolstoy's western European readers overlooked this aspect, or took it
in their stride as splashings of Russian local colour. A case can be made
for arguing that wars directed and managed by political systems
dominated by the upper class, as before 1815, produced far less
literature than wars directed and managed by political systems
dominated by the middle class, as after 1914. The career of the
aristocratic Tolstoy, as the greatest individual influence on war literature
in the period of apparent transition between upper-class and middle-
class dominated political systems, suggests the limitations of this kind
of sociology; perhaps what was developing was not so much a new
class system but, out of the old class system, a new idea of classlessness,
of citizens equal in their obligation to serve and to risk their all for
the collective. Tolstoy would fit in better with that view of what was
happening. On the other hand, his nationalism suggests some sort
of common ground with Deroulède and Henty, and the enthusiasts
who organized the *Verein zur Feier des 19. Oktober* in Leipzig and the
University Rifle Volunteers in Oxford. The rise of European nationalism was so strongly involved with the rise of the middle class that it is
easy to assume that the processes were identical, or organically con-
nected; but the social and ideological roots of nationalism in Russia
do not seem to have been at all the same as in Britain and France:
the fact is we are still a very long way from possessing a unified field
theory of historical change that will enable us to make a neat expository package of such relationships.[18]

   What one can see in the later nineteenth century is the accumulation of materials for a tradition of writing about war such as did not
exist a century earlier. It may be that the real input did not relate
primarily to war at all. The increasingly egalitarian and democratic
nature of western society in the later nineteenth century sponsored
the evolution both of a more realistic, naturalistic literature dealing

---

[18] Paul Boyer, *Chez Tolstoi: entretiens à Iasnaia Poliana* (Paris, 1950), p. 40.

with the real lives of real people and, by a complex reflex, also of a tradition of romantic evasion and chivalrous fantasy. Opposing tendencies reinforced one another. Romanticism had legitimized subjectivism in literature but had not made it compulsory to go off into odd corners of the world in order to experience the unique: but exploration of odd corners was precisely what was encouraged by the nineteenth century's growing list of true life adventure stories. What one sees in the nineteenth century is not so much the growth of war literature as a kind of traditional discourse, but the maturing of all its potential ingredients. By 1914 one could have said that all that was needed to carry the tradition forward was a really big war for people to write about.

And at the beginning of August 1914 just such a war broke out.

Part Two

The First World War

CHAPTER 4

$$\overline{}$$

Poets

FIRST SOME facts and figures. No other commonly shared but essentially objective and external experience has generated anything like the quantity of poetry, fiction and reminiscences inspired by the two world wars of the twentieth century. Léon Riegel notes that the New York Public Library's *Subject Catalog of the World War I Collection*, dating from 1961, lists 1350 novels 'mainly in English'. First-hand non-fiction accounts of the war are probably equally numerous: Jean Norton Cru's *Témoins*, an analysis of eye-witness accounts of the First World War published in French, which appeared in 1929 at a time when many such testimonies were still to appear, deals with the work of forty-nine novelists and 202 authors of memoirs, journals, letters and reflections. In 1919 Edmund Gosse estimated that 500 volumes of war poetry had been published in Britain between August 1914 and November 1918: the British Museum's *Subject Index of the Books Relating to the European War, 1914–1918* lists only 239, but it is evident that a large number of volumes printed for private circulation or issued by small provincial publishers never reached the British Museum. Gosse's figure may even be an underestimate: *Whitaker's Almanack* states that the number of volumes in the poetry and drama category published in 1911 alone was 538, and the war seems to have affected the subject-matter of poetry rather than altered the quantity being produced. In 1917 William Hudson thought for some reason that not enough verse was being written and produced some doggerel entitled 'Why Are the Poets Silent?':

> Why is the harp untouched, the singer dumb . . .?
> Bards hear not poesy in German hate,

Or Belgian massacre, or French death-pain,
Or British anguish, or aught of the fate
Endured in battle-trenches.

But in the following year William S. Murphy expressed what was probably a juster view of wartime poetry when he stated, 'Measured by
quantity alone, it is unique; at no time has so great a volume of verse
been produced in as short a period'. Although scholars accord First
World War poetry an importance in English Literature that it does
not have in the literary annals of other countries, Britain was far
from having a monopoly of war poets. 'From the bloody earth of
the trenches sprouted a magnificent literary flowering', wrote a
Frenchman in 1916. Jean Vic's five volume *La littérature de la guerre:
manuel méthodique et critique des publications de langue française*, which
only goes up to the Armistice, has eighteen pages of listings of poetry
books, including such forgotten treasures as Emmanuel Soy's *Des
palmes sur les tombes* (1916), Gilles Normand's *La voix de la fournaise*
(1916), Sous-lieutenant André Dollé's *Pages de gloire, d'amour et de
mort* (1916), *La muse et les ailes* by J.M. Renaitour, *Pilote aviateur* (1917)
and Jean-Fontaine-Vive's *Jeunesse ardentes* (1918). At least forty war
poets writing in Flemish made themselves known during the first
seventeen months following the invasion of Belgium, though the
most interesting of the younger Flemish poets of the time, Paul van
Ostaijen, spent the war in Antwerp working hand in glove with the
German occupation authorities. Over 300 authors who published
volumes of war poems are listed in Julius Bab's *Die deutsche Kriegslyrik*
of 1920, but according to a professor at Munich university writing
in 1915 the total number of war poems produced by German authors
in the first six months of hostilities was three million. That's approximately 17,000 a day, but a later expert thought the figure was
underestimated. The Italians versified on a less heroic scale, though
their finest twentieth-century poet, Giuseppe Ungaretti, produced
his best work while *soldato semplice della 19ª Fanteria*, an ordinary
soldier of the 19th Infantry Regiment.[1]

---

[1] Léon Riegel, *Guerre et littérature: le bouleversement des consciences dans la littérature
romanesque inspirée par la Grande Guerre (littératures française, anglo-saxonne et allemande),
1910–1930* (Nancy, 1978), p. 559; Edmund Gosse, *Some Diversions of a Man of Letters*
(1919), p. 264; *Whitaker's Almanack, 1913*, p. 764; William Hudson, *Wilhelm and His*

One of the most persistent images of the First World War – only sketchily adumbrated in earlier conflicts – is of young men being herded to their deaths at the behest of bloodthirsty older men who were making a good thing of the war at a safe distance from the guns:

> If I were fierce, and bald, and short of breath,
>   I'd live with scarlet Majors at the Base,
> And speed glum heroes up the line to death.
>   You'd see me with my puffy petulant face,
> Guzzling and gulping in the best hotel,
>   Reading the Roll of Honour. 'Poor young chap',
> I'd say – 'I used to know his father well . . .'

There is an element of truth in this. As early as December 1914 *The Egoist* jeered:

> At the sound of the drum,
> Out of their dens they come, they come,
> The little poets we thought were dead,
> The poets who certainly haven't been read . . .

One of the people the author of these verses had in mind was probably would-be Poet Laureate William Watson who, at the age of fifty-six, decided that he wanted his war poems to be 'so much in evidence that people [would] be saying that W.W. is the real national poet in this crisis'; he managed to have sixteen war poems printed in different newspapers within the first six weeks. Even those present found something grotesque in the meeting of prominent British writers who assembled at government request to discuss efforts to counter German propaganda:

> It was an extraordinary gathering. Galsworthy, cool, bald and solemn; Conan Doyle, strong, solid and good-humoured; R. Bridges a glorious sight, wavy

continued
Gods: and Other War Sonnets [1917], p. 47; William S. Murphy, *The Genesis of British War Poetry* (1918), p. 13; Maurice d'Hartoy, *Au Front* (Paris, 1916), p. vii, preface by the Marquis de Ségur; Jan Bernaerts, Hendrik Heyman, eds, *Oorlogspoëzie: verschenen in 1914 en 1915 en onuitgegeven gedichten* (Port Villez, 1916); Ernst Volkmann, *Deutsche Dichtung im Weltkrieg, 1914–1918* (Leipzig, 1934), p. 8, cf. W.G. Randall, 'The German War and the German Poets', *Contemporary Review*, 111 (June 1917), pp. 747–53, at p. 748.

hair, black coat, huge red tie, light trousers, white socks, patent leather shoes; he sat in a tilted chair, looking at his ease, calmly indifferent, every now and then craning his head backwards out of an open window . . . Wells – fat, brown and perky, very smart; Chesterton enormous, streaming with sweat, his hair dripping . . . Hugh next him looking hot; Hardy very old and faded . . . Barrie small and insignificant. Arnold Bennett very pert and looking every inch a cad, Newbolt cool and anxious.

Catherine W. Reilly's *English Poetry of the First World War: A Bibliography* (1978) lists 2225 British First World War poets, only 417 of whom actually wore uniform. But it would be unjust to pretend that the folks back home had no feeling (other than *Schadenfreude*) for the ordeal of their sons and brothers in the trenches. One recalls Kipling's little poem on his son, killed in action while serving with the Irish Guards:

> My son was killed while laughing at some jest, I would I knew
> What it was, and it might serve me in a time when jests are few.[2]

In any case the war intruded physically into the Home Front to a much greater extent than the French wars had done. On 16 December 1914 German battlecruisers shelled Scarborough, Whitby and Hartlepool; in the latter town ninety-three people were killed and 436 injured. On 31 May 1915 a German airship bombed London:

> From a blur of female faces
> Distraught eyes stand out,
> And a woman's voice cries:

---

[2] Siegfried Sassoon, 'Base Details', in *Counter-Attack and Other Poems* (1918), p. 25 – see also Osbert Sitwell's 'Armchair', in *Argonaut and Juggernaut* (1919), pp. 116–18; Herbert Blenheim [pseud.], 'Song in Wartime' *The Egoist*, 1, no. 23 (1 December 1914), p. 446b; John Moorcroft Wilson, *I Was an English Poet: A Critical Biography of Sir William Watson (1858–1936)* (1981), p. 188; David Newsome, *On the Edge of Paradise: A.C. Benson the Diarist* (1980), p. 312.

The earliest instance I know – pointed out to me by Martin Ceadel – of a contrast being drawn between the horrors of life in the trenches (in this case in the Crimean War) and the complacency of those who advocated the war, 'comfortably snoring in their beds' at home, is in a letter Cobden wrote to Bright on 15 August 1855, British Library, Add. MS 43650, fos 125–26. When Britain went to war with France in 1793 both prime minister and foreign secretary were thirty-three and the man nominated to command the troops sent to the Continent was twenty-nine – i.e. they were much the same age as men serving in the ranks; in 1914 both the prime minister and the commander of the British Expeditionary Force were sixty-two.

'The Zeppelins – they are attacking us;
Kingsland Road is alight,
Stoke Newington is burning.
Did you not hear the guns?
Oh, what shall we do!'

By 11 November 1918 the Germans had carried out fifty-one raids on English towns with airships, and fifty-two with aeroplanes. Though it was England's centres of population that experienced the heaviest air-raids of the war, there were also thirty-four attacks on Venice, and by the time of the Armistice the Royal Air Force, hitherto unable to reach targets east of Stuttgart, was finalizing plans for raiding Berlin with four-engined bombers. The scale of destruction in the pioneer raids of the First World War was far from negligible: on 22 June 1916 nearly a hundred children were killed in a French raid on Karlsruhe when a direct hit was scored on a circus, and on 11 November of the same year ninety-three people attempting to find shelter in the old fortifications at Padua were killed by a single bomb from an Austrian aeroplane. On 16 February 1918 a German four-engined Zeppelin-Staaken RV 1 dropped a bomb weighing one metric ton on London, destroying a wing of the Royal Hospital at Chelsea (the wing was rebuilt and again demolished by a German rocket on 31 January 1945). Scarce resources had to be held back from the battle zone to meet these attacks

We wandered through the chill autumnal Park,
And spoke of courage and the youthful dead,
And how the boldest spirit may be cowed
By indiscriminate terror. Overhead,
The moon rode high on her predestined arc,
Steadfast through tidal waves of sombre cloud.
Like vast antennæ, search-lights swept the sky,
When, suddenly, as if in swift reply,
Out of the south, with jets of luminous smoke,
And coughing clatter, hidden guns awoke.

But counter-measures might be almost as dangerous as the attacks themselves: on 7 July 1917 a daylight raid on London by twenty-one Gotha twin-engined bombers resulted in the death of ten people, and the injury of fifty-five, from cascading fragments of anti-aircraft shells,

in addition to the forty-four killed and 125 injured by German bombs.
The Germans also employed long-range guns. At first it was only the
Scarlet Majors at the Base who were at risk: on 27 June 1917 the Casino
Hotel at Dunkirk, housing the HQ of the British 15th Corps, was hit by
a 38 cm. shell fired from an emplacement at Leugenboom near Ostend,
twenty-four miles away, though fortunately no staff officers were in the
building at the time: 'Casualties among clerks and orderlies – ten killed,
fifteen wounded. Corps Commanders', BGGS', CE's, DA & QMG's, G,
Q, and several other offices were all destroyed'. Nine months later, on
23 March 1918, the German army began shelling Paris with 21 cm. guns
positioned in railway sidings sixty-seven miles away near Laon: one of
the shells brought down the roof of a crowded church, killing eighty-
eight worshippers. And even without being directly involved in such
incidents, people were at once enormously energized and enormously
worried by the war: not least those, like Bertrand Russell and D.H.
Lawrence, who bitterly opposed the war on principle but were exempted,
by age or medical condition, from active participation.[3]

Though one might be somewhat irritated by civilians writing things
like 'We ate our breakfast lying on our backs/Because the shells were
screeching overhead', at its best the work of non-participants – if indeed
it is fair to call them that – achieved genuine pathos. The following is
by the Marquess of Crewe, who was a cabinet minister at the outbreak
of the war:

> Here in the marshland, past the battered bridge,
>   One of a hundred grains untimely sown,
> Here with his comrades of the hard-won ridge,
>   He rests, unknown.
>
> His horoscope had seemed so plainly drawn:
>   School triumphs, earned apace in work and play:
> Friendships at will; then love's delightful dawn
>   And mellowing day;

[3] F.S. Flint, 'Zeppelins', in *Other World: Cadences* (1920), p. 54; Giovanni Scarabello,
Il martirio di Venezia durante la grande guerra e l'opera di difesa della marina italiana (2
vols, Venice, 1933), i, p. 59; A.D. Harvey, *Collision of Empires: Britain in Three World
Wars, 1793–1945* (1992), p. 392, 394, 396; Henry Head, 'To Courage, Seated', in *Destroy-
ers and Other Verses* (1919), p. 14; Public Record Office, WO 95/922, 15th Corps General
Staff War Diary, 27 June 1917; H.W. Miller, *The Paris Gun: The Bombardment of Paris by
the German Long-Distance Guns and the Great Offensives of 1918* (1930), passim.

Home fostering hope; some service to the State;
    Benignant age; then the long tryst to keep
Where in the yew-tree shadow congregate
      His fathers sleep.

Was here the one thing needful to distil
    From life's alembic, through this holier fate,
The man's essential soul, the hero will?
      We ask; and wait.

Writing at a distance, authors on the Home Front were sometimes betrayed by the recalcitrance of facts of which they were uninformed. When W.B. Yeats was inspired by the death of 'my dear friend's dear son', Major Robert Gregory, to write his poem 'An Irish Airman Foresees His Death' –

I know that I shall meet my fate
Somewhere among the clouds above

– he did not know that Gregory had crashed into the side of a hill obscured by low cloud, during a test flight. On the other hand no one nowadays asks how much Laurence Binyon of the British Museum knew about the reality of war when he wrote:

They shall grow not old as we that are left grow old.
Age shall not weary them, nor the years condemn.
At the going down of the sun and in the morning
We will remember them.

Indeed the most famous verses of the war years (though their fame came only in another war a generation later) were written during basic training, before the author had even heard a shot fired in anger:

Vor der Kaserne
vor dem grossen Tor
stand eine Laterne
und steht sie noch davor,
so wollen wir uns da wiedersehn
bei der Laterne wolln wir stehn
wie einst, Lili Marleen

(In front of the barracks, in front of the great gate, there stood a wicket entrance, and it's still standing there, we still want to see each other again, we want to stand at the wicket, like we used to, Lili Marleen.) A version of this was recorded by the singer Lale Andersen in 1938. In 1941, the German army broadcasting station in Belgrade, for want of other suitable records, transmitted it frequently and it quickly became popular all over the Mediterranean war zone, being eventually translated into twenty-six languages and providing the subject for a British feature film of 1944 misleadingly entitled *The True Story of Lili Marleen.*[4]

A certain physical remoteness from the worst horrors might even have been of assistance to someone trying to describe the realities of war. In August 1914 John Masefield was in his mid-thirties. He greeted the outbreak of war with a fine elegiac poem –

> And silence broods like spirit on the brae,
> A glimmering moon begins, the moonlight runs
> Over the grasses of the ancient way
> Rutted this morning by the passing guns.

– and in 1915, having worked for a period in a French military hospital sixty miles behind the lines, was sent to the Dardanelles to help organize the evacuation by motor boat of soldiers wounded in Gallipoli fighting. He saw a great deal of suffering and – from a reasonably safe distance – the places where the suffering had been incurred, but was never in much danger of sharing it personally. After a successful propaganda tour in the United States, he was commissioned to write a popular history of the Gallipoli campaign. Not surprisingly, considering the time when it was written and the nature of the information

[4] Wilfred Gibson, 'Breakfast', published in his collection *Battle* (1916): Gibson joined the army in 1917; The Marquess of Crewe, 'A Grave in Flanders', originally published *The Harrovian: War Supplement*, 3 (February 1915), p. 1; Public Record Office, AIR 1/1567/204/80/54, and AIR 1/1575/204/80/76: the family tradition that Robert Gregory was shot down in error by an Italian plane (see A. Norman Jeffares, *W.B. Yeats: A New Biography*, 1988, p. 236) is not confirmed by official records; the weather conditions were so bad that an aerial interception would have been unlikely; Laurence Binyon 'For the Fallen', stanza 4, originally printed in *The Times*, 21 September 1914, p. 9c-d; Johan Daisne 'Zur Geschichte von Lili Marleen', in *Hans Leip: Leben und Werke* (Hamburg, 1958), pp. 69–71.

made available to him, the resulting book was something of a whitewash as far as the military aspects were concerned. A later generation, more accustomed to anti-war than to pro-war propaganda, may give a double meaning to the judgement of one of Masefield's contemporaries that 'It is on a level with Tennyson's "Charge of the Light Brigade", only it is in prose', but it remains perhaps the finest book of its type ever written:

> Those who wish to imagine the scene must think of twenty miles of any rough and steep sea coast known to them, picturing it as roadless, water-less, much broken with gullies, covered with scrub, sandy, loose, and dif-ficult to walk on, and without more than two miles of accessible landing throughout its length . . . Then let them imagine the hills entrenched, the landing mined, the beaches tangled with barbed wire, ranged by howitzers and swept by machine guns, and themselves three thousand miles from home, going out before dawn, with rifles, packs, and water-bottles, to pass the mines under shell fire, cut through the wire under machine-gun fire, clamber up the hills under the fire of all arms, by the glare of shell-bursts, in the withering and crashing tumult of modern war, and then to dig themselves in in a waterless and burning hill while a more numerous enemy charge them with the bayonet . . . Let them imagine themselves driven mad by heat and toil and thirst by day, shaken by frost at midnight, weakened by disease and broken by pestilence, yet rising on the word with a shout and going forward to die in exultation in a cause foredoomed and almost hopeless . . . But as they moved out these things were but the end they asked, the reward they had come for, the unseen cross upon the breast . . . They went like kings in a pageant to the im-minent death. As they passed from moorings to the man-of-war anchor-age on their way to the sea, their feeling that they had done with life and were going out to something new welled up in those battalions; they cheered and cheered till the harbour rang with cheering. As each ship crammed with soldiers drew near the battleships, the men swung their caps and cheered again, and the sailors answered, and the noise of cheering swelled, and the men in the ships not yet moving joined in, and the men ashore, till all the life in the harbour was giving thanks that it could go to death rejoicing . . .[5]

[5] John Masefield, 'August 1914', last stanza; Maurice V. Brett and Lionel Viscount Esher, eds, *Journals and Letters of Reginald Viscount Esher* (4 vols, 1934–38), iv, p. 57, Esher to John Charteris, 16 October 1916; John Masefield, *Gallipoli* (1916), pp. 7–8, 34–35.

Masefield's *Gallipoli* was published in September 1916. At that stage
one of the chief problems for writers who had seen the reality of war
from an even closer viewpoint was that they were mostly still in the
thick of it. A battlefield, even a static one, was not the best environ-
ment for the production of literature. Roland Dorgelès explained that
he did not write on the front line 'not only for want of spare time,
but also and above all for lack of liberty of mind . . . As far as I'm
concerned I knew nothing more incompatible with the duties of a
novelist than those of a machine-gun corporal.' Patrick MacGill, by
then wounded and unfit for further service, claimed in the preface
to his wartime novel *The Great Push* (1916) that 'the chapter dealing
with our last night at Les Brebis, prior to the Big Push, was written in
the trench between midnight and dawn of September the 25th' – i.e.
during the hours immediately prior to the commencement of the Battle of Loos – but one is not quite sure whether to believe him:

> I poked my head through the upper window of our billet and looked
> down the street. An ominous calm brooded over the village, the trees which
> lined the streets stood immovable in the darkness, with lone shadows cling-
> ing to the trunks . . . My mind was suddenly permeated by a feeling of
> proximity to the enemy. He whom we were going to attack at dawn seemed
> to be very close to me. I could almost feel his presence in the room. At
> dawn I might deprive him of life and he might deprive me of mine. Two
> beings give life to a man, but one can deprive him of it. Which is the
> greater mystery? Birth or death? They who are responsible for the first
> may take pleasure, but who can glory in the second? . . . To kill a man . . .
> To feel for ever after the deed that you have deprived a fellow being of
> life!
>
> 'We're beginning to strafe again', said Pryor, coming to my side as a
> second reverberation shook the house.

It certainly seems odd that MacGill managed to write so much while
apparently taking part in the dialogue he recorded:

> 'And who will I write to for you, Bill?' I asked.
> Bill scratched his little white potato of a nose, puckered his lips, and
> became thoughtful. I suddenly realised that Bill was very dear to me.
> 'Not afraid, matey?' I asked.
> 'Naw', he answered in a thoughtful voice.
> 'A man has only to die once, anyhow', said Felan.

'Greedy! 'Ow many times d'yer want ter die?' asked Bill.[6]

MacGill's eve-of-battle chapter is just under 4000 words long; Trollope, who at least had his own desk to sit at, used to average 10,000 words a week. Other frontline writers were more sparing in their use of ink and paper. Richard Aldington wrote of composing haiku:

> One frosty night when the guns were still
> I leaned against the trench
> Making for myself *hokku*
> Of the moon and flowers and of the snow.

> But the ghostly scurrying of huge rats
> Swollen with feeding upon men's flesh
> Filled me with shrinking dread.

One wonders too if the most distinctively novel feature of Giuseppe Ungaretti's frontline poems, their short disjointed lines, does not owe something to their having been written on scraps of paper resting on the author's knee – rather thin boney knees too – with frequent glances up to check if anything stirred in No Man's Land:

> Una intera nottata
> buttato vicino
> a un compagno
> massacrato
> con la sua bocca
> digrignata
> volta al plenilunio
> con la congestione
> delle sue mani
> penetrata
> nel mio silenzio
> ho scritto
> lettere piene d'amore

> Non sono mai stato
> tanto attaccato
> alla vita

[6] Roland Dorgelès, *Souvenirs sur les croix de bois* (Paris, 1929), p. 39; Patrick MacGill, *The Great Push* (1916), pp. vii-viii, 50–51, 58.

(For one entire night thrown next to a comrade butchered with his mouth gnashing at the full moon with the swelling of his hands sticking into my silence I wrote letters full of love. Never have I been so attached to life.) Quite independently a reserve lieutenant in the German army, August Stramm, had been experimenting with a similar technique in his own language:

> Die Erde blutet unterm Helmkopf
> Sterne fallen
> Der Weltraum tastet
> Schauder brausen
> Wirbeln
> Einsamkeiten.
> Nebel
> Weinen
> Ferne
> Deinen Blick

(The earth bleeds under its helmeted head – stars fall – space fumbles – shudders heave – lonelinesses whirl. Fogs weep distance from your look.) By the time Ungaretti was writing at the front however, Stramm had already been killed in action, sixty kilometres beyond Brest-Litovsk.[7]

In fact a great deal was written in the trenches, and not only letters to wives and parents, and the occasional prohibited diary. The relatively

---

[7] Anthony Trollope, *An Autobiography* [1883], pp. 88–89; Richard Aldington 'Living Sepulchres', in *Collected Poems* (1929), p. 75: the *haiku*, a poem of seventeen syllables, originally a Japanese form, had enjoyed a minor vogue in England since the late 1890s; Giuseppi Ungaretti 'Veglia' ('Vigil') in *Allegria di Naufragi* (Florence [1919]), pp. 62–63, originally published in *Il porto sepulto* (Udine, 1916). Ungaretti dated this poem 'Cima 4 il 23 dicembre 1915' – Peak 4 23 December 1915; August Stramm, 'Wunde' ('Wound'), August Stramm, *Das Werk* (Wiesbaden, 1963), p. 69, originally published in *Der Sturm*, Jahrgang 5, no. 19/20 (January 1915). If one reads for content rather than style one may also find a parallel between Ungaretti's 'Veglia' and Géza Gyóni's 'Őrségen' ('On Guard Duty'), the second stanza of which may be rendered:

> Death lurks beyond this bridge
> Drizzle falls from swirling clouds
> And on the Vistula bridge
> The soldier thinks of a fairy-tale woman

Géza Gyóni *Lengyel Mezőkön: Tábortűz Mellett* (Przemysl, 1914), p. 11.

small Belgian army, operating in the last unoccupied corner of its homeland and to a large extent cut off from all family contact, gave birth to no less than 290 trench newspapers, and the French army had perhaps 400, of which 170 published by the French land forces in France itself have survived in libraries. The editors were in some cases subaltern officers; there was one uncommissioned soldier amongst the eleven editors of *Le diable au cor*, 1915–18, whereas *L'argonnaute* was edited by five privates and three corporals. These men were actually at the front, and in many cases died in action: units of the French army which operated in the rear and had access to better facilities produced magazines relatively rarely. In the British army 107 frontline magazines have been identified, the first being the *Fifth Gloucester Gazette*, produced under the direction of the chaplain of the 5th Battalion Gloucestershire Regiment in April 1915. They were usually printed in England by commercial printers (as were the numerous magazines produced by home-based units) but the famous *Wipers Times* (later the *BEF Times*), produced by the 12th Battalion Sherwood Foresters, was printed with Belgian fount and presses found in the Ypres Salient. At least one rear-areas magazine, *The Strafer*, edited by Army Service Corps captains at '3 GHQ A.M. Park' was partly roneoed, no doubt on government-issue roneo machines. Many of these magazines were short-lived but those that survived were likely to increase their circulation: *The 7th Manchester Sentry* in England claimed a print-run of 26,000 in May 1916 and on the Western Front *The Listening Post* (7th Battalion Canadian Expeditionary Force) claimed 20,000 in October of the same year (this may be compared to the 47,000 circulation of *The Times* before the war, or the 20,000 claimed by the *Cambridge Magazine*, which could be described as the trench journal of the war's opponents back in England). In the Italian and Austro-Hungarian armies frontline journals were usually official initiatives by HQ staff (as was later the case with the British army in the 1939–45 war): the novelist Robert Musil, as a *Landsturmoberleutnant*, edited one such, the *Soldaten-Zeitung*, in the Bolzano sector from July 1916 till April 1917. The Germans also had a number of army newspapers organized by HQs of larger formations (the largest circulation of any soldiers' newspaper in the 1914–18 – 52,000 copies – was achieved by the *Zeitung der 10. Armee oder Armee-Zeitung Scholz* on the Eastern Front late in 1916), but there were also fifty-five frontline journals issued by units of the German army, below divisional level, including *Hohnacker neueste Nachrichten*, which was first produced in a run of eighty hectographed copies on a quiet stretch of the Vosges front by men of the *4. Kompagnie* of the *2. Bayerische Landwehr Regiment* as early as 14 September 1914: this, the very first such small-unit paper in any army, was later extended to cover the entire brigade, with a circulation of 2000.[8]

Frontline soldiers read as well as wrote: 'It is really remarkable how you learn to read at the front', Otto Braun told a family friend: 'only a few books up till now, Faust, Hölderlin, and Zarathustra, but, as should be, learning them almost by heart'. Ernst Jünger later claimed that during the British offensive of August 1918 he occupied what spare moments he had with *Tristram Shandy* 'which imprinted itself on my memory more deeply than all the events of combat'. He finished it in hospital after being wounded for the fourteenth time. Edmund Blunden found comfort in a text of the same vintage: 'At very spare moment I read in Young's *Night Thoughts on Life, Death and Immortality* and I felt the benefit of this grave and intellectual voice, speaking out of a profound eighteenth-century calm.' (A review of Blunden's *Pastorale* in the *Times Literary Supplement* led to his being summoned to battalion HQ and appointed Field Works Officer, his colonel being 'overjoyed at having an actual author in his battalion'). Osbert Sitwell sought not calm in his reading but a kind of commentary on what he was living through:

> As a pessimist, and in an effort to make this existence seem more tolerable, in general I avoided works of a cheerful tendency, and once more abandoned myself to the genius of Dostoievsky . . . When after reading

[8] André Charpentier, *Feuilles bleu horizon, 1914–1918* (Paris, 1935), p. 377; Stephane Audoin-Rouzeau, *Men at War, 1914–1918: National Sentiment and Trench Journalism in France during the First World War* (Providence, Rhode Island, 1992), pp. 8–9; J.G. Fuller, *Troop Morale and Popular Culture in the British Armies, 1914–1918* (Oxford, 1990), pp. 7, 9; Patrick Beaver, ed., *The Wipers Times: A Complete Facsimile etc.* (1973), pp. xi, xiii; for the *Cambridge Magazine*, see A.D. Harvey, 'Jaw, Jaw about the War, War', *Times Higher Education Supplement*, 4 October 1991, p. 19a-f; for Second World War British Army papers, see *Union Jack: A Scrapbook. British Forces' Newspapers, 1939–1945* (1989), pp. 7–9, 251–54; Karl Corino, *Robert Musil: Leben und Werk in Bildern und Texten* (Reinbek bei Hamburg, 1988), pp. 245–46; Karl Kurth, *Die deutschen Feld- und Schützengrabenzeitungen des Weltkrieges* (Leipzig, 1937), pp. 88–92, 133, 207. See also Mario Isnenghi *Giornali di trincea, 1915–1918* (Turin, 1977).

The Brothers Karamazov, Crime and Punishment and *The Idiot, King Lear* or *Othello*, I needed a change of feeling, I turned to the novels of Dickens again . . .With what certainty he would have comprehended and rendered a night of duty: rats and mud, and the particular horror they hold for human beings, he already understood (think of the opening of *Our Mutual Friend* on the waters of the Pool of London!), and he would at once have captured the feeling of these coffin-like ditches, where death brooded in the air after the same manner that some fatal disease, such as malaria, hangs suspended, but ever-present, over the deserted marshlands of Italy and Greece.

Harold Duke Collison-Morley, like Sitwell a career officer – in September 1915 he was commanding the 19th Battalion London Regiment (the St Pancras Battalion) – wrote home, 'There is no hardship or terror or doubt that happens out here that Shakespeare does not touch on or give advice for'. A few days later the British army launched the second of its major offensives, at Loos, and Collison-Morley was 'killed at the head of his men, after being twice wounded, just before reaching the German trenches'; a copy of *Henry V* was found on his body. The continuing relevance of *Henry V* was also acknowledged by David Jones, when he recalled years later, 'Trench life brought that work pretty constantly to mind.' Siegfried Sassoon recorded 'reading *Tess of the D'Urbervilles* and trying to forget about the shells which were humping and hurrooshing overhead', and later, when waiting to be sent into action, found 'A sort of numb funkiness invaded me. I didn't want to die – not before I'd finished reading *The Return of the Native* anyhow'. Another Thomas Hardy novel, *Far From the Madding Crowd* provided Wilfrid Ewart with distraction at Ypres in 1916. Edgell Rickword wrote a cruel little poem about reading Donne and Tennyson aloud to the 'gaping, mackerel-eyed' corpse of a dead friend:

> I tried the Elegies one day,
> But he, because he heard me say
> 'What needst thou have more covering than a man?'
> Grinned nastily, and so I knew
> The worms had got his brains at last . . .
> There was one thing that I might do
> To starve the worms; I racked my head
> For healthy things and quoted 'Maud'.

His grin got worse and I could see
He laughed at passion's purity.
He stank so badly, though we were great chums
I had to leave him; then rats ate his thumbs.[9]

Rickword himself later recalled picking up a copy of Siegfried Sassoon's *Counter-Attack* when returning to France from leave and finding it 'devastating because he was the first poet I knew of who dealt with the war in the vocabulary of war'. Blunden also mentioned on one occasion having to 'thrust aside my *Cambridge Magazine* with Siegfried Sassoon's splendid war on the war in it'. Indeed the soldiers in the front line had the unprecedented experience of being able to read substantial literary treatments of a war they were still engaged in. Franz Marc read the poems of August Stramm printed in the issue of *Sturm* that announced his death in action, noting, 'for him language was neither a form nor a vessel in which you offer ideas . . . instead it was material from which he struck fire, marble which he wanted to awaken to life, like a true sculptor'. Jean Norton Cru remembered that, 'During our attack of late June 1916 at Verdun on the eastern slope of the Vignes ravine I had in my haversack Genevoix's *Sous Verdun* and Paul Lintier's *Ma pièce*'. Henri Barbusse's *Le feu* sold 200,000 copies by the time of the Armistice and many of these found their way into the hands of soldiers. Sassoon recalled of Wilfred Owen, 'And didn't I lend him Barbusse's *Le feu* which set him alight as no other war book had done?' Cru regarded Barbusse's novel as a tissue of inaccuracies and implausibilities, but noted that even frontline soldiers who admitted its inaccuracy found it a refreshing change from the romantic picture of war that was being circulated on the home

---

[9] Julie Vogelstein, ed., *The Diary of Otto Braun: With Selections from his Letters and Poems* (1924), p. 139, Braun to Julie Vogelstein, 20 March 1915; Julien Hervier, *Entretiens avec Ernst Jünger* (Paris, 1986), pp. 24–25; Edmund Blunden, *Undertones of War* (1982, Penguin edn), p. 217; ibid., p. 78; Osbert Sitwell *Laughter in the Next Room: Being the Fourth Volume of Left Hand, Right Hand!* (1949), p. 83–84; Lacy Collison-Morley, *Shakespeare in Italy* (Stratford, 1916), Dedication; David Jones, *In Parenthesis* (1963, edn), p. 196, notes to part 3; Siegfried Sassoon, *Memoirs of an Infantry Officer* (1930), pp. 65–66, 110; Wilfred Ewart, *Scots Guard* (1934), p. 91; Edgell Rickword, 'Trench Poet', in *Behind the Eyes* (1921), p. 44. ('What needst thou have more covering than a man?' is the last line of John Donne's Elegie XIX 'To His Mistris Going to Bed'.) See also Paul Fussell, *The Great War and Modern Memory* (1975), pp. 161–69.

front: he quoted a captain, *un vrai poilu*, as saying 'Of course its inaccurate, but look how long they've been stuffing the heads of the people in the rear with rubbish about our life here, and Barbusse now says the exact opposite'.[10]

André Bridoux wrote in 1930 of *Le feu* passing from hand to hand in the trenches of Champagne:

> The men sought to take stock of themselves; they were eager to find a precise rendering of the confused but stirring picture they had formed of themselves and their new destiny; they counted on the writer to help them achieve a clearer awareness of what they saw around them and what they felt within themselves.

At the same time a great deal of both reading and writing was expressive of an urge to escape from the awfulness of the present. One of the earliest soldier poets, F.W. Harvey, wrote mainly about the Gloucestershire countryside and in introducing a volume of his poems the colonel of his battalion explained, 'Mud, blood and Khaki are rather conspicuously absent. They are, in fact, the last things a soldier wishes to think or talk about'. Even Siegfried Sassoon admitted the truth of this:

> Soldiers are dreamers; when the guns begin
>   They think of firelit homes, clean beds, and wives.
>
> I see them in foul dug-outs, gnawed by rats,
>   And in the ruined trenches, lashed with rain,
> Dreaming of things they did with balls and bats,
>   And mocked by hopeless longing to regain
> Bank-holidays, and picture shows, and spats,
>   And going to the office in the train.

Partly perhaps it was a matter of fixing one's thoughts on beauty, fresh air and calm when surrounded by ugliness, cordite fumes and man-made racket. 'If only this fear would leave me I could dream of Crickley

---

[10] Donald E. Stanford, *British Poets, 1914–1945* (Detroit, 1983), p. 307; Blunden, *Undertones of War*, p. 196; Klaus Lankheit, Uwe Steffen, eds, *Franz Marc: Letters from the War* (New York, 1992), p. 66, to Maria Marc, 23 September 1915; Jean Norton Cru, *Témoins* (Paris, 1929), p. 4; Jean Vic, *La littérature de la guerre: manuel méthodique et critique des publications de langue française* (5 vols, Paris, 1918–23), iii, p. 257; Siegfried Sassoon, *Siegfried's Journey* (1945), p. 60; Cru, *Témoins*, pp. 557–65; ibid., p. 565.

Hill', wrote Ivor Gurney; and Ford Madox Hueffer elaborated much
the same idea in his poem 'The Iron Music':

> The French guns roll continously
> And our guns, heavy, slow;
> Along the Ancre, sinuously,
> The transport wagons go,
> And the dust is on the thistles
> And the larks sing up on high . . .
> *But I see the Golden Valley*
> *Down by Tintern on the Wye . . .*
>
> Dust and corpses in the thistles
> Where the gas-shells burst like snow,
> And the shrapnel screams and whistles
> On the Becourt road below,
> And the High Wood bursts and bristles
> Where the mine-clouds foul the sky . . .
> *But I'm with you up at Wyndcroft,*
> *Over Tintern on the Wye.*[11]

Yet even the ability to day-dream, let alone to read books or compose
poems, represented something of a triumph of the human spirit
over material reality. In a letter to his mother Wilfred Owen wrote:
'I can't tell you any more Facts. I have no Fancies and no Feelings,
Positively they went numb with my feet.' T.E. Hulme told a friend:
'My mind is a corridor. The minds about me are corridors. Nothing
suggests itself. There is nothing to do but keep on'. Robert Graves
confessed, 'I feel exactly like a man who has watched the "Movies"
for a long evening and then suddenly found himself thrown on the
screen in the middle of scalp-hunting Sioux and runaway motor cars'.
Rupert Brooke, recalling his baptism of fire at Antwerp, confessed
'most of the time I was thinking of food, or marching straight, or

---

[11] André Bridoux, *Souvenirs du temps des morts* (Paris, 1930), p. 9; F.W. Harvey, *A
Gloucestershire Lad: At Home and Abroad* (1916), p. viii, preface by Colonel J.H. Collett;
Siegfried Sassoon, 'Dreamers', in *Counter-Attack and Other Poems* (1918), p. 19; Ivor
Gurney, 'De Profundis', in P.J. Kavanagh, ed., *Collected Poems of Ivor Gurney* (Oxford,
1982), p. 41; Ford Madox Hueffer, 'The Iron Music', in *On Heaven: and Poems Written
on Active Service* (1918), pp. 35–36.

what to say to the men, or, mostly, not thinking at all'. While in the trenches Siegfried Sassoon confided to his diary, 'I wonder what Thomas Hardy would think of the life out here. How the Pre-Raphaelites would have loathed it'. Later he wrote of 'the veritable gloom and disaster of the thing called Armageddon . . . a place of horror and desolation which no imagination could have invented . . . a place where a man of strong spirit might know himself utterly powerless against death and destruction'.[12]

There were of course moments when even men like Wilfred Owen who hated the war passionately found themselves caught up and energized by the vast drama:

> There was an extraordinary exultation in the act of slowly walking forward, showing ourselves openly. There was no bugle and no drum for which I was very sorry. I kept up a kind of chanting sing-song:
>
> > Keep the Line straight!
> > Not so fast on the left!
> > Steady on the Left!
> > Not so fast!
>
> Then we were caught in a Tornado of Shells. The various 'waves' were all broken up and we carried on like a crowd moving off a cricket-field. When I looked back and saw the ground all crawling and wormy with wounded bodies I felt no horror at all but only an immense exultation at having got through the Barrage.

R.H. Tawney, a pillar of the Fabian Society and later a Professor of Economic History, also no lover of war, found exhilaration merely in the discovery that he was not at all frightened at being shot at:

> we went forward, not doubling, but at a walk . . . I hadn't gone ten yards before I felt a load fall from me. There's a sentence at the end of *The*

[12] John Bell, ed., *Wilfred Owen: Selected Letters* (Oxford, 1985), p. 210, Wilfred Owen to his mother Susan Owen, 7 January 1917; Alun R. Jones, *The Life and Opinions of T.E. Hulme* (1960), p. 182, 'TEH Poem: Abbreviated from the Conversation of Mr T.E.H.: Trenches St Eloi'; Paul O'Prey, ed., *In Broken Images: Selected Letters of Robert Graves, 1914–1946* (1982), p. 32, Graves to Eddie Marsh, 22 May 1915; Geoffrey Keynes, ed., *The Letters of Rupert Brooke* (1968), p. 654, Brooke to John Drinkwater, 18–25 January 1915; Rupert Hart-Davis, ed., *Siegfried Sassoon: Diaries, 1915–1918* (1983), p. 96, 19 July 1916; Siegfried Sassoon, *Memoirs of an Infantry Officer* (1930), p. 216.

Pilgrim's Progress which has always struck me as one of the most awful things imagined by man: 'Then I saw that there was a way to Hell, even from the Gates of Heaven, as well as from the City of Destruction.' To have gone so far and be rejected at last! Yet undoubtedly man walks between precipices, and no one knows the rottenness in him till he cracks, and then it's too late. I had been worried by the thought: 'Suppose one should lose one's head and get other men cut up! Suppose one's legs should take fright and refuse to move!' Now I knew it was all right. I shouldn't be frightened and I shouldn't lose my head. Imagine the joy of that discovery! I felt quite happy and self-possessed.

But such moments were few and far between: neither Richard Aldington nor Ford Madox Hueffer, for example, ever took part in a set-piece attack, though they served for months at the front.[13]

> No flame we saw, the noise and the dread
> Was battle to us,

wrote Ivor Gurney. According to Max Deauville, the 'heaps of corpses, the terrible hand-to-hand combats' never existed:

The face of war is more sober, more dull, more formed out of boredom, fear, moral constraint, cafard, slavery and melancholy. It is ugly and uninteresting, it never satisfied the instinct for struggle and combat which sleeps in men's hearts. Heroes were killed without glory, without knowing how or by whom, without seeing anything, in an unleashing of hidden forces amidst which only chance ruled.

Recollecting his first days on the Western Front, Vivian Gilbert wrote:

Who has not experienced or read of the trenches in France? The mud, the flies and the stench, and death forever waiting round the next traverse! And, worst of all, the dreary monotony of inaction, the crushing out of individualism and the fatalistic anticipation of conflict! I had come out from England prepared to fight, eager to do my share, but somehow this did not seem like real fighting; never to see one's opponent; to stand for hours with liquid mud up to one's thighs – for the heavy shelling brought

---

[13] *Wilfred Owen: Selected Letters*, pp. 243–44, Wilfred Owen to Colin Owen, 14 May 1917; R.H. Tawney, *The Attack and Other Papers* (1953), pp. 13–14 (originally printed in the *Westminster Gazette*, August 1916).

constant rain; to fire machine guns at unseen targets for pre-arranged periods throughout the night on elevations worked out with map, compass and clinometer; and then if one *did* have any time to oneself, to spend it like a rat in a deep, damp dugout. It was so unlike all my pre-conceived notions of warfare.

It was also unlike most people's idea of what a writer would want to write about. Adding to the general sense of monotony and malaise was the numbing effect of the sheer physical degradation of frontline conditions:

> They talk about the glory of war, but they should see this place; the stench of it is too terrible, bodies and bits of bodies everywhere, covered with enormous maggots and awful big green flies which leave the piece of putrefaction as you pass and swarm all around your face . . .

And again and again it was the sheer ugliness of it all that obsessed the men who had to live with it:

> I suppose I can endure cold, and fatigue, and the face-to-face death, as well as another; but extra for me there is the universal pervasion of *Ugliness*. Hideous landscapes, vile noises, foul language and nothing but foul, even from one's own mouth (for all are devil ridden), everything unnatural, broken, blasted; the distortion of the dead, whose unburiable bodies sit outside the dug-outs all day, all night, the most execrable sights on earth. In poetry we call them the most glorious. But to sit with them all day, all night . . . and a week later to come back and find them still sitting there, in motionless groups, THAT is what saps the 'soldierly spirit' . . .

One man succeeded in making art out of that ugliness: Paul Nash, the greatest painter of the war, but also amongst the greatest of English letter writers:

> The ground for miles around furrowed into trenches, pitted with yawning holes in which the water lies still and cold or heaped with mounds of earth, tangles of rusty wire, tin plates, stakes, sandbags and all the refuse of war. In the distance runs a stream where the stringy poplars and alders lean about dejectedly, while farther a slope rises to a scarred bluff the foot of which is scattered with headless trees standing white and withered, hopeless, without any leaves, done, dead. As shells fall

in the bluff, huge sprouts of black, brown and orange mould burst into the air amid a volume of white smoke, flinging wide incredible debris, while the crack and roar of the explosion reverberates in the valley. In the midst of this strange country, where such things happen, men are living in their narrow ditches, hidden from view by every cunning device, waiting and always on the watch, yet at the same time, easy, careless, well fed, wrapped up in warm clothes, talking, perpetually smoking, and indifferent to anything that occurs . . . As night falls the monstrous land takes on a strange aspect . . . the horizon brightens and again vanishes as the Very lights rise and fall, shedding their weird greenish glare over the land, and acute contrast to their lazy silent flight breaks out the agitated knocking of the machine guns as they sweep the parapets . . .[14]

The number who simply could not bear it was perhaps fewer than one would expect. The Austrian poet Georg Trakl had a breakdown after only a month as pharmacist in a field hospital on the Galician Front; and after a month under medical care managed to kill himself with an overdose of cocaine. Robert Nichols lasted three weeks as a second-lieutenant in a field battery. Ivor Gurney, who wrote 'War brings greater self-control – or breakdown', was gassed in September 1917, rehospitalized in February 1918 because of the recurrence of symptoms of gas-poisoning and transferred to a hospital specializing in neurasthenia cases in May 1918. He spent most of the rest of his life in asylums. But the ideal age for military service is also the age at which people are most likely to begin showing the symptoms of mental illness: Ivor Gurney seems to have been a classic case of schizophrenia; the nature of Nichols's breakdown is not clear but he too might have had psychiatric problems even without the war; Trakl had been a drug addict for at least a year before the war broke out. The official verdict in the British army was that 80 per cent of war psychosis cases had a family history of nervous or

---

[14] Ivor Gurney, 'On Somme', in P.J. Kavanagh, ed., *Collected Poems of Ivor Gurney*, p. 157; Max Deauville [Maurice Duvez], *La boue des Flandres* (1964 edn), p. 10 (Avant-propos); Vivian Gilbert, *The Romance of the Last Crusade: With Allenby to Jerusalem* (New York, 1923), pp. 43–44; Herbert Buckmaster, *Buck's Book: Ventures – Adventures and Misadventures* (1933), p. 146; *Wilfred Owen: Selected Letters*, p. 217–18, to Susan Owen, 4 February 1917; Paul Nash, *Outline: An Autobiography and Other Writings* (1949), pp. 105–6, Paul Nash to Margaret Nash, 6 April 1917.

mental disease. At the beginning of the war army medics had known nothing about 'shell shock' but by the second half of 1916 it was being diagnosed comparatively freely. Later, when it was discovered that the symptoms often disappeared after a period of rest, the reported incidence of battle neurosis went down. In the American Expeditionary Force in 1918 sixty-five out of every 100 soldiers who complained of symptoms of neurasthenia were returned to duty from Field Hospitals, and a further twenty from the specialist neurological hospitals attached to each of the two armies composing the American Expeditionary Force: and of the 15 per cent who ended up at Base Hospital 117, where longer-term battle neurosis cases were dealt with, only one in fifteen was sent back to America for further treatment: the others eventually returned to duty. As the criteria for diagnosis and the stage at which statistics were collected varied at different stages of the war, it is difficult to assess the actual incidence of battle neurosis: the British Army's statistics for the second half of 1916 suggest a ratio of one battle neurosis case for every thirteen men killed, whereas the AEF statistics for October 1918 show one battle neurosis case reporting to Field Hospitals for every five men killed, and one case admitted to Base Hospital 117 for every thirty killed. The total of battle neurosis cases in the British army in France and Belgium was estimated at 80,000 (as compared to 1,937,364 killed and wounded). In 1922 50,000 British ex-soldiers were receiving government pensions for neurasthenic disablement, which seems a very poor recovery rate: possibly the majority of these cases were men whose psychiatric problems, though first manifesting themselves in the army, would have occurred in any case. On the other hand, it was perfectly normal for ex-soldiers who suffered no obvious psychiatric disablement to have nightmares about the war for the rest of their lives: if they slept. William Linton Andrews claimed in 1930:

> For many years after the War, like many, many others who had been there a long time, I woke almost every night in terror from a nightmare of suffocation by gas, or of being trapped by a bombardment from which I ran this way and that, or of fighting a bayonet duel with a gigantic Prussian Guardsman.

And Ugo Dell'Aringa of the Italian army had precisely one hour's sleep in thirty-nine years after his return home from the war.[15]

Soldiers suffering from battle trauma were not necessarily lacking in enthusiasm. One doctor recorded the case of a former student of University College, Aberystwyth, twice wounded in action on previous occasions, who was struck deaf and dumb – a not infrequent phenomenon – by a shell exploding close beside him. By means of scribbled notes he requested and obtained permission to stay and participate in the next attack instead of going to the rear. In the attack he operated a Lewis Gun with his usual competence, was wounded a third time and sent to hospital. 'I've been too long up there to look on it with any fear', he wrote. He recovered his power of speech under ether eleven days later, and was eventually returned to duty.[16]

After the war it was claimed that some men had only been able to keep themselves going by heavy drinking. Mark Plowman wrote of his company commander,

> He is just a good-natured fellow, with any amount of pluck, whose morals have been damaged by the war and its whisky. The amount of whisky he

[15] R.K.R. Thornton, ed., *Ivor Gurney: War Letters* (Ashington, 1983), p. 207, Ivor Gurney to Marion Scott, 26 September 1917; Michael Hurd, *The Ordeal of Ivor Gurney* (Oxford, 1978), pp. 121, 123, 195–98; H.C. Marr, *Psychoses of the War: Including Neurasthenia and Shell Shock* (1919), p. 48; Norman Fenton, *Shell Shock and its Aftermath* (1926), p. 23 figure 2, p. 28 figure 6 and p. 29. (Despite its London imprint this is the main authority for shell shock in the American Expeditionary Force); W. Johnson and R.G. Rous 'Neurasthenia and War Neuroses', in W.G. Macpherson et al., *Medical Services: Diseases of the War* (2 vols, 1923), ii, pp. 1–67, at p. 4, table III, and cf. *Statistics of the Military Effort of the British Empire during the Great War, 1914–1920* (1922), pp. 263–64; Johnson and Rous, 'Neurasthenia and War Neuroses', pp. 7, 8, cf. *Military Effort*, p. 249; William Linton Andrews, *Haunting Years: The Commentaries of a War Territorial* [1930], p. 5; *The Guinness Book of Records* [1958], p. 221.

[16] Charles S. Myers, *Shell Shock in France, 1914–18* (Cambridge, 1940), pp. 73–75. For a general discussion of war neurosis during the First World War, see Eric J. Leed, *No Man's Land: Combat and Identity in World War I* (Cambridge 1979), pp. 163–92; for its occurrence in earlier wars see John Talbott, 'Combat Trauma in the American Civil War', *History Today*, 46, March 1996, pp. 41–47, Anthony Babington, *Shell Shock: A History of the Changing Attitudes to War Neurosis* (1997), pp. 13–20, and R.L. Richards 'Mental and Nervous Diseases during the Russo-Japanese War', *Military Surgeon*, 26 (1910), p. 177–93.

and Mallow, the bombing-officer, can drink is astonishing. Every time Mallow reaches for the bottle he repeats the parrot phrase, 'This war will be won on whisky or it won't be won at all', apparently intending to float home on whisky himself.

A school-boy hero transmogrified into whisky-toping company commander featured in R.C. Sherriff's hit play *Journey's End*, first staged in January 1929. It may have been the furore provoked by *Journey's End* that encouraged Robert Graves to state in his memoir *Good-Bye to All That*, published in November of the same year, that officers who stayed too long in the trenches often became dipsomaniacs:

> I knew three or four who had worked up to the point of two bottles of whiskey a day before being lucky enough to get wounded or sent home in some other way. A two-bottle company commander of one of our line battalions is still alive who, in three shows running, got his company needlessly destroyed because he was no longer capable of taking clear decisions.

One has only to think of how many units were needlessly destroyed as a result of clear decisions made when stone-cold sober to find something suspicious in this, and a writer in the *Times Literary Supplement* remarked 'One of the chief impressions that many of us took away from *Journey's End* was that Stanhope and his friends were very lucky to have such lavish supplies of whiskey at their disposal'. Nevertheless official statistics show that, relative to the total number of officers serving abroad who were court-martialled, the percentage who were charged with drunkenness fell by more than a quarter after the Armistice.[17]

---

[17] Mark VII [Mark Plowman], *A Subaltern on the Somme in 1916* (1927), p. 23; letters in *The Times* from Brigadier-General Robert Pigot, General Sir Ivor Maxse and Lieutenant-Colonel Graham Seton-Hutchinson, *The Times*, 16 April 1930, p. 10e, and 17 April 1930, p. 17e; Robert Graves, *Goodbye To All That*, p. 144; *Times Literary Supplement*, 12 June 1930, p. 485d; *Statistics of the Military Effort of the British Empire*, p. 660: in the year ending 30 September 1918 there were 980 trials of officers by court martial outside the UK, of which 387 were for drunkenness, and in the year ending 30 September 1919, 1001 trials of officers by court martial, of which 293 were for drunkenness.

Robert Graves's 'two-bottle company commander' is identified as 'Jack Greaves', i.e. Captain R.C.J. Greaves, in a copy of *Good-Bye to All That* formerly belonging to,

Not everyone was adversely affected by the atmosphere of the battle zone however: some men found it positively bracing. According to Wyndham Lewis,

> Arrival at 'the Front' for us was not unlike arrival at a big Boxing Match, or at a Blackshirt Rally at Olympia. The same sinister expectancy, but more sinister and more electric, the same restless taciturnity of stern-faced persons assembling for a sensational and bloody event, their hearts set on a knockout. Somebody else's, of course.

Charles Carrington recalled of joining a battalion in the line: 'It was far more like stepping out from the pavilion to bat for the first time in a match, than like waiting with horrid anticipation at the dentist's door'. Later he reflected:

> As for the danger, it must be remembered that most men like adventures. Anyone who has ever been through a street accident, anyone who has climbed a mountain, knows that. It is one of the strange attributes of the mind that we enjoy what makes our flesh creep, and no one was very long at the front without sometimes feeling a thrill of excitement which quite banished the dragging fears of anticipation.

A.W. Smith wrote:

> As a whole, in between the moments of intensity I remember great arid stretches of drabness and mild boredom. They are overshadowed by the dark cloud of an immense tiredness. Sleep seemed the only thing that mattered – to be let alone to sleep.
>
> Being at the front flattered my conceit. I was on the stage – if only in the chorus. I was one of the initiated. I was the centre of interest of my relations and friends.
>
> I did not dislike being at the front.[18]

Some people even attempted to make a joke of it:

continued

and annotated by, Captain J.C. Dunn (the medical officer in Graves's battalion) now in the possession of the Royal Welch Fusiliers – see Robert Graves *Good-Bye to All That*, ed. Richard Percival Graves (Oxford 1995), p. 345, note to p. 158 line 12e.

[18] Wyndham Lewis, *Blasting and Bombardiering* (1937), p. 119; Charles Carrington ('Charles Edmonds'), *A Subaltern's War* (1929), pp. 20 and 195; A.W. Smith, *A Captain Departed* (1934), p. 44.

Except for the banal booming and flashing of the guns one might be at one of those old-fashioned balls in Arthur Grenfell's garden at Roehampton – the same tiresome noise of electricity being generated in the too near foreground, the same scraggy oaks, the same scramble for sandwiches, the same crowd . . . the same band playing the same tunes, the same moon in the same sky.

In the same vein perhaps was the suggestion of an officer in the Grenadier Guards that the trenches were not as bad as prep school:

At least there were no masters, matrons, or compulsory games. The discomfort was, at times, perhaps a little greater, the food, though tinned, perhaps a little more palatable . . . Through the long course of Samurai-like discipline to which they were, with few exceptions, obliged to submit in their most impressionable years, the children of the former British governing classes had been taught to bear with composure a high degree of physical hardship and spiritual misery, while enclosed in an atmosphere of utmost frustration . . . certainly the young of this class could bear bodily suffering and exhaustion, and a sense of the cruellest isolation, with a stoical equanimity unknown among those who came from good working-class homes and had been brought up, right from their earliest years to manhood, in an unaltering atmosphere of domestic affection.

There may have been something in that: after having been caught in No Man's Land by a German bombardment an Old Etonian wrote home:

It was good fun while it lasted . . . You never exist long in this battalion, so I expect it will be my turn next. Still we're very cheerful. It does seem funny to be playing a gramophone and roaring with laughter at everything, when you're only about half a mile from the German trenches.

The poet Edward Thomas – who had also been at Public School but as a day boy – was another who saw little essential difference between life at the front and peacetime existence:

Physical discomfort is sometimes so great that it seems a new thing, but of course it is not . . . Of course, one seems very little one's own master, but then one seldom does seem so . . . An alternation of comfort and

discomfort is always a man's lot. So is an alternation of pleasure or happiness or intense interest with tedium or dissatisfaction or misery. I have
suffered more from January to March in other years than in this.[19]

Cyril McNeile, the inventor of Bulldog Drummond, thought people
tended to forget the worst moments in any case:

> What are the moments that stick out like landmarks in my mind as I
> look back? Those of palsied fright, when, cowering behind a blade of grass,
> ears numbed with the inferno of noise around, it seemed merely a ques-
> tion of seconds before the inevitable end? Honestly – I don't think so.
> Those of intense physical discomfort, when, wet to the skin and well nigh
> frozen to the bone, teeth chattering, eyes full of mud, nostrils full of stench,
> it seemed as if the limit of human endurance had been reached? Honestly
> – I don't think so. Those when one heard suddenly that the fellow whose
> leg you had pulled two hours before had stopped an odd one in the brain?
> No: not even those . . .

What he remembered was 'the spirit of camaraderie' and the epicurean
pleasure of a decent dinner and a decent bed when one came out of
the line. Similarly Charles Carrington wrote:

> If no man now under thirty can guess the meaning of twenty-four hours'
> bombardment, nor has he any notion of the joy of ninety-six hours' rest.
> Who has never been drenched and frozen in Flanders mud, has never
> dreamed of the pleasure derivable from dry blankets on a stone floor.[20]

Some people positively thrived in the line:

> The horrors of the Great War and the miseries of those who were called
> upon to take part in it have been described by innumerable writers. For
> my own part I have to confess that I look back on the years 1914–1918 as
> among the happiest I have ever spent. That they contained moments of

---

[19] John Joliffe, ed., *Raymond Asquith: Life and Letters* (1980), p. 277, Raymond Asquith
to Lady Diana Manners, 21 July 1916; Sitwell, *Laughter in the Next Room*, p. 80; letter
from an Old Etonian in the 2nd Battalion Coldstream Guards, printed in *The Zep-
pelin: Piloted by Present Etonians*, 26 March 1915; George Thomas, ed., *Edward Thomas:
Selected Letters* (Oxford, 1995), to Julian Thomas, 30 March 1917.

[20] Cyril McNeile, *Sapper's War Stories: Collected in One Volume* [1930], pp. 9–10
(Foreword); Carrington, *A Subaltern's War*, p. 195.

boredom and depression, of sorrow for the loss of friends and of alarm for my personal safety is indeed true enough. But to be perfectly fit, to live among pleasant companions, to have responsibility and a clearly defined job – these are great compensations when one is very young.

That was written seventeen years after the end of the war but was by no means an instance of viewing the past through a romantic haze: the same officer wrote to his mother six and a half weeks after the Armistice (and after the best part of four years at the front as a subaltern in the 4th Battalion Oxford and Buckinghamshire Light Infantry), 'it will be very hard to leave the regiment after so many years . . . Could you ever have guessed how much I should enjoy the war?'[21]

It would not be difficult in fact to compile a thick anthology of first-hand accounts of the war that testify to its having been a positive, even life-enhancing experience. The retrospective view we have of the horrors of the First World War is a social construct, composed not merely from the most successful – that is, *commercially* the most successful – literary accounts of the Western Front, but also from the attitudes which became prevalent after the 1939–45 war, especially during the 1960s when military technology finally reached a *reductio ad absurdam* and the world seemed poised on the brink of total annihilation by thermo-nuclear weapons. Yet the testimony of those who fought in the First World War, as it has come down to us, is not only refracted and distorted to our gaze by the events of the intervening years, but is also, in its very origins, subject to bizarre anomalies and asymmetries. It may for example be simply one of those meaningless agglomerations of coincidence which one now and again encounters when studying human groups that, with more than a hundred infantry regiments in the British army in 1914, the authors of three of the best memoirs of the war, Siegfried Sassoon, Robert Graves and Bernard Adams, should have served together as officers in the same battalion, the 1st Royal Welch Fusiliers, in December 1915; and that Frank Richards, J.C. Dunn and Wyn Griffith, who also wrote notable accounts of the war, the poet David Jones, and Vivian de Sola Pinto, the critic who in middle age launched the post-Second World War revival

---

[21] Graham H. Greenwell, *An Infant in Arms: War Letters of a Company Officer, 1914–1918* (1935), p. ix; ibid., p. 305, Greenwell to his mother, 26 December 1918.

of interest in the 'trench poets', should have been in other battalions of the same regiment. Similarly the authors of two of the best novels about the war, Henry Williamson and Victor Yeates, had been contemporaries in the same house at the same obscure south London grammar school. Perhaps less of a coincidence was that Nicolae Vulovici, the leading Romanian poet of patriotic militarism, was killed in action within a fortnight of Romania's entry into the war, and the two other leading Romanian poets of military age were killed within the next few weeks, whereas the two most interesting younger Portuguese poets kept out of the war altogether, Mário de Sá-Carneiro committing suicide in Paris, apparently before the authorities got round to calling him up, and Fernando Pessoa having already drunk himself into physical unfitness. Meanwhile all but one of the most notable Russian poets of the earlier part of this century managed to avoid frontline service in the war with Germany which helped bring down the Tsarist regime, though they were mostly caught up in the Revolution that followed. Gumilev volunteered and became a hero, winning two St George's Crosses and a commission, but Pasternak failed his medical, and it is probable that Mandelshtam was not conscripted for the same reason; Mayakovsky, initially turned down for military service for political reasons – something only possible in Russia – was, when finally inducted into the army, assigned to the Petrograd Automobile School because he was a qualified draughtsman; Blok served as an artillery officer at Pinsk; Yesenin, initially exempted because of poor eye-sight, eventually became a clerk on an ambulance train based at Tsarskoe Selo; Khlebnikov, sent to hospital with a skin disease soon after being called up, was still begging his commanding officer to assign him to active service when the Revolution came. This is part of the reason why most of the best poets of the First World War were British: apart from Gumilev, the Russian poets simply never got close enough to write about it.[22]

---

[22] *Colfensia: The Chronicles of Colfe Grammar School*, no. 19 (1913) p. 21–22, shows that Yeates, in Form VA, was a vice-captain for sport in Buff House while Williamson, a sixth former, was captain of the Buff House harrier team; Eugen Marinescu, *Cîntăretul Luptelor Şi Al Biruinţelor: căpitanul-poet Nicolae Vulovici* (Bucharest, 1977), p. 107–10 (the other two poets were Mihail Săulescu and Constantin Stoika); Leonid I. Strakhovsky, *Craftsman of the Word: Three Poets of Russia* (Cambridge, Massachusetts, 1949), p. 31; Christopher Barnes, *Boris Pasternak: A Literary Biography*, i (1989), pp. 179,

British war poets also had another advantage. The conditions in which, in every army, the rank and file lived in the frontline were appreciably worse than those experienced by their officers; in the French and German and Russian armies the officers either were pre-war professional soldiers, all three armies having much larger officer cadres in 1914 than the British, and conserving this resource better by having fewer officers in front line units, or else temporary officers promoted from the ranks because distinguished by their enthusiasm and military competence. The British officers who wrote poetry were predominantly 'temporary gentlemen' who had been commissioned mainly because of their class and education, rather than their military bearing. It is difficult to believe Ford Madox Hueffer (later Ford Madox Ford) or Richard Aldington would ever have become officers in the French or German armies; and Wilfred Owen and Robert Graves would certainly not have been commissioned as quickly as they were. Osbert Sitwell had already been an officer in the Grenadier Guards when war broke out, but it was precisely the fact that they had officers like Osbert Sitwell which made the Brigade of Guards different from the elite formations of other countries' armies:

> We are the greatest sheep in the world;
> There are no sheep like us.
> We come of an imperial bleat;
> Our voices,
> Trembling with music,
> Call to our lambs oversea.
> With us they crash across continents.
>
> We will not heed the herdsmen,
> For they warned us,
> 'Do not stampede';
> Yet we were forced to do so.
> Never will we trust a herdsman again . . .

continued

182; Wiktor Woroszylsk, *The Life of Mayakovsky* (1972), p. 141; Avril Pyman *The Life of Aleksandr Blok* (2 vols, Oxford, 1979–80), ii, pp. 234–35; Gordon McVay, *Esenin: A Life* (1976), pp. 73–77; Charlotte Douglas, ed., *Collected Works of Velimir Khlebnikov*, i, *Letters and Theoretical Writings* (Cambridge, Massachusetts, 1987), p. 106 and, especially, p. 116 letter 91.

> We are stampeding to end stampedes.
> We are fighting for lambs
> Who are never likely to be born.
>
> When once a sheep gets its blood up
> The goats will remember . . .

Censorship conditions were also more favourable in Britain: in Germany and France the *Cambridge Magazine*, which published several of Siegfried Sassoon's anti-war poems, would almost certainly have been suppressed, whereas in Britain it merely had to put up with surveillance by the Special Branch and a rather pointless dirty tricks campaign conducted by the Foreign Office. The importance of the *Cambridge Magazine* cannot be overstated: in publishing Sassoon's work it provided a platform for the man whose anti-war poems encouraged Wilfred Owen and Osbert Sitwell to write their own.[23]

Such factors may have had more influence in determining the distinctive quality of the war literature of the various belligerent nations than more substantial institutional differences, such as conscription. Till 1916 the British armed forces were composed entirely of volunteers: before the war France, Germany and Russia had maintained large peacetime armies by means of a system of compulsory military service, and those who had already completed their military service obligation were available for call up as reservists once a general mobilization had been ordered. The British contribution to the literature of the First World War is unique in that it was written almost entirely by volunteers. One hundred and twenty years earlier, Coleridge and Wordsworth had kept out of the war at least in part because they saw themselves as poets: for the writers of the 1914 generation it was precisely *because* they were writers that they felt they had to join in. For Richard Aldington the war was 'the biggest thing that ever happened'; Arnold Toynbee, hearing of the death of one of his friends at the front, wondered, 'when there is all

---

[23] Osbert Sitwell, 'Sheep-Song', in *Argonaut and Juggernaut* (1919), pp. 97–98 (dated September 1918); for the petty persecution of the *Cambridge Magazine* by the authorities see A.D. Harvey, 'Watching the Intellectuals: The Government and *The Cambridge Magazine* in 1916', *Cambridge Review*, 112, no. 2315 (December 1991), pp. 184–86; for wartime censorship in Germany, see John D. Halliday, *Karl Kraus, Franz Pfemfert and the First World War* (Passau, 1986), pp. 169, 172–73.

this going on, why am I not in it?' Such a question had never occurred to the intellectuals of the 1800s. Yet the uniqueness of Britain's volunteer army was an institutional rather than a psychological phenomenon: that peculiar quality of outrage which one detects in the poetry of Sassoon and Owen, as if they had volunteered for service in the belief that the war would be much less terrible than it turned out to be, is to be found also in the writings of draftees in the German and French armies, like Remarque or Giono. Nor can there be any doubt that if France and Germany had *not* had conscription, they too would have been able to raise armies on a volunteer basis. Before the war, in fact, the Germans had needed to call up only part of each age-group to man the army, and many of those who went to the front in 1914 were men who had enlisted voluntarily, including thousands of teenagers like the Gymnasium-students in Erich Maria Remarque's *Im Westen Nichts Neues* who volunteered for service months ahead of becoming old enough to be called up in the routine way. (In real life Remarque was drafted, but, for example, Ernst Jünger and Gorch Fock were volunteers.) There were also volunteers in the French army, including the pioneer Surrealists Guillaume Apollinaire and Blaise Cendrars. Joseph Roth and Józef Wittlin volunteered together in Austria, and even in Bulgaria, which mobilized a higher percentage of the country's adult male population than any other belligerent, Dimcho Debelianov, the most notable Bulgarian writer to be killed in the war, enlisted of his own free will despite being exempted because of his technical qualifications. And once one had volunteered, of course, one was faced with the same assault on one's values, intellect and sensibilities as any conscript.[24]

One also ran the same risk of sudden death. Ernest Psichari and Nicolae Vulovici have already been mentioned: amongst other authors snuffed out by the war before they had any real chance to write about it were the poet and essayist Charles Péguy, killed on 5 September 1914 during the Battle of the Marne, Henri Alain-Fournier, author of *Le Grand Meaulnes*, killed on 22 September 1914, and Hermann Löns, killed 26 September 1914, whose 'Blood and Soil' poetry was

---

[24] Verna Coleman, *The Last Exquisite: A Portrait of Frederic Manning* (Melbourne, 1990), p. 118, quoting Aldington to Harriet Monroe, 7 August 1914; Gordon Martel, 'The Origins of the Chatham House Version', in Edward Ingram, ed., *National and International Politics in the Middle East: Essays in Honour of Elie Kedourie* (1986), pp. 66–83, at p. 74, quoting Arnold Toynbee's letter to his mother of 12 November 1914.

later esteemed by the Nazis and whose novel *Der Wehrwolf* (1910), about peasants defending themselves against marauding foreign troops during the Thirty Years' War, provided the name adopted for the underground resistance groups organized when Allied forces began encroaching on German territory at the end of 1944. Péguy, Alain-Fournier, Löns and Vulovici may be regarded as belonging amongst the Lost Voices of First World War literature: had they lived the course of the war would not have been perceptibly altered, but the way we remember it might have been different.

CHAPTER 5

Artists

AMONGST THOSE who survived long enough to make any sort of artistic statement about the war, it seems to have been painters rather than writers who were most immediately influenced by the vagaries of the military machine, though in painting as much as in literature the effect of outward institutional factors was balanced by more recondite mechanisms of cause and effect.

It may be argued that the hundred years of material progress in Europe after Waterloo, the development of factories, of railways, of international money markets, made a conflict on the scale of the First World War inevitable, but the premise that sooner or later neighbouring states will find occasion to go to war is in fact no truer for the industrial era than for the pre-industrial – indeed experience since 1945 suggests it may be less true. In any case events as such are only part of the historical process: even more important is the sequence and timing of events. Though the outcome of the First World War might have been much the same if it had broken out before the aeroplane had been invented, and though Britain might still have gone to war with Germany for the sake of Belgium even if there had not been a ten-year build up of Anglo-German tension over Germany's desire to have a stronger battle fleet, all the details of what actually happened are inextricably bound up with the fact that they happened when and in the order they did. And one of the things that happened was that the war came just as artists, at least pictorial artists, were becoming, artistically speaking, ready for it.

In suggesting that artists were ready for the war in August 1914 one inevitably brings to mind Italian Futurism. The Futurist leader

F.T. Marinetti had already declared that war was the only hygiene of
the world in 1912, and Italy's war in what is now Libya in 1911–12,
and the Balkan Wars of 1912–13, which took place in a zone where
the Italians counted on increasing their influence, provided plenty
of warlike images. Marinetti wrote an evocation of the Battle of Tripoli
in relatively decorous French, and of the siege of Adrianople in
demented Italian. But the Futurists did not have a monopoly of warlike special effects. The German Expressionist Ludwig Meidner's
Apocalyptic Landscape paintings, his *Revolution*, and his ink, pencil and
gouache composition *Bombing a City*, all dating from 1913, seem to
have been inspired by his perception of the violent energies mobilized
by contemporary urban life rather than by any prophecy regarding
the outbreak of war, while the military scenes painted by French Cubists
such as Roger de La Fresnaye and Jacques Villon seem to have had
less to do with bellicosity than with the way the angularity and regular-
ity of peacetime military parades, their merging of individuals into
masses, lent themselves to the compositional preoccupations of the
Cubist movement. Such paintings can be seen as making only the tini-
est contribution to the general assumption that war was a natural and,
sooner or later, inevitable phenomenon. When the politicians (admirers of Landseer and Winterhalter almost to a man) decided on war,
Marinetti was prominent amongst those in Italy who campaigned for
Italian participation, but even if it is pretended that the Futurists had
an important role in bringing Italy into the war in May 1915, it was
after all a war that had started without them nine months earlier. The
timeliness of Futurism, Expressionism, Cubism is not that they facilitated
the outbreak of war, but that they provided the ideal expressive medium
for depicting it.[1]

Surprisingly enough, the best of this depicting did not occur in
the heartlands of the pre-war *avant garde*. William Rothenstein was
too cautious when he wrote, 'the work produced by English painters
during the war remains a significant contribution to the European
art of our times'. In fact the British produced the most important
paintings of the war, just as they produced the most important poetry.

[1] *La bataille de Tripoli, 26 octobre 1911, vécue et chantée par F.T. Marinetti* (Paris, 1912);
for Ludwig Meidner, see Richard Cork, *A Bitter Truth: Avant-Garde Art and the Great
War* (New Haven, 1994), pp. 13–15.

As suggested in the last chapter, poets in the British army had certain advantages compared to poets in other armies, but institutional advantages and opportunities do not automatically generate poetry. They may however make all the difference to a painter's ability to get on with his painting. In 1914 most European countries had conscription. Young artists were enrolled in the army, went to the front, and were buried there – often literally. In this way Germany lost Franz Marc (1886–1916), August Macke (1887–1914), Wilhelm Morgner (1891–1917), Hermann Stenner (1891–1914) and the more academically-inclined Hans Fuglsang (1889–1917) and Albert Weisgerber (1878–1915). (Weisgerber had so far succeeded in becoming a respectable citizen, though an artist, that he was a reserve officer when the war broke out.) With regard to August Macke, his friend Max Ernst later wrote:

> The attitude of Macke baffled us. Influenced by Futurism he accepted the war not merely as the most grandiose expression of contemporary madness but also as a philosophical necessity (war necessary for achieving the concept of humanity!) His bellicosity was however in no way coloured by patriotism, as was that of Apollinaire who – we later learnt – also allowed himself to be thrown off course by events. For those who have come to believe in the black irony of fate it is worth remembering that these two men who knew and loved each other, and who were haunted by the same ideas, perished as 'enemies', the one just after the declaration of war, the other on the eve of the armistice.

France lost the sculptor Henri Gaudier-Brzeska (1891–1915); Georges Braque, like the poet Guillaume Apollinaire, was wounded in the head and underwent brain surgery. In the Italian army Umberto Boccioni met a fate by no means appropriate for a Futurist – he died as a result of falling from a horse, though admittedly it was an artillery horse.[2]

Once they were in the army many artists continued to make sketches, but the conditions in which they had to live were even less encouraging for art than for literature. Max Ernst, who managed to spend the war at HQs and base depots, and even found time to continue with

---

[2] William Rothenstein, *Men and Memories* (2 vols, 1931–32), ii, p. 350; Max Ernst, *Écritures* (Paris, 1970), pp. 24–25.

his writing and painting, nevertheless wrote later, 'Max Ernst died on the 1st of August 1914', and on another occasion, '1914–1915 Black Out'. His final verdict was:

> In the shit for four years. 'Victorious, we are going to beat France, die as brave heroes!' we had to sing, with raging hearts, during the long marches at night.
>
> What can one do against military life – its stupidity, its ugliness, its cruelty. To yell, swear, throw up in anger is no use. The temptation to abandon oneself to the therapeutic virtues of the contemplative life doesn't get one very far.

Ludwig Meidner was so depressed by the war that even though not called up till 1916 he painted relatively little during the first eighteen months of hostilities: once in the army, unable to paint or draw, he began to write and for a while even 'dreamt of becoming a second Byron, Heine or Victor Hugo'. Otto Dix became a sergeant in a machine-gun unit but found his comrades in arms contemptible, telling a visiting fellow-artist, 'You know, they think I'm mad, anything they can't eat they can't understand'. Oskar Schlemmer, an infantryman on the Russian Front, was pleased by the colours he saw, noting down 'the tents from inside, the greys transparent and grey-green, the browns rust-red – the colour of my pictures', but even as he amused himself with the way natural and unnatural shades combined his depression and weariness with the army leaked through: 'I am seeing my fill of the splendour of colours, the differently green ground, the grey soldiers, and I eat and smoke and seek calm, the buddhist calm which I now only manage on the march'. Ernst Ludwig Kirchner did not even reach the front; he had a nervous collapse during preliminary training. Paul Klee, assigned to the German army air department to guard aircraft in transit, varnish fuselages and paint on registration numbers with templates, eventually became a paymaster's clerk at a flying school; about the nearest he ever came to the frontline was at Cambrai, where he was shocked by the sight of troops coming out of the line:

> an overwhelming sight. Everything yellow with mud. The unmilitary, matter-of-fact appearance, the steel helmets, the equipment. The trotting step. Nothing heroic, just like beasts of burden, like slaves. Against a background of circus music.

But rather than give him new ideas, the war merely consolidated old ones:

> The more horrible the world (as today, for instance), the more abstract our art, whereas a happy world brings forth an art of the here and now.
> I have long had this war inside me. This is why, interiorly, it means nothing to me.[3]

The sheer uninterestingness of the war, in artistic terms, was also insisted upon by Gaudier-Brzeska in a kind of manifesto published in Wyndham Lewis's magazine *Blast*:

> THE BURSTING SHELLS, the volleys, wire entanglements, projectors, motors, the chaos of battle DO NOT ALTER IN THE LEAST the outlines of the hills we are besieging. A company of PARTRIDGES scuttle along before our very trench.
> IT WOULD BE FOLLY TO SEEK ARTISTIC EMOTIONS AMID THESE LITTLE WORKS OF OURS.
> THIS PALTRY MECHANISM, WHICH SERVES AS A PURGE TO OVERNUMEROUS HUMANITY . . . .
> *MY VIEWS ON SCULPTURE* REMAIN ABSOLUTELY *THE SAME* . . .
> I have made an experiment. Two days ago I pinched from an enemy a mauser rifle. Its heavy unwieldy shape swamped me with a powerful IMAGE of brutality
> I was in doubt for a long time whether it pleased or displeased me.
> I found that I did not like it.
> I broke the butt off and with my knife I carved in it a design, through which I tried to express a gentler order of feeling, which I preferred.
> BUT I WILL EMPHASIZE that MY DESIGN *got its effect* (just as the gun had) FROM A VERY SIMPLE COMPOSITION OF LINES AND PLANES
>
> GAUDIER-BRZESKA

---

[3] William A. Camfield, *Max Ernst: Dada and the Dawn of Surrealism* (Munich, 1993), p. 41, quoting *View* 1942 and exhibition catalogue Paris 1959; Ernst, *Écritures*, p. 25; Lothar Brieger, *Ludwig Meidner: mit einer Selbstbiographie* (Leipzig, 1919), p. 13; Otto Griebel, *Ich war ein Mann der Strasse: Lebenserinnerungen eines Dresdner Malers* (Halle, 1986), p. 59; Oskar Schlemmer, *Idealist der Form: Briefe, Tagebücher, Schriften, 1912–1943* (Leipzig, 1990), p. 20–21; Felix Klee, ed., *The Diaries of Paul Klee, 1898–1918* (1965), p. 355 no. 1026a, 6 December 1916; ibid., p. 313, nos 951 and 952, 1915.

(This text was followed by an announcement of Gaudier-Brzeska's death in action at Neuville St-Vaast on 5 June 1915.)[4]

In France wartime chauvinism encouraged an anti-modernist, anti-avant-garde tone in much art criticism, and the turning away from innovation detectable in the work of Dufy, Picasso and Matisse may perhaps be related to this, yet the objective conditions of the war zone encouraged some Cubist experimentation by artists like André Mare, who had been on the fringes of Cubism before 1914 but kept well away from it after 1918, and André Fraye, who was not involved with Cubism either before or after the war. Fernand Léger, a sapper during the war, even experienced a minor epiphany: 'I was dazzled by the open breach of a 75-millimetre gun in the sunlight, by the magic of the light on the white metal . . . That open breach of a 75 in the full sunlight has taught me more for my plastic development than all the museums of the world'. Derain, in an infantry regiment, seems however to have turned against Cubism because of its emphasis on form at the expense of meaning:

> On leave I saw plenty of things that didn't fill me with enthusiasm from the painting angle. It's the mess too . . .
> Cubism is a really idiotic thing which revolts me more and more . . .
> I had some ideas about what should concern painters: simply the unknown. No more mechanics, that's to say no more means of expression, colours, line etc. – but just the unexplainable.

But the main burden of his wartime letters was the awfulness, ugliness and uninterestingness of the war:

> The artillery! The artillery – always artillery. The mud – the rain or the dust – Nothing to tuck into, nothing to lie on and always like that, with never any letting up.
> And the shells, and the aeroplanes, the night . . .
> It's less picturesque than one could ever have believed and yet full of continual surprises . . .
> If you knew the dumbness of the soldiers, it's beyond imagining. They don't understand a thing, nothing at all. You really couldn't have believed the generality of men were so stupid.

[4] *Blast*, 2 (July 1915), pp. 33–34.

At least three *avant-garde* painters who served in the French army, Jacques Villon, André Dunoyer de Segonzac and Roger de La Fresnaye, were assigned to painting camouflage. This line of work resulted in some notable woodcuts and a striking canvas, now in the National Gallery of Canada, by Edward Wadsworth, who had worked on camouflage in the Royal Navy, and it made Jacques Villon interested in colour theory, but it seems to have contributed little to the artistic development of Dunoyer de Segonzac: as for Roger de La Fresnaye, he contracted TB in 1918 and, having produced a few last paintings in an agreeably derivative style, died in November 1925. The French artist who had perhaps the best opportunities to draw what he liked at the front was Paul Maze, who was attached to the British army as an interpreter and was able to make frequent use of his sketchbook. In his memoirs he quotes a British colonel at Mametz saying, 'I am afraid you won't find the landscape very inspiring', and judging by the bright, cheerful Impressionist style of his work from other periods, this was probably true: some of his sketches were passed on to the British staff for their topographical value but he seems to have destroyed most of the rest of his wartime work. One feels on the whole that the French *avant garde* failed to come to grips with the war; and perhaps the most eloquent depictions of the war to be painted in France were by conservative, eclectic artists, the Swiss-born Félix Vallotton, already forty-nine in 1914, and George Leroux, aged thirty-seven in 1914, who had won the Prix de Rome, accolade of academic respectability, back in 1906. Leroux's *L'enfer*, now in the Imperial War Museum, says as much about the sheer mind-boggling awfulness of the war as Otto Dix's *War Tryptich* of 1932 and *Flanders* of 1934–36, despite Dix's bitter unsmiling humour and stylish reminiscences of Breughel and Altdorfer and Hans Baldung Grien. It seems to have required the defeat of his country to make Dix see the war in terms of unendurable horror and degradation, for at the period when Leroux was painting *L'enfer*, Dix, possibly by way of distracting himself from the awful company he had to keep in the trenches, was producing crayons such as *Going Over the Top, Dying Warrior, Hand to Hand Fighting, Direct Hit* which are full or organic energy and fecundity.[5]

---

[5] Kenneth E. Silver, *Esprit de Corps: The Art of the Parisian Avant-Garde and the First World War, 1914–1925* (Princeton, 1989), pp. 79–80, 85; *Fernand Léger, 1881–1955* (Catalogue of Exhibition at the Palais de Beaux Arts, Brussels, October-November

In Britain conditions were substantially different from those in France and Germany. There was no conscription till 1916: Christopher Nevinson, who was to emerge as one of the two outstanding painters of the war, first encountered its horrors as a volunteer medical orderly behind the French lines. In 1916 the British government decided to send official war artists to the front (as the Germans had done virtually since the beginning), and in March 1917 approved a scheme for a National War Museum (now the Imperial War Museum) which would exhibit the work of war artists. And whereas German war artists like Theodor Rocholl and Wilhelm Schreuer were usually men too old for combat service, the British employed a number of younger painters who had been serving as soldiers at the front and might thus be counted on to see things from the point of view of participants rather than onlookers: notably Wyndham Lewis and Paul Nash.[6]

One of the organizers of the war artists' scheme, Campbell Dodgson, Keeper of Prints and Drawings at the British Museum, thought that 'Nash is decidedly post-impressionist, not cubist, but "decorative", and his art is certainly not what the British public will generally like'. Few Keepers of Prints and Drawings have been more mistaken. The spokesmen of public opinion were ready for novelty, quickly recognizing that the new fashion of warfare could not be depicted in an old-fashioned way. Even the *Illustrated London News* did not hesitate to condemn paintings which were accurate enough in matters of detail but which seemed too nineteenth-century in spirit:

> The general character of this work reminds us too closely of the battle-pieces of thirty years ago: there is nothing save in detail, to identify it with the New War. And there, in a nutshell, is the weakness of three-fourths of the year's war pictures – they do not belong to the year.

A contributor to another weekly wrote:

> These scenes are freshly observed, but what are we to say of the battle-charges and turbulent horses, executed in the dear old manner, and familiar

continued
1956), p. 30; Maurice Vlaminck, ed., André Derain, *Lettres à Vlaminck* (Paris, 1955), p. 221, 227; ibid., pp. 221, 224, 225; Paul Maze, *A Frenchman in Khaki* (1934), p. 145.

[6] Theodor Rocholl had been born in 1854, Wilhelm Schreuer in 1866; see *Kriegsfahrten deutscher Maler: Selbsterlebtes im Weltkrieg, 1914–1915* (Bielefeld, 1915), pp. 9–84 for Rocholl, pp. 87–106 for Schreuer.

to us for a hundred years, and which at best were good enough for the old-fashioned papers – in which, I hasten to add, such 'fancy' subjects no longer appear! The impression we gather is that it is difficult to paint, realistically, the din and horror of a modern battle; and that War must be treated synthetically, and its various aspects suggested to the mind rather than, brutally, to the eye.[7]

One of the out-of-date middle-aged establishment artists complained of in this last quotation was John Lavery who later fully admitted the error of his ways:

> Instead of the grim harshness and horror of the scenes I had given charming colour versions, as if painting a bank holiday on Hampstead Heath . . . I felt nothing of the stark reality, losing sight of my fellow-men being blown to pieces in submarines or slowly choking to death in mud. I saw only new beauties of colour and design.

The efforts of some established artists to use conventional representational techniques in combination with a disconcerting irony and an element of hyper-realism that came near to suggesting delirium were not appreciated by the Young Turks. Wyndham Lewis recalled meeting William Orpen in France:

> He came to our table and produced from his pocket a flask of whisky. 'Will y'have some?' he croaked in his quavering Dublin patter, which he had taken good care never to get rid of. 'It's good stuff – I know ut's good. It's from Haig's Mess. I gottut there this morning!'
>   I drank to the health of the High Command . . . Upon hearing that I was with a battery in the Salient, he gazed in a half-mocking stare, twisting his eyebrows and smiling his wry Irish mockery at me.
>   'It's hell isn't it? It must be hell!' quickly he chattered under his breath.
>   I said it was Goya, it was Delacroix – all scooped out and very El Greco. But hell, no . . .
>   'Ah yes, it must be hell!' he said. He pronounced hell, 'hail'.
>   'Hell sometimes for the infantry. But it's merely a stupid nightmare – it's not real.'
>   'Same thing!' said he.

[7] Campbell Dodgson quoted in Cork, *A Bitter Truth*, p. 197; *Illustrated London News*, 8 May 1915, p. 592, and *Sketch*, 12 May 1915, p. iv, both quoted in Peter Harrington, *British Artists and War: The Face of Battle in Painting and Prints, 1700–1914* (1993), p. 306.

Orpen however may be regarded as a pioneer of a style somewhere between what the Germans called *Neue Sachlichkeit* and the Italians *Realismo magico* (a term coined in 1919 by Giorgio di Chirico, who had spent the war in the Italian infantry, not at the front but reflecting on art in a barracks in Ferrara). The British, who have an excessive tendency to take their artistic fashions from the French, have no term for this style, though one of its classic exemplars is *The Kensingtons at Laventie* painted in 1915 by Eric Kennington, who later specialized in portraits of individual frontline soldiers. Orpen's war paintings stand somewhat on their own because of his odd sense of humour, but another artist who produced a *Neue Sachlichkeit/Realismo magico* type of picture, before the Germans and Italians found a label for the style, was Henry Lamb, whose *Advanced Dressing Station on the Struma* was painted for the Manchester City Gallery in 1920. From the German or Italian point of view the new style was a reaction to Expressionism or Post-Impressionism: from Kennington's or Orpen's or Lamb's point of view it was more directly a reaction to the war, and the problems of finding an iconological language in which to convey its realities.[8]

The man who succeeded most dramatically in finding the right painterly means of showing what was going on was Christopher Nevinson. A devoted disciple of Marinetti, the Italian Futurist, he had also known Picasso and was familiar with Cubism. In February 1915 he told the *Daily Express* 'This war will be a violent incentive to Futurism, for we believe that there is no beauty except in strife, and no masterpiece without aggressiveness'. In 1913 Boccioni, the most considerable artist amongst the Futurists, had stated that they were working 'to destroy the old pictorial, idiotic, traditional, realistic, decorative, smoke-blackened museum stuff', but his specific programme sounded rather like a more animated Cubism: Impressionism, Boccioni wrote, is 'the first step towards the creation of a plastic organism constructed out of the pure lyrical interplay (of masses, lines, and lights) between object and setting . . . It points towards the *plastic fact*, towards creating what only we Italian Futurists have proclaimed and

[8] John Lavery, *The Life of a Painter* (1940), p. 148; Wyndham Lewis *Blasting and Bombardiering* (1937), p. 180; for 'Realismo magico' see *Grande Dizionario Enciclopedico UTET* (20 vols, Turin, 1984–91), xvii, p. 119, and cf. Franz Roth *Nach-Expressionismus-Magischer Realismus: Probleme der neuesten europäische Malerei* (Leipzig, 1925).

produced: the *style of sensation*, the *impression eternalized*, and *dynamism*'. Nevinson believed all that: the problem was how to reconcile this aggressive, cocksure celebration of modern forms and the modern spirit with what he had seen and felt as a hospital orderly in France. What for the Futurists was a celebration, with Nevinson became an indictment: his paintings show human individuals slotted together into a mass, like the components of a machine, or forced to become robot-like extensions of machines, or reduced at last to shadowy beings whose bandages have more individuality than their faces. As John Rothenstein later wrote, Cubism gave Nevinson 'an instrument in tune with the machines, which could represent a modern war with shattering effect . . . it was a kind of magnificent shorthand, perfectly adapted to convey the simplified essence of a mechanized apocalypse'; but it was the apocalypticalness, not the cubishness, that Nevinson was interested in. The critics responded enthusiastically to the way that Nevinson's formal technique fitted in with the physical appurtenances of machine-era warfare:

> Were there ever objects more appropriate for geometrical composition, for statement in terms of angles, curves and cubes, than guns and gun-carriages, lorries, planks and sleepers, aeroplanes, searchlights, the parallel rifles of troops on the march? The very steel helmets of the men in the trenches are so many ready-made arcs.

The *Westminster Gazette* saw Nevinson's way of depicting soldiers in positive terms: 'The soldiers themselves look as though they were the component parts of a formidable engine, drawn together by some irresistible attraction'. The *Times Literary Supplement* however recognized and endorsed Nevinson's evocation of the horrendously negative aspect of his subject:

> Nearly all war pictures in the past have been merely pictures that happened to represent war. Paolo Uccello's battle scenes are but pretexts for his peculiar version of the visible world. They might just as well be still life for all the effect the subject has had upon his treatment of it. Tintoret's battle scenes are parade pictures. Those of Rubens are like his hunting scenes or his Bacchanals, expressions of his own overweening energy. In none of these, except perhaps in Lionardo's, was there implied any criticism of war, or any sense that it is an abnormal activity of man. The men who take part in it are just men fighting; they

are not men seen differently because they are fighting, or in any way robbed of their humanity because of their inhuman business . . .

In Mr Nevinson's war pictures, now to be seen at the Leicester Gallery, there is expressed a modern sense of war as an abnormal occupation; and this sense shows itself in the very method of the artist. He was something of a Cubist before the war; but in these pictures he has found a new reason for being one; for his Cubist method does express, in the most direct way, his sense that in war man behaves like a machine or part of a machine, that war is a process in which man is not treated as a human being but as an item in a great instrument of destruction, in which he ceases to be a person and becomes lost in a process. The Cubist method, with its repetition and sharp distinction of planes, expresses this sense of mechanical process better than any other way of representation . . . Samuel Butler imagined a future in which machines would come to life and make us their slaves; but it is not so much that machines have come to life as that we ourselves have lost the pride and sweetness of our humanity; not that the machines seem more and more like us, but that we seem more and more like the machines.[9]

The *Times Literary Supplement*'s reviewer was far from being enamoured by Cubism however:

there is the same incongruity between the cubist effort to see the visible world as a mechanical process and art itself. The cubist seems to force himself with a savage irony into this caricature of nature; we have emptied reality of its content in our thought and he will empty it of its content to our eyes . . . This irony we find in Mr Nevinson's pictures of the war, whether it be a despairing irony or the rebellion of an unshaken faith. He has emptied man of his content, just as the Prussian drill sergeant would empty him of his content for the purposes of war; and only a Prussian drill sergeant could consent to this version of man with any joy.

This seems to have chimed with what was increasingly Nevinson's own way of thinking. His experiences of machine-era warfare seem to have weaned him away, not merely from a Futurist admiration of machines,

---

[9] Nevinson in the *Daily Express*, quoted Cork, *A Bitter Truth*, p. 71; Ester Coen, *Umberto Boccioni* (New York), pp. 244, 246 (text originally published in *La fiera letteraria*, 10 July 1927); John Rothenstein, *Modern English Painters* (3 vols, 1984 edn), ii, p. 51 – first published 1956; Campbell Dodgson and C.E. Montague, *British Artists at the Front*, i, *C.R.W. Nevinson* (1918), p. 3; *Westminster Gazette*, 2 October 1916, p. 7; *Times Literary Supplement*, 5 October 1916, p. 469b.

but from any interest in machines, or even in Cubism, with its simplified masses and straight lines and suggestion of mathematical relationships. In 1917 he was forbidden to exhibit a painting entitled *Paths of Glory* which showed two dead British soldiers face down beside a barbed wire entanglement, and was summoned to the War Office for an official reprimand when the picture was exhibited with a diagonal strip of brown paper bearing the word 'Censored' pasted across the two bodies. Apart from the steel helmets of the dead men there was nothing in the picture to suggest that it depicted the present: its painterly technique was as old as Manet. One almost suspects that for Nevinson the picture worked as well with the diagonal strip of brown paper as without: the message was 'Young men are being slaughtered uselessly', and it did not depend on the medium. A slightly later picture showing an overweight gentleman of somewhat Germanic appearance, with a distant, perhaps merely self-hypnotized, look in his eyes, sitting on a chair with an anti-macassar next to a marble fire-place, bell-push and ornately framed oil painting, has its entire point in its title: 'He Gained a Fortune but He Gave a Son'. The same message is contained in a poem written at about this time by Osbert Sitwell and dedicated to Siegfried Sassoon:

> His purple fingers clutch a large cigar –
>   Plump, mottled fingers, with a ring or two.
> He rests back in his fat armchair. The war
>   Has made this change in him. As he looks through
> His cheque-book with a tragic look he sighs:
>   'Disabled Soldiers' Fund' he reads afresh,
> And through his meat-red face peer angry eyes –
>   The spirit piercing through its mound of flesh.
>
> They should not ask me to subscribe again!
>   Consider me and all that I have done –
> I've fought for Britain with my might and main;
>   I make explosives – and I gave a son . . .

In both painting and poem, there is not much to take account of other than the message and the local colour, though the poem does suggest some ambiguities that may also be traceable in the painting. Sitwell's war profiteer is named Mr Abraham – presumably Jewish (surely Sitwell realised that Sassoon was Jewish too?). Is Nevinson's

war profiteer Jewish too? He certainly doesn't look very English. The
Sitwell coal mines did rather well out of the war, and since neither
Osbert nor his brother Sacheverell managed to get themselves killed,
they stood to benefit eventually. Nevinson was himself a kind of war
profiteer, making a better income painting the war than he would
have done as a corporal fighting it. Perhaps his recognition of this
contributed to his sense of defeat and depression. By 1917 he had
lost his way as an artist, and seems never to have found it again.[10]

What Nevinson, in his best pictures, did for the frontline soldiers,
Paul Nash did for the landscape of the war zone. His letters show
him to have been a meticulous and highly intelligent observer of
nature, but his pre-war artistic work seems feathery in concept as
well as in composition. The war changed that. In 1917 he sketched
the battlefield of Passchendaele, finding it 'the most frightful
nightmare of a country more conceived by Dante or Poe than by
nature . . . one huge grave, and cast up on it the poor dead. It is
unspeakable, godless, hopeless'. Some of the paintings he executed
from these sketches in 1918 and 1919 have merely topographical
captions – *The Mule Track, The Menin Road* – others had more polemi-
cal titles, *Void,* or *We Are Making a New World.* They all show a landscape
denatured by human destructiveness, reduced to repetitive forms
littered with shattered human artefacts, with humans visible, if at
all, as vermin scuttling surreptitiously between cover: and, in the
foreground of *The Menin Road,* a couple of beautifully-observed weeds
growing in the mud. Nash was not the only artist to see that during
the war man had reduced nature to a set of ugly abstract shapes. It
was Wyndham Lewis who wrote:

> War, and especially those miles of hideous desert known as 'the line' in
> Flanders and France, presented me with a subject-matter so consonant
> with the austerity of that 'abstract' vision I had developed, that it was an
> easy transition. Had you at that time asked me to paint a milkmaid in a
> landscape of buttercups and daisies I should probably have knocked you
> down. But when Mars with his mailed finger showed me a shell-crater
> and a skeleton, with a couple of shivered tree-stumps behind it, I was still
> in my 'abstract' element.

[10] Ibid., p. 469d; C.R.W. Nevinson, *Paint and Prejudice* (1937), p. 110; Osbert Sitwell,
'The Modern Abraham' – dated 1917 – in *Argonaut and Juggernaut* (1919), p. 106.

But none of Wyndham Lewis's creative efforts, whether literary or artistic, were ever as interesting as his programmes and commentaries. It was only really Nash and Nevinson who found in *avant-garde* art the means with which to paint Armageddon.[11]

---

[11] Paul Nash *Outline: An Autobiography and Other Writings* (1949), pp. 210–11; Wyndham Lewis, *Rude Assignment: A Narrative of My Career Up-to-Date* [1950], p. 128.

CHAPTER 6

Truth

IN PAINTING there may be no real distinction between what one wants to say and how one says it: after all, one does not actually *say* anything, one puts paint on a canvas. Some critics would claim the distinction does not exist in literature either; nevertheless this chapter deals primarily with *what* writers said about the First World War, and the next chapter primarily with *how* they said it.

From the very beginning governments recognized the propaganda value of first-hand accounts of the fighting. At home the relatives of those at the front line, and all those others whose lives had been disrupted and energized by the mobilization of national resources, wanted – or thought they wanted – to know what was happening; abroad there were neutral states whose opinion-formers needed to be won over or at least placated. When the Swedish explorer Sven Hedin made his way to Germany to investigate the war, he was given every facility by the German Foreign Ministry and General Staff: the resulting book was regarded as a major coup for German propaganda. In Vienna authors like Rainer Maria Rilke the poet, Hugo von Hofmannsthal the playwright, Stefan Zweig and Franz Werfel were employed (though not all at the same time) in the archives of the Ministry of War to write or touch up stories of frontline heroism suitable for use by the newspapers, while artists like Rudolf Konopa and Géza Maróti were sent to sketch at the front. In 1915 the British War Office permitted five correspondents from the London press to go out to the Western Front on a permanent basis but despite the award of KBEs to four of them after the war their work remains no more than higher journalism, written from the point of view of the onlooker. John Masefield's book on Gallipoli has already been mentioned. A number of the more successful aviators were officially encouraged to write up their exploits – Richthofen, Bishop, McCudden – and managed to present themselves on paper as mindlessly gung-ho youths of no literary sensibility. Robert Nichols, a poet who had survived three weeks in a field battery before having some sort of nervous breakdown, was commissioned to write an account of the frontline work of the Royal Engineers but only managed two chapters. Nichols's later activities however suggest that officialdom, in Britain at least, may have attached less importance to literature than to painting; when he was sent on a propaganda mission to the United States in 1918 literature was only part of his remit. 'My first public act on landing was to place a wreath on the catafalque of Joyce Kilmer, one of their soldier poets. This created, I think, a favourable impression', he reported, and he also gave interviews on 'the most modern developments of British Art, Literature and Music': but his chief responsibility was to help with the publicity for an exhibition of paintings by Christopher Nevinson, John Lavery and Wyndham Lewis. Perhaps it was recognized that while art depended to a large extent on an institutional framework, literature would go its own way whatever attempts were made to manipulate it.[1]

Literature in fact went in several directions. Ezra Pound – not in the forces – had a vivid impression of

> frankness as never before
> disillusions as never told in the old days
> hysterias, trench confessions
> laughter out of dead bellies

[1] Sven Hedin, *With the German Armies in the West* (1915), pp. 9–14, 45–46 – first published as *Från Fronten i Väster: September-November 1914* (Stockholm, 1915): Hedin, who as a young man had known Ibsen, later became an admirer and personal friend of Adolf Hitler; see also Karl Hildebrand, *Ett starkt folk* and *Donaumonarkien i krig* (both published Stockholm, 1915, and quickly translated into German); Scott D. Denham, *Visions of War: Ideologies and Images of War in German Literature Before and After the Great War* (Bern, 1992), p. 73, cf. Stefan Zweig *The World of Yesterday* (1943), p. 178. Public Record Office, FO 395/222/46969, contains the draft of the first two chapters of Nichols's projected book on the Royal Engineers: judging by the quality, he was probably advised not to continue; see A.D. Harvey, 'Robert Nichols in the Public Record Office', *P N Review*, 91 (May-June 1993), pp. 10–11; Public Record Office, FO 395/221/242479/41719 and FO 395/227/241379/241379.

but for obvious reasons the bulk of what was written at the front, whether addressed to fellow soldiers or to loved ones at home, aimed at keeping up the spirits of both writer and reader. The French trench journal *On progresse* claimed, 'The rank stupidity of the Army and the vastness of the sea are the only two things which can give an idea of infinity', but it was the *Cambridge Magazine* back in England which printed Siegfried Sassoon's bitter denunciations of the war. The first page of the first issue of *The Dud* (11th Battalion King's Shropshire Light Infantry) announced:

> The Editors are not setting out to reform the world, nor do they expect to create any undue sensation amongst literary circles. The origin of this paper – briefly stated – is as follows: the Editor and the Art Editor have long been sending contributions to the best known Journals, all of which have invariably been rejected! Therefore they determined to publish their respective efforts and spite the publishers.
>
> If in so doing they amuse you for a few moments, then they will account their venture a success.

A fair specimen of the usual tone of whimsy in these productions may be found in another *Dud*, this time produced by the 14th Battalion Argyll and Sutherland Highlanders:

> 'It's queer', said Black, 'how near we are to home. The gramaphone is playing the latest revue rubbish, this cake was made by my sister only four days ago, and I am reading this week's *Punch*.'
>
> 'And I', I said, 'am trying to sleep', but the words were hardly out of my mouth before all thought of sleep vanished, for mother suddenly appeared in the dug-out, and the voice I loved best in the world said: 'The old story I see, James – breakfast in bed', and she smiled indulgently. 'By the way, too, you don't look after your servants very well, those stairs haven't been dusted for *weeks*.' Poor mother! She also must have reversed engines in descending those stairs. Thank heaven she didn't come when it was wet.
>
> 'Will you have some tea?' I asked, 'we're just at breakfast – Bones!'
>
> Bones appeared, lifted a dirty cup with a grimy paw, vanished into the darkness, and speedily reappeared with his vessel full of a brown tepid liquid. Mother did her best with it.
>
> 'He has a nice pleasant face,' she said, 'but he can't make tea, and, my dear boy, you must speak to him about the state of his hands.'

'Oh, they aren't so bad', said I uneasily, 'It's the shadows. It's pretty dark down here.'

'Disgracefully dark', assented mother. 'I could hardly find my way in, but', she added plaintively, 'I didn't dare to complain, I thought it was one of the hardships out here, perhaps.'

'We'll soon cure that', I replied stoutly, and lit a couple of extra candles. 'There, that's better.' It wasn't. Candles are hard to get, and in any case the cuttings from the *Vie Parisienne* became much too obvious. There was a gloomy silence whilst she regarded the walls of the dug-out. . .[2]

Some books were published which attempted to present honest, unbiased accounts of what was going on, but as the war prolonged itself attitudes with regard to what it was that was really going on necessarily changed. For the first eighteen months or so of the war the best writing about it by men in the firing line consisted of cool, detailed rather detached prose accounts of what they had seen and of reflections, in both prose and poetry, on what they had experienced. The detailed, rather detached prose accounts would come back after the war. From 1916 onwards however the intensification of the fighting and of its horrors shifted frontline writing in a new direction. It was no longer necessary to describe war to contemporaries who had seen it for themselves, or to the folks back home who had been saturated with first-hand accounts and obviously preferred something a little less unnerving, such as *The Love of an Unknown Soldier: Found in a Dug-Out* (a best-seller in 1918), which purported to be the love letters of an unknown and probably dead artillery subaltern to an American girl he had met in Paris. The best frontline writing of the second half of the war was addressed to one's fellow soldiers. Michele Campana for example, finishing his book *Perchè ho ucciso?* ('Why did I kill?') in October 1918, wrote 'Only my comrades can understand and like this

---

[2] E.P. [Ezra Pound], *Hugh Selwyn Mauberley* (1920), p. 12, part 4, iv; Stéphane Audoin-Rouzeau, *Men at War, 1914–1918: National Sentiment and Trench Journalism in France during the First World War* (Providence, Rhode Island,, 1992), p. 60, quoting *On progresse*, 1 April 1917. *The Dud* (11th Kings Shropshire Light Infantry), June 1916, p. 1; 'Mother in the Trenches', *The Dud* (14th Argyll and Sutherland Highlanders), November 1916, p. 21 – this and the previous item are in the British Library, call mark PP 4039 wba.

book, because it is they who have created it with their blood and I who have faithfully transcribed it'.[3]

The best of this sort of writing came from the British army, and the best of all from Wilfred Owen, who thought, 'All a poet can do today is warn. That is why the true poets must be truthful':

> Bent double, like old beggars under sacks,
> Knock-kneed, coughing like hags, we cursed through sludge,
> Till on the haunting flares we turned our backs
> And towards our distant rest began to trudge.
> Men marched asleep. Many had lost their boots
> But limped on, blood-shod. All went lame; all blind;
> Drunk with fatigue; deaf even to the hoots
> Of tired, outstripped Five-Nines that dropped behind.
>
> Gas! GAS! Quick, boys! – An ecstasy of fumbling,
> Fitting the clumsy helmets just in time;
> But someone still was yelling out and stumbling
> And flound'ring like a man in fire or lime. . .
> Dim, through the misty panes and thick green light,
> As under a green sea, I saw him drowning.
>
> In all my dreams, before my helpless sight,
> He plunges at me, guttering, choking, drowning.
>
> If in some smothering dreams you too could pace
> Behind the wagon that we flung him in,
> And watch the white eyes writhing in his face,
> His hanging face, like a devil's sick of sin;
> If you could hear, at every jolt, the blood
> Come gargling from the froth-corrupted lungs,
> Obscene as cancer, bitter as the cud
> Of vile, incurable sores on innocent tongues, –
> My friend, you would not tell with such high zest
> To children ardent for some desperate glory,
> The old Lie: Dulce et decorum est
> Pro patria mori.[4]

---

[3] Michele Campana, *Perchè ho ucciso* (Florence, [1918]), p. 153, '*congeda*', dated 10 October 1918, written in hospital in Florence.

[4] Wilfred Owen, *Poems* (1920), Preface; Wilfred Owen, 'Dulce Et Decorum Est'.

A Muse of Fire

Poetry was the obvious medium for such statements, if only because its compression made it the most convenient format – Patrick MacGill was almost unique in claiming to be able to write at length in the trenches. Poetry also, despite Wordsworth's famous claim that it took its origin 'from emotion recollected in tranquillity', offered a kind of immediacy, which may be the reason why very little poetry written from a frontline perspective was produced once the war was over. The war poems of Anton Schnack and David Jones's *In Parenthesis* are perhaps the only notable exceptions. Wilfred Owen and Isaac Rosenberg had been killed in the last days of the war of course, but if they had survived it is unlikely they would have stuck with the war as a favoured subject. Sassoon, Graves, and Blunden survived to write more poetry but decided that prose offered the best medium for what they had left to say about their time in the army: in July 1919 Graves told Blunden, 'War poetry is played out I'm afraid, commercially, for another five or ten years. Rotten thing for us, but it's no good blinking at it'.[5]

It is sometimes claimed that, once the fighting was over, there was no real interest in war literature till the late 1920s, with 1929, the year of the book version of Erich Maria Remarque's *All Quiet on the Western Front*, R.C. Sherriff's *Journey's End*, Richard Aldington's *Death of a Hero* and Robert Graves's *Goodbye to All That* perhaps marking the breakthrough. At the end of the Second World War, when Godfrey Winn wanted to write up his experiences, Lord Beaverbrook told him:

> in ten years' time, the war will be 'news' again. It was last time. Remember *All Quiet*? In ten years' time, that's when you will get the sales. *Now's* the time for you to be out and about, with your nose to the scent. The war's over. The public are sick of war books, anything to do with the war. Ask your publisher, ask any bookseller. Now it's the future, the problems of reconstruction you should think about, write about, interest your readers in.

But Beaverbrook had his facts the wrong way round. One of the most celebrated of English war novels, Ernest Raymond's *Tell England*, came out in 1920 – the first half, dealing with its protagonists' schooldays, had been written before the war anyway – and Wilfrid Ewart's *Way of*

[5] For Anton Schnack see Patrick Bridgewater, *The German Poets of the First World War* (1985), pp. 96–119; Paul O'Prey, ed., *Robert Graves: In Broken Images. Selected Correspondence* (New York, 1988), p. 113, Graves to Blunden, 2 July 1919.

Revelation enjoyed a brief vogue in 1921. (Fourteen months after his novel was published Ewart was dead, accidently shot by a New Year reveller in Mexico City.) John Dos Passos's *Three Soldiers* was published in 1922. In Italy all the best work to appear about the war had appeared by 1921, with the exception of Carlo Salsa's *Trincee* ('Trenches'), which came out in 1924. The year 1921 is also more or less the cut-off point for the Portuguese, who declared war on Germany in 1916 and thereafter made something of a speciality of insipid books with striking titles like *The Avalanche* (1918), *Iron and Fire* (1919), and *The Macabre Symphony* (1920). The most influential of German war memoirs, Ernst Jünger's *In Stahlgewittern*, was published in 1920, though six years later Jünger still thought 'it required a longer and harder labour for us to become clear about the meaning of events'.[6]

Like Jünger, Hugh MacDiarmid considered in 1923 that it was still too soon to come to terms with what their generation had lived through, claiming, 'the real literature of the war could not possibly be written for a few years – possibly for a good few years – if ever', and it may be a mistake to assume that the literature we have is the best we might or should have had. *In Stahlgewittern* might never have been published if Jünger's father had not put up the money to pay the printer. Georg von der Vring's *Soldat Suhren*, completed in 1923, was rejected by eighteen publishing houses before finally being accepted by a Swiss firm in 1927. Edmund Blunden hastened to set down his reminiscences in 1918 but did not publish them for ten years, finding it necessary to rewrite his text completely because, 'although in its details not much affected by the perplexities of distancing memory, [it] was noisy with a depressing gaiety then very much the rage'. Charles Carrington wrote down his memories of the Battle of the Somme and the Battle of

---

[6] Ernest Richards suggested as early as 1931, in the preface to his schools anthology *Tales of the Great War*, that 'the bonds of memory were suddenly loosed' in 1928; Godfrey Winn, '*PQ 17* (1947), p. 8 – Lord Beaverbrook is not actually named but his identity is sufficiently obvious from the context; Ernest Raymond *The Story of My Days: An Autobiography, 1888–1922* (1968), pp. 132–33; Stephen Graham, *Life and Last Words of Wilfrid Ewart* (1924), pp. 257–58, and Public Record Office, FO 369/1837, p. 130, Mexico City Legation to Foreign Office, 15 January 1923; Ernst Jünger, *Feuer und Blut: einer kleiner Auschnitt aus einer grossen Schlacht* (2nd edn, Berlin 1926), Preface.

The Portuguese books referred to are Albino Forjaz de Sampaio's *A avalanche* (1918), Eduardo Augusto Pereira Pimenta's *A ferro e fogo* (1919) and the anonymous *A sinfonia macabra* (1920).

Passchendaele in 1919 and 1920 but later confessed 'for several years modesty prevented me from showing them even to my friends'; eventually he published them under a pseudonym in 1929. Other manuscripts may have been, not merely delayed, but fumbled over for years before being finally binned. J.B. Priestley, who had enlisted in September 1914 and had been wounded twice in the trenches, did not publish anything about his experiences till the early 1960s, when what he mainly recalled was how boring it all was:

> Except at certain rare moments, and these were far outnumbered by their peacetime counterparts, I did not discover any deeper reality in war . . . Its obvious one-sidedness soon made it seem to me a vast piece of imbecility.

At the time he had written to his father from the trenches of 'a vast exultation of the soul at the expense of the body', and one cannot help wondering if the negative picture he eventually gave in his memoirs was not coloured by creative blockages encountered over forty years earlier.[7]

War books, it should be remembered, were not simply caused by the war: soldier-writers were not simply virgin wombs who in 1914 were waiting to be impregnated by a dose of trench-fighting. When Siegfried Sassoon acknowledged, 'a war was needed to wake me up and give me my incentive to write', he did not mean that he had not written poems before 1914, merely that they had not been very good. And afterwards, though there were very large numbers of war books by authors who published nothing else, the majority of the best-known works were by professed men of letters, some of whom had already made a name for themselves before 1914: the war, however inescapable it seemed while everyone was in uniform, became just one out of a list of possible topics once peacetime necessities reasserted

---

[7] C.M. Grieve ['Hugh MacDiarmid'], 'A Four Years' Harvest', in *Annals of the Five Senses* (Montrose, 1923), pp. 59–121, at p. 65; Heimo Schwilk, ed., *Ernst Jünger: Leben und Werk in Bildern und Texten* [Stuttgart, 1988], p. 89; Hans-Harald Müller, *Der Krieg und die Schriftsteller: Der Kriegsroman der Weimarer Republik* (Stuttgart, 1986), pp. 101–102; Edmund Blunden, *Undertones of War* (1982, Penguin edn), p. 7; Charles Carrington ('Charles Edmonds'), *A Subaltern's War* (1929), p. 7; J.B. Priestley, *Margin Released: A Writer's Reminiscences and Reflections* (1962), p. 89; Vincent Brome, *J.B. Priestley* (1988), p. 48.

themselves. Both the books that were written and the moment at which their authors chose to write them related to the motivations and career strategies of a very disparate set of individuals.[8]

The choice of whether to write a war novel, a slightly fictionalized and tidied up memoir of what the author has really seen and felt, or a scrupulously faithful record in which only a few names have been changed, has also to be seen in relation to certain characteristics which distinguish the majority of war memoirs from most other examples of autobiographical writing. War memoirs tend to say less about what the author did and who he met than about what he suffered and experienced passively. With a few exceptions like Siegfried Sassoon's George Sherston sequence, they also give unusually little sense of their protagonists changing and developing as human beings, though in the four year period described the writers had often been promoted from junior dogsbody to positions of considerable responsibility. These books are unusual too in being written mostly by *young* men – often still under thirty – and at a time when the events described were still recent and raw enough to give nightmares: that is to say, they were written in psychological conditions not dissimilar to those in which the romantic subjective, whingeing type of first novel is generally produced.

Not surprisingly some war reminiscences seem to be more an exercise in forgetting than remembering. When Elliott White Springs left Culver Military Academy, Indiana, his class yearbook recorded, 'His ambition is to be a writer of dime novels'. Five years later he was a flight commander in the 148th Squadron of the US Army Air Corps and on the way to becoming America's sixth-ranking fighter ace: and not enjoying it. In July 1918 he wrote home:

> I'm all shot to pieces . . . Few men live to know what real fear is. It's something that grows on you day by day, that eats into your constitution and undermines your sanity . . . While I am waiting around all day for the afternoon patrol, I think I am going crazy. I keep watching the clock and figuring how long I have to live . . . When I go out to get in my plane my feet are like lead – I am just barely able to drag them after me.

[8] Rupert Hart-Davis, ed., *Siegfried Sassoon: Diaries, 1920–1922* (1981), p. 100, 7 February 1922.

Nothing of this appears in the sketches based on his experiences which he later published under the title *Nocturne Militaire*: in these the would-be dime novelist asserted himself with a vengeance.

> I got caught diving on a two-seater over by Armentières. I got underneath him according to the instructions and blue prints from GHQ – see page 14, paragraph 6, 'How to attack a two-seater'. I was all set to hit him with my first burst, but when I pressed my triggers nothing happened. Both guns had jammed and so did my heart! While I was trying to clear my guns, the two-seater began to manoeuvre, and before I woke up to what was happening, the observer had taken a good long crack at me and the hot oil was streaming back in my face to call attention to the fact that my oil lead was hit. I started back at a thousand feet with the whole Hun army shooting at me and those that weren't shooting were throwing rocks and old shoes.

But perhaps Elliott White Springs really had forgotten his pre-mission nerves by the time he came to write *Nocturne Militaire*; perhaps in any case he had exaggerated his nervous prostration in his letter home out of a desire to obtain sympathy from his parents, or to inflict some obscure revenge on them. There is an element of posing in the wartime letter as much as in the post-war reminiscence, which is hardly surprising since the same man wrote both; but we cannot be sure that the authentic Elliott White Springs is to be found somewhere between the two poses, because we cannot know how many others there were in his repertoire.[9]

Any autobiographical writer has to choose what he feels to be an appropriate voice. Some may do so without quite realising the range of possibilities on offer, but it took Edmund Blunden several years to get the undertone right in *Undertones of War* and Siegfried Sassoon was perfectly aware of what he was doing when he reinvented himself as a juvenile gentile in *Memoirs of an Infantry Officer*. Yet finding an appropriate voice is only a means to an end. The prime motive of most ex-servicemen who wrote about the war was nothing more or less than an urge to tell the truth about what they had experienced. As early as 1917 Vernon Bartlett stated in an 'Apologia' at the beginning of his *Mud and Khaki: Sketches from Flanders*:

[9] Burke Davis, *War Bird: The Life and Times of Elliott White Springs* (Chapel Hill, North Carolina, 1987), p. 23; ibid., pp. 78–79; Elliott White Springs, *Nocturne Militaire* [1927], p. 250–51.

There has been so much written about the trenches, there are so many war photographs, so many cinema films, that one might well hesitate before even mentioning the war – to try to write a book about it is, I fear, to incur the censure of the many who are tired of hearing about bombs and bullets, and who prefer to read of peace, and games, and flirtations.

But, for that very reason, I venture to think that even so indifferent a war book as mine will not come entirely amiss . . . If, to a minute extent, anything in these pages should help to bring home to people what war really is, and to remind them of their debt of gratitude, then these little sketches will have justified their existence.

Ernst Jünger wrote in 1920, 'I am not a reporter, I am not putting forward a collection of heroes, I don't wish to describe how it could have been, but how it was.' In 1925 Cyril McNeile remarked in the Preface to his novel *Shorty Bill*:

Books on the war are no longer popular, but I cannot help thinking, from remarks that have been made to me, that there are still people who would like to be reminded, and others, of a younger generation, who would like to learn.

For T.W. White, author of an account of his escape from Turkish captivity, publication of his book in 1928 was an act of piety:

My excuse for putting a war story before the public at so late a date is that I feel that this gist of a diary recording the doings and sufferings of prisoners of war in Turkey should be published, if for no other reason than as a tribute to those who died.[10]

Yet simply writing down the truth as one remembered it was not as easy as it sounded: as the Hungarian novelist József Lengyel later wrote 'If the author wished to write down everything, even the biography of an ant would fill more than a hundred volumes.' And though three or four years of military service might provide almost too many incidents to select from, while one was trying to make one's selection the memory itself was making a selection of its own. In the mid-1930s Victor Yeates did not find this a problem:

[10] Vernon Bartlett, *Mud and Khaki: Sketches from Flanders and France* (1917), p. 11; Ernst Jünger, *In Stahlgewittern* (1920), Preface; [Cyril McNeile], *Shorty Bill* [1926], Preface, dated February 1925; T.W. White, *Guests of the Unspeakable: The Odyssey of an Australian Airman – Being a Record of Captivity and Escape in Turkey* (1928), p. 7, 'Apologia'.

I was writing a novel that was to be an exact reproduction of a period and an exact analysis and synthesis of a state of mind: for these purposes an overwhelming and untidy accumulation of detail seemed necessary.

But at exactly the same period John Gibbons was finding both details and states of mind increasingly hard to recall:

All Quiet on the Western Front [the best-selling novel by Erich Maria Remarque] probably made a fortune for its publishers and for some gentlemen in Hollywood, but it could hardly have had any public at all from the men who had actually done the fighting . . .
     I see that I shall have to write my own War Book. And I shall have to write it soon, if I am to get it into print in time for the next part of the War and before the thing is on us again. Also I shall have to get the story down before I have forgotten half of it. Which again is curious. For perhaps two years after 1918 I would wake night after night trembling with the nightmare of the filth and terror of the trenches; and now all that has long left me, and I catch myself remembering only the jolly bits and the funny stories of cheating the sergeant.

Less than five years after the war K.L. Harris, sitting down to compose an essay on his 'Service Experiences' for the RAF Staff course at Andover, noted that 'the distance of time that has elapsed has caused the incidents and impressions to become merged into one conglomerate mass, from which it is hard to extract the true metal and discard the dross'. Charles Carrington, who had written down his recollections of the Somme and Passchendaele in 1919 and 1920, thought in 1929 that 'no war book written now, ten or fifteen years after the event, can secure the authenticity attaching to these two stories'.[11]
     Only a few months earlier Paolo Monelli had come to a similar conclusion, explaining:

---

[11] József Lengyel, *Prenn Drifting* (1966), p. 292 (originally published as *Prenn Ferenc hányatott élete* (Budapest, 1959); V.M. Yeates, *Winged Victory* (1961 edn), p. 6, note by Yeates written on the flyleaf of Henry Williamson's copy of the first edition; John Gibbons, *Roll On, Next War! The Common Man's Guide to Army Life* (1935), p. 3; Public Record Office, AIR 1/2386/228/11/26, staff college essay by K.L. Harris. W.E. Theak in the 1931 intake was of the same opinion, cf. AIR 1/2392/228/11/185; Carrington, *A Subaltern's War*, p. 9.

The man who undertook today, in good faith, to narrate his memories as a fighting man would write a false book. Not by his own fault, but because of the qualities of human nature. The most faithful and humble memory distorts long-past events. The shells fall closer, the actions are enormously exaggerated, the periods of waiting lose their length, the intermediate moments disappear: the falsehoods and the rhetoric of others act unconsciously upon us. With what that should neither be conventional nor hypothetical could I now fill in the frightful silence that, in my memories, enwraps the battle of December 4th, 1917, on the saddle between Monte Tondarecar and Castelgomberto? Certainly that afternoon of fighting at close quarters, that struggle at a few dozen metres' distance, that wearisome disengaging from enemy encirclement, and those *mêlées* round the machine-guns, must have been enveloped in a tremendous din; but, while I have still very clear recollections of the lie of the ground, the rocks, the mountain pines, the men, the wounded, the dead, the advancing German masses, the blood flowing from the forehead of corporal-major De Boni, and the wide, staring eyes of Altin, nothing remains to me of the voices, the shouts, the noises, or the explosions, as though I had lived through that scene – a vain image among other vain images – on the screen of a cinema.

Those critics were wrong who, rather disdaining these humble jottings of mine published immediately after the great tempest, said: 'Only the years to come will give us the books that really describe the war'. Completely wrong. The books that really describe war are those written shortly after the fight, immediately outside it. Even among these there are false ones, mark you, at least for us ex-soldiers, if our judgment – and some people doubt it – is to be of any value; false, because written by men in the back areas, or by boasters whom no war ever cured, or by people who took into the front line too many literary or humanitarian preconceptions.[12]

It was not enough simply to have been there and seen it. Jean Norton Cru, in his analytical treatise *Témoins*, was not afraid to say when he thought frontline soldiers got it wrong: for example Roland Dorgelès, author of one of the classics of French war literature *Les croix de bois*, served fourteen months at the front but represented for Cru 'one of

[12] Paolo Monelli, *Toes Up* (1930), p. 220 – for the original Italian text of this see pp. viii-ix of the 1928 (4th) edition of *Scarpe al sole*.

the most ignorant writers there is on the subject of combat experience and the sufferings of the common soldier'. André Bridoux complained:

> One could cite books that are false from softness, one might even say, feebleness, and from being intended to give an idea of war that would fit in with children's picture books, but one would find more that are false from excess and from wanting to shake the reader's nerves with a display of suffering and butchery. Apart from the fact that they are repugnant and useless, such descriptions are psychologically false, for the horror depended less on the spectacle itself than on one's state of mind at the time, and when one went into the line in a bad sector, seeing a wounded man, or even an empty stretcher, affected the imagination more than all the rubble over which one had marched up to the line.

Edmund Blunden was another who thought that it was difficult to strike the right note:

> a peculiar difficulty would exist for the artist to select the sights, faces, words, incidents, which characterized the time. The art is rather to collect them, in their original form of incoherence. I have not noticed any compelling similarity between a bomb used as an inkpot and a bomb in the hand of a corpse, or even between the look of a footballer after a goal all the way and that of a sergeant inspecting whale-oiled feet. There was a difference prevailing in all things.[13]

In André Bridoux's view Blunden, an officer who spent much of his time at the front attached to battalion headquarters, needn't have bothered:

> weeks, months, weren't enough to learn in: it needed years for the life of the soldier to get into one's skin, for one to take on its habits and its spirit; above all, it was necessary to have been a soldier, and I mean soldier, rank and file, for those who were only officers will always lack direct knowledge of the real rank and file, the essential component of the army.

---

[13] Jean Norton Cru, *Témoins: essai d'analyse et de critique des souvenirs de combattants édités en français de 1915 à 1918* (Paris, 1929), pp. 559, 563, 588–93, 631 etc.; ibid., p. 592; André Bridoux, *Souvenirs du temps des morts* (Paris, 1930), pp. 10–11; Edmund Blunden, *Undertones of War* (1982, Penguin edn), p. 182.

Not everyone agreed. Cyril McNeile, later a well-known writer of thrill-ers, was a captain in the Royal Engineers when the war broke out: hence his pseudonym 'Sapper'. Apart from the fact that he won the Military Cross, was twice mentioned in despatches, and ended the war as a lieutenant-colonel commanding the 18th Battalion of the Middlesex Regiment, the nature of his frontline service is unclear: he probably became a brigade major (i.e. chief staff officer) of an infantry brigade in 1916 but till he was appointed to command his battalion he would never, as an engineer officer, have had infantry-men under his direct orders. In 1917 he published a novel entitled *No Man's Land* dedicated 'To the Infantrymen', and in the Preface he wrote 'I offer these pages as a small tribute . . . to the men who have saved the world – to the Infantrymen'. *No Man's Land* recreated the life of the infantry from both the common soldiers' and the subalterns' point of view: in a later work, *Shorty Bill* (1926) he took one of his Other Rank characters from *No Man's Land* and made him the central character. Though the sub-Kipling dialogue now jars somewhat, both books are convincing and, if read at a sufficiently early age, even moving. A better known work is *Krieg* ('War', 1928) by Ludwig Renn, one of the classic accounts of the war from the ordinary soldier's point of view. The real identity of its author was Arnold Vieth von Golssenau, who had been a lieutenant in the Guards in Saxony when war broke out and was subsequently promoted to captain. He later explained:

> in the First World War ordinary soldiers often took the initiative if their officers were dead or absent. I wanted to give an account of these obscure individuals whom I had learnt to respect and love as the real heroes of the war. None of the war reporters or scribblers in the service of the rul-ing classes had written about them, because they did not know these soldiers and were forever on the look out for conspicuous deeds of personal hero-ism: and what came of that was empty phrases which we 'frontline swine' merely despised because they were all false or biassed.

Vieth von Golssenau (as one might have guessed) was a com-munist, having joined the party after his family lost its money in the inflation of the early 1920s: it is ironical that he should have adopted an authorial strategy similar to that of the creator of 'Bulldog Drummond'. Humphrey Cobb went even further. An American

citizen, he served in the Canadian Expeditionary Force as a teenager,
and was wounded and twice gassed. His death from thrombosis in
his mid-forties may have had its ultimate cause in his wartime injuries:
he certainly had a close enough look at the war from the Canadian
soldier's point of view to write a book about it. Instead he wrote
Paths of Glory (1935), about soldiers in the French army who refused
to advance in a doomed offensive, were court-martialled and
executed by firing squad. He may have heard about such things
happening in the French army, whereas in the Canadian Expeditionary Force the same scenario would not have been quite convincing. In rejecting personal experience in favour of a viable plot, Cobb
was following in the footsteps of the author of the most famous of
American novels about the First World War: Ernest Hemingway's *A
Farewell To Arms* (1929) in which the protagonist is with the Italian
army from 1915 onwards: the defeat of the Italian army at Caporetto
and the retreat to the Tagliamento, which provides the novel's climax,
occurred while Hemingway was a cub reporter in Kansas City.
Hemingway only arrived at the Italian front, as a Red Cross
ambulance driver, the following June, and was wounded by an
Austrian trench mortar three weeks later. The only battle he saw
was the Italian army's defensive victory on the Piave, by which, at
the time, he was most impressed:

> I was all through the big battle and have Austrian carbines and am-
> munition, German and Austrian medals, officer's automatic pistols, Boche
> helmets, about a dozen Bayonets, star shell pistols and knives and almost
> everything you can think of. The only limit to the amount of souvenirs
> I could have is what I could carry for there were so many dead Austrians
> and prisoners the ground was almost black with them. It was a great
> victory and showed the world what wonderful fighters the Italians are.

In retrospect however he decided the Piave was neither dramatic
enough nor disastrous enough for his story-line, and posed problems
of chronology. He may also have thought readers would be unable to
sympathize with a red-blooded American hero who deserted his army
when it was winning.[14]

---

[14] Bridoux, *Souvenirs du temps des morts*, p. 12; 'Ex-Private X' expressed a similar
view in *War is War* (1930), p. 5; 'Ludwig Renn' (Arnold Vieth von Golssenau), *Anstösse*

The benefit of hindsight inevitably coloured even writing that purported to be honest reportage. 'The most successful war books of today', complained the Czech journalist Egon Erwin Kisch in 1930, 'present the facts of that time on the basis of the experiences, circumstances and views of today'. After he had had a considerable popular and critical success with his memoir *Good-Bye to All That* Robert Graves wrote to the *Times Literary Supplement* asking:

> But what is meant by the *truthfulness* of war-books? . . . It was practically impossible (as well as forbidden) to keep a diary in any active trench-sector, or to send letters home which would be of any great post-War documentary value; and the more efficient the soldier the less time, of course, he took from his job to write about it. Great latitude should therefore be allowed to a soldier who has since got his facts or dates mixed. I would even paradoxically say that the memoirs of a man who went through some of the worst experiences of trench warfare are not truthful if they do not contain a high proportion of falsities. High-explosive barrages will make a temporary liar or visionary of anyone; the old trench-mind is at work in all over-estimation of casualties, 'unnecessary' dwelling on horrors, mixing of dates and confusion between trench rumours and scenes actually witnessed. General Crozier [of whom more later] honestly admits that his memory was in the later stages of his long service badly affected by the strain; but, as writers of books of this sort should, gives units, dates, places wherever possible as a pledge of intended truthfulness.

Graves's own deviations from strict accuracy include his endorsement of the picture in R.C. Sherriff's play *Journey's End* of company commanders awash with whisky, and some fashionable sneers at the Church of England:

> For Anglican regimental chaplains we had little respect. If they had shown one-tenth the courage, endurance, and other human qualities that the regimental doctors showed, we agreed, the British Expeditionary Force might well have started a religious revival. But they had not, being under

continued

in meinem Leben (1980), p. 70; Jeffrey Meyers, *Hemingway: A Biography* (1985), p. 29–31, and Michael S. Reynolds, *Hemingway's First War: The Making of Farewell to Arms* (Princeton, 1976), pp. 123–28, 134; Carlos Baker, ed., *Ernest Hemingway: Selected Letters, 1917–1961* (1985, paperback edn), p. 12, Hemingway to his family, 21 July 1918.

orders to avoid getting mixed up in the fighting and to stay behind with
the transport. Soldiers could hardly respect a chaplain who obeyed these
orders, and yet not one in fifty seemed sorry to obey them . . . the Roman
Catholic chaplains were not only permitted to visit posts of danger, but
definitely enjoyed to be wherever fighting was, so that they could give
extreme unction to the dying. And we never heard of one who failed to
do all that was expected of him and more. Jovial Father Gleeson of the
Munsters, when all the officers were killed or wounded at the first battle
of Ypres, had stripped off his black badges and, taking command of the
survivors, held the line.

It is certainly true that several Catholic chaplains won the DSO for
bravery under fire, as did the Rev. Michael Adler, 'Senior Jewish
Chaplain to the Forces', and some clergymen of the Anglican Church
preferred to go to the front not as chaplains but as combatant officers, including the Rev. Percy William Beresford, who won a DSO
commanding a battalion and was killed in action, and the Rev. Arthur
Aston Luce, later Chancellor of St Patrick's Cathedral, Dublin, who
won the MC. But the Rev. Theodore Bayley Hardy, VC, DSO, MC, a
former headmaster who died of wounds complicated by pneumonia
in October 1918 at the age of fifty-two and who was described by
his battalion adjutant as 'the most wonderful man I have ever met',
the Rev. Edward Mellish, VC, MC, the Rev. William Addison, VC
and the Rev. Harry Blackburne, DSO, MC, seven times mentioned
in despatches, afterwards Dean of Bristol, all distinguished themselves
under fire as Anglican pastors. (No Catholic chaplains won the VC.)
One should also mention the Rev. P.T.B. 'Tubby' Clayton, founder
of Toc H, and the Rev. G.A. Studdert Kennedy *aka* 'Woodbine Willie',
both of whom won the MC and who certainly did as much as two
men could to reverse the long-term decline of the Church of
England's hold on the popular imagination. (Graves's suggestion
that more effective chaplains could have started a religious revival,
incidentally, is a direct crib from C.E. Montague's *Disenchantment*,
published in 1922.) As for the jovial Father Gleeson, he is mentioned
six times in Captain Stouppe McCance's *History of the Royal Munster
Fusiliers* but only in his ecclesiastical character, and the War Diary
of his battalion, which does not mention him, gives little indication that the Munsters ran out of officers during the First Battle of
Ypres: *11 November 1914* (the worst day of the battle): '1.30 a.m.

Line taken over. 8 a.m. Capt. Reymes-Cole killed by a sniper in B Coy Trenches. Attacks were made by enemy during the day. Lt Philby was killed. Night very wet; all quiet.. . . .' *19th November 1914* '7 officers granted 96 hrs leave out of country . . .' They would certainly not have sent seven officers home on leave if there had not been enough officers to command the surviving troops.[15]

Graves was later quite frank in admitting the degree of calculation that had gone into writing *Good-Bye to All That*: 'I have more or less deliberately mixed in all the ingredients that I know are mixed into other popular books, specifically food and drink, murders, ghosts, kings, one's mother, T.E. Lawrence and the Prince of Wales'. A similar calculatedness may have been behind the stream of grittily realistic war novels that followed in the wake of Erich Maria Remarque's best-selling *Im Westen Nichts Neues*, which was serialized in the influential Berlin newspaper *Vossische Zeitung* in November and December 1928. It appeared in book form in January and immediately became an international publishing sensation, its frankness on such topics as defecation, delousing and the patriotism of elderly non-combatants earning it hyperbolical reviews and vast sales wherever it appeared. The English translation, under the title *All Quiet on the Western Front* was reprinted eight times in April 1929 alone. (By the 1990s it had been translated into at least forty-nine languages, with world sales in excess of four million.) The military historian Cyril Falls noted sourly 'it is common gossip that several writers sat down to produce one in the same vein after watching Herr Remarque's sales go soaring into the hundred thousands'. These writers may be taken as including J.F. Snook, author of *Gun Fodder*, a novel full of denunciations of officers and featuring a visit to a brothel in Calais, F. Haydn Hornsey, whose novel *Hell on Earth*

[15] *Times Literary Supplement*, 26 June 1930, p. 534b; Robert Graves *Goodbye to All That* (1960, paperback edn), pp. 158–59; M. Hardy, *Hardy VC: An Appreciation* [1920], p. 44: and see also, William Purcell, *Woodbine Willie: An Anglican Incident. Being Some Account of the Life and Times of Geoffrey Anketell Studdert Kennedy Poet, Prophet, Seeker after Truth, 1883–1929* (1962), p. 117–19; C.E. Montague *Disenchantment* (1922), p. 78 – pp. 66–79 of this book are a discussion of the ineffectiveness of wartime army chaplains; Captain S. McCance *History of the Royal Munster Fusiliers* (2 vols, privately printed, 1927), passim; Public Record Office, WO 95/1279, War Diary 2nd Battalion Royal Munster Fusiliers.

describes a visit to what seems to have been the same brothel (apparently not a very appealing concern as neither author seems to have partaken of the wares on offer), Charles Yale Harrison, author of *Generals Die in Bed,* in which the protagonist spends an entire ten days leave with a girl who picked him up in a Shaftesbury Avenue restaurant, which he has innocently entered in search of his first meal in London, and Helen Zenna Smith whose *Not So Quiet . . . Stepdaughters of War* – note the title – was based on her experiences as an ambulance driver in France and Belgium and features bodily functions –

> Pools of stale vomit from the poor wretches we have carried the night before, corners the sitters have turned into temporary lavatories for all purposes, blood and mud and vermin and the stale stench of stinking trench feet and gangrenous wounds

– extramarital sex –

> 'And the men, making love to you one day and dead the next. I've been on leave twice with different subs and they're both dead'.

– and incomprehending mothers, rendered insensible by jingoism –

> 'I am proud of his blindness and his disability . . . If the sight of his blindness shames one of the cowards then he has not suffered vainly. As Shakespeare puts it. . . .'

These four novels all appeared in 1930, but perhaps the most blatant attempt to cash in on the post-*All Quiet on the Western Front* mood came out in the early Summer of 1931: Wilfred Saint-Mandé's *War, Wine and Women.*[16]

---

[16] Robert Graves, 'Postscript to *Goodbye to All That*', in *But Still It Goes On: An Accumulation* (1930), pp. 13–56, at pp. 13–14; Thomas F. Schneider, *Erich Maria Remarque: In Westen Nichts Neues. Bibliographie der Drucke* (Bramsche, 1992), pp. 6, 9, 39; Cyril Falls, *War Books: A Critical Guide* (1930), p. x; Helen Zenna Smith, *Not So Quiet . . . Stepdaughters of War* (1987 edn), pp. 59, 200, 229–31, and see also pp. 30–31 and 173. See also Sassoon, *Memoirs of an Infantry Officer,* pp. 152–53, for 'David Cromlech's' (i.e. Robert Graves's) second-hand information regarding 'the ubiquity of certain establishments in France' and his correspondence with Graves

Though now virtually forgotten, during the early 1930s *War, Wine and Women* sold at least as well as Edmund Blunden's *Undertones of War* or Siegfried Sassoon's *Memoirs of a Fox-Hunting Man*. On 18 June 1931 the *Times Literary Supplement* carried an advert announcing '1st Edition Exhausted 2nd Impression Ready': the advert was framed in a decorative border of barbed wire, and showed a steel helmet, insouciantly tilted, strap hanging loose, a large butterfly perched on the crown and this art-work by no means misrepresents the contents of the book. (The barbed wire and the helmet were of course already stock symbols of the World War; the butterfly seems to have been the one seen by Paul Bäumer just before the bullet got him at the end of Lewis Milestone's 1930 film version of *All Quiet on the Western Front*.) The British Library's copy of *War, Wine and Women* is of the tenth edition of 1936: it was also published in a New York edition under the title *Sons of Cain*. (None of Wilfred Saint-Mandé's other books achieved a second printing.) The *Times Literary Supplement*'s anonymous reviewer confessed to having difficulty in deciding what to make of the book:

> If it were not extremely readable and exciting, it would not be worth puzzling over, so blatant are its faults and so bad its taste . . . A man writing an autobiographical fragment is entitled to say what he likes about himself, but it is hard to believe that he would say of his wife – if a real wife – what is said here.

The book seems however to have been universally accepted as a genuine autobiographical memoir. In the American National Union Catalog for example it is cross-referenced under 'European War, 1914–1918 – Personal Narratives, English'.[17]

Although Wilfred Saint-Mandé claimed in the book to be a member of a family of wine-merchants, the offhand manner in which

continued
on the subject in Paul O'Prey, ed., *Robert Graves: In Broken Images. Selected Correspondence, 1914–46* (New York, 1988), pp. 201–5, February-March 1930, and Charles Carrington, *Soldier from the Wars Returning* (1965), pp. 162–67.

[17] *Times Literary Supplement*, 18 June 1931, p. 485c-d; ibid., 25 June 1931, p. 508c. Despite being advertised in the *Times Literary Supplement* it is of course possible that *War, Wine and Women* had a different readership from, e.g., *Memoirs of an Infantry Officer*, but there is no way of establishing this, cf. A.D. Harvey *Literature into History* (Basingstoke, 1988), p. 92ff.

he refers to alcoholic merry-making does not seem to justify the inclusion of 'wine' in his title. The 'war' is obviously far more important. He tells how he enlisted in August 1914, served in the Ypres Salient, at the Battle of the Somme and during the German offensive of March 1918. He was wounded several times and in 1918 transferred to the Royal Air Force, becoming a pilot in a squadron of Bristol Fighters and shooting down six German aircraft before being himself shot down and wounded, his left arm being subsequently amputated. The fighter-pilot bit is handled with the most cursory detail, but though the descriptions of trench warfare are much more leisurely and detailed, they are not especially individual or well-articulated:

> At 7.30 our barrage lifted, the whistles sounded and once more we clambered over the top. Once more Jerry swiftly got his machine-guns into position and mowed us down in heaps. The captain was one of the first to fall, blown to pieces by a shell. I felt sorry for him, for it is shocking to see a man rent asunder, even if he is a rotter. The religious man's prediction came true: his head was blown off by a trench-mortar bomb. Smoke grew thicker over the battlefield, intense artillery fire rolled, rumbled and thundered overhead and all round. Many of my comrades fell, many to rise no more. (p. 286)

The only thing distinctive about this is the reference to the captain and to the religious man's prediction coming true. There are scores of better-written, more vividly-realized, eye-witness accounts of the battles of the First World War. Saint-Mandé was perhaps unusual in the emphasis he gave to the smelly side of war:

> The swollen corpses lying out in front were punctured by bullets or burst spontaneously and sent over the vilest of stinks. (p. 222)

or:

> The usual chemical-soaked blanket hung in the doorway and the ventilation was nil. The steam from our wet clothes, and the sweat from our filthy bodies, concocted the vilest fog I've ever known. I fell asleep from utter exhaustion, and in spite of the lice, did not wake until next morning. (p. 262)

Saint-Mandé also devoted particular attention to the loathsome and horrendous injuries suffered by the combatants, for example:

A bomb had burst in his face, destroying both eyes and mutilating him so frightfully that he would have been better dead. There was a bloody hole where the nose had been and the lower jaw was shattered so that the mouth hung askew in a horrible grimace. I wish a photograph of that charnel-house could be hung in every school in the world. (p. 155)

The last sentence quoted is perhaps a give-away: photographs of war-mutilated faces and limbs were often employed by anti-war propagandists in the 1920s and 1930s and Saint-Mandé's lingering on such details seems to suggest a similar propaganda intention: and clearly, it was welcomed as such by his readers.[18]

The horrific descriptions are set off by lengthy philosophical and literary disquisitions and accounts of sexual adventures. This combination of elements reminds one in retrospect of Frank Harris's *My Life and Loves*, the first volume of which had been printed in Paris in 1922. *War, Wine and Women* is a would-be classic evocation of a young man at the outset of adulthood, bursting with intellectual and sexual energy, caught up in the death-machine of the world war. The intellectual energy aspect is not entirely convincing. Saint-Mandé claimed in his book that he had won 'a modern languages scholarship at Oxford' just before the outbreak of war (as well as playing cricket and rugby for his school). He presents himself as knowing some Italian, and is able to quote the rather obscure late seventeenth-century Italian poet Vincenzo Filicaja (p. 23). His French of course is excellent, and he not only recounts word for word a number of stilted conversations in that language, and refers to his reciting verses by Béranger, Hugo and Deroulède, but also quotes verbatim from Lamartine, Buffon and Ronsard. His German was also evidently fluent as he was able to act as interpreter when a German prisoner is interrogated, and to understand him when he announced 'It is time the *dulce et decorum est pro patria mori* stunt be shown up' – a rather tricky sentence in the original German, surely, especially in view of the idiosyncratic English-style

---

[18] Photographs of physical mutilations were originally published in medical treatises such as Harold Gillies's *Plastic Surgery of the Face* (1920): an example of their use as anti-war propaganda is Ernst Friedrich's *Krieg dem Kriege*, published in 1924 with German, French, English and Dutch captions.

Page references are to the 1st edition of *War, Wine and Women*: subsequent printings seem to be identical.

pronunciation of Latin Saint-Mandé would have learnt at school
in Britain (p. 383). Earlier he lingers over a 'copy of Lessing's *Laocoon*
that I had taken from a dead German'. He is fascinated by and repeats
to himself the lines:

> As the depths of the sea always remain calm, however violently the surface
> may rage, so the expression in the figures of the Greeks, under every form
> of passion, shows a great and self collected soul . . . (p. 301)

As it happens, these words, in the first paragraph of the first chapter
of *Laokoon*, are not by Lessing himself but are a quotation from
Winckelmann; considering that they are difficult to translate from
the original German the fact that Saint-Mandé's version scarcely differs from that given in E.C. Beasley's translation, published in 1888
by Bohn's Shilling Library, suggests that while great minds think alike
hacks prefer to copy from one another.[19]

Needless to say, English Literature is not neglected. Saint-Mandé
only got round to Oscar Wilde's *Picture of Dorian Gray* and Thomas
Browne's *Religio Medici* after the war and never seems to have got round
to Milton or Wordsworth at all, but R.L. Stevenson's *Travels with a
Donkey*, J.A. Froude's *Short Studies in Great Subjects* and Henry Fielding's
Journal of a Voyage to Lisbon provide timely quotations. In a characteristic
passage Saint-Mandé describes his liaison with ' a most voluptuous
woman' who has abandoned her husband, 'a typical American with
big spectacles and a clean-shaven face' (p. 430). He gives her a lesson
on early eighteenth-century English Literature and she admits that
she 'had at one time tried to read Hegel and had given it up as hopeless'. Fortunately there is a copy of Thoreau's *Walden* in the bookcase
and the narrator is able to turn up a favourite passage. After that the
woman changes into silk pyjamas and they have sexual intercourse
(pp. 436–39).

Unfortunately it was not always possible to maintain this intellectual level, for as Saint-Mandé confesses:

---

[19] E.C. Beasley's version has 'however much the surface may be raging' rather
than 'however violently the surface may rage' but in other respects the two versions
are identical. The unlikelihood of this being a coincidence, given the style of the
original German, will be seen from a comparison with the other available English
translations of *Laokoon*. Beasley's rendering was originally published in 1853.

One often reads highfalutin accounts of philosophic meditations on the battle-field. For my part I lived like a brute. My mind was numbed and incapable of any thought, beyond brooding over the fiendish discomforts that we had to endure. (p. 407)

Nevertheless, shortly before the great German offensive of March 1918, he asks his parents to send 'a few books, including if possible:

> *Aucassin et Nicolette*
> *The Decameron*
> *The Memoirs of Benvenuto Cellini*
> *The Plays of Aristophanes*
> *Representative Men*, Emerson
> *Principles of Human Knowledge*, Berkeley   (p. 519)

This list probably gives a fair representation of the author's intellectual interests at this juncture. But there was one other preoccupation which evidently predominated, for it receives the main emphasis in the text as well as in the title of *War, Wine and Women*.

Wilfred Saint-Mandé is not one of your unscrupulous sexual opportunists. A young peasant woman with two small children offers herself, 'pressing against me and exacerbating my desire', but he remembers 'the words of Christ that if a man offended a little child it were better for him to hang a millstone round his neck and drown himself in the depths of the sea', and muttering '*parce que vous avez des enfants*' he 'strode rapidly down the hill, afraid my resolution would weaken unless I hurried' (p. 279). A little earlier, recovering from wounds behind the lines, he had showed less firmness. Marie, a young barmaid whose parents had been executed by the Germans as *franc-tireurs*, is eager to give herself to him:

> I could not be sure whether it was to prove her love or merely to satisfy her sex-impulse. In the trenches I yearned for such an opportunity with all the fervour of a strong and healthy frame. But when it was offered I had scruples. It seemed dishonourable to have sexual intercourse with a girl whom one would never see again, and my early education implanted in me a wholesome respect for virginity.

On Marie's birthday however they 'drank old wine out of bottles covered with cobwebs' and he allowed himself to be over-persuaded. 'That night was the prelude to many others' (pp. 249–50).

But Saint-Mandé's best adventures are with Anglo-Saxon girls. When he first meets Jean, his future wife, they merely discuss Platonic Love and cuddle on a greatcoat spread out on a mossy bank at the foot of an old oak (pp. 100–102). While he is away at the Western Front Jean marries a wealthy, well-connected man three times her age who, instead of consummating the marriage, runs off to Paris to be with his mistress and to have a VD cure. When Saint-Mandé is wounded he is taken to her stately home which, as part of the war effort, she is running as a hospital, and it is not long before she summons him to her private quarters. She tells him that she still loves him and, despite having recently been wounded in the left arm and right shoulder, he carries her to a couch:

> The fragrant perfume of her hair, the freshness and flexibility of her body, the delightful caresses and prolonged kisses, the exquisite soft-ness of her skin and the beauty of her face, all enraptured me to such a pitch that the world and the war were forgotten in those divine mo-ments. (p. 171)

But, perhaps because Jean was his future wife, Saint-Mandé gives less by way of explicit detail than in the case of some of his other adventures. There is Daphne, for example, who has read 'for Honours in Philosophy of all things' at Newnham College, Cambridge, and has been briefly married to a captain in the Scots Guards who 'lost both legs at Le Cateau, and shot himself rather than live the life of a *cul-de-jatte*' (p. 110). They meet in a night club before Saint-Mandé embarks for France and after two minutes' conversation they ensconce themselves in an alcove:

> Daphne placed her feet on a balcony rail in front and pulled back her skirt to avoid creasing it at the knee. The fine silk stockings emphasized the slender ankles and shapely calves. I kissed her while caressing the firm little breasts which stood out challengingly, instead of drooping like the flaccid apologies one sees on so many anaemic maidens, who starve their bodies to keep them slim, and sacrifice their health in the process. (p. 109)

But Saint-Mandé has more than sex and anorexia on his mind:

> 'Were you brought up in a Christian home?' I wondered.

'Why do you ask?'

'Merely to know if your emancipation from the servile thraldom that masquerades as Christianity was similar to my own'. (p. 114)[20]

Though not above going with French prostitutes providing they seemed to be amateurs (pp. 312–14), and enjoying a tender friendship with an American nurse (pp. 365–67), Saint-Mandé also has a significant relationship with the Hegel-reading American already mentioned.

> Her figure was slim but not thin. The waist was very slim but the buttocks were well developed and moved up and down with a peculiar snaky motion as she walked. The legs were shapely even when naked. (p. 430)

She is at least ten years his senior – not yet in need of surgical stockings it seems, though it may have been a mistake to leave off the girdle. Another promising encounter with an older woman – the wife of the vicar back home, no less – soon approaches its consummation:

> 'Wilfred, what would the world be without love – I mean passionate, rapturous embraces?' she asked suddenly.
>
> 'Not worth living in', I replied fervently, rushing at her and crushing her in my arms. (p. 450)

They are interrupted by the return home of the vicar; but one can see why Jean often seems to wish to break off their engagement.

Needless to say, so enthusiastic an indulger of healthy natural urges had no time for perversion. At one of the many base hospitals he passed through, he 'picked up a book called *À rebours* by Huysmans and sat up half the night reading it'. His verdict on the book may well give an idea of what his literature classes were like in later years when he was a university lecturer:

---

[20] *Cul-de-jatte* may be literally translated as 'basin-arse' and is a customary vulgarism in France for a legless cripple.

There is of course no Honours School of Philosophy at Cambridge: only the Moral Sciences Tripos. *The Newnham College Register* (2 vols, Cambridge [1965]), suggests two possible originals for the emancipated Daphne. Gladys Todd was at Newnham 1910–1913, reading Moral Sciences and later Medieval and Modern Languages: when *War, Wine and Women* was published she was buyer for the Times' Book Club. Marjorie Gabain read Moral Sciences at Newnham, 1911–1914, and became an actress: no details survive of her career after leaving Newnham, and this may suggest a Bohemianism that fits in with Saint-Mandé's description. Neither woman is recorded as having married; but as will be seen there are other reasons for doubting Saint-Mandé's account.

The curious hero of the work is one Des Esseintes, who is morbid and decadent in every possible way. The book is a series of filthy scenes wrapped up in an odour of mysticism. Years later I read Oscar Wilde's *Picture of Dorian Gray*, and was struck by the resemblance between the two books . . . The book, neurotic and morbid as it is, is written with much talent; it is an able study of a diseased soul. (p. 381)

The sheer philistinism of all this seems almost a guarantee of authenticity but in the preface to one of his later books Saint-Mandé confessed that *War, Wine and Women* 'was meant to be nothing more than a novel with war as a background'. At first glance this seems no more than a change of marketing strategy, since the book had obviously been received as a true account and, however much exaggerated and padded out, would probably strike the most sceptical reader as *mainly* autobiographical. The suspicion that Wilfred Saint-Mandé is a pseudonym – taken from the name of a Paris suburb – is not in itself cause to doubt the book's authenticity: many memoirs of the First World War were published pseudonymously. The fact that the account given of Saint-Mandé's descent from a French emigré family which 'never deserted the wine business in London, which is still today one of the most important in the country' is demonstrably fictitious is not in itself of major importance. What is crucial to the status as an authentic memoir of *War, Wine and Women* is that, while it purports to be an account of the experiences of an infantryman in and out of the trenches, its author turns out to have been in the Royal Field Artillery.[21]

The RFA was the branch of the artillery which in the First World War operated 13-pounder field guns within three miles of the front line. Especially in conditions of open warfare (as in March 1918) its members were frequently exposed to enemy bombardments and even small arms fire. Many artillerists were decorated for gallantry during

[21] Wilfred Saint-Mandé, *No Repentance* (London, 1935), Foreword. Note that the accent on the final 'e' of the author's name is not used in this, his last publication.
   Amongst the more notable First World War memoirs that were published pseudonymously are *A Subaltern's War* (1929) by Charles Carrington, originally published under the name 'Charles Edmonds'; *Fighter Pilot* (1936) by R.J. MacLanachan, published under the name 'McScotch'; and *Flying Minnows* (1936) by Vivian Voss, published under the name 'Roger Vee'. The 1977 edition of *Flying Minnows* gives a key to the altered names in the text.

the First World War: but not the author of *War, Wine and Women*. His protagonist found that one new officer 'was very impressed by my [medal] ribbons' (p. 477) and the American older woman had read in the newspapers how he 'had already become distinguished' (p. 431): the real-life author seems to have obtained only the usual campaign medals. Given the amount of equipment involved in artillery work, it is even possible that the author never served with a front-line battery, but only somewhere in the rear.

Wilfred Saint-Mandé's real name was John Henry Parkyn Lamont and at the time of writing *War, Wine and Women* he was senior lecturer in French at Transvaal University College, Pretoria, which became the University of Pretoria during the period he worked there. Actually he was the only member of the French department and got away with giving his qualifications in the university calendar as M.A. (Wales) and B. ès L. (Besançon), the latter title being the professionally worthless baccalaureat, equivalent to GCE A-level or graduation from High School.[22]

War, Wine and Women belongs to the period during which Frank Harris's *My Life and Loves*, James Joyce's *Ulysses* and D.H. Lawrence's *Lady Chatterley's Lover*, though (or because) banned in Britain, were establishing their reputation as classics of sexual frankness, and it was not long since Robert Keable, an ex-missionary, had enjoyed a runaway success with *Simon Called Peter*, a novel about an army chaplain who, as his faith wobbles in the rear lines in France, betrays his chaste almost-fiancée Hilda in the liberated embrace of a fast-living nurse named Julie. Sex had also been one of the things the *Times Literary Supplement*'s reviewer had objected to in *All Quiet on the Western Front* when complaining of Remarque's 'preoccupation with bodily functions', though in fact *All Quiet on the Western Front* was positively virginal by comparison with another book published in Germany in 1929, Hans

---

[22] 'Wilfred Saint-Mande is identified as H.P. Lamont, 'Formerly lecturer in French in the University of Pretoria', in E.R. Seary, *A Biographical and Bibliographical Record of South African Literature* (Grahamstown, 1938), p. 33. His full name is given in Prifysgol Cymru, *The Guild of Graduates* ([Cardiff], 1975). Further information was kindly provided by Rosemarie Dillon of the Registrar's Department, University College Cardiff, in a letter of 3 August 1989. See further biographical details in A.D. Harvey '"Oh, What a Literary War!" An Alternative Version', *London Magazine*, 33, no. 9/10 (December/January 1993–94), pp. 43–57, at pp. 51–53.

Otto Henel's *Eros im Stacheldraht* ('Eros in the Barbed Wire') which deals with frontline brothels, VD, marriages failing because the husband is at the front, etc. The reaction against nineteenth-century pieties, already evident before 1914, received enormous impetus from the First World War, especially since many younger men came to believe that those who were the most mealy-mouthed about sex and religion were also the most prone to romanticizing the slaughter in the trenches. This equation is very evident in, for example, Aldington's *Death of a Hero* and Henel's *Eros im Stacheldraht*, and is one of the sub-texts of *Lady Chatterley's Lover.*

Amongst those who saw themselves in the vanguard of the assault on prudery and hypocrisy was Henry Parkyn Lamont, M.A., B. ès L. In one of his later works, *Halcyon Days in Africa* describing the experiences of the young 'Professor of French at Krugersburg University College', his protagonist encounters a Miss Elizabeth Werger at a conference of the Senate of the University of South Africa, held at Murraytown; running into her later on the same day he goes back to her hotel room where she declares, 'I want you to give me a baby'. He obliges but some months later receives a tear-stained letter from her informing him that she has killed herself: amusing herself in Berlin while awaiting the birth of their child, she has contracted syphilis ('Drink and drugs destroyed my will. I sold my soul for cocaine. Night after night I lowered myself to hell'). The thought of her disease rotting not only her lovely body but also her unborn child has driven her to suicide. This book was published by Eric Partridge's Scholartis Press but, despite Partridge's well-known scatological sympathies, the narrative is on occasion interrupted by rows of asterisks, though given the unevenness of Lamont's prose style it is difficult to tell which parts of the *mise en scène* have been bowdlerized. That was in 1934. Next year Lamont brought out two novels with the obscure firm of Lincoln Williams. The Foreward of *The Devouring Flame* announced 'Like certain other efforts of mine, it has been mutilated in order to ensure reasonably safe publication'. He also complained that 'there are, unfortunately, many evilly-disposed persons who persistently misrepresent the high moral purpose of my work'. The Foreward of *No Repentance* discusses the public reaction to *War, Wine and Women*:

'Nasty', 'Disgusting', 'Pornographic' and 'Revolting' were hurled at me for not remembering that England is the last refuge of sexual cant, prudery and hypocrisy. I used to think America would beat us in this respect, but even there, *Ulysses* has been admitted, whereas it is still banned here.[23]

Lamont was also abreast of fashion in having a chip on his shoulder about social class. The imaginary family background of affluent wine-merchants and the improbable open scholarship to Oxford have already been noted. The women bedded by the protagonist of *War, Wine and Women* all seem to have been picked for their connections as well as their looks. The young French woman with children whom he rejects is merely a peasant 'whose husband was in a road gang' and who is worried about the cost of living (p. 279) but Jean, his future wife, has a notably rich and snobbish family, Daphne with her Newnham degree and Guards Brigade husband clearly has a superior background, Juliet the American nurse has puritanical but rich and materialistic parents (p. 365) and the Hegel-reading Stella is married to a wealthy banker (p. 430). Even Marie Masson, whose parents have been shot as *franc-tireurs*, 'had been able to secure part of her father's fortune, with which she acquired the modest inn'. (p. 248)

Though more than once urged to apply for a commission (pp. 309, 410), the narrator of *War, Wine and Women* has little time for most of the officers set over him through the workings of the British class system: 'a tall dark fellow with an evil scowl [who] delighted in punishing men for the slightest offence' (p. 80), 'he looked a raving maniac and had probably been drinking. He flourished his revolver, and seemed ready to use it' (p. 197). Not all the officers are like this of course but those who are not, like Captain Ray (p. 310) and Captain Ewen (pp. 466–67), are emphatically noted as exceptions. One of the rare 'good' officers acknowledges:

> I admit there are both officers and non-coms who make one sick. . . .
> They lack the most elementary qualities of leadership and make up for it
> by bullying and cursing the men. (p. 200)

---

[23] *Times Literary Supplement*, 18 April 1929, p. 314c; Wilfred Saint-Mandé, *Halcyon Days in Africa* (1934), p. 240; Wilfred Saint-Mande, *No Repentance* (1935), foreword. For the question of a single work being representative of more than one literary genre, see A.D. Harvey's *Literature into History*, pp. 109–10.

This kind of thing found a ready audience in the 1930s. Both the disastrous casualties of the First World War and the post-war failures on the economic and social front were widely thought to be the fault of traditional governing classes which nevertheless remained the model for social emulation. Charles Carrington had complained in 1929 that, 'After the war was over a fashion set in for decrying the efforts and defaming the characters of all those in authority in the war'. Lamont's combination of snobbishness and anti-authoritarianism, while typical of the period, was also perhaps a reflection of the fact that his own rise in the social scale had not been entirely unproblematic.[24]

War, Wine and Women must be regarded as a successfully calculated piece of book-making – one that brought its own poetic retribution in the failure of Lamont's later books to meet his expectations – and as such presumably related more to the author's assessment of what readers expected than to personal agonies that needed to be exorcized. And yet the author *was* in the war, and though not killed or, like his protagonist, mutilated, the war presumably made as big a hole in his life as it did in the lives of other participants. *War, Wine and Women* may be tosh but it is still an ex-soldier's best attempt to salvage some sort of literary statement from what he had lived through.

War, Wine and Women may be taken as representing one extreme, but even those writers at the other end of the spectrum of veracity, who made it their mission to tell the unvarnished truth, however unpleasant or discreditable to themselves personally, might have problems with objective and ascertainable fact. During the 1930s Frank Percy Crozier (reputedly the best brigade commander in the British army during the First World War, though in retrospect horrified by how much he had enjoyed it) was making a second career for himself as a platform speaker in the cause of world peace, and one of the ideas he was anxious to put across was that it was quite normal for soldiers to be exhilarated by combat, and to be carried forward on a surge of homicidal glee. At the same time he never forgot how good he had been at his job and nurtured a considerable resentment with

[24] Charles Carrington ('Charles Edmonds'), *A Subaltern's War* (1929), p. 17.

regard to the circumstances which led to the loss of half his brigade on 9 April 1918.[25]

The only thing most people know about the expeditionary corps which the Portuguese sent to the Western Front in 1917 is that in April 1918 the second of the German spring offensives was directed against the section of the line held by the Portuguese 2ª Divisão, resulting in a break-through on a nine mile front: it was two days later, with the gap in the British front still widening, that Haig issued his famous order of the day, 'With our backs to the wall and believing in the justice of our cause each one of us must fight on to the end'. The 119th Infantry Brigade, which Crozier commanded, had been on the Portuguese left flank. Of his three infantry battalions, the 18th Batallion Welch Regiment lost all but its CO, signalling officer and twenty Other Ranks, and the 13th Batallion East Surrey Regiment lost eighty-nine killed and wounded and 455 'missing'.[26]

In his war memoirs, *A Brass Hat in No Man's Land*, published in 1930, Crozier recorded that the Portuguese simply bolted, adding:

> The uniforms of the Germans and Portuguese are not dissimilar. Hundreds of Portuguese were mown down by our machine guns, and rifle fire. After all, 'fire at all field grey advancing towards us', was a legitimate order!

The Portuguese authorities learnt of Crozier's remarks from a review in the *Daily Mail* and complained to the British Ambassador in Lisbon. The latter passed on the complaint to the Foreign Office in London:

3rd May, 1930

Sir,

At an interview which I had with the Minister for Foreign Affairs yesterday His Excellency showed me a copy of the *Daily Mail* in which was published, under fairly sensational headlines, a review of a book upon the War recently written by a certain Brigadier-General Crozier. Commander Branco pointed with great indignation to references made by the Brigadier to the behaviour of the Portuguese Army in France – references which he stigmatised as

---

[25] For Crozier's reputation as the best brigade commander in the British army, see *The Times*, 4 September 1937, p. 12c.

[26] For Haig's Order of the Day, see James Edmonds, *Military Operations: France and Belgium, 1918*, ii (1937), pp. 249 and 512.

completely unfounded and most malicious. He asked me whether something could not be done in the matter and requested that I should, at any rate, call the attention of my Government to the publication in question.

2. I told His Excellency that, as he knew, the press was completely free in England to publish what it liked on condition that it was ready to run the risk of actions for libel; and, although my knowledge of the law was limited, I did not think that the Portuguese Government could successfully prosecute the *Daily Mail* for the article which he had showed me. I must confess that I had hardly ever in my life read a number of the *Daily Mail*, nor was it one of the newspapers taken in by any member of my staff. The paper carried no weight with any sensible person in England, and made a speciality of sensational news and headlines. Nor had I read the Brigadier's book but, judging by the passages in the review which he had shown me, it appeared to me to be one of those numerous publications issued since the War by disgruntled people who considered that their military genius had not been adequately recognised by the British authorities and who, under a regime less humanitarian than our own, would probably never have had the opportunity of publishing anything at all. I promised, as he had asked me, to draw your attention to the article in question.

3. I regret to say that I did not take note of the issue of the *Daily Mail* of which Commander Branco complained, but I will endeavour to ascertain this and send the Department of the Foreign Office concerned a private note indicating the date.

I have the honour to be with the highest respect, Sir, Your most obedient, humble Servant,

F.O. Lindley

The Foreign Office does not seem to have been especially concerned, and the matter was dealt with at a junior level. Charles Duff, a press officer, minuted,

What Brig. Gen. Crozier says about the Portuguese is substantially true: I was attached to them as interpreter for several months & I think Brig. Gen. Crozier lets them off very lightly.

R.A. Gallop, formerly second secretary at the Athens legation, and not yet thirty, noted,

I do not think anything would be gained by asking the WO [War Office] whether they can substantiate Gen. Crozier's charges and have amended the draft [letter to the Lisbon embassy] accordingly. Unless the Portuguese MFA [Minister of Foreign Affairs] reverts to the question with Sir. F. Lindley I think no further action need be taken.[27]

This was not exactly Brigadier-General Crozier's view, for in a subsequent book, an anti-war tirade entitled *The Men I Killed*, he again referred to the Portuguese troops' disorderly retreat across his section of the line, stating 'I ordered the shooting, by machine-gun and rifle fire, of many Portuguese, in order to stem the tide'. This time it was a Portuguese newspaper *Diario de noticias* which drew the matter to the Portuguese government's attention, and again a complaint was forwarded to London. At the prompting of Sir George Mounsey, assistant under-secretary of state at the Foreign Office – i.e. no. 4 in the official hierarchy – the question was referred to Stephen Gaselee, the Foreign Office's librarian and adviser on literary matters. Gaselee minuted:

> The General is now dead (*vile damnum*) and it might almost be worth while quoting to the Portuguese the words in the *Times* obituary notice about his last publication:
> 'In kindness to him his last book, *The Men I Killed*, is best forgotten. Most of it was written in the worst of taste. The allegations he made against the conduct of soldiers at the front aroused great indignation among ex-Service men and the relatives of those who lost their lives in the War.'
> In fact, we are just as angry as the Portuguese.

Mounsey added a final note to the file:

---

[27] F.P. Crozier, *A Brass Hat in No Man's Land* (1930), pp. 201, 204; Public Record Office, FO 395/447/P1059; Sir Francis Lindley PC, KCMG (1872–1950) was ambassador at Lisbon 1929–31, at Tokyo 1931–34; Fernando Augusto Branco (1880–1940), Portuguese Foreign Minister 1930–32, had commanded the Portuguese submarine flotilla during the First World War and had been naval attaché in London, 1919–24. Though Lindley's letter was dated 3 May, it was stamped on arrival at the Foreign Office only on 12 May, and both Duff and Gallop's minutes are dated 15 May. Charles Duff (1894–1966), author of *A Handbook on Hanging* (1928) and numerous other books, had been awarded the *Medalha de Valor Militar* for his work as an interpreter with the Portuguese during the war. R.A. Gallop (1901–48) was in Lisbon as second secretary, 1931–35, and published editions of Portuguese folk songs.

Good, then we can make our assurances whole-hearted.[28]

There is no doubt that Crozier was an excitable, over-emphatic individual, and a great believer in the idea that in the heat of battle it was natural for men to be carried away by blood-lust. Here is part of his account of the events of 9 April 1918:

> Strictly from the military point of view I have no regrets for having killed a subaltern of British infantry on that same morning I ordered our machine-guns and rifles to be turned on the fleeing Portuguese. It happened on the Strazeel Road. It was a desperate emergency. I had to shoot him myself, along with a German who was running after him. My action *did* stem the tide; and that is what we were there for.
>
> Vividly, I still remember that scene. It might have been only yesterday. Never can I forget the agonized expression on that British youngster's face as he ran in terror, escaping from the ferocious Hun whose passions were a madness and who saw only red.
>
> As I stood on the road, almost alone, after the incident, a car drove up. In it were a GSO2 and a CRE. One of them shouted out to me. Was all well? And he looked at the smoking revolver in my right hand.
>
> Yes – all was well! And I *laughed*.
>
> Perhaps you, reader, would not have laughed . . .
>
> I do not believe, had you been in my shoes, that you would have known either what you might do next or what you might have done. It is even conceivable that you might have run away, too, and not known it. I nearly did.

But we only have his word for it. There may have been no one else nearby when he shot the British subaltern but it is odd that there is no confirmation from other sources of his ordering his men to fire on the Portuguese. The war diaries of the 119th Infantry Brigade, its three component infantry battalions and the 40th Battalion Machine Gun Corps, which manned the Vickers Guns in Crozier's brigade area, are all available in the Public Record Office. The 119th Infantry Brigade

---

[28] F.P. Crozier, *The Men I Killed* (1937), p. 49; Public Record Office, FO 371/21269/W16242, and cf. *The Times*, 1 September 1937, p. 14d. Sir George Mounsey KCMG (1892–1986) was assistant under-secretary of state at the Foreign Office, 1929–39. Stephen Gaselee (1882–1943) was librarian at the Foreign Office, 1920–43: his views on James Joyce are in FO 395/209/128688 and there are no doubt other literary appraisals by him to be found elsewhere in FO 371 and FO 395.

diary, the 21st Middlesex diary and the 'Narrative of Events 9th April to 14th April 1918', written on 16 April to supplement the exiguous diary of the virtually defunct 18th Welch, mention the Germans on the Portuguese front, but make no reference to Portuguese troops as such. The 13th East Surrey diary states, 'the enemy broke through the Portuguese on our Right flank, and the Battalion was surrounded'. The 40th MGC's 'Report on Operations 9th–14th April' says the enemy 'having pressed back the PORTUGUESE were gradually encircling our men'. There are no other references to the Portuguese, let alone to shooting them.[29]

Brigadier-General Crozier's soldier servant, David Starrett – later a close friend – left his own account of the events of 9 April 1918, in a typescript that may be examined in the Imperial War Museum. He wrote that, 'Some "Pork-and-Beans" as we called the Portuguese appearing, they were chased away as huntsmen chase foxes'. He makes no mention of their being fired on with rifles and machine-guns, and his huntsmen image scarcely suggests that this was what he had in mind: even a member of the servant class would have known huntsmen do not shoot foxes.[30]

Nor did Crozier refer to the machine-gunning of the Portuguese in the letter he wrote in September 1927 to Brigadier-General James Edmonds with the object of establishing that he had been certain beforehand that the Germans would attack and that his superiors had ignored his suggestions for precautionary measures, though he did take the opportunity to reflect both on the Portuguese and on his own Corps Commander:

---

[29] Crozier, *The Men I Killed*, p. 54: a GSO 2 was a grade 2 staff officer, a CRE a staff officer responsible for Royal Engineers: they were presumably from 40th Division HQ, Public Record Office, WO 95/2601 (the war diary of 40th Battalion Machine Gun Corps – attached to 40th Division, of which Crozier's brigade formed part), WO 95/2605 (119th Infantry Brigade), WO 95/2606 (13th East Surrey and 21st Middlesex), WO 95/2607 (18th Welch). Denis Winter, *Haig's Command: A Reassessment* (1991), p. 309–10, claims that what the Public Record Office has is for the most part not the war diaries themselves but sanitized summaries by Charles Atkinson, Director of the Historical Section of the Committee of Imperial Defence from 1915 to 1918, but the war diaries cited here are undoubtedly the originals, in some cases partly comprising jottings in blue pencil on squared sheets of paper from a note pad.

[30] Imperial War Museum, Papers of David Starrett, TS entitled 'Batman', p. 112.

> But the most astounding thing of all to my mind was the mentality which permitted the Portuguese to hold the line *at all*!! and thus expose the whole front to danger.
>
> I have no wish whatever to make insinuations against Du Cane, my Corps Cdr of those days, with whom I have been on terms of Friendship for years but I do say that the Corps was 'thinking wrong' in early 1918.

Given the general tone of this letter, it may even seem a little odd that Crozier makes no allusion to something to which he was later to attach some considerable significance.[31]

It is worth noting that Crozier nowhere states that the advancing German troops were mixed up with the retreating Portuguese, or were immediately behind them, or were using them as a screen. Despite his claim in *The Men I Killed* that he saw a British subaltern being chased down a road by a German soldier and shot them both with his revolver, there would generally have been some distance between fleeing British and Portuguese and attacking Germans, and consequently no reason why British troops would have wanted to fire on the Portuguese, at a time when it would have been desirable to conserve ammunition for the Germans. Crozier may well, in his anger and excitement, have ordered his troops to shoot at the Portuguese, but even if he did see a mob of Portuguese being mowed down by a traversing machine-gun, in the midst of a large-scale battle he would have had no way of being sure which machine-gun it was that fired the bullets, even if he had been standing right next to the machine-gunner responsible. And in 1930 he stated merely that the Portuguese had been shot and that this was consistent with orders: the claim that he had specifically instructed them to be shot only materialized in 1937.[32]

The only other account I have found of the Portuguese being machine-gunned by the British is in F. Haydn Hornsey's *Hell on Earth*,

---

[31] Public Record Office, WO 95/2605, Crozier to Edmonds 24 September 1927, pasted into 119th Infantry Brigade war diary for April 1918. In spite of his hints about Sir John Du Cane, his corps commander, Crozier had presumably not forgotten that the Portuguese 2ª Divisao was part of the *neighbouring* corps, commanded by Sir Richard Haking.

[32] Crozier, *The Men I Killed*, p. 54.

published two months after *Brass Hat in No Man's Land*. Hornsey was apparently in the 11th Battalion Suffolk Regiment in the 34th Division, separated from the Portuguese by Crozier's brigade and the 121st Brigade, and he describes the incident as having occurred on the fifth or sixth day of the German offensive, by which time the Portuguese had been withdrawn from the line. He mentions that the Portuguese 'wore a uniform which at a distance resembled the field grey of the Germans'. Crozier had made the same point: one suspects Hornsey added the passage at the last minute after he had read Crozier's book.[33]

There is no doubt however that the Portuguese brigade next to Crozier's, the 4ª Brigada de Infantaria, also known as the Brigada do Minho, was more or less obliterated. Tenente-coronel Eugenio Mardel Ferreira, the acting brigade commander, was wounded and captured, along with thirty-two of his officers and approximately 1600 of his men; twenty-seven officers and eighty-eight Other Ranks were treated for wounds at British aid posts; fifteen officers and about 200 Other Ranks were killed. Considering the violence of their onslaught this does not seem an excessively large number to attribute to the unassisted effort of the attacking Germans. More than three-quarters of a century later the details do not perhaps matter very much – is responsibility or guilt simply a question of whose finger was on the trigger in any case? For our purposes the most interesting aspect is how unconvincing Crozier's efforts were when he tried so manfully to tell the truth.[34]

---

[33] F. Haydn Hornsey, *Hell on Earth* (1930), pp. 90–91: cf. p. 16 (where he states he was in the 34th Division: the Public Record Office's file index of awards of campaign medals has a Frank H. Hornsey in the Suffolk Regiment, of which the 11th Battalion was in the 34th Division) and p. 100.

[34] Vasco de Carvalho, *A 2ª. divisão portuguêsa na batalha do Lys (9 de Abril de 1918)* (Lisbon, 1924), p. 324; and Manuel de Oliveira Gomes da Costa, *O corpo de exército português na Grande Guerra: a batalha do Lys, 9 de Abril de 1918* (Porto, 1920), p. 169.

On the eve of the battle the 4ª Brigada had ninety officers and 3020 men. Eugenio Mardel Ferreira's memoirs, *A brigada do Minho na Flandres* have proved impossible to track down. He was complimented by the general commanding the German division that defeated him, and decorated by the Portuguese, French, Italian, Belgian and Spanish governments, but received no medal from the British.

Perhaps the real point is that every attempt to tell the truth is as much a matter of motives and previous commitments as making up lies and inventing falsehoods.

CHAPTER 7

Technique

IT IS the message of First World War literature rather than its technique that one remembers, yet in 1914 many younger writers were as preoccupied by questions of technique as the painters of the day.

In the event the only movement related to literature to obtain significant additional energy from the First World War was Surrealism, which was robbed of its founding father during the war itself and did not emerge to the public gaze till the mid-1920s. Guillaume Apollinaire, the most influential of Surrealism's pioneers, volunteered for the French army – he was a Russian citizen – rose from private to *sous-lieutenant*, and seems to have had a marvellous time, a kind of second adolescence without hang-ups, till wounded in the head in March 1916. He died in Paris from influenza and emphysema two days before the Armistice, and as with other writers who die relatively young one can only speculate whether his extinction came before or after he had had a chance to produce his best work. What is most striking however about his wartime writings, and those of his *avant-garde* associates, was how much they had in common with the work of other combatants.

Apollinaire's enjoyment of the war seems to have had little philosophical rationale, and his poetry suggests that what appealed to him most were the spectacular stage effects, and perhaps the ever-present sense of menace:

> Que c'est beau ces fusées qui illuminent la nuit
> Elles montent sur leur propre cime et se penchent pour regarder

Ce sont des dames qui dansent avec leurs regards pour yeux bras
    et coeurs

J'ai reconnu ton sourire et ta vivacité

C'est aussi l'apothéose quotidienne de toutes mes Bérénices
    dont les chevelures sont devenues des comètes
Ces danseuses surdorées appartiennent a tous les temps et à toutes
    les races
Elles accouchent brusquement d'enfants qui n'ont que le temps
    de mourir

(How lovely the rockets which light up the night
They rise to their limit and stoop to look
They are dancing women attentive to eyes arms and hearts

I recognized your smile and your liveliness

They're also an everyday apotheosis of all my Berenices whose
    hair has become comets
These gilded dancers belong to every age and every race
They off-handedly bring forth children who have only time to
    die)

(The poem of which this is part is entitled 'Merveille de la guerre',
'Wonder of War'.) One can see the same frigid detachment in Paul
Éluard's

Toujours, très lente
Camions, canons, mi-roues renouvelées dans les blés

(For ever and ever, very slowly, wagons, field-guns, half-wheels renew-
ing themselves in the corn fields). Yet though the concept of Surrealism had still to be officially promulgated, the Surrealist quality
of the war was recognized by great numbers of those who fought in
it. Éluard's phrase, 'the machine-gun, like a person stammering',
Apollinaire's comparison of the noise made by a salvo of shells
exploding with the sound of four people shaking a carpet to make
the dust come out, or Blaise Cendrars's description of an artillery
barrage as resembling 'old puffers entering the station . . . locomotives in the air, invisible trains, concertinaings, collisions . . . Gratings.

Lispings. Hootings. Whinnyings . . . Chimaeras of steel and mastodons in rut', had their counterpart in the writings of frontline veterans of much smaller literary ambition.[1]

For the civilians herded into the ranks the sounds of shell and bullet were strange and unexpected as well as frightening and called out for description. At close quarters an artillery barrage sounded 'as though the earth were cracking up like an egg of super-gigantic proportions tapped by a gargantuan spoon': it created, according to the same witness, 'A veritable crescendo of sounds, so continuous as to merge and blend into a single annihilating roar, the roar of a train in a tunnel magnified a millionfold: only the rattle of the machine-gun barrage, like clocks gone mad, ticking out the end of time in a final breathless reckoning, rises above it'. At a greater distance it was 'like someone kicking footballs – a soft bumping, miles away', or a noise, felt rather than heard 'like the beating of one's heart after running'. A German infantry officer recalled, 'If you put your hands over your ears and then drum your fingers vigorously on the back of your head, then you get some idea of what the drumfire sounded like to us'. The sound of an approaching shell, it was claimed, 'can be imitated by a suitable rendering of the sentences, "Who are you? I am (these words being drawn out to full length) – (a slight pause) – Krupp (very short and sharp!)"'[2]

---

[1] Guillaume Apollinaire, 'Merveille de la guerre', in *Oeuvres poétiques* (2 vols, Paris, 1965), i, p. 273, originally published in *Calligrammes: poèmes de la paix et de la guerre* (Paris, 1918): Berenice's Hair is the name of a constellation near the tail of Leo; Paul Éluard, *Oeuvres complètes* (2 vols, Paris, 1968), i, p. 14, originally published in *Le devoir* (Paris, 1916); ibid., i, p. 26, 'Notre mort II', originally published in *Le devoir et l'inquiétude, poèmes suivis de Le rire d'un autre* (Paris, 1917); Apollinaire, 'Cote 146' *Oeuvres poétiques*, ii, p. 241; Blaise Cendrars, 'J'ai tué', *Oeuvres* (8 vols, Paris, 1960–65), iv, p. 150, dated 3 February 1918. The word 'chuintements' in Cendrars's text, here rendered as 'lispings', actually refers to the pronunciation of 's' as 'sh' but it has been assumed that few readers will know the English word for this, which is 'sigmatism'.

[2] Carroll Carstairs, *A Generation Missing* (1930), pp. 88, 103; Sassoon *Memoirs of an Infantry Officer*, p. 114; Sherard Vines, *The Dark Way* [1919], p. 141; Martin Middlebrook, *The Kaiser's Battle, 21 March 1918: The First Day of the German Spring Offensive* (1978), p. 147, quoting Leutnant Rudolf Hoffmann; S.W. Beeman, 'The Artillery', in Harry Golding, ed., *The Wonder Book of Soldiers for Boys and Girls* (4th edn, 1916), pp. 178–83, at p. 182.

Some writers attempted to marshal all the onomatopoeic resources of their language, just as Robert Southey had done a hundred years earlier in a poem for children about a waterfall:

> The Cataract strong
> Then plunges along,
> Striking and raging
> As if a war waging
> Its caverns and rocks among:
> Rising and leaping,
> Sinking and creeping,
> Swelling and sweeping,
> Showering and springing,
> Flying and flinging
> Writhing and ringing . . .

The repetitive 'i' sounds and the concussive 'n's in Isaac Rosenberg's lines 'And shells go crying over them/From night till night and now' were no serendipitous accident, nor were the sibillants of Nikolai Gumilev's

> Kak sobaka na tsyepi tyazhyeloi
> Tyavkayet za lyesom pulyemyet
> I zhuzhzhat shrapneli, slovno pchyeli
> Sobiraya yarko-krasni med.

(Like a dog on a heavy chain barks a machine-gun in the wood and shrapnel buzzes like bees gathering bright red honey). The most successful ventures with this technique during the First World War were by the German poet August Stramm, though admittedly one of his efforts was taken up by several German newspapers and printed as an example of what war poetry should *not* be like. This is his poem 'Granaten' (Shells):

> Das Wissen stockt
> Nur Ahnen webt und trügt
> Taube täubet schrecke Wunden
> Klappen Tappen Wühlen Kreischen
> Schrillen Pfeifen Fauchen Schwirren
> Splittern Klatschen Knarren Knirschen

Stumpfen Stampfen
Der Himmel tapft
Die Sterne schlacken
Zeit entgraust
Sture weltet blöden Raum

(Knowledge stops – only perception weaves and deceives – dove deafens terrible wounds – flap fumble burrow shriek – shrill pipe spit whirr – splinter chip creak crunch – stump stamp – the sky trudges – the stars become slag – time becomes more horrid – stubbornness populates stupid space.)[3]

It was easier though to make up one's own onomatopoeic words. This had been done, as already mentioned, by Aristophanes, and, on a modest scale, by Tolstoy in *War and Peace* ('*Trakh-ta-ta-takh!* came the frequent crackle of musketry'). Early in 1914 the Futurist writer F.T. Marinetti made this practice a particular feature of a book intended to capture the noises and atmosphere of the Balkan Wars:

tza tzu tatatatatata la gomena puzzare fumare **crrrr prac-prac** troppo tardi inferno al diavolo il ponte angolo ottuso arco teso gonfiare il suo ventre **apriiiiirsi aaaaahi patapum-patatraack** maledizione canaglia canaglia gridare gridare uriare muggire **scoppio di cuori turchi** squarciagola sfrangiarsi scapigliamento di **hurrrrrrraaah tatatatatata hurrrrrraaah tatatatata** PUUM PAMPAM PLUFF **zang-tumb-tumb hurrrrraaah tatatatatata hurrrraaah**

(Even the ordinary vocabulary of this is syntactically so jumbled that it is scarcely translatable.) In English onomatopoeic words like 'twang' and 'boom' and 'crash' had been acceptable usages as far back as the sixteenth century: 'ping', for the noise made by a rifle bullet, seems to have entered the language in the nineteenth century; but onomatopoeic coinages seem to be especially characteristic of twentieth-century English, and can be seen as an aspect of the democratization, vulgarization, vernacularization of language in the era of the mass-market and mass-democracy, as in Henry Williamson's *The Patriot's Progress*:

---

[3] Robert Southey, 'The Cataract of Lodore'; Isaac Rosenberg, 'Dead Man's Dump', in Ian Parsons, ed., *The Collected Works of Isaac Rosenberg* (1979), p. 109, lines 12–13; Nikolai Gumilev, 'Voina', in *Sobranye Sochynenyi* (4 vols, Regensburg, 1947), ii, p. 69, first published in *Kolchan* (1915); August Stramm, 'Granaten', in Stramm, *Das Werk* (Wiesbaden 1963), p. 94, first published in *Der Sturm*, Jahrgang 6, no. 11/12 (September 1915).

Drubber drubber drub continuous gunfire over and through all the living and the dead . . . Brutal downward dronings of 5.9's. Ruddy flashes
in front. Cra-ash. Cra-ash. Cra-ash. John Bullock breathed faster. Cries
from far in front. Drivers crouched over their mules. For Christ's sake get
a move on in front! They waited. The woo-r, woo-r, woo-r plop, woo-r plop,
of gas-shells, the corkscrewing downward sigh, the soft plop in the mud.
Another and another. Gas-shells – them. From behind a voice crying, 'Pass
the word up from the Second-in-Command to move on!' Other mes-
sages. Erz-z-z-z-z-ZAR, another salvo over them like runaway tramcars, red-
smoky glares and spark-scatters and colossal rending crashes.[4]

Everyone could invent their own sound-imitating string of letters. For
Robert Graves the noise a shell made was 'whoo-oo-ooo-oooOOO-bump-
CRASH!' followed by 'a curious singing noise in the air, and then flop!
flop! little pieces of shell-casing came buzzing down all around'. J.D.
Strange transcribed the sound of an incoming shell as 'Wheeeeee-ee-
hurrunch!' but Cecil Lewis thought it was more a case of 'Wheeeeee
. . . wheeee . . . whee-ow . . . whe-ow . . . whow . . whow . whow . . . Zonk!'
According to Richard Aldington a complete salvo made a crescendo
noise, 'ZWIING, CRASH! CRAASH! CLAAANG' Bernard Adams described trench
mortars as going 'whizz-sh-sh-sh-h-h' – silence – 'THUD' and the sound
of a richocheting rifle bullet as 'Ping-g-g-g,' while for Ford Madox Ford
the noise of a passing bullet was 'F-R-R-R-r-r-r! A gentle purring sound!'
For Hugh Dalton machine-guns made a 'wooden-sounding *clack-clack-
clack*', whereas Richard Aldington wrote of the 'Zwiss, zwiss, zwiss, zwiss
. . . of bullets, following the rapid rat-tat-tat-rat-tat-tat-rat of a machine-
gun'. For Ford Madox Hueffer it was more of a *wukka wukka* noise:

> Then, far away to the right thro' the moonbeams
> '*Wukka Wukka*' will go the machine-guns,
> And, far away to the left
> *Wukka Wukka.*
> And sharply,
> *Wuk* . . . *Wuk* . . . and then silence
> For a space in the clear of the moon.[5]

---

[4] Leo Tolstoy, *War and Peace*, x, chapter 30 (World's Classics, 1933 edn, ii, p. 506);
F.T. Marinetti, *Zang Tumb Tuum: Adrianopoli Ottobre 1912* (Milan, 1914), p. 145; Henry
Williamson, *The Patriot's Progress* (1930), pp. 97, 99–100.

[5] Robert Graves, *Goodbye to All That* (1960, Penguin edn), p. 82; J.D. Strange, *The*

Of course it was not always possible to identify what it was actually making a noise:

> We ducked, then got up again and witnessed the horrifying spectacle of Harvey blown into the air. I shuddered as a piece of something hit my helmet with a 'tink'. It might be a piece of Harvey's skull!

And often enough the sounds were in elaborate combinations even when one was some miles to the rear:

> Shells falling on a church: these make a huge '*corump*' sound, followed by a noise like crockery falling off a tray – as the roof tiles fall off. If the roof is not tiled you can hear the stained glass, sifting mechanically until the next shell. (Heard in a church square, on each occasion, about ninety yards away.) Screams of women penetrate all these sounds – but I do not find that they agitate me as they have done at home.

Nearer the firing line the orchestration of different varieties of killing device was even more complex:

> Close by, a quickfirer is pounding away its allowance of a dozen shells a day. It is like a cow coughing. Eastward there begins a sound (all sounds begin at sundown and continue intermittently till midnight, reaching their zenith at about 9 p.m. and then dying away as sleepiness claims their makers) – a sound like a motor-cycle race – thousands of motor-cycles tearing round and round a track, with cut-outs out: it is really a pair of machine guns firing. And now one sound awakens another. The old cow coughing has started the motor-bikes: and now at intervals of a few minutes come express trains in our direction: you can hear them rushing toward us; they pass going straight for the town behind us: and you hear them begin to slow down as they reach the town: they will soon stop: but no, every

continued
Price of Victory (1930), p. 119; Cecil Lewis, *Sagittarius Rising* (1942 edn), p. 111; Richard Aldington, *Death of a Hero* (1965 edn), p. 296; Adams, *Nothing of Importance*, p. 28; ibid., p. 24; Ford Madox Ford, *A Man Could Stand Up –* (1926), p. 93; Hugh Dalton, *With British Guns in Italy: A Tribute to Italian Achievement* (1919), p. 241; Aldington, *Death of a Hero*, p. 276; Ford Madox Hueffer, 'Clair de Lune', in *On Heaven and Poems Written on Active Service* (1918), p. 43–44.

time, just before they reach it, is a tremendous railway accident. At least, it must be a railway accident, there is so much noise, and you can see the dust that the wreckage scatters. Sometimes the train behind comes very close, but it too smashes on the wreckage of its forerunners. A tremendous cloud of dust, and then the groans. So many trains and accidents start the cow coughing again: only another cow this time, somewhere behind us.

The closer one was, the less pleasant the sounds:

> More terrible – not to be forgotten – were the salvoes of the German batteries close in front, which fired almost together every three minutes. Boom-boom-boom-boom – they threatened to burst the brain, they caused a racking headache, these terrible tornadoes of sound. The machine-gun and the rifle-fire were as nothing after these. The rat-tat-tat, the clack-clack, the ping-ping sent their messages well overhead to the trenches behind and the still-advancing troops. Much other noise came to puzzle the ears, to weary the brain: the faint shouting of men, the clink-clink of the entrenching-tools as soldiers dug themselves in, the great hollow explosions which resounded afar off amid the ruins of Aubers and Neuve Chapelle.
>
> And the groans, the moans, the crying of those who lay around!

Richard Aldington described a battle as 'an immense rhythmic harmony, a super-jazz of tremendous drums, a ride of the Walkyrie played by three thousand cannon. The intense rattle of the machine-guns played a minor motif of terror'. Wilfred Owen played with the idea that these noises carried some sort of message:

> The Bullets chirped – In vain! vain! vain!
> Machine-guns chuckled – Tut-tut! Tut-tut!
> And the Big Gun guffawed

But in another of his poems it was simply a matter of 'the monstrous anger of the guns, / Only the stuttering rifles' rapid rattle'.[6]

---

[6] J.F. Snook, *Gun Fodder* (1930), p. 221; Richard M. Ludwig, *Letters of Ford Madox Ford* (Princeton, 1965), p. 73, Ford Madox Hueffer (as he then was) to Joseph Conrad 6 September 1916; *The Letters of Charles Sorley: With a Chapter of Biography* (Cambridge, 1919), p. 287, Charles Sorley to Prof. W.R. Sorley, his father, 15 July 1915; Wilfrid Ewart, *Scots Guard* (1934), p. 56; Aldington, *Death of a Hero*, p. 321; Wilfred Owen,

It was not only the British who went in for the game of trying to find exact equivalents for the sounds of modern warfare. Paul Lintier was reminded of the sea:

> From the unknown country beyond the hills came the terrific noise of the battle: the rattle of musketry and the roar of machine-guns, like great rollers being sucked back on a pebbly shore, and the thunder of artillery enveloping and uniting all these noises into a single voice like that of a storm in mid-ocean, with heaving, crashing waves, deep, thudding undertones and the shrill whistle of the wind through the surf.

Henri Barbusse wrote of 'les sifflements et les tapements des balles, le souffle des obus qui passent: des rugissements et des miaulements, très exactement, et des halètements de locomotives lancées à toute vitesse', the whistling and pattering of bullets, the whisper of passing shells, roarings and miaowings, literally, and the panting of locomotives hurtling at full speed. Jean Galtier-Boissière noted down the sound of shrapnel as 'Dzin-baiing! . . . Psiou . . . Brainggn! . . . Dzin . . . brâon . . . Dzion . . . brâon . . . Dchin . . . bingh!' The combination of noises made by machine-guns mounted on motor vehicles inspired one French armoured car unit to christen their unit magazine *TacaTacTeufTeuf*. For the German writer Otto Riebicke, bullets went 'päng . . . päng', grenades 'rrrumsch . . . rrrumsch', machine-guns 'rattarattatt'. In his novel *Krieg* Ludwig Renn, according to a British critic, 'imitates the noise made by the shells with a meticulous care that is almost comic': 'S – kramm! ram! ram! ram! ram! . . . Sch – p! [a dud] . . . Bramm! . . . Wramm . . . Ramm! App! Ramms! Karr! . . . Pramm! harp! Kötsch! Rur-rum-pa! ra! hrätsch! Parr! . . . Ra – Ramms! S-parr! Schr – kräpp!' Werner Beumelburg, who almost certainly disapproved of Renn's work, followed his example in this at least: 'sssss kreng . . . Ssssss . . . kreng krach. Sssss . . . petsch [another dud] . . . Sssss . . . sssss . . . wwumm wwumm'. He even made a kind of joke of it:

> How many men have you still got? . . . A nice simple calculation. . . . There were thirty-four of them at Azannes . . . wummm rrranggg . . . Comma, line. Got it? Go on. Twenty-four in the Orne Gorge . . . krrranggg

continued
'The Last Laugh' and 'Anthem for Doomed Youth'. See also Rolf Greifelt, *Der Slang des englischen Soldaten im Weltkrieg, 1914–1918* (Marburg, 1937), p. 12–13.

rrenggrenggrrrenggg . . . write it down in a column, subtract . . . sss krrangg
. . . four from four equals zero . . . wummm krrranggg . . . three from four
leaves one . . . rrrang brummm . . . makes ten . . .

Even neutrals got in on the game. Thomas Dinesen, the brother of
Karen Blixen, joined the Canadian army, won the VC, and wrote his
memoirs – in his native language, which was Danish:

> Hele natten igennem drøner kanonerne, med spredte skud, både nær
> ved og langt, langt borte mod nord og syd . . . bum – – – bum – – bum
> bum – – BUM! lige bag os, – og vi hører granaterne suse gennem luften.
> De små, langt borte, knirker som en cykel på en grussti; andre hvæser tæt
> over hovedet på én som en Rolls-Royce i fuld fart. De engelske
> maskingeværer skratter, med mellemrum, natten igennem, – da-da-
> da-da – – – – da-da-da-da-da-da – – – – – da-da-da –, men de bør jo ikke
> være farlige for os, selv om kuglerne pister lige over vore hoveder.
> SVUP! der ryger en dart, en stor granat fra en skyttegravsmorter, op et
> sted ovre i mørket fra Frits' forreste linie, 2–300 meter borte.

This was translated into English, with the orthography of the sound-
effects revised to suit an English readership:

> boom . . . boom . . . boom . . . boom-boom . . . BOOM! Just behind us we
> hear the shrapnel whizzing through the air. The small shells, when far
> away, creak just like a cycle on a gravel path; others hiss immediately above
> one's head, like the sound of a big Rolls-Royce going at top speed. In
> between, comes the sound of the English machine-guns, suddenly stop-
> ping, then commencing again all through the night: *dah-dah-dah . . . dah-
> dah-dah . . . dah-dah-dah-dah!* Of course, they ought to be our best friends,
> but all the same some of the shots come very close, whizzing just above
> our heads! *SWU-UPP!* . . .[7]

[7] Paul Lintier, *My Seventy-Five: Journal of a French Gunner (August-September 1914)*
(1929) p. 55 – first published as *Ma pièce: souvenirs d'un cannonier, 1914 (avec une batterie
de .75)* (Paris, 1916); Henri Barbusse, *Lettres de Henri Barbusse à sa femme, 1914–1917*
(Paris, 1937), p. 47; Jean Galtier-Boissière, *En rase campagne 1914: un hiver à Souchez,
1915–1916* (Paris, 1917), pp. 42–43; André Charpentier, *Feuilles bleu horizon, 1914–1918*
(Paris, 1935), p. 302; Otto Riebicke, *Ringen an der Somme und im Herzen* (Magdeburg,
1917), p. 31; J. Knight Bostock, *Some Well-Known German War Novels, 1914–1930* (Oxford,
1931), p. 16; Ludwig Renn *Krieg* (Frankfurt, [1929]) pp. 129, 198, 216, 253, 261,
266, 289, 296; Werner Beumelburg, *Die Gruppe Bosemüller* (Oldenburg, 1930), pp.
14, 15, 103, 279: see also Adam Scharrer *Vaterlandlose Gesellen: das erste Kriegsbuch eines*

Yet no amount of ingenuity in transcribing sound effects could provide a basis for a sustained literary treatment of the war, and though the *idea* of war literature had emerged clearly enough in the later nineteenth century, it seems that developments in literary technique – more especially in poetry – gave less direct assistance to writers than the developments in painting in the two decades before 1914 did to artists.

In poetry, in Britain, the Imagist movement seemed initially to offer some useful prescriptions on how to write a war poem, though a manifesto published in 1915 was anxious to deny their novelty:

These principles are not new; they have fallen into desuetude. They are the essentials of all great poetry, indeed of all great literature, and they are simply these:

1. To use the language of common speech, but to employ always the *exact* word, not the nearly exact, nor the merely decorative word.

2. To create new rhythms – as the expression of new moods – and not to copy old rhythms, which merely echo old moods . . . In poetry, a new cadence means a new idea.

3. To allow absolute freedom in the choice of subject. It is not good art to write badly about aeroplanes and automobiles; nor is it necessarily bad art to write well about the past. We believe passionately in the artistic value of modern life, but we wish to point out that there is nothing so uninspiring nor so old-fashioned as an aeroplane of the year 1911.

4. To present an image (hence the name: 'Imagist'). We are not a school of painters, but we believe that poetry should render particulars exactly and not deal in vague generalities, however magnificent and sonorous . . .

5. To produce poetry that is hard and clear, never blurred nor indefinite.

6. Finally, most of us believe that concentration is of the very essence of poetry.

continued
Arbeiters (Vienna, 1930), pp. 83, 94, and Thor Goote, *Wir fahren den Tod* (Gutersloh, [1930]), pp. 246, 268, 379 etc.; Thomas Dinesen, *No Man's Land: en Dansker med Canadierne ved Vestfronten* (Copenhagen, 1965 edn), p. 85, cf. the English translation, *Merry Hell: A Dane with the Canadians* [1930], p. 113. The Danish text was first published in 1929.

Another Thomas Dinesen, a Schleswig Dane, fought in the German army on the Russian front: see Thomas Dinesen, *Pligtens Tunge Bud: en sønderjydes erindringer fra verdenskrigen, 1914–18* ([Esbjerg], 1978).

These words were written by Richard Aldington, but his poetic practice was less impressive either than his preaching or, later on, his novel *Death of a Hero*:

> These antique prostitutions –
> Am I dead? Withered? Grown Old?
> That not the least flush of desire
> Tinges my unmoved flesh,
> And that instead of women's living bodies
> I see dead men – you understand? dead men
> With sullen, dark red gashes
> Luminous in a foul trench?[8]

In fact almost none of the best English poetry of the First World War is technically innovative: Wilfred Owen's panting half-rhymes are in no sense as mould-breaking as the experiments of Ungaretti in Italian and Stramm in German:

> It seemed that out of battle I escaped
> Down some profound long tunnel, long since scooped
> Through granites which titanic wars had groined.
> Yet also there encumbered sleepers groaned,
> Too fast in thought or death to be bestirred,
> Then, as I probed them, one sprang up, and stared . . .

One may even read something of a hidden agenda in T.S. Eliot's claim that David Jones belonged to the same innovative generation as himself, James Joyce and Ezra Pound, for Jones's *In Parenthesis*, unlike the rest of the best poetry of the war, was written years afterwards, long after Owen and Rosenberg had been carried to their graves on the battlefield.[9]

There is indeed no mention of Owen and Rosenberg in Eliot's correspondence: his verdict on a public reading of war poetry in October 1917 was 'the only one who has any merit is a youth named Siegfried

---

[8] *Some Imagist Poets: An Anthology* (1915), pp. vi-vii (Preface by Richard Aldington); Richard Aldington 'Concert', in *Collected Poems* (1929), p. 95.

[9] For Owen's rhymes, see Dennis Welland, *Wilfred Owen: A Critical Study* (1978 edn), pp. 104–24; Wilfred Owen 'Strange Meeting'; T.S. Eliot, introduction to 1961 paperback edition of David Jones, *In Parenthesis*.

Sassoon (semitic) and his stuff is better politics than poetry'. The word 'youth', though not totally inappropriate when applied to Sassoon's habitual demeanour, was probably meant satirically: already in his thirties, Sassoon was two years older than Eliot. The degree to which the creator of 'Prufrock' was disengaged from what was going on is suggested by a bogus letter, purportedly by a lady named Helen B. Trundlett, which he wrote shortly afterwards as a space-filler for a literary journal he helped edit: this spoof described the 'dross' in Rupert Brooke's earlier poetry as having been 'purged away (if I may be permitted this word) in the fire of the Great Ordeal which is proving the well-spring of a Renaissance of English poetry'. Presumably Eliot thought otherwise. He may already have been working out his ideas for his influential essay on 'The Metaphysical Poets', first printed in 1921, in which he put forward the idea of a 'disassociation of sensibility' which had prevented English poets since the seventeenth century from writing genuine poetry about current intellectual and moral concerns: a point of view that implies a complete dismissal of the attempts of Owen and other First World War poets to give poetic form to their experiences.[10]

Owen himself claimed of his own work 'The Poetry is in the pity', and some of the most successful poems of the war years depend on their subject and the chance memorable phrase rather than any real poetic excellence. Both Rupert Brooke's

> If I should die think only this of me
> That there's some corner of a foreign field
> That is for ever England

or Alan Seeger's

> I have a rendezvous with Death
> At some disputed barricade

would have weathered less well if their authors had survived to edit the *Daily Telegraph* or become ambassador at Stockholm, though neither the hill-top olive grove on Skyros where Brooke was buried nor the meadow near Belloy-en-Santerre where Seeger was riddled by a traversing

---

[10] Valerie Eliot, ed., *Letters of T.S. Eliot*, i, *1898–1922* (1988), p. 205, Eliot to Eleanor Hinkley, 31 October 1917.

machine-gun were quite what their poems evoked. One suspects in any
case that luck has a great deal to do with the reputation of such pieces:
Ewart Alan Mackintosh, a classical scholar at Christ Church, produced
a couple of volumes of rather late-Victorian verse, of which one poem
at least is as fine as anything Brooke or Seeger wrote, even if later readers might have preferred to have foregone 'the crash of Victory' in the
last stanza quoted – though perhaps after all it conveys well enough the
callous satisfaction of a man throwing hand grenades ('a bomber') when
one of his grenades detonates exactly where he intended:

> Though grasses grow on Vimy,
> And poppies at Messines,
> And in High Wood the children play,
> The craters and the graves will stay
> To show what things have been.
>
> Though all be quiet in day-time
> The night shall bring a change,
> And peasants walking home shall see
> Shell-torn meadow and riven tree,
> And their own fields grown strange.
>
> They shall hear live men crying,
> They shall see dead men lie,
> Shall hear the rattling Maxims fire,
> And see by broken twists of wire
> Gold flares light up the sky.
>
> And in their new-built houses
> The frightened folk will see
> Pale bombers coming down the street,
> And hear the flurry of charging feet,
> And the crash of Victory.[11]

Mackintosh's verses seem to owe something to the tone and pace
of a much better-known piece by John MacCrae:

[11] Wilfred Owen, *Poems* (1920), Preface; Ewart Alan Macintosh, 'Ghosts of War
(Sent from France in October 1917)'; in *War the Liberator and Other Pieces* (1918), pp.
38–39 (Mackintosh won the MC in May 1916, was gassed on the Somme, and killed
at Cambrai in 1917; the poem is given here minus its first and last stanzas).

> In Flanders fields the poppies grow
> Between the crosses, row on row
> That mark our place: and in the sky
> The larks still bravely singing, fly
> Scarce heard amid the guns below.

MacCrae himself, who had been born in 1872 and had served as a major in the Royal Artillery during the Boer War, had been one of those who had thrilled to A.E. Housman's *A Shropshire Lad* when it had first become famous in the late 1890s, and despite the differences in prosody one is probably justified in seeing Housman as the most influential of his literary forebears.[12]

Rupert Brooke also had his imitators, though the echo of his famous sonnet in the first line of the following is presumably ironic:

> If I should die, be not concerned to know
>   The manner of my ending, if I fell
> Leading a forlorn charge against the foe,
>   Strangled by gas, or shattered by a shell.
> Nor seek to see me in this death-in-life
>   Mid shirks and curses, oaths and blood and sweat,
> Cold in the darkness, on the edge of strife,
>   Bored and afraid, irresolute, and wet.
>
> But if you think of me, remember one
>   Who loved good dinners, curious parody,
> Swimming, and lying naked in the sun,
>   Latin hexameters, and heraldry,
> Athenian subtleties of δης and τοις,
>   Beethoven, Botticelli, beer, and boys.

(The author, Phillip Bainbrigge, had been a sixth-form master at Shrewsbury before his call-up, and the reference to 'boys' is unlikely to have any homoerotic significance – even if the war did play havoc with pre-war cautions.) Other poets chose less obvious models, for example Keats:

---

[12] John MacCrae's 'In Flanders Fields' was first published in *Punch*, 8 December 1915; he served as a lieutenant-colonel in the Royal Army Medical Corps, attached to the Canadian Expeditionary Force, and died of pneumonia on 28 January 1918.

A little moment more – O, let me hear
(The thunder rolls above, and star-shells fall)
Those melodies unheard re-echo clear
Before the shuddering moment closes all.
They come – they come – they answer to my call,
That Grecian throng of graven ecstasies,
Hyperion aglow in blazing skies,
And Cortez with the wonder in his eyes.

Southey perhaps (but with a curious prefiguring of the poem by Wilfred Owen quoted a couple of pages back):

I tracked a dead man down a trench,
  I knew not he was dead.
They told me he had gone that way,
   And there his foot-marks led.

The trench was long and close and curved,
   It seemed without an end;
And as I threaded each new bay
   I thought to see my friend.

I went there stooping to the ground.
   For, should I raise my head,
Death watched to spring; and how should then
   A dead man find the dead?

At last I saw his back. He crouched
   As still as still could be,
And when I called his name aloud
   He did not answer me.

The floor-way of the trench was wet
   Where he was crouching dead:
The water of the pool was brown,
   And round him it was red.

I stole up softly where he stayed
   With head hung down all slack,
And on his shoulders laid my hands
   And drew him gently back.

> And then, as I had guessed, I saw
> His head, and how the crown –
> I saw then why he crouched so still,
> And why his head hung down.

Or Browning:

> Who but the guns shall avenge him? *Battery – Action!*
> Load us and lay to the centremost hair of the dial-sight's refraction;
> Set your quick hands to our levers to compass the sped soul's assoiling
> Brace your taut limbs to the shock when the thrust of the barrel recoiling
> Deafens and stuns!
> Vengeance is ours for our servants: trust ye the guns!

A.P. Herbert, in *The Bomber Gipsey*, obviously took his title from Matthew Arnold, though one of the poems in this collection, 'Beaucourt Revisited', echoed William Johnson Cory's 'They Told Me Heracleitus . . .':

> I wandered up to Beaucourt, I took the river track
> And saw the lines we lived in before the Boche went back . . .

Charles Sorley's best-known poem, found in his kit-bag after he was shot through the head, suggests a debt to Christina Rossetti:

> When you see millions of the mouthless dead
> Across your dreams in pale battalions go,
> Say not soft things as other men have said,
> That you'll remember. For you need not so.
> Give them not praise. For, deaf, how should they know
> It is not curses heaped on each gashed head?
> Nor tears. Their blind eyes see not your tears flow.
> Nor honour. It is easy to be dead.
> Say only this, 'They are dead'. Then add thereto,
> 'Yet many a better one has died before'.
> Then, scanning all the o'ercrowded mass, should you
> Perceive one face that you loved heretofore,
> It is a spook. None wears the face you knew.
> Great death has made all his for evermore.

Isaac Rosenberg, despite his admiration for Walt Whitman ('I have written a few war poems but when I think of "Drum Taps" mine are absurd') and his qualified view of Blake ('The drawings are finer than his poems'), seems to have modelled himself more on the latter:

> I snatched two poppies
> From the parapet's ledge
> Two bright red poppies
> That winked on the ledge.

Even in his 'Break of Day in the Trenches' there is an echo of Blake, with a rat instead of a tiger:

> What do you see in our eyes
> At the shrieking iron and flame
> Hurled through still heavens?
> What quaver – what heart aghast?[13]

Similar lines of descent will be traceable in the work of French and German war poets: and the oddest instance of a wartime poem, or rather song, that derives from an earlier model is an English adaptation of a German original. There are innumerable different versions of this song. 'The German generals crossed the Rhine . . .', or perhaps they were merely officers, no rank specified, and there may have been

---

[13] Phillip Bainbrigge's poem was printed, apparently for the first time, in Nevil Shute *Slide Rule* (1954), p. 29: soon after writing this poem Bainbrigge was killed in action; Geoffrey Dearmer, 'Keats before Action', in *Poems* (1918), p. 41 – see also the sonnet 'Keats' in the same collection; untitled poem by W.S.S. Lyon in *Easter at Ypres, 1915, and Other Poems* (Glasgow, 1916), pp. 12–13: these verses are printed with the note 'Written in the trenches by "Glencorse Wood" 19–20th April 1915': Lyon, a young Edinburgh lawyer and sub-warden of the Edinburgh University Settlement, was killed less than three weeks later; Gilbert Frankau 'The Voice of the Guns', in *The Guns* (1916), p. 34; A.P. Herbert, 'Beaucourt Revisited', in *The Bomber Gipsey and Other Poems* (1918), p. 29 – originally published in *The Mudhook: Journal of the 63rd (RN) Division*, 1 September 1917; Charles Hamilton Sorley, *Marlborough and Other Poems* (Cambridge, 1922), p. 78; Parsons, ed., *Collected Works of Isaac Rosenberg*, p. 267, Rosenberg to Joseph Leftwich, 8 December 1917, and p. 198, Rosenberg to Winifreda Seaton, December 1912–January 1913, and cf. p. 102, 'In the Trenches', and p. 103, 'Break of Day in the Trenches'.

three of them, and it may have been the *line* rather than the Rhine –
front line? Armistice line? Different versions have different refrains:
'*Skibboo, skibboo, ski-bumpity-bump skibboo!*' or '*Taboo, taboo, tabollocky eye
taboo!*' but the most usual is '*Parley-voo*', which provided the name by
which the song was known in the neighbourhood of Colchester barracks in the late 1950s: the title *Mademoiselle from Armentières*, which is
sometimes used, properly refers only to the tune:

> The German generals crossed the line, *parley-voo*
> The German generals crossed the line, *parley-voo*
> The German generals crossed the line
> To fuck the women and drink the wine
> *Inky-pinky parley-voo*
>
> They came to the door of a wayside inn, *parley-voo*
> They came to the door of a wayside inn, *parley-voo*
> They came to the door of a wayside inn
> Pissed on the mat and walked right in
> *Inky-pinky parley-voo*
>
> 'O landlord have you a daughter fair, *parley-voo*
> O landlord have you a daughter fair, *parley-voo*
> O landlord have you a daughter fair
> With lily-white tits and golden hair?
> *Inky-pinky parley-voo*

This is undoubtedly derived from Ludwig Uhland's well-known ballad 'Der Wirtin Töchterlein', written in 1809 and published in his
Gedichte of 1815:

> Es zogen drei Bursche wohl über den Rhein
> Bei einer Frau Wirthin, da kehrten sie ein
> 'Frau Wirthin! hat Sie gut Bier und Wein?
> Wo hat Sie Ihr schönes Töchterlein?'

In Uhland's version the landlady (not landlord) takes the three *Bursche*
(batmen or orderlies, or perhaps merely 'lads') to a bedroom and
shows them her daughter's corpse, and each of the orderlies declares
that he had been in love with her. In the British First World War version

At last they got her on the bed [repeated twice, with refrain]
And shagged her till her cheeks were red
And then they took her to a shed [repeated twice, with refrain]
And shagged her till she was nearly dead
They took her down a shady lane [repeated twice, with refrain]
And shagged her back to life again.

How and when the transformation of Uhland's verses occurred is a mystery: Eric Partridge, the folklorist of English filth, thought it might even have happened as far back as the time of Waterloo, though there is no real evidence to sustain this theory. At any rate 'Parley-voo' serves both as a warning against trying to 'explain' poems in terms of their sources and as a useful corrective to those who wish to think of the British trenches as populated solely by idealistic young poets who were half in love with each other.[14]

Prose writers also needed models. If there was less difficulty, *pace* Blunden, about tone and phrasing than with poetry (prose being closer to everyday discourse) there was more difficulty with regard to structure and organization, since a novel or a book-length memoir would have to contain far more words than a poem: as Somerset Maugham explained in the Preface to his collection of short stories based on his First World War career as a British secret service agent,

Fact is a poor story-teller. It starts a story at haphazard, generally long before the beginning, rambles on inconsequently and tails off, leaving loose ends hanging about, without a conclusion. It works up to an interesting situation, and then leaves it in the air to follow an issue that has nothing to do with the point; it has no sense of climax and whittles away its dramatic effects in irrelevance. There is a school of novelists that looks upon this as the proper model for fiction. If life, they say, is arbitrary and disconnected, why, fiction should be so too; for fiction should imitate life. In life things happen at random, and that is how they should happen in a story; they do not lead to a climax, which is an outrage to probability, they just go on. Nothing offends these people more than the punch or the unexpected twist with which some writers seek to surprise their readers, and when the circumstances they relate seem to tend towards a dramatic

[14] John Brophy and Eric Partridge, *Songs and Slang of the British Soldier, 1914–1918* (1930), p. 49, establishes the link between 'Parley-voo' and 'Der Wirthin Töchterlein'.

effect they do their best to avoid it. They do not give you a story, they give you the material on which you can invent your own.[15]

One model was *War and Peace*. Wilfrid Ewart's debt to Tolstoy was acknowledged by his biographer:

> The next idea was to give to England a book which might be the equivalent of Tolstoy's *War and Peace*. He read the whole of *War and Peace* with that in mind. His greatest difficulty was naturally the technical one of novel-writing. He had the experience, he had the gift of writing, but he had no known equipment for telling a story.

The result was *Way of Revelation*, which enjoyed considerable success when it was published in 1921. The *Times Literary Supplement* wrote:

> The central figures of the drama – Adrian Knoyle and Eric Sinclair – stand on the threshold of adventure. Adrian has become engaged, unofficially, to Lady Rosemary Meynall, while his friend maintains a desultory court-ship of Faith Daventry. Then comes the war, and the remainder of the book is devoted to a study of the reactions of this set of characters to the new conditions.
> It is of course, the obvious way in which to treat the war. The same thing has been done a great many times already, occasionally with suc-cess. *Way of Revelation* conforms to the pattern. There is no story. Pictures of warfare and trench routine alternate with pictures of London society. Most of the women fill a portion of their spare time with nursing and charity entertainments. Some of the men obtain soft jobs at the Admiralty. The majority of them go to France, where some are killed and whence others return maimed . . . In the treatment of an obvious theme he has made use of the obvious characters, the obvious situations, the obvious emotions, and yet, because of his sincerity, because of his faith in his vi-sion of life, he has reached, through the obvious, to the universal.[16]

Rather less obvious (and perhaps less universal) was Ford Madox Ford's *Parade's End* tetralogy (1924–28) in which Tolstoy's Pierre Bezukhov becomes anglicized (though with a Dutch surname) as a captain in the Glamorganshires. Gilbert Frankau's *Peter Jackson: Cigar Merchant*

---

[15] W. Somerset Maugham, *Ashenden* (1928), Preface.

[16] Stephen Graham, *Life and Last Words of Wilfrid Ewart* (1924), p. 134; *Times Liter-ary Supplement*, 24 November 1921, p. 769a; ibid., 5 February 1920, p. 85a-b.

and Richard Aldington's *Death of a Hero* may be seen as variations on the *War and Peace* model too (though the critic F.R. Leavis also noted in *Death of a Hero* 'tributes to Samuel Butler and Mr Aldous Huxley' and the occasional 'patch of H.G. Wells [and] of D.H. Lawrence'), but not inappropriately the war novel most reminiscent of Tolstoy was written by a Russian. Peter Nikolayevich Krasnov, a colonel in the Tsar's cavalry at the outbreak of war, and to all appearances twin brother to one of the minor characters in *Anna Karenina*, had risen by 1917 to the command of the Third Cavalry Corps stationed near Petrograd. After an unsuccessful bid to eject the newly-installed Soviet regime he fled south, was elected Ataman of the Don Cossacks with German support, and after the Civil War took refuge in Germany. His *Ot Dvuglavago Orla k Krasnomy Znamyeni, 1894–1921* was published in Berlin in, it seems, 1922. The 1552-page English version, *From the Two-Headed Eagle to the Red Flag, 1894–1921*, was published in Berlin in 1923, and an abridgement of the English text appeared in 1928. The earnestness of Krasnov's attempts to follow his great predecessor are evident throughout his book, as is his inability to sustain the effort. Only about a third of the novel deals with the First World War as such: *From the Two-Headed Eagle to the Red Flag* covers nearly four times the time-span of *War and Peace*. Krasnov also managed to live almost as long as Tolstoy and to die harder. In 1943 he undertook to raise and lead a Cossack army to help overthrow the Soviet government. After the defeat of Hitler he was tried by a Red Army tribunal, being then in his seventy-eighth year, and subsequently hanged. It does not seem that his authorship of *From the Two-Headed Eagle to the Red Flag* was an item in his indictment: perhaps the Soviet prosecutors had not been able to find a copy.[17]

Though Gilbert Frankau's *Peter Jackson: Cigar Merchant* was praised by the *Times Literary Supplement* as 'a novel of the old type . . . it has "a beginning, a middle, and an end"', some writers felt that a story-line was not everything. This after all was the era of James Joyce, of whom Henry Williamson (of *Tarka the Otter* fame) was briefly a disciple:

> Chaps going on forward. He was on his feet in the sissing criss-cross and stinking of smoking earth gaping – hullo, hullo, new shell-holes, this must

[17] *Cambridge Review*, 51, p. 61 (25 October 1929), review by F.R. Leavis; *Great Soviet Encyclopedia* (32 vols, New York, 1973–1983), xiii, p. 483.

be near the first objective. They had come three hundred yards already! Cushy! Nothing in going over the top! Then his heart instead of finishing its beat and pausing to beat again swelled out its beat into an ear-bursting agony and great lurid light that leapt out of his broken-apart body with a spinning shriek and the earth was in his eyes and up his nostrils and going away smaller and smaller into blackness

and tiny far away

Rough and smooth. Rough was wide and large and tilting with sickness. He struggled and struggled to clutch smooth, and it slid away. Rough came back and washed harshly over him. He cried out between the receding of rough and the coming of smooth white, then rough and . . . [18]

Another experimental work was Edlef Köppen's *Heeresbericht* (1929 – an English translation was published under the title *Higher Command*), which interwove a fictional account of the experiences of a young artillerist with official communiqués, official letters, speeches, excerpts from newspapers and encyclopedias and apparently genuine (in fact fictional) extracts from private letters and diaries. In general however the prose writers of the war generation were little more interested in experimentation than the poets. It was almost as if they felt their material was too serious, too important, for fancy footwork. Apart from *War and Peace*, it seems to have been Barbusse's *Le feu* which had the largest influence on later writers.

Before the war Henri Barbusse had been a writer in the French naturalist tradition. One of his earlier novels, *L'enfer*, recently filmed by Claude Chabrol, is a study in depressingness and obsession which may, if one wishes, be taken as demonstrating that his naturalism had advanced significant stages beyond that of Flaubert or Zola. Contrary to what is sometimes claimed, Barbusse served several months as a rifleman in the trenches before being assigned to a first aid post. *Le feu: journal d'une escouade* was published in France in 1916 and in Britain, in Fitzwalter Wray's translation, with the title *Under Fire: The Story of a Squad*, during the following year. Its harrowing evocation of the meaningless sufferings of the frontline troops had the advantage of priority (though in fact conditions had become even worse since the period Barbusse described), but other

---

[18] The passage quoted is from Henry Williamson, *The Patriot's Progress* (1930), pp. 169–71.

writers, and painters like Georges Leroux, were already squaring
up to the problem of showing the same thing. Barbusse's master-
stroke was to seize on the small group and the interaction of its
members as an expository model.[19]

Mulvaney, Ortheris and Learoyd in Kipling's *Soldiers Three* (1888)
are merely a little clique within a unit stationed on Britain's imperial frontier. They are cross-sectional only in the same sense that
the Scots officer, the Irish officer and the Welsh officer in
Shakespeare's *Henry V* are cross-sectional, and their sufferings together
are much less in evidence than their united torturing of the English
language. In *Le feu* the group is larger and it is experiencing the
horrors of war as a complex entity. Siegfried Sassoon wrote 'for an
infantry subaltern the huge unhappy mechanism of the Western Front
always narrowed down to the company he was in'. For the private
soldier or lance-corporal it was not even the hundred or so men of
the company that provided the group one belonged to, it was one's
platoon or even section:

> trench life is very domestic, highly atomic. Its atom, or unit, like that of
> slum life, is the jealously close, exclusive, contriving life of a family housed
> in an urban cellar. During the years of trench war a man seldom saw the
> whole of his company at a time. Our total host might be two millions strong,
> or ten millions; whatever its size a man's world was that of his section – at
> most, his platoon; all that mattered much to him was the one little boatload
> of castaways with whom he was marooned on a desert island and making
> shift to keep off the weather and any sudden attack of wild beasts. Absorbed
> in the primitive job of keeping alive on earth naked except in the matter
> of food, they became, like other primitive men, family separatists.

After the war a few novels such as Josef Magnus Wehner's *Sieben vor
Verdun* ('Seven before Verdun') dealt with the experiences of a number
of soldiers who were in different units, but this approach was
exceptional. First World War novels which were not fictionalized
memoirs of individuals were most commonly novels about *groups*.
Roland Dorgelès's *Les croix de bois* (1919; published in English as *Wooden*

[19] For Barbusse's war service, see *Lettres de Henri Barbusse à sa femme, 1914–1917*,
p. 22, 26 December 1914, and p. 148, 20 June 1915; Jean Vic, *La littérature de la guerre*,
iii, p. 257.

Crosses in 1920) was second only to *Le feu* as the best-known French novel of the war and followed Barbusse's format. Philip MacDonald's *Patrol* (1927), describing a cavalry patrol in Mesopotamia which becomes lost and is picked off one by one by hostile Arabs, Liam O'Flaherty's *Return of the Brute* (1929), in which a member of another patrol adds to the normal attrition of war by killing one of his comrades with a grenade and throttling the corporal before allowing himself to be mown down by a German machine-gun, and Frederic Manning's *Her Privates We* (1931), which focuses on three friends in a section in a company in an unnamed battalion, are perhaps the most notable British instances of the same approach. (J.B. Priestley, who did not write a war novel, used the same formula in his best-selling *The Good Companions*, in which a Yorkshire mill-worker, a colonel's daughter from Gloucestershire and a Cambridge-educated prep school master form a concert group to tour England in the depths of the depression.) American examples on the same model are James B. Wharton's *Squad* (1928) and William March's *Company K* (1930).[20]

The Germans showed a particular fondness for novels about groups of protagonists welded together by their shared experiences in the trenches. An early example was Fritz von Unruh's *Opfergang* ('Way of Sacrifice'), written at about the same time as *Le feu* but not published till 1919. Erich Maria Remarque's *Im Westen Nichts Neues*, published in book form in 1929, focuses on the experiences of four youths who had been in the same class in Gymnasium and had joined the army together as volunteers, and their trench-comrades Tjaden the locksmith, Haie Westhus the peat-digger, Detering the peasant, and Stanislaus Katczinsky the cobbler. The year 1929 also saw Karl Bröger's *Bunker 17: Geschichte einer Kameradschaft* (translated 1930 as *Pill Box 17: The Story of a Comradeship-in-Arms*); *M.G.K.* – i.e. 'Machine-Gun Company' – by Franz Seldte, who lost an arm in the war, became leader of the right-wing veterans' organization 'Stahlhelm', and, though never in Hitler's inner circle, minister of labour in the Nazi government, 1933–45; Ernst Johannsen's *Vier von der Infanterie* (published in English 1930 as *Four Infantrymen on the Western Front, 1918*), in which it was explained 'These four men –

[20] Siegfried Sassoon, *Memoirs of a Fox-Hunting Man* (1942 edn), p. 224; C.E. Montague, *Disenchantment* (1922), p. 35.

Job, Lornsen, Müller and the student – form a tiny comradeship within the greater one that takes in the whole front' – this was the book which was the basis for G.W. Pabst's unforgettable movie *Westfront 1918*, and Alfred Hein's *Ein Kompagnie Soldaten: In der Hölle von Verdun*, which, though largely from the point of view of Lindolf, the company runner, ends:

> Once more the company went forward in the winter night through the desolation of the front, their hearts illumined and purified by the still steady flame of human comradeship.

In 1930 appeared Werner Beumelburg's *Die Gruppe Bosemüller* ('Bosemüller's Squad') which, though only moderately successful in the last years of the Weimar Republic, became a million-seller after the Nazis came to power and banned Remarque's *Im Westen Nichts Neues* because of its negative attitude to war. The experiences of a squad were also described in Ernst Weichert's *Jedermann* of 1931, though with particular emphasis on the inner core of four soldiers: their representative status was of course sign-posted by the title, which means 'Everyman'.[21]

The group provided not merely a narrative device but a kind of symbol. Roland Dorgelès, for example, was fully aware of how the small group could serve to represent a whole army's whole experience of the war:

> I learnt to suffer, to bear witness in the name of those who have suffered so much . . . Not for an instant did I think of keeping a diary of my regiment. I had a higher ambition – not to tell the story of *my* war but of *the* war. Throw out the dates, delete the names of the actors, forget the unit numbers, and draw from myself would-be memories so replete with truth that each ex-soldier would cry out, 'They're mine too'.

Symbolic representations of a more elaborate kind were rare. In Remarque's *Im Westen Nichts Neues* the narrator becomes lost during a patrol, blunders into a French soldier in the dark, stabs him

---

[21] Ernst Johannsen *Four Infantrymen on the Western Front* (1930), p. 11. Later contributions to the 'group-experience' war novel were Hubert E. Gilbert's *Drei Krieger* (1934) and Erich Hoinkis's *Er und seine Kompanie* (1936).

with 'my little dagger' and when daylight comes finds that his victim, a 'man with a small pointed beard', is still alive. Frantically, Remarque's narrator puts on field dressings, but by the middle of the afternoon the Frenchman is dead. It is too dangerous to leave the cover of the shell hole. 'Soon the silence is more unbearable than the groans. I wish the gurgling were there again, gasping, hoarse, now whistling softly and again hoarse and loud.' He begins to talk to the corpse. He takes out the Frenchman's wallet. 'It slips out of my hand and falls open. Some pictures and letters drop out.' He copies out the dead man's address. 'I have killed the printer, Gerard Duval. I must be a printer, I think confusedly, be a printer, printer . . .' A shell hole also features in Vernon Bartlett's *No Man's Land* (1930), about a wounded soldier left to die in one, and in Hans Fallada's *Die Eiserne Gustav* (1938; translated as *Iron Gustav*, 1940), in which the protagonist Otto Hackendahl and a lieutenant from another unit engage in a pivotal dialogue while stranded together in a shell crater between the two front lines. The only First World War novelist who attempted to go much further than this was another German, Arnold Zweig, in *Der Streit um den Sergeanten Grischa* (1928; English translation published in the same year under the title *The Case of Sergeant Grischa*) and *Erziehung vor Verdun* (published in exile, in Amsterdam, in 1935, and in English as *Education Before Verdun*, in 1936). In *Der Streit um den Sergeanten Grischa* an escaped Russian prisoner of war is sentenced to death as a result of a mix-up and is eventually executed out of expediency. In *Erziehung vor Verdun* a young NCO objects to the other NCOs setting up their own kitchen and hogging the beer and the best food, and writes about it to an uncle, who is a senior officer. His letter is intercepted by the postal censors, who order that the young NCO should be court-martialled, but the trial is postponed, and the NCO is sent to a position of danger where he is conveniently killed. The novel functions quite well as a panoramic depiction of the Battle of Verdun, but the *cause célèbre* which is supposed to provide the essential narrative thread seems forced and scarcely capable of bearing the weight Zweig evidently wished to give it. The issue of German NCOs monopolizing the best sausages does not seem so very important in the context of the German army having violated Belgian neutrality, overrun almost the entire country, and laid waste half a dozen French *départements*: it is also disconcertingly reminiscent of the picture conjured up by Charles Carrington's remark, half a dozen years earlier, 'No corrupt sergeant-majors stole my rations or accepted my bribes . . . No casual staff officers ordered me to certain death, indifferent to my fate'.[22]

Zweig's own war experience perhaps explains both the symbolic ambitions and the failure of his novels. After thirteen months on the Verdun front, he was assigned to a department of the HQ on the Eastern Front responsible for producing German-language publications for circulation in the occupied areas of the Russian Empire. Zweig, himself Jewish, found himself amongst a group of Jewish intellectuals, with access to censored books (including Barbusse's *Le feu*). One imagines that Zweig and his colleagues looked increasingly askance at the activities of the General Staff officers – not all Prussians, of course, but all members of aristocratic, army-orientated families – whose policies they were employed to dress up in palatable form for public consumption. The Sergeant Grischa story-line seems to have been based on a real incident; at any rate the unsuccessful moral stands at the centre of the two novels tends to suggest that during his stint at HQ it had at least crossed Zweig's mind to take up similarly high-minded positions of principle. Even if this had not occurred to him at the time, the propaganda aspect of his work would have given him good reason to reflect on the moral ambiguities that arise in wartime.[23]

Curiously enough, the best-known of all novels by a frontline veteran in which a much-put-upon individual is raised to symbolic status as the representative of his class, race, age group or whatever, actually had its genesis before the war. Jaroslav Hasek's classic piss-take *Osudy Dobrého Vojáka Švejka za Světové Války* ('The Adventure of Good Soldier Svejk in the Great War', 1921–23, translated 1930 as *The Good Soldier Schweik*) is almost identical in tone to five stories Hašek wrote in 1911 about the idiotic Švejk's peacetime military service. Evidently for Hašek, as for Klee and Marinetti, the war was

[22] Roland Dorgelès, *Souvenirs sur les croix de bois* (Paris 1929), pp. 25, 33–34; Erich Maria Remarque, *All Quiet on the Western Front* (1930), pp. 235, 238–39, 242, 245, 247; Charles Carrington ('Charles Edmonds') *A Subaltern's War* (1929), p. 17.

[23] Manuel Wiznitzer, *Arnold Zweig: das Leben eines Deutsch-Jüdischen Schriftstellers* (Königstein, 1983), pp. 24–25.

less of a surprise than it was for some other people: Clausewitz's famous dictum, that war is merely the continuation of politics with the admixture of other means is sometimes as applicable to literary studies as it is to military history.[24]

---

[24] Jaroslav Hašek, *The Red Commissar* (1981), p. 192, 'Introduction' by Sir Cecil Parrott to the section comprising the five pre-war Šveik stories.

CHAPTER 8

Heroes

THE LAST four chapters have dealt with how writers and artists rose to the challenge of describing what they had experienced in the front line but there were other ways of responding creatively to the war besides writing and painting. The coincidences of opportunity and chronology, and what Wilfred Owen called 'Chance's strange arithmetic' in the front line, operated not just for those who recorded the war for posterity but for their whole generation.[1]

In Ernest Raymond's *Tell England* the colonel says to the two teen-age heroes:

'Eighteen, confound it! It's a virtue to be your age, just as it's a crime to be mine . . . Eighteen years ago you were born for this day. Through the last eighteen years you've been educated for it. Your birth and breeding were given you that you might officer England's youth in this hour. And now you enter upon your inheritance. Just as this is *the* day in the history of the world so yours is *the* generation. No other generation has been called to such grand things, and to such crowded, glorious living . . .'

Of course no one timed things that deliberately. Before August 1914 most of the men who fought in the First World War had had lives which they didn't think they were finished with, and many of them were still young enough to revert occasionally to childhood behaviour patterns. Here is one officer's diary account of a moment of relaxation:

Lying here on the soft grass we ate our lunch, basking in the hot rays of the sun and finding life sweet. Then smoking and talking we made brooches

[1] Wilfred Owen, 'Insensibility', stanza 2.

and bows out of sedgegrass and tiny flowers. In order not to desecrate the happy little ruin we buried our sandwich paper and replaced the turf (though there were dozens of empty tins lying round). Then we threw our empty bottles into the stream and raced beside them, each cheering his own craft – TT versus Toper – until after about half a mile they were caught in the weeds and we lay down and panted on the bank.

Strolling quietly back in silence, we found a dead pigeon and buried him, railing in his grave with little sticks and chains of plaited sedgegrass, and in his coverlet of pimpernels we erected a tiny white cross.

Then we went out on to the hot white road where our troops lay under the hedge . . .

Albert Ball, VC, DSO and two bars, MC, one of the great heroes of the war, seems to have regressed under the pressure of combat to the behaviour and language of an eight-year-old newly installed at his first boarding school: 'Oh, I am so poo-poo, for I do so want a rest', he wrote home; and on another occasion complained 'really things are desperate just now, and my mind is full of poo-poo thoughts'. In July 1916 he wrote 'I am having a very poo time, but most interesting. On the 6th three topping chaps went off and never returned. Yesterday four of my best pals went off'. In fact he did not have any pals. Except at meals he avoided the other officers (who were all bigger than him and no doubt inclined to be a little rowdy in their horseplay), and lived in a hut beside his aeroplane 'in solitary state with his violin and little garden – so much so that we called him the "Lonely Testicle, or Pill"'.[2]

It is remarkable how many of the outstanding writers of the war had had personal problems before August 1914. Ivor Gurney had shown symptoms of what may have been the psychiatric disorder which hospitalized him for the last part of his life. Rupert Brooke's unresolved bisexuality had brought him to the verge of a break-down. Wilfred Owen was homosexual, with the classic homosexual thing about his mother ('Love is not quenched, except the unenduring flickerings thereof. By your love, O Mother, O Home, I am protected from Fatigue

---

[2] Ernest Raymond, *Tell England* (1953 edn), pp. 168 – first published 1920; Edwin Campion Vaughan, *Some Desperate Glory: The Diary of a Young Officer, 1917* (1981), p. 107, 1 May 1916; Chaz Bowyer, *Albert Ball VC* (1977), pp. 50, 54–55, 63, 83, quoting his letters home and the reminiscences of Air Vice-Marshal Stanley Vincent. 'Pill' is early twentieth-century slang for 'bore'.

of life and the keen spiritual Cold', he wrote to his 'own dear Mother' on 7 January 1917). Robert Graves was in love with a boy in a lower form at Charterhouse when he joined up. Sassoon, repressing his sexuality – also male-orientated – led a schizoid life before the war pretending simultaneously to be a man of letters and a fox-hunting squire, and covered this up not unsuccessfully in *Memoirs of a Fox-Hunting Man* and *Memoirs of an Infantry Officer* by presenting his narrator as a callow youth from a modest county family, rather than a twenty-eight year-old scion of a dynasty of wealthy Indian Jews. In 1921 he recalled his 'pre-war isolation from the people who can interest me', and the life he had lived amongst 'people who are definitely antipathetic to my career as an artist'. T.E. Lawrence also had a problem with his sexuality as he hinted, perhaps inadvertently, in *Seven Pillars of Wisdom*:

> The men were young and sturdy; and hot flesh and blood unconsciously claimed a right in them and tormented their bellies with strange longings. Our privations and dangers fanned this virile heat, in a climate as racking as can be conceived. We had no shut places to be alone in, no thick clothes to hide our nature. Man in all things lived candidly with man.
>
> The Arab was by nature continent; and the use of universal marriage had nearly abolished irregular courses in his tribes. The public women of the rare settlements we encountered in our months of wandering would have been nothing to our numbers, even had their raddled meat been palatable to a man of healthy parts. In horror of such sordid commerce our youths began indifferently to slake one another's few needs in their own clean bodies – a cold convenience that, by comparison, seemed sexless and even pure. Later, some began to justify this sterile process, and swore that friends quivering together in the yielding sand with intimate hot limbs in supreme embrace, found there hidden in the darkness a sensual co-efficient of the mental passion which was welding our souls and spirits in one flaming effort. Several, thirsting to punish appetites they could not wholly prevent, took a savage pride in degrading the body, and offered themselves fiercely in any habit which promised physical pain or filth.

Ernest Raymond was less fussed by such issues, not even recognizing the connection between his older-brotherly interest in young officers and his sexual instincts till he re-read *Tell England* much later:

> Another thing that is a cause of wonder to me as I re-read the book is the indubitable but wholly unconscious homosexuality in it. The earlier

part was written when I was eighteen or nineteen; the latter part in my
twenties, and in those far-off days 'homosexuality' was a word which –
absurd as this may seem now – I had never heard. It was not then the
daily topic in newspapers and converse that it is today . . . I did not know
that homosexuality could exist in embryo without even knowing itself for
what it was, or desiring the least physical satisfaction, till the time came
for it to die and be transcended by full and normal manhood. Its pres-
ence in the book is one more evidence of its author's unusually slow progress
towards maturity. A fellow clubman, a witty Irishman, who, though fifty
or sixty now, persists in loving *Tell England* always delights me when he
says, as he has more than once, 'I have just read that damned book again,
and as usual I've been surprised that your Radley [the hero schoolmaster
in the first part] does not reappear in the Gallipoli chapters, but then, of
course, I suddenly remember that he'd have been doing his five years in
jug'.[3]

Not everybody was gay in the British army of course. Henry Lamont,
alias Wilfred Saint-Mandé, had probably begun his career as a fantasist,
if not his second career as a lady-killer, even before war broke out.
Richard Aldington had already given himself up to the loathing of
parents and the love of manipulative women which he was to write
about so eloquently in *Death of a Hero*, in which George Winterbourne's
wife is modelled on Hilda Doolittle, whom Aldington had married in
1913, and George Winterbourne's useless father – 'an inadequate
sentimentalist [who] messed up his children's lives by being weak and
sentimentalist with them and by losing his money' – is a portrait of
Albert E. Aldington, who in 1912 lost so much money in unlucky business speculation that poor Richard's university studies had to be
curtailed and in 1915, though an official in the Ministry of Muni-
tions, had insufficient pull to wangle Richard a commission, even
though the latter had seen from the very beginning of the war that it

---

[3] John Bell, ed., *Wilfred Owen: Selected Letters* (Oxford, 1985), p. 210, Owen to Susan
Owen, 7 January 1917; Rupert Hart-Davis, *Siegfried Sassoon: Diaries, 1920–1922* (1981),
p. 30, 10 January 1921; T.E. Lawrence, *Seven Pillars of Wisdom: A Triumph* (1976,
paperback edn), pp. 8–9 – first printed for private circulation 1926; Ernest Raymond,
The Story of My Days: An Autobiography, 1888–1922 (1968), pp. 180–81: the witty
Irishman's tasteless joke refers of course to the fact that male homosexual practices
were illegal till 1967, though two rather than five years was the normal gaol sentence.
   See also Adrian Caesar, *Taking It Like a Man: Suffering and Sexuality and the War
Poets Brooke, Sassoon, Owen, Graves* (Manchester, 1993), p. 225.

was 'going to be the biggest thing in history'. Mrs Winterbourne in *Death of a Hero* is May Aldington, though her son doesn't mention her status as the best-selling author of books such as *Love Letters that Caused a Divorce* and only in later life recorded his opinion of them as 'hideously vulgar and illiterate'. Parental problems may also have been behind eighteen-year-old Ernst Jünger's running away to join the French Foreign Legion in November 1913: bearing in mind that his father had formerly worked in a university laboratory, it is interesting to note that the official entry in his Foreign Legion pay book was 'can neither read nor write'.[4]

So many of the best books about the First World War were written by misfits – people who were misfits before the war and remained misfits after it – that one tends to forget what a wonderfully successful time it was for some people: and not just armaments manufacturers. The war produced no heaven-born generals, except perhaps Nikolai Nikolayevich Yudenich in the Caucasus and Paul von Lettow-Vorbeck in East Africa – his most recent biographer describes the latter as 'the most successful guerilla leader in world history' – but it provided several young men with a connecting link between outstanding school careers and success in later life: men such as H.W. Yoxall, school captain at St Paul's, MC and bar during the war, later managing director of Condé Nast, and T.F. Tallents, head of school at Harrow, MC and bar, twice wounded in action, promoted major in the Guards Machine Gun Regiment at the age of twenty-three, later chairman and managing director of the New Zealand and Federal Shipping Company.[5]

Other men were unable to settle after the fighting ended, and at moments of stress might burst out with exclamations of incredulity at the post-war existences they had slipped into, like the preparatory

---

[4] Charles Doyle, *Richard Aldington: A Biography* (Basingstoke, 1989), pp. 1, 3, 9–11, 53, and Verna Coleman, *The Last Exquisite: A Portrait of Frederic Manning* (Melbourne, 1990), p. 118, quoting Aldington to Harriet Monroe, 7 August 1914; Hans Peter Des Coudres and Horst Muhleisen, *Bibliographie der Werke Ernst Jüngers* (Stuttgart, 1985), p. 197.

[5] For Yudenich, see Holger M. Herwig and Neil M. Heyman, *Biographical Dictionary of World War I* (Westport, 1982), pp. 362–63; for Lettow-Vorbeck, see his *My Reminiscences of East Africa* [1920], and Edwin P. Hoyt, *Guerilla: Colonel von Lettow-Vorbeck and Germany's East African Empire* (New York, 1981), especially p. 206; Ivo Elliott, *The Balliol College Register: Third Edition, 1900–1950* (Oxford, 1953), pp. 203, 205.

school master recalled by Robin Maugham who would shout at unsatisfactory boys, '*Do* you think I fought in the trenches of Flanders – *do* you think I waded through gore and mud in order to sit in a classroom teaching Latin to a little idiot like you . . .?' Even Siegfried Sassoon, rereading his diary for June 1916 five years later, noted 'I wish I could "find a moral equivalent for war" . . . I feel as if I were only half-alive'. The fictional Captain Hugh Drummond, DSO, MC, 'late of His Majesty's Royal Loamshires' placed an advert in the newspaper: 'Demobilised officer, finding peace incredibly tedious, would welcome diversion. Legitimate, if possible; but crime, if of a comparatively humorous description, no objection. Excitement essential'. Drummond's real-life counterparts joined organizations such as the *Freikorps* in Germany, or the Blackshirts in Italy, or the Auxiliary Division of the Royal Irish Constabulary. Tim Birkin found a substitute for the war in driving racing cars:

> I was in the Air Force, and when Armistice came, found the view of my future life, as I then beheld it, a very dull and confined one . . . I was lucky enough to have the money to look round for an occupation, and not accept the first that offered; and of all that I considered, motor racing provided the energy, adventures, and risks most like those of the battlefield. It had, moreover, the promise of a great future, and there was the same chance of unexpected disaster, the same need for perfect nerves, with a presence of mind that must never desert you, the same exhilaration of living in the shadow of death that often came so suddenly and gloriously, that it seemed to have no shadow. There was, besides, the peculiar delight of being responsible for your own calamities, since, once off the mark, you were at liberty to take risks or avoid them as you pleased, a state of independence few individuals enjoyed in the war.[6]

Other men had discovered a talent for homicide that could find no application in civilian life after 1918: men like Lance-Corporal Henry Norwest of the Canadian Expeditionary Force who obtained 115 observed 'kills' as a sniper on the Western Front; or Sergeant Alvin

[6] Robin Maugham, *Escape from the Shadows* (1972), p. 39; Hart-Davis, ed., *Siegfried Sassoon: Diaries, 1920–1922*, pp. 73, 30 June 1921; [Cyril McNeile], *Bull-Dog Drummond* [1920], p. 25, and cf. p. 24; A.D. Harvey, 'Who Were the Auxiliaries?', *Historical Journal*, 35 (1992), pp. 655–59; Sir Henry Birkin, *Full Throttle* [1932], pp. 25–26.

York of the American Expeditionary Force who won the Congressional Medal of Honour for killing twenty-eight Germans and capturing another 132, with thirty-five machine-guns, at the Argonne on 8 October 1918; or Rittmeister Manfred Freiherr von Richthofen, who with eighty victories in aerial combat was the leading fighter pilot of the war and, of the millions of combatants, probably the only one who will still be a household name in the twenty-first century. The First World War sponsored new techniques, new aesthetics in other areas besides literature and painting:

> Behind nearly every traverse we come on a dead body with the blood coming from numerous wounds caused by thin sharp splinters from hand grenades. It is a brief glance only, for our eyes are more in the air than on the ground. It is not a hard death: the force of the explosion takes life and consciousness away at once. It is a strange feeling to leap forward over these dead whom you have never seen alive. The satisfaction is a purely practical one, as though you saw before your eyes the expected result of an intelligent calculation and gave it a final assent. If it were oneself that was hit in such a moment, as I have been more than once, one would feel no more than the wonder of being so suddenly and incomprehensibly arrested, while the whole being was so bent on victorious activity that nothing else had any reality whatever.

Thus Ernst Jünger: and it seems that what was unusual about Jünger was less his self-immersion in combat than the way he wrote about it afterwards.[7]

It was one of the paradoxes of industrialization that, in making it possible to bring unprecedented numbers of soldiers to the battlefield, and by providing the technical means to fight battles in an unprecedentedly complicated and investment-intensive way, it also provided scope for new types of individual skill. In 1930 Ernst Jünger

---

[7] For Norwest, see *Canada in the Great War: An Authentic Account of the Military History of Canada from the Earliest Days to the Close of the War of Nations* (6 vols, Toronto, 1917–21), iii, p. 312–13: like the other leading snipers of the Canadian Expeditionary Force, Ballendine (fifty 'kills'), Philip McDonald (forty) and Riel (thirty-eight), Norwest was a Native American; Ernst Jünger *Copse 125: A Chronicle from the Trench Warfare of 1918* (1930), translation of *Das Wäldchen 125: eine Chronik aus dem Grabenkämpfen 1918* (Berlin, 1926), p. 253.

edited a book entitled *Krieg und Krieger* ('War and Warriors') which contained a 'Schöpferische Kritik des Krieges', a creative critique of the war, which argued:

> War and the forms of war are a part of general cultural history. It is impossible to consider them outside their time and the spiritual currents of their time. Purely practical grounds have never produced wars or determined the nature and form of weapons, as the materialists used to believe; it is rather that in every period universal, not easily explicable, yet dominant spiritual forms, ideological entities exist, to which the style and forms of war conform. A history of style in war ought to be written: the form of combat and tactics, armaments and uniforms are just as revealing for the character of races and the spiritual content of different epochs as the corresponding sections of Art History: the changing history of the spirit of struggling humanity is at least as evident in their symbolism, sometimes more so.

One may query the notion of 'dominant spiritual forms' (*'beherrschende Geistesformen'*) in this context but, for example, it was not only the means by which Norwest and Richthofen disposed of their victims that was characteristic of industrial era warfare, but also the number of their victims, and even the fact of their enumeration.[8]

It took over 2000 years of so-called civilization, in which wars were fought by literate and numerate combatants, for it to become established practice for the more successful practitioners to keep a running score of the enemies they had personally offed. In Roman times, as we now know from graffiti on the walls at Pompeii, the more successful gladiators fought and won more than fifty separate contests: 'Severus, freedman, fifty-five fights, has just won again'; 'Auctus of the Julian troop has won fifty times'; but these were sporting achievements, of interest only to people who frequented the amphitheatres and the betting booths, and the death of the losers, which was not automatic, was incidental and often subsequent to the applause. In the wars which the Romans fought, battles were too confused and crowded for anyone to think of keeping a score: it was in the nature

---

[8] Wilhelm von Schramm, 'Schöpferische Kritik des Krieges', in Ernst Jünger, ed., *Krieg und Krieger* (Berlin, 1930), pp. 33–49, at p. 33.

of hand-to-hand (or spear-to-spear) combat by men fighting in close ranks that when an adversary recoiled under a blow, another one pushed forward. Some non-European cultures attempted to provide statistics for individual mayhem. In the Gempei War in twelfth-century Japan, the warrior monk Tsutsui Janyo Meishu distinguished himself defending a bridge across the River Uji, allegedly killing twelve enemy samurai and wounding eleven others with twenty (sic) arrows, cutting down five more with his *naginata* (pole-handled sword) and, when the blade of his *naginata* broke, felling eight others with his ordinary sword, before withdrawing with sixty-three arrows sticking in his armour, only five of which arrows had penetrated – which rather contradicts the account given both in this and other contemporary narratives of skewering two armoured men with the same arrow: but one can believe the bit about the *naginata* breaking. In Europe the appeal of knowing how many people one has personally butchered seems not to have occurred to the best-documented heroes of *arme blanche* warfare. William the Marshal (1146–1219) fought innumerable tournaments in the 1170s and 1180s but wasn't even interested in the injuries he caused, for the whole object of his fighting was to acquire his opponents' valuable equipment. On his death bed he was reported to have claimed

> j'ai pris .v. cents chevaliers
> Dont j'ai & armes & destriers
> Et tot lor herneis retenu

(I have taken 500 knights whose arms and horses and all their armour I kept). In the course of more than fifteen years of jousting it is more than likely that a couple of score men received fatal injuries as a result of losing a bout with William but that was not the aspect he chose to remember. Robert the Bruce (1274–1329), King of Scotland, was probably the most successful soldier of his day, but he is specifically recorded as having slain only two men: John Comyn, stabbed treacherously in the Franciscan church at Dumfries (and even then it required a second dagger-thrust from Roger Kirkpatrick to finish him off); and Humphrey de Bohun, with an axe-blow to the head, in a preliminary skirmish just before the Battle of Bannockburn. Much later, during the French Wars of 1793–1815, Robert Rollo Gillespie, 'the bravest man that ever wore a red coat', carried out innumerable feats of heroism and was wounded countless times but the only men whom he is known for certain to have killed were the opposing principal in a duel in which he was a second – he was put on trial for this piece of bad sportsmanship but acquitted – and six West Indians who broke into his quarters with cutlasses and pistols one night when he was adjutant general at St Domingo in 1796. Neither incident suggests that when he led his troops into action he stood and watched them do all the work.[9]

The actual collection of trophies that demonstrated that one has killed an enemy is – or used to be – characteristic of certain illiterate societies, notably the Sepik in New Guinea, the Dayaks in Borneo, the Jívaros and Mundurucù in Brazil. Amongst the Dayaks, a man could not marry, or wear a machete, unless he had been on a head-hunting expedition, and heads were also needed for important funerals and naming ceremonies. But the preparations for head-hunting expeditions took two or three months, so they cannot have been very frequent. Among the Jívaro head-taking raids were organized by a *kakaram*, a 'powerful one', who had killed 'at least three or four persons', and most neighbourhoods had a couple of such heroes. After leading several head-taking raids a *kakaram* would become a *ti-kakaram*, a 'very powerful one' but by this stage he would already be quite elderly. It is doubtful whether any individual Dayak or Jívaro ever killed as many as a dozen enemies, for both societies consisted of very small, demographically insecure populations. Even the Maoris, at their peak, numbered fewer than 60,000. Individuals with the desire and ability to kill twenty enemies in a day would not have fitted in.[10]

The blood-letting in European duels also seems to have been exaggerated. In March 1803 Captain J. of the British army and Lieutenant W. of the Royal Navy killed each other in a duel but, though the

[9] Jack Lindsay, *The Writing on the Wall: An Account of Pompeii in its Last Days* (1960), p. 63; Stephen R. Turnbull, *The Book of the Samurai: The Warrior Class of Japan* (1982), pp. 31–33; Paul Meyer, ed., *L'histoire de Guillaume le Maréchal . . . poème français* (3 vols, Paris, 1891–1901), ii, p. 305, lines 18483–85, and cf. iii, p. xl; J.W. Fortescue, *A History of the British Army* (13 vols, 1899–1930), xi, p. 129, cf. Eric Wakeham, *The Bravest Soldier: Sir Rollo Gillespie, 1766–1814. A Historical Military Sketch* (1937), passim.

[10] Carl Bock, *The Head-Hunters of Borneo: A Narrative of Travel up the Mahakkam and down the Barito* (1881), pp. 216, 219; Michael J. Harner, *The Jívaro: People of the Sacred Waterfall* (1973), pp. 115–16, 183; Fortescue, *A History of the British Army*, xiii, pp. 395–96 n. 2.

English custom of duelling with pistols was more likely to end in death than the continental fashion of duelling with swords, fatalities – or for that matter duels – were not especially common. In Britain duelling seems to have reached its peak between 1790 and 1830: two prime ministers of the day fought bloodless duels (Pitt in 1798, the Duke of Wellington in 1829) and in 1809 Viscount Castlereagh wounded George Canning in a duel shortly after they had both resigned from the cabinet. But in this period there is no authentic record of anyone killing more than one opponent in successive duels, and the record number of duels fought in the British Isles by an individual – John Philpot Curran (1750–1817), later Master of the Rolls in Ireland – is five, all apparently bloodless. Later in the nineteenth century the O'Gorman Mahon was said to have fought thirteen duels, and to have a pistol bearing two notches, but there are no authentic details. The O'Gorman spent nearly thirty years abroad, rising (almost simultaneously) to the rank of general in the Uruguayan army, colonel in the Brazilian army and commodore in the Chilean navy, and his duels presumably occurred for the most part outside Europe. One of his contemporaries, Henry Ronald McIver, served in the British, Italian, American Confederate, Mexican, Brazilian, Argentine, Cretan, Cuban, French, Egyptian, Carlist, Herzegovinian and Serbian armies, finishing up as a general in the Greek army: He fought in six duels, three or four of which were fatal to his opponents: unusually he seems to have been more lethal with a sword than a pistol.[11]

If it is true that the O'Gorman cut notches in the butt of his pistol as a record of the men he had killed, he probably got the idea from the Wild West. The precise 'scores' of the most successful American gun-slingers is in fact rarely recorded. Wyatt Earp's total may have been as few as three, that of William Bonney, Billy the Kid, perhaps as many as twenty-one. Wild Bill Hickok, who owes his fame essentially to the fact that he was the first man to make a name for himself with a six-shooter, killed seven men (one by accident) before himself being gunned down in 1876: his preferred weapons incidentally were

[11] *Annual Register* (1803), p. * 9; for J.P. Curran and the O'Gorman Mahon, see the *Dictionary of National Biography*; for McIver, see W.D. L'Estrange, *Under Fourteen Flags: Being the Life and Adventures of Brigadier-General McIver, a Soldier of Fortune* (2 vols, 1884).

not Colt .45s in twin holsters, as in the movies, but two .36 Colt 1851 navy-model revolvers which he carried butts forward tucked into a silk sash. As it happened, it was the most successful gun-fighter of the West who was the only one of note to write his memoirs: John Wesley Hardin. He shot his first adversary in 1868 when nearer fifteen than sixteen years old. 'This was the first man I ever killed, and it nearly distracted my father and mother when I told them.' He went on the run and shot dead three soldiers who were hunting him. During the course of the next nine years he killed another forty men, always at more or less risk to his own life, but was arrested in 1877, tried and sentenced to twenty-five years' gaol for second-degree murder. Shortly after being released after serving two-thirds of his sentence, he was shot in the back by a policeman in El Paso.[12]

No doubt a considerable degree of skill was evinced by people like Bruno Lüdke, who murdered eighty-five women in various German towns between 1928 and 1943, but it was skill in catching people off guard, not the kind of face-to-face courage of men like John Wesley Hardin: and no other criminal since Hardin has been so successful in disposing of other people while in immediate risk of his own life. Louis Buchalter alias Lepke (1897–1944), of Murder Incorporated, is said to have ordered the elimination of over seventy people, and international terrorist Ilich Ramírez Sanchez alias Carlos, on his arrest in August 1994, admitted responsibility for the deaths of eighty-three people, but in both cases someone else usually pulled the trigger. Vincenzo Gibaldi, alias Machine Gun Jack McGurn (1903–36), killed at least twenty-two people for reasons of private spite or at the behest of Al Capone; Abe Reles, who turned states evidence in the Murder Incorporated trial and was subsequently thrown from a window, is believed to have personally killed a dozen people. Dominic 'Mad Dog' McGlinchey of the Provisional IRA, later of the INLA, claimed to have killed over thirty policemen and soldiers in Ulster, though when he was eventually convicted of murder it was for killing an unarmed postmistress: all pretty small beer compared to what law-abiding citizens

---

[12] For Hickok's guns see Joseph G. Rosa, *They Called Him Wild Bill: The Life and Adventures of James Butler Hickok* (Norman, Oklahoma, 1974 edn), p. 7; Robert G. McCubbin, ed., *The Life of John Wesley Hardin: As Written by Himself* (Norman, Oklahoma, 1961), pp. 13–14.

showed themselves capable of when they put on their country's uniform.[13]

Roughly contemporary with the career of the unfortunate John Wesley Hardin there occurred a development which contributed much more directly than the careers of Western gunslingers to making it socially acceptable to keep a score of the people one had killed. It had been customary since the eighteenth century – the period in which most English traditional sports became formalized – for men who indulged in the recreational slaughter of grouse and pheasant to keep a record of how many they had killed; but grouse and pheasant, though tricky to hit, were totally defenceless and fell out of the sky quite easily when winged, and with servants to provide a constant succession of loaded guns it was not impossible to massacre hundreds in one August day. Big-game hunting was much more of a challenge. It was physically demanding – big game wasn't available a pony-trap ride from the ducal castle – and it was dangerous. It provided the most extreme form of that strenuous sportiness which, with Britain in the lead, became an upper-class fashion in nineteenth-century Europe. Roualeyn Gordon Cumming's *Five Years in a Hunter's Life in the Far Interior of South Africa*, published in 1850 – third edition, under the title *The Lion Hunter of South Africa*, 1856 – was probably the first book to be devoted to the pleasures of pursuing animals dangerous enough to destroy human life. With the appearance of *The Hunting Grounds of the World by 'The Old Shekarry'* (i.e. Henry Astbury Leveson) in 1860 and William Charles Baldwin's *African Hunting from Natal to the Zambesi. . . . from 1852 to 1860* in 1862 the vogue of big-game hunting might already seem to have established itself, but in fact its real take-off depended on technical innovations.

Loose powder-and-ball ammunition was not really suitable for rapid reloading in a tropical forest: brass cartridges loaded at the breech only became standard in the 1870s. Apart from the Winchester, which only fired pistol ammunition, magazine rifles were not generally available till the 1880s, and though Purdy had developed a high-velocity

[13] Burton P. Turkus and Sid Feder, *Murder, Inc.* (1957, paperback edn), p. 201; *Financial Times*, 16 August 1994, p. 16d; Robert J. Schoenberg, *Mr Capone* (1993), pp. 185–86; Turkus and Feder, *Murder, Inc.*, p. 6; *The Times*, 11 February 1994, p. 1b. McGlinchey's conviction was later quashed on appeal.

rifle in 1859, the 'express' was only widely available more than two decades later. Easy reloading and extra penetrative power were a *sine qua non* before amateurs were going to take on, alone or with a few companions, animals like elephants, rhinoceroses and African buffaloes. An early use of the term 'big game' was in Sir John Christopher Willoughby's *East Africa and its Big Game*, of 1889: it was followed by *American Big-Game Hunting* by Theodore Roosevelt and G.B. Grinnell, of 1893, and Clive Phillipps Wolley's *Big Game Shooting* of 1894. Rowland Ward's *Horn Measurements and Weights of the Great Game of the World: Being a Record for the Use of Sportsmen and Naturalists* came out in 1892; his earlier *The Sportsman's Handbook to Practical Collecting . . . To Which is Added a Synoptical Guide to the Hunting Grounds of the World* had originally had 103 pages: the seventh edition of 1894 had 192 pages, which were increased to 303 in the tenth edition of 1911. The classic works of Roualeyn Gordon Cumming and William Charles Baldwin were also reprinted in the 1890s, as was F.C. Selous's *A Hunter's Wanderings in Africa*, which had first appeared in 1881 and had a fourth edition in 1895. Clearly big-game hunting was not simply a newly-created tradition, it was also an aspect of a newly-created *literary* tradition.

Part of the fun of big-game hunting was bringing home the trophies: the larger homes of Britain (and France and Germany) began to fill up with antlers and stuffed heads, and inscribing the details of when and where and by whom these melancholy objects had been collected provided a remunerative business for metal engravers. When, in 1915, the Big Game ethic transferred itself to aerial combat, successful fighter pilots often made a point of collecting trophies from aircraft they had brought down – propellers, rudders, national insignia – and hanging them on the walls of their quarters or unit mess. The hunting analogy was frankly confessed by Richthofen who, in an account he wrote of hunting aurochs, confessed 'in the moment when the bull advanced I had the same feeling, the same hunting fever, as seizes me if I sit in my aeroplane, see an Englishman, and have to fly for five minutes to come up with him'. William Avery Bishop, the British Empire's leading ace, also insisted on the sporting analogy. In his war memoirs *Winged Warfare: Hunting the Huns in the Air* he wrote:

> The excitement of the chase had a tight hold on my heartstrings, and I felt that the only thing I wanted was to stay right at it and fight and fight and fight in the air. I don't think I was ever happier in my life. It seemed

that I had found the one thing I loved above all others. To me it was not a business or a profession, but just a wonderful game. To bring down a machine did not seem to me to be killing a man; it was more as if I was just destroying a mechanical target, with no human being in it. Once or twice the idea that a live man had been piloting the machine would occur and recur to me, and it would worry me a bit. My sleep would be spoiled perhaps for a night. I did not relish the idea even of killing Germans, yet, when in a combat in the air, it seemed more like any other kind of sport, and to shoot down a machine was very much the same as if one were shooting down clay pigeons. One had the great satisfaction of feeling that he had hit the target and brought it down; that one was victorious again.

On the other hand a member of the same flight as Albert Ball in No. 11 Squadron RFC noted, as if with surprise, 'There was in his attitude none of that sporting element which to a certain extent formed the basis of many scouts pilots' approach to air fighting'.[14]

It was no coincidence that though the most successful fighter pilots of the 1914–18 War were all brilliant marksmen, many of them were notably poor pilots. G.F. Smylie of the Royal Naval Air Service later remarked, 'The man who flew in a really finished manner, who was a joy to watch, was not usually the man to go into a fight. On the other hand the Hungetter was often a potential crash every time he landed'. A case in point was R.A. Little of the RNAS, with forty-seven 'kills' the top-scoring Australian pilot of the war: he was famous for his clumsy landings, though the crash that eventually killed him was caused by the fact that he was already bleeding to death from a bullet-wound in the groin. Even Albert Ball, who piloted his planes 'very safely and accurately' 'never flew for amusement'. It was not till after 1918 that skill in handling motor-driven machines came to be regarded as a manly accomplishment on a par with marksmanship.[15]

[14] Manfred von Richthofen, *Der rote Kampfflieger* (Berlin, 1917), p. 178; W.A. Bishop, *Winged Warfare* (New York, 1981 edn), p. 141 – first published 1918: and see also, James Thomas Byford McCudden, *Five Years in the Royal Flying Corps* [1919], pp. 286, 311, 325; W.M. Fry, *Air of Battle* (1974), p. 79.

[15] Public Record Office, AIR 1/2392/228/11/169; *Australian Dictionary of Biography* (14 vols so far published, Melbourne 1966–), x, p. 120–21; Cecil Lewis, *Sagittarius Rising* (1966 edn), p. 173, 174 – first published 1936.

The Big Game Hunter approach did not manifest itself only in aerial combat: Richard Meinertzhagen, while a staff officer at the War Office in August 1918, took a trip to France and was very pleased with himself for having 'accounted for' twenty-three 'Huns' during a day spent operating a Hotchkiss machine-gun in a Canadian armoured car. Some of the most lethal marksmen had been brought up in more plebeian traditions of sport. 'Every time a head come up I knocked it down', recalled Sergeant Alvin York of the day he killed twenty-eight German soldiers, no doubt thinking of a fair-ground booth: and describing how he used a pistol to dispose of a German officer and five men who charged him from twenty-five yards away, he explained:

> I tetched off the sixth man first, then the fifth; then the fourth; then the third; and so on. That's the way we shoot wild turkey at home. You see we don't want the front ones to know that we're getting the back ones.[16]

Sergeant York's exploits were never equalled (or even approached) by anything known to have taken place in the Wild West, but were sometimes all but topped by other combatants on the Western Front. Captain Robert Gee of the Royal Fusiliers, having been taken prisoner, killed his guard with the spiked stick he carried in action, collected two revolvers from dead bodies and charged a machine-gun nest, killing eight Germans. Lieutenant Joseph Maxwell of the Australian Imperial Force shot three Germans with his revolver and took prisoner four others in a machine-gun nest, reloaded and shot dead five more Germans manning another machine-gun. Then a German prisoner told him that some of the other men in his company were ready to surrender. With two other Australians Maxwell climbed down into the German trench and was immediately overpowered and disarmed. Having recovered his breath he produced an automatic pistol from his gas mask container, shot dead two more Germans and escaped with his companions in the resulting confusion.[17]

---

[16] Richard Meinertzhagen, *Army Diary, 1899–1926* (Edinburgh, 1960), p. 242; Tom Skeyhill, ed., *Sergeant York: Alvin C. York. His Own Life Story and War Diary* (Garden City, 1928), p. 227–28.

[17] A.D. Harvey, 'Revolver VCs', *Guns Review*, 32, no. 11 (November 1992) p. 858–59, and cf. Joseph Maxwell, *Hell's Bells and Mademoiselles* (Sydney, 1932), pp. xiii-xiv.

Twenty-two soldiers in the British and British Empire forces won the VC by their prowess with the revolver or automatic pistol; ninety-seven won it by their skill with that coarsest of weapons, the hand grenade. (This doesn't include the nine men who won the VC by throwing themselves or stepping on grenades, or hurling them away at the last minute, to prevent their comrades being killed.) Invented in the sixteenth century the grenade had fallen out of favour by the mid-eighteenth, partly because there were fewer sieges than in the period of Louis XIV's wars, but chiefly because of the development of infantry tactics: whereas in the seventeenth century infantry formations combined a variety of weapons – pikes, muskets, grenades – eighteenth-century infantry were exclusively armed with muskets equipped with ring bayonets, thereby maximizing both fire-power and capacity for self-defence against attacking cavalry. A throwable missile charged with gunpowder was not sufficiently effective to be worth the diversion of man-power. The development of more powerful explosives in the second half of the nineteenth century, and the use of improvised grenades at the siege of Port Arthur during the Russo-Japanese War of 1904–5, caused the international military community to take a fresh look at this economical weapon. The British army's first modern hand grenade, a device with a sixteen-inch throwing handle designated Hand Grenade No. 1, was introduced in 1908. It was not till after the First World War had begun however that it was realised that the grenade was the perfect weapon for trench warfare – nobody had quite expected trench warfare anyway. Grenades also had the advantage of being relatively easy to manufacture: in the second half of 1914 only 2164 were made in Britain, but in the final quarter of 1915 9,489,765. British army doctrine (which also emphasized the crucial importance of bayonet training at a time when the Germans were increasingly counter-attacking without fixed bayonets) tended to insist that the function of the grenade was 'solely to amplify and facilitate the use of the Rifle'. The rifle was far more accurate at a far longer range and it took far longer to use up one man's stock of rifle ammunition, but at short range, and especially in the confined space of a trench, the grenade was immeasurably more lethal. It was less effective against inanimate objects:

Another point to be borne in mind as regards the ordinary grenade is that it will *not* destroy doorways. There is a popular misconception among troops that the ordinary Mills hand grenade, if placed upon a doorstep and the pin withdrawn, will, when it explodes, burst open an ordinary door in such a manner as to allow troops to pass through. This is not so. The usual effect will merely be to make a number of shrapnel holes in the door, with probably a fairly large hole close to the spot where the bomb was placed.

But closed doors were not generally a problem on the Western Front, and till the adoption of the Bergmann sub-machine-gun by the German army in the last months of the war the grenade represented the only really effective infantry assault weapon available: portable machine-guns prior to the Bergmann were either too heavy, like the Lewis Gun or the German army's MG 08/15, or too slow-firing and unreliable, like the French Chauchat, or too rapid-firing and therefore needing constant reloading like the Italian Villar Perosa. The exploits with pistols mentioned previously were possible only for people with immense innate skill or arduous practice. The hand grenade of all weapons was the one that depended most on the man and least on his military training:

One of the men of my platoon was shot through the lungs, or some such place. He gasped terribly for breath, and fell behind me. Easing his head with my left hand, I threw bombs with the right, also saying a few cheering words to the boys. Presently I felt his head drop back – his fight was over. I was just preparing another bomb, with the upper part of my head and chest well above the parapet, when a German bomb burst near my neck, blowing away the left side of same and part of jaw, lower teeth and gum and upper teeth. Left arm was blown round my neck, and the biceps muscle was contracted like a ball on the top of left shoulder. Jugular vein, windpipe and carotid artery were fully exposed, and shoulder-blade badly out of place. My head lay helplessly on my arm, and sometimes almost rolled on my back. For a moment I was dazed, as I had already been hit three times with shrapnel in the early part of the morning while organising men of some other unit, who had lost their officers and NCOs, but I was soon clear again; still, what with loss of blood and almost blinded with it, I had to leave the boys, but I did not go far, only to the first line, where I lay in a shell-hole and watched how things progressed. But feeling myself becoming weaker and weaker, I set off to find a doctor. I had not gone far when I met the remnants of a carrying party. I wrote on a piece of paper asking for a dressing station, and they asked for the direction the boys had advanced. They were carrying bombs and the boys wanted them, so, staggering away, I took them up through the barrage. Five parties I led back, but the last one never got there, for a shell came over, killed three of them, and broke my jaw in another two places, so, almost blinded with blood and falling at every three or four steps, I left the field.

One suspects that the grenade's sheer nastiness as a weapon militated against its ever obtaining the publicity accorded aerial combat.[18]

John Buchan claimed, 'half the magic of our Flying Corps was its freedom from advertisement': but since Buchan was employed by the Department of Information, responsible for propaganda, his remark may be taken with a pinch of salt. The Germans, French and Italians published the names of their aces in the regular army communiqués which were printed in the press, whereas the identity of their British counterparts only 'leaked out by way of the supplement to the *London Gazette*' when they were awarded decorations for gallantry. On the other hand, when Billy Bishop, eventually the British Empire's top-scorer, appeared in the *London Gazette* as having been awarded the Military Cross on 26 May 1917, the Distinguished Service Order three weeks later, the Victoria Cross eight weeks after that, and a Bar to his DSO six weeks after his VC, people were likely to notice. In the early days shooting an enemy aeroplane down seemed so unusual and difficult that it received immediate recognition: Max Immelmann's first aerial victory on 1 August 1915 was followed by the award of the Iron Cross First Class within twenty-four hours, and French pilots were receiving the coveted *Médaille Militaire* for their first kill as late as August 1916. By the time of his death Immelmann, whose score of sixteen was soon to be vastly outdistanced, had been decorated with the Order *pour le mérite*, the Iron Cross First and Second Class, the Order of St Heinrich, the Albrecht Order with Swords, the Order of the House of Hohenzollern with Swords, the Bavarian Order of Merit, the

[18] A.D. Harvey, 'The Hand Grenade in the First World War', *RUSI Journal*, 138, no. 1 (February 1993), pp. 44–47; H.J. Cupper, *Hints on Grenade Work (Tactical)* (1917), p. 5: the author was Chief Instructor VII Corps Bombing and Trench Mortar School; 'Egyptforce', *Street Fighting: For Junior Officers* [1919], pp. 40–41; O'Moore Creagh and E.M. Humphris, *The VC and DSO: A Complete Record . . . with Many Biographical and Other Details* (3 vols, 1924), i, p. 224, account by Lance-Sergeant Fred McNess of the Scots Guards of his exploits at Ginchy in September 1916.

Hanseatic Cross and the Turkish Iron Crescent. After his sixth kill he was summoned to dinner by his army commander, the Crown Prince of Bavaria: Immelmann's own King, Friedrich August III of Saxony, was among the other guests. Oswald Boelcke, on leave after receiving the Order *pour le mérite*, found himself the centre of attention wherever he went:

> it is worse than having a warrant out against you. They stared at me all the time in the streets, both in Frankfurt and in Wiesbaden, where I was on Wednesday afternoon. Also the people in the Opera crowded round me in each interval – it was terrible.
>
> But the worst was yet to come. When the opera-singer Schramm sang the well-known aria 'Father, Mother, Sisters, Brothers' he was loudly applauded and encored. At last he reappeared to start his encore. But just imagine – I could hardly believe my ears – the fellow did not sing the proper words but a verse in my honour which they had hastily strung together behind the scenes – it sounds like it. The singer himself sent me a copy round:

> > Listen friends, our brave airman
> > Lieutenant Boelcke is in the house!
> > Many times he's been the victor
> > Against the enemy in mighty struggle.
> > May he yet succeed
> > In vanquishing a hundred foes!
> > Oh how splendid and how nice,
> > If we see him again soon![19]

The deaths of the better-known aces were regarded as big news. When Albert Ball was killed the *Nottingham Evening Post* printed his photograph and a column and three-quarters about him on the front page. The Lord Mayor of Nottingham had broken the story at that afternoon's council meeting:

---

[19] John Buchan, *Mr Standfast* (1919), p. 24; *Days on the Wing: Being the War Memoirs of Major the Chevalier Willy Coppens de Houthulst* (1934), p. v, Foreword by Marshal of the Royal Air Force Sir John Salmond; Bishop, *Winged Warfare*, p. 248; Johannes Werner, *Knight of Germany: Oswald Boelcke, German Ace* (1933), p. 164. I have substituted my own, more literal rendering of the German verses, as given in Johannes Werner, *Boelcke der Mensch, der Flieger, der Führer der deutschen Jagdfliegerei* (Leipzig, 1932), p. 151, for Claud W. Sykes's rhyming version in the English edition of 1933.

When the history of the war comes to be written no name will stand out more prominently than that of our gallant young citizen-airman, and I propose to immediately issue an appeal to the citizens of Nottingham and the country, and in fact to all his admirers, to subscribe to a fund to raise a statue to his memory in Nottingham.

When Richthofen was killed the *Berliner Lokal-Anzeiger* of 23 April 1918 gave half of its front page to the story, including a portrait drawing of '*Unser Fliegerheld Rittmeister v. Richthofen*'. When Georges Guynemer was reported dead the French Chamber of Deputies voted unanimously that his name should be inscribed on the walls of the Pantheon. His body was never recovered: Henri Lavedan of the *Académie Française* wrote, 'later on people will say: the ace of aces one day flew so high in combat that he never returned to earth'. In fact Guynemer, whose last victim – shot down in self-defence – was a British two-scater which persisted in firing at him, had crashed between the British and German lines, and before the Germans could do more than send out a medical team to examine his body *in situ*, the British began a bombardment of the entire sector which lasted fifteen days. At the end of two weeks there was no trace of the French air ace: it was thought advisable to pretend that he had just disappeared.[20]

But fame, like survival, could be something of a lottery. Edward Mannock, who is sometimes credited with shooting down even more planes than Billy Bishop, and who certainly accounted for fifty-one German aircraft and a part-share of twenty-three others, was virtually unknown at the time of his death, his Victoria Cross being gazetted posthumously. And Manfred von Richthofen, though officially credited with the largest score, was by no means the most accomplished of these aerial serial killers. Only twenty-four of his eighty victims were single-seat fighters, as fast and manoeuvrable as his own aeroplane: fifty-six of Billy Bishop's seventy-two victims were single-seat fighters. Bishop also spent only about half as long as Richthofen at the front. Richthofen's record, equalled by James McCudden, W.G. Barker and Georges Guynemer, was to shoot down four enemy planes in a day:

[20] Robert Wohl, *A Passion for Wings: Aviation and the Western Imagination, 1908–1918* (New Haven, 1994), pp. 233–35; Philippe Ochsé, *Les avions de Guynemer* (Rennes, [1985]), p. 24.
The statue to Albert Ball was erected in the grounds of Nottingham Castle.

Bishop managed five in one day and the French ace René Fonck twice destroyed six – officially confirmed – in one day. On another occasion Fonck shot down three German aircraft in ten seconds: they all crashed within a 400 metre radius. 'Mon record', he noted modestly. Richthofen also had the advantage that he generally fought over his own lines, so that the aircraft he shot down landed in German-held territory; Allied fighter pilots, operating over the German lines, were not always able to obtain confirmation that the enemy plane they had fired at had crashed. René Fonck, who was officially credited with seventy-five victories, five less than Richthofen, also claimed a further fifty-one which had fallen behind enemy lines.[21]

Sometimes the folks back home objected to their young men keeping scores:

> In view of these many 'numbers' mother will be saying again that it is not right to number our victims in this unfeeling way. But we don't really do it – we do not number the victims who have fallen, but the machines we have brought down. That you can see from the fact that it only counts as one victory when two inmates are killed, but that it still remains a 'number' when both the inmates escape unhurt. We have nothing against the individual; we only fight to prevent him flying against us. So when we have eliminated an enemy force, we are pleased and book it as one up to us.

The convention however was to pretend that aerial combat was a revival of the values of medieval chivalry. Fighter pilots were frequently referred to as Knights of the Air. 'They are the knighthood of this War, without fear and without reproach', said Lloyd George, the British prime minister. Though it was prohibited in the British service, pilots of other nations often adopted personal liveries for their aircraft. Manfred von Richthofen's all-red paint job earned him the posthumous soubriquet the 'Red Baron', but he seems to have copied it from the French pilot Jean Navarre's red Nieuport, which had become a familiar sight in the skies over Verdun during the spring and early summer of 1916.

---

[21] Christopher Shores, Norman Franks, Russell Guest, *Above the Trenches: A Complete Record of the Fighter Aces and Units of the British Empire Air Forces, 1915–1920* (1990), pp. 64, 256, 269: according to p. 115 of this book Raymond Collishaw of the Royal Naval Air Service reported shooting down six German planes on 6 July 1917, ten months before René Fonck's first such claim, but Collishaw was unable to obtain confirmation by independent witnesses; René Fonck, *Mes combats* (Paris, [1920]), pp. 231–46.

Godwin Brumowski, the leading Austrian fighter ace, also adopted a red livery; Josef Jakobs chose black; the Belgian André de Meulemeester had his Hanriot painted yellow but discovered that this 'set the British Flying Corps at his heels'. Interestingly enough one form of display that was to become customary in the Second World War was almost unknown in the 1914–18 period: painting rows of small symbols on one's plane to indicate how many of the enemy one had shot down. W.G. Barker seems to have pioneered this fashion by having white flashes painted on the struts of his Sopwith Camel during the last months of the war.[22]

Except in Italy, where torpedo-boat commander Luigi Rizzo won almost twice as many medals as air ace Franco Baracca, it was fighter pilots who held the record in the First World War for the largest number of decorations for gallantry awarded to an individual. René Fonck had, beside the *Medaille Militaire* and the *Croix de Chevalier de la Légion d'Honneur*, a *Croix de Guerre* with twenty-seven *palmes* (equivalent to bars) necessitating an extended ribbon which hung from his heart to his belt (and with which, apparently, he flew in combat). Mannock, McCudden and Barker each received six British decorations for gallantry. Oddly enough however the three most impressive accumulations of gallantry awards in the British army were by men whose job did not involve shooting at other people. F.W. Lumsden of the Royal Marine Artillery won the Victoria Cross and the Distinguished Service Order (at that time Britain's second highest gallantry award) with three bars as a staff officer and brigade commander: no doubt he brandished a revolver occasionally but his main business was organizing other people under fire. Lance-Corporal W.H. Coltman, VC, DCM and bar, MM and bar, the most highly decorated British Other Rank did not carry a weapon of any

<hr />

[22] Werner, *Knight of Germany*, p. 212; A.D. Harvey, *Collision of Empires: Britain in Three World Wars, 1793–1945* (1992), p. 388–89; *Hansard: House of Commons*, vol. 98, col. 1247, 29 October 1917; Public Record Office, AIR 1/1589/204/82/74; Bruce Robertson, ed., *Air Aces of the 1914–18 War* (Letchworth, 1959), p. 29, photo caption: but Lieutenant-Commander Max Horton flew a Jolly Roger with a bar for each German ship sunk when entering harbour in his submarine as early as the winter of 1914–15 – Richard Compton Hall, *The Underwater War, 1939–45* (Poole, 1982), p. 62.

Incidentally only some of Richthofen's planes were painted red all over: see Alex Imrie, *The Fokker Triplane* (1992), p. 79.

sort: he was a stretcher-bearer. Captain Noel Chavasse, VC and bar, MC was a battalion medical officer.[23]

But perhaps the most eye-catching hero of the war was the Italian Enrico Toti, killed shortly after his thirty-fourth birthday on Hill 85, east of Monfalcone and posthumously awarded the Italy's Gold Medal for Valour, and commemorated by a statue in the Pincio, in his native Rome. In his teens he had served in the Italian navy and had later become a fireman on the railways. His pre-war exploits as a cyclist – he had cycled to Lapland in 1911, to the Sudan in 1913 – enabled him to overcome official opposition and enlist in a Bersaglieri cyclist unit when Italy entered the war in 1915. Operating in rugged mountain terrain, the Italian army had little use for cycle troops, and it was as a simple soldier, albeit in a crack light infantry unit, steel helmet adorned with the famous Bersaglieri feathers, that Toti met his death, charging the enemy lines – despite having had one leg amputated, above the knee and too high up for an artificial limb to be fitted, as a result of a railway accident in 1908.

By getting himself killed Toti at least solved the problem of what to do after the war. The British army's most decorated private, Henry 'Napper' Tandey, VC, DCM, MM, five times mentioned in despatches – in September 1918, it is said, Tandey took Adolf Hitler prisoner but he escaped back to the German lines – said of his war service, 'I went

---

[23] Proportionately fewer medals were awarded in the British army to Other Ranks than to officers: in the 1914–18 war 9002 officers received the Distinguished Service Order (counting first awards only) and 37,104 the Military Cross; 24,620 Distinguished Conduct Medals and 115,589 Military Medals were awarded to Other Ranks. Only 472 first bars to the DCM were awarded as compared to 708 first bars to the DSO: P.E. Abbott, J.M.A. Tamplin, *British Gallantry Awards* (1981) p. 82, 126, 220, 226. The DCM was regarded as 'the best all-round medal of the Army': Tom Bridges *Alarms and Excursions: Reminiscences of a Soldier* (1938), p. 155.

Mannock was awarded the VC, DSO and two bars, MC and bar, Barker the VC, DSO and bar MC and two bars, and McCudden (promoted from the ranks) the VC, DSO and bar, MC and bar and MM; four other pilots received five British gallantry awards: apart from Lumsden, who was killed in action, and Coltman the only member of the British ground forces to be decorated five times was Lord Gort, VC, DSO and two bars, MC.

In Italy, Luigi Rizzo was awarded two gold and four silver medals for military valour, as compared to the air ace Franco Baracca's one gold and three silver medals. Rizzo's feats included the sinking of *two* Austro-Hungarian battleships, the pre-dreadnought *Wien* and the more modern *Szent István*.

to be a soldier and did an ordinary soldier's job'. After it was over he returned to his pre-war employment as an engineer in a hotel in Leamington Spa. Coltman became a municipal gardener. Other people found it more difficult to adjust to civilian life. The enduring psychological trauma of the war became one of the clichés of the 1920s. 'Why else, may I ask, should those who were once the flower of our youth form today so disproportionate a number of the down and out?' asked General Sir Ian Hamilton in 1929. In a prefatory note to *Im Westen Nichts Neues* Erich Maria Remarque claimed he was telling the story of 'a generation of men who, even though they may have escaped the shells, were destroyed by the war'. Wilfred Saint-Mandé wrote a novel about 'how the War debased a young man, who subsequently failed to control his passions, until he came to a tragic and premature end'. In his 'Author's Foreword' he asked:

Since the War how many thousands of ex-soldiers have been sent to prison for crimes that would never have been committed had it not been for the atmosphere of bloodshed and rapine in which so many of my generation lived for over four years? There is at least one case on record of a man wounded in the head fighting for his country, and subsequently executed for a murder of which he almost certainly would not have been guilty had he not been taught to kill as a duty a few years previously. And a large proportion of those who came through the War with skins intact were wounded in more insidious ways.[24]

Of course there were some people who assessed what had happened from a completely opposite point of view:

A particularly malignant falsehood is being propagated in the name of 'pacificism', to the effect that the wounds and nervous shock inflicted upon soldiers by the experience of war constituted an injury to racial qualities . . . Let it at least be firmly understood by the noble women who choose to espouse these men that the injuries of war last but for one generation, and that their children will receive, as a natural dower, a constitution unimpaired, and the power to become all that their father might have been . . .

[24] *Leamington and District Morning News*, 22 December 1977, p. 1b-e: obituary of Henry Tandey VC; *Burton Observer and Chronicle*, 4 July 1974, p. 3c-f; obituary of W.H. Coltman VC; Sir Ian Hamilton, 'The End of War', *Life and Letters*, 3 (November 1929), p. 403; Wilfred Saint-Mandé, *The Devouring Flame* (1935), Author's Foreword.

The one thing that nobody doubted was that the war had changed both the men who had fought it and the national communities that had asked them to fight. The big question after 1918 was, what would this change lead to?[25]

[25] 'Broken Soldiers', *Eugenics Review*, 7 (October 1915), p. 202, quoted in Seth Koven, 'Remembering and Dismemberment: Crippled Children, Wounded Soldiers and the Great War in Britain', *American Historical Review*, 99 (1994), pp. 1167–1202, at p. 1189.

CHAPTER 9

Lessons

BOTH A poem and an act of heroism might confer a kind of meaning on an aspect of the war but such a devastatingly total experience also demanded an explanation of what it meant as a whole.

During the war itself it was inevitable that a great deal of the rhetoric should have derived from pre-1914 preoccupations and pre-1914 cultural traditions. The best-selling book by a frontline author in Germany during the war was Walter Flex's *Der Wanderer zwischen beiden Welten* (1917: 'The Wanderer between the Two Worlds') in which the narrator encounters a young man who before the war had been a *Wandervögel,* one of the German youths who had spent their summers roaming the country, toughening themselves in the fresh air and communing with Nature. 'All that was bright and healthy in the German future seemed to him to come from the spirit of the *Wandervögel,* and if I were to think of him as embodying this spirit purely and clearly I would only be doing him justice . . .' Flex himself told his brother:

> I am inwardly as committed to the war as I was on the first day. I am not thus, and was not, like so many of my friends, from national but from moral fanaticism. It's not national but moral challenges that I hold up and represent. What I have written about the eternity of the German people and of the world-redeeming mission of German-ness has nothing to do with national egoism but is a moral belief which can realize itself in defeat, or as Ernst Wurche would have said, in the heroic death of a people . . .

In *Der Wanderer zwischen beiden Welten* Flex wrote:

> The thought of the heroic death of a people is not more terrible than the thought of the violent death of a man. Only dying is ugly for men and

for peoples. But if a man receives a fatal shot which rips into his guts, then that's it. What follows is ugly and no longer belongs to him. The great and beautiful bit, the heroic life, is over. It must be the same if a people, in its honour and greatness, receive a death blow: what happens next should not be seen as part of its living, it has no part of it . . .[1]

The same exhilarated sense of destiny that left no space for thoughts of tomorrow was later recalled by Ernst Jünger:

> We had left lecture room, class room, and bench behind us. We had been welded by a few weeks' training into one corporate mass inspired by the enthusiasm of one thought . . . to carry forward the German ideals of '70. We had grown up in a material age, and in each one of us there was the yearning for great experience, such as we had never known. The war had entered into us like wine. We had set out in a rain of flowers to seek the death of heroes. The war was our dream of greatness, power, and glory. It was a man's work, a duel on fields whose flowers would be stained with blood. There is no lovelier death in the world . . . anything rather than stay at home, anything to make one with the rest.

But when the war turned out to be so different from what had been expected and became a matter of enduring day after day, week after week, horrors which seemed certain to persist into a long futurity which one would not oneself live to see, perspectives began to change. Exhilaration gave way to the sternest determination to endure. Obliviousness of the morrow gave way to a resolute intention to survive, minute by minute, for as long as was necessary:

> a battle was no longer an episode that spent itself in blood and fire; it was a condition of things that dug itself in remorselessly week after week and even month after month. What was a man's life in this wilderness whose vapour was laden with the stench of thousands upon thousands of decaying bodies? Death lay in ambush for each one in every shell-hole, merciless, and making one merciless in return.

During the war itself Otto Riebicke wrote:

> These German soldiers in their German Siegfried helmets with their fists on their hot rifles, with bronzed features of courage, love and horror,

---

[1] Walter Flex, *Der Wanderer zwischen beiden Welten* (Munich, 1924 edn), p. 12; ibid., p. 100 (Afterword by Martin Flex); ibid., p. 36.

these heroes for whom mines and shell-fire again and again flatten out and fill up everything so that they have to lie out in the open, with only a couple of handfuls of sand in front of them, and the enemy beating at them from stronger positions and hurling ten thousand tons of High Explosive in clattering trench-mortar bombs so that the sky is full of razor-sharp slashing, rotating knives and the earth spurts as high as houses against the sky – these men on the Somme are the barrier against the monstrous hurricane of the war, behind which the homeland goes on to the harvest carefree and full of confidence.

Perspectives rooted in pre-war notions began to be replaced by a sense of novelties that were at once horrifying and thought-provoking. 'The Europe of to-day appeared here for the first time on the field of battle', wrote Jünger later:

all the frightfulness that the mind of man could devise was brought into the field; and there, where lately there had been the idyllic picture of rural peace, there was as faithful a picture of the soul of scientific war. In earlier wars, certainly, towns and villages had been burned, but what was that compared with this sea of craters dug out by machines? For even in this fantastic desert there was the sameness of the machine-made article. A shell-hole strewn with bully-tins, broken weapons, fragments of uniform, and dud shells, with one or two dead bodies on its edge . . . this was the never-changing scene that surrounded each one of all these hundreds of thousands of men. And it seemed that man, on this landscape he had himself created, became different, more mysterious and hardy and callous than in any previous battle. The spirit and the tempo of the fighting altered, and after the battle of the Somme the war had its own peculiar impress that distinguished it from all other wars. After this battle the German soldier wore the steel helmet, and in his features there were chiselled the lines of an energy stretched to the utmost pitch, lines that future generations will perhaps find as fascinating and imposing as those of many heads of classical or Renaissance times.

There was even a kind of exhilaration in the sheer hideousness of it all:

Hellrot fällt Mondlicht auf meinen harten Helm. Der Schatten wird matt, zerstirbt im Phantastischen.
Ich klettere durch einen Granattrichter hoch – in die Sommeschlacht.

> Weit hinten stirbt Bapaume in Pulver, Rauch und Qualm.
>
> In tausendjährigen Katakomben harren deutsche Soldaten des Rufes zum Sturm, Männer mit Siegfriedhelmen und Siegfriedstreue.
>
> Darauf hämmern Englands schwere Granaten ihren brüllenden Zorn.

(Bloodred falls the moonlight on my hard helmet. The shadows become faint, fading into the fantastic. I clamber up through a shell hole – into the Battle of the Somme. Far behind Bapaume dies in dust, fumes and smoke. In thousand-year-old catacombs German soldiers await the signal for the assault, men with the helmets of Siegfried and the loyalty of Siegfried. On them England's heavy shells pound their bellowing anger.)[2]

For Jünger and Riebicke the real meaning of what they had endured was revealed in November 1918 when they discovered that their four-year ordeal, and the deaths of more than a million and a half of their comrades in arms, had been in vain – worse than in vain, the prelude and justification for disgrace, loss of territory, humiliating restrictions. Someone like Ezra Pound who was on the winning side – even inadvertently – could write of myriads dying

> For an old bitch gone in the teeth
> For a botched civilization

but those who had risked all and lost did not even have the old bitch for comfort. Yet with final defeat Jünger reconsidered his experiences and thought he began to understand:

> Now I looked back: four years of development in the midst of a generation predestined to death, spent in caves, smoke-filled trenches, and shell-illumined wastes . . . in short, a monotonous calendar full of hardships and privation, divided by the red-letter days of battles. And almost without any thought of mine, the idea of the Fatherland had been distilled from all these afflictions in a clearer and brighter essence. That was the final

---

[2] Ernst Jünger, *The Storm of Steel: From the Diary of a German Storm-Troop Officer on the Western Front* (1929), p. 1; ibid., pp. 109–10; Otto Riebicke *Ringen an der Somme und im Herzen* (Magdeburg, 1917), p. 27; Jünger, *Storm of Steel*, p. 109; Riebicke, *Ringen an der Somme*, p. 136.

winnings in a game on which so often all had been staked: the nation was no longer for me an empty thought veiled in symbols; and how could it have been otherwise when I had seen so many die for its sake, and been schooled myself to stake my life for its credit every minute, day and night, without a thought? And so, strange as it may sound, I learned from this very four years' schooling in force and in all the fantastic extravagance of material warfare that life has no depth of meaning except when it is pledged for an ideal, and that there are ideals in comparison with which the life of an individual and even of a people has no weight. And though the aim for which I fought as an individual, as an atom in the whole body of the army, was not to be achieved, though material force cast us, apparently, to the earth, yet we learned once and for all to stand for a cause and if necessary to fall as befitted men ...

And if it be objected that we belong to a time of crude force our answer is: we stood with our feet in mud and blood, yet our faces were turned to things of exalted worth. And not one of that countless number who fell in our attacks fell for nothing. Each one fulfilled his own purpose.[3]

Ernst Jünger's account of his First World War experiences, *In Stahlgewittern: aus dem Tagebuch eines Stosstruppführers* (1920; translated into English as *The Storm of Steel*, 1929) was a best-seller in Germany during the 1920s. Joseph Goebbels, later Hitler's propaganda minister, was a keen admirer, calling it 'Das Evangelium des Krieges. Grausamgross!' (the gospel of the war. Grisly-great!). Nevertheless it did nothing like as well as Gunther Plüschow's cheerful narrative of how he outwitted and escaped from the English in *Die Abenteuer des Fliegers von Tsingtau* ('The Adventures of the Airman of Tsingtao') which sold over 600,000 copies between 1923 and 1927. Walter Flex's *Der Wanderer zwischen beiden Welten* also continued to sell well; even Barbusse's *Le feu*, published in German translation in Zurich in 1918 and on sale in Germany after the Armistice, seems to have also kept ahead of the sales of *In Stahlgewittern* till the time of Hitler's coming to power in 1933. Jünger's version of the war may be seen indeed as one of several rival versions which were in competition during the period of the

[3] E.P. [Ezra Pound], *Hugh Selwyn Mauberly* (1920), p. 13, part 5; Jünger, *Storm of Steel*, pp. 316–17. I have altered the last word, given as *resolve* in the 1929 translation: the German is 'Und jeder der Unzähligen, die wir auf unserem Sturmgange verloren, ist nicht umsonst gefallen, er hat seinen Sinn erfüllt'. *Sinn* means 'sense', 'meaning', 'significance', 'tendency' – something more intrinsic and innate than 'resolve'.

Weimar Republic. The publication in the late 1920s of Georg von der Vring's unheroic *Soldat Suhren*, which deals mainly with training and life in a quiet section of the front, with battle and wounds only at the end, of Ludwig Renn's *Krieg*, Moritz Frey's *Die Pflasterkasten*, an occasionally almost Schweikish account of a medical orderly's worm's eye view of life behind the lines, and Erich Maria Remarque's *Im Westen Nichts Neues* might even suggest that the Jünger version of the war was finally swamped by that of his rivals, especially in view of the huge success of Remarque's novel, sales of which approached one million by the time Jünger was at the 100,000 mark. In reality *In Stahlgewittern* was one of those books which influenced other writers and intellectuals as much, or more, than publications that enjoyed considerably larger sales. In particular it was calculated to have much more appeal than, for example, Barbusse's novel to those who remembered the war but had been too young to fight in it – a group prominent in the Nazi party in the late 1920s. By the end of the 1920s moreover its message was taking on a new topicality.[4]

Having survived open civil war, attempted coups and the collapse of the currency, the Weimar Republic was by the beginning of 1929 at least as firmly established as the Third Republic in France. The latter had been born in comparable circumstances of defeat and national humiliation and still, after nearly sixty years, had all the glamour and convincingness of the botched-up temporary compromise that it was, but had demonstrated that it was not necessary that the citizenry should believe in it, so long as there was no agreement on how to replace it. The world economic recession of 1929 threw all the governments of Europe into crisis, and the Weimar regime was not particularly less capable of dealing with the economic catastrophe than the governments of other European states. As elsewhere, rocketing unemployment provided recruits for extremist parties which had first flourished during the years just after the war and which had been perfecting their organization and

---

[4] Ralf Georg Reuth, ed., *Joseph Goebbels: Tagebücher, 1924–1945* (5 vols, Munich 1992), i, p. 221, 13 January 1926. The 63–67,000th copies of the Zurich edition of *Das Feuer* (i.e. *Le feu*) were printed in 1929 and the 68–82,000th in 1930. The 22–25,000th copies of *In Stahlgewittern* were printed in 1927, the 116–125,000th in 1935.

The literal meaning of Jünger's title *In Stahlgewittern*, incidentally, is not 'The Storm of Steel' but 'In Steel-Storms'.

techniques, though with little chance of seizing power, during the comparatively affluent mid-1920s.

The economic and social crisis of 1929 seems also to have fostered a revaluation of the world war: this was perhaps the one phenomenon of the time that was more marked in Germany than elsewhere. In the foreword of his popular history of the war, *Sperrfeuer um Deutschland* (1929), Werner Beumelburg wrote of wanting to 'fuse together the military events with the spiritual events. In this way a picture will be produced that, based on the results of reliable research, places on record the living face of the war'. *Sperrfeuer um Deutschland* ('Artillery Barrage around Germany') attempted to present the whole nation as the protagonist in the war: a similar message was embodied in the various novels of the period dealing with groups of frontline soldiers. Both Communists and Nazis held up the common man, the common soldier, as the embodiment of the corporate ideal: 'Don't ask yourself what this war did for me, for you, for anybody in particular', wrote Erwin Zindler, 'rather ask what this war meant for the great Unknown Soldier. We are all merely a part of him. But he is the visible, willing, self-sacrificing Germany, which lives through his dying'. Ulrich Sander claimed, 'It was the war that first brought us into touch with the common man. It was through the war that we first found the sources of our race'. Among the critically acclaimed novels of the period was one by Franz Schauwecker, who during the 1920s had been associated with Jünger in the Stahlhelm, the right-wing veterans' organization. In its English translation it is called *The Furnace* but the original German title – *Aufbruch der Nation* – is not easy to interpret: the obvious meaning is 'Departure of the Nation' but it could mean 'The Emergence of the Nation' or even 'The Guts of the Nation'. The novel ends with the end of the war: the two protagonists sit in a cafe and discuss why it is that no one from the front line does anything to oppose the revolution that is sweeping through Germany's cities. One of them concludes that they should discover why Germany lost the war: 'We had to lose the war, in order to win the nation'. 'And with that they left the room and went to the station. Nobody observed them. No-one knew them.' They were, in fact, part of the great

Unknown Soldier, setting out to survive the Weimar Republic and to prepare the way for rebirth.[5]

German academics – much more responsive to contemporary literature than British academics, especially at this period – observed literary developments with not entirely disinterested attention. Ernst Jünger himself appeared in the 1931 edition of *Brockhaus* – the standard German-language encyclopedia – as 'opposing to Pacifism a "heroic realism" which decisively affirms the idea of the nation and raises military spirit above bourgeois security: he is one of the most influential representatives of the "new nationalism"'. Not bad for a man still aged only thirty-six. In the same year Herbert Cysarz published his *Zur Geistesgeschichte des Weltkriegs: die dichterischen Wandlungen des deutschen Kriegsbilds, 1910–1930* ('Towards an intellectual history of the world war: the poetic transformation of the German view of the war.') This argued against the existence of any essentially new intellectual current, claiming that Expressionism, the movement to which, for example, Ludwig Meidner had belonged, had been 'from 1910 to 1914 a prophet of the war, from 1914 to 1918 a measure of the war and its cultural crisis, from 1918 to 1923 the after-tremor of the war'. But political developments in Germany soon made it unfashionable to trace anything of significance in contemporary life back beyond 1914. Hitler's accession to power in 1933 (officially known as the *seizure* of power) made the correct attitude to First World War literature *de rigueur*. Remarque's *Im Westen Nichts Neues* was banned, as was the *Vossische Zeitung*, the newspaper that had first published it as a serial. Importations of Barbusse's *Das Feuer* from Switzerland were stopped. Ernst Glaeser's somewhat mawkish account of the impact of the war on youngsters on the Home Front, *Jahrgang 1902*, which had sold 100,000 between 1929 and 1931, went out of print, though it was to be popular enough when reprinted after the Second World War. Arnold Zweig fled abroad: his manuscript of *Erziehung vor Verdun* was confiscated.

---

[5] Werner Beumelburg, *Sperrfeuer um Deutschland* (Oldenburg, 1929), Vorwort; Erwin Zindler, *Auf Biegen und Brechen* (Leipzig, 1929), p. 256; Ulrich Sander, *Das feldgraue Herz* (Jena, 1934), p. 12; Franz Schauwecker, *Aufbruch der Nation* (Berlin, 1930), p. 410.

Two excellent recent books on the Weimar Republic are Theo Balderston, *The Origin and Course of the German Economic Crisis: November 1923 to November 1932* (Berlin, 1993); and Richard Bessel, *Germany after the First World War* (Oxford, 1993).

Before 1933 the war had been presented by German writers from at least as many different points of view as in other countries: after 1933 only the pro-war point of view was permitted. And not merely permitted: it is difficult to understand how Werner Beumelburg's dull and creakingly ironic *Die Gruppe Bosemüller* sold a million copies in the Nazi period unless it was officially promoted, and Franz Schauwecker's appearance in *Brockhaus* as standing 'next to Ernst Jünger' and amongst 'the leading writers of militarism' had little to do either with his prose style or his mediocre sales, for *Aufbruch der Nation* was evidently too heavy-going to qualify for the popular-classic status enjoyed by *Die Gruppe Bosemüller*.[6]

In academic circles the question of 'Leader and Led' (*'Führer und Geführte'*) quickly established itself as one of the key issues of literary criticism. Even before Hitler had come to power Heinz Grothe had announced, 'The Führer is the mirror of his men . . . For as the Führer is, so is his troop . . . The most beautiful thing is of course when the leaders somehow feel an inner call to take their place at the head of their troops'. Herbert Weyand's dismissive *Der Englische Kriegsroman* (1933, 'The English War Novel') found that the question of 'Leader and Led' was discussed by British writers only from a negative point of view, and only with regard to the higher national level: the reason for this, in Weyand's view, was that 'The English spirit draws its nourishment from the English soil. Its realm is reality . . . It sees in the first instance facts . . . The Englishman limits himself to the appearance of facts'. The following year Hermann Pongs, Professor at Stuttgart Technical University, published an article on 'War as National Destiny in German Writing' in the periodical *Dichtung und Volkstum*, and later issued the same piece as a pamphlet. He gave special emphasis to 'the structure of the whole: men and

---

[6] Herbert Cysarz, *Zur Geistesgeschichte des Weltkriegs: die Dichterischen Wandlungen des deutschen Kriegsbilds, 1910–1930* (Halle, 1931) p. 84n. ; for the confiscation of Zweig's manuscript see W.K. Pfeiler, *War and the German Mind: The Testimony of Men of Fiction at the Front* (New York, 1941), p. 137.

The publishing history of Reichsminister Joseph Goebbels's novel, *Michael: ein deutsches Schicksal,* illustrates the commercial advantage enjoyed by literary works that were seen to be in tune with the regime. It was first published in 1929, and had a second edition in 1931. That would probably have satisfied ordinary demand: but in the ten years that followed Goebbels's appointment as propaganda minister there were *fifteen* more editions.

officers, people and Führer': he began by quoting a recent speech
by Dr Goebbels. Walther Linden meanwhile contributed an article
on 'Popular Literature of the World War and Post-War Period' to
Zeitschrift für Deutschkunde ('Journal of German Studies') of which
he was co-editor: he wrote of 'the comradeship of a nation's frontline
soldiers forged together in blood and suffering' and of how 'A new
manhood was forged in the fire of the front'. He complained that
for Remarque war was only cruelty, meaningless murder, spiritual
destruction and that the huge sales of a work so nihilistic as *Im Westen
Nichts Neues* 'will for ever remain a disgrace'. He did not approve of
Ernst Glaeser or Arnold Zweig either, but concluded 'German war
literature is in the truest sense one of the most valuable constituents
of contemporary literature in Germany . . . It is a people's literature
[*völkische Dichtung*] which bears witness to the German collectivity's
immense experience of destiny . . .' From the war, he claimed, 'a
new Man was born, who demanded quite different life structures
and political structures from the pre-war, bourgeois ones. This is
the inward transition which led from the Second Reich [1871–1918]
to the Third Reich'.[7]

Somewhat less overtly political was Privy Councillor Dr Ernst
Volkmann's anthology *Deutsche Dichtung im Weltkrieg, 1914–1918*, which
even included a selection from Georg Trakl, though care was taken
to mention the failure of Trakl, 'dieses dem Kriege seelisch nicht
gewachsener und am 3. November 1914 im Garnisonsspital in Krakau
aus dem Leben geschiedenen Dichters', to develop spiritually in step
with the war. Volkmann approvingly quoted Hitler's *Mein Kampf* in
his introduction and made an interesting remark, not amplified but
soon to be taken up by younger critics: 'The longer the troops lay
before the enemy and under fire, the stronger grew the spiritual value

---

[7] Heinz Grothe, *Das Fronterlebnis: eine Analyse, gestaltet aus dem Nachleben* (Berlin,
1932), p. 32; Herbert Weyand, *Der Englische Kriegsroman* (Bonn, 1933), p. 42; ibid.,
p. 18–19; Hermann Pongs, *Krieg als Volksschicksal im deutsche Schrifttum* (Stuttgart, 1934),
p. 25; Walther Linden, 'Volkhafte Dichtung von Weltkrieg und Nachkriegzeit', *Zeitschrift
für Deutschkunde Jahrgang*, 48 (1934), p. 1–22, at pp. 3, 9; ibid., pp. 6–7; ibid., pp.
19–20.

of Leadership and Followership [*Führertum und Gefolgschaft*] as also of true comradeship for man and society'.[8]

A caveat has to be entered here. Having their origin in a common language spoken thousands of years ago, and to some extent modified with reference to one another in more recent centuries, most European languages resemble each other relatively closely in sentence structure and in distinctions between concepts – certainly much more closely than they resemble Chinese or Eskimo or Zulu. But the words of one language are rarely absolutely and unambiguously the same in meaning and resonance as words in another language, and peculiarities of syntax mean that a sentence in one language will have a different emphasis from a sentence in another language with the same general meaning. I have for example quoted Walther Linden as writing of 'the comradeship of a nation's soldiers forged together in blood and suffering', which could be a rendering of 'die in Blut und Leiden zusammengeschmiedete Kamaradschaft der Frontkämpfer eines Volkes' but is actually meant to be a translation of 'die Kameradschaft der in Blut und Leiden zusammengeschmiedeten Frontkämpfer eines Volkes'. It is not the comradeship but the frontline soldiers who have been forged together in blood and suffering, which sounds pretty odd in English: and the word 'forged', though better than 'welded' (for Linden doesn't use the normal word for 'welded') is very weak compared to *zusammengeschmieden,* which suggests having been smithied together. Similarly I have had to translate *völkische Dichtung* as 'a people's literature' and *Volksgemeinschaft* as 'collectivity' and *Volksschicksal* as 'national destiny' but the word *Volk* has a resonance in German that cannot be represented in English – certainly not by using the cognate form 'folk'. The Nazis in any case had a quite distinct concept of *das Volk* which, since they only needed to express themselves in their own language, does not mitigate the problems of translation: for example they regarded *Volk,* as a natural, organic collective, as quite distinct from *Nation,* an artificial collective. Hermann Pongs seems to have had a special fondness for compounds using the root *volk*: he appears to have been responsible for changing the name of the journal

---

[8] Ernst Volkmann, *Deutsche Dichtung im Weltkrieg, 1914–1918* (Leipzig, 1934), p. 25.

Euphorion to *Dichtung und Volkstum*, of which the only non-risible transla-
tion is *Literature and National Character* though its meaning is closer to
Poetry and Peoplishness. When he wrote, for example, 'Hier ist
Volkszusammenhang, zwischen Führer und Mann' he obviously
pretended to mean more than the connection, hanging together
(*Zusammenhang*) of *Führer* and Man.[9]

Amongst the most problematic words is *Führer*. When Mussolini
established his dictatorship in Italy he revived an archaic word to
describe his office: *Duce*. Hitler did not revive an archaic word: he
expropriated one of the commonest nouns in the German language.
Before 1914 *Führer* was in everyday use to mean a driver, a guide, a
guidebook, a person who leads something or someone somewhere.
During the 1914–18 war the word came to take on an almost mystical
import. A senior commander was a *Befehlshaber*, a command-haver; a
middle-rank commander was a *Kommandeur*; but the man who actually led the troops into battle, and got shot at while leading them, was
a *Führer*. The word took on as much importance as one's nominal
rank in the army, as one can still see from the memorials to fallen
officers in German civic cemeteries: *Leutnant u. Kompagnieführer*, *Major
u. Bataillonführer*. Jünger's *In Stahlgewittern* is sub-titled *Aus dem Tagebuch
eines Stosstruppführers*, from the diary of a shock-troop-commander. The
fighter ace Ernst Udet, when commanding a fighter squadron on the
Western Front in 1918, signed himself 'Udet *Oberlt d. R. und Führer*' It
was the natural word for an ex-soldier leading a para-military organization to adopt, though one cannot help wondering if Hitler, amongst
the many chips on his shoulder, did not have one about not having
been in a position to lead anyone in the war (for though an NCO he
was a company runner rather than in charge of a section.)[10]

'That was perhaps the most important thing for us, the emergence
of a Führer to whom one paid unconditional allegiance' (Another
attempt to translate the untranslatable: '*dies Herauschristallisieren eines
Führers, dem man unbedingte Gefolgschaft zollte*'). So wrote Fritz Baur, in
a book published in Vienna in 1929. From the time and place of

---

[9] Pongs, *Krieg als Volksschicksal*, p. 27.

[10] For the word *duce*, see *Enciclopedia italiana di scienze, lettere ed arti* (35 vols, Milan,
1929–37), xiii, p. 247; for Udet see report reproduced between p. 104 and p. 105 of
his *Mein Fliegerleben* (Berlin, 1935): *Oberlt d. R.* means senior lieutenant of the Reserve.

publication it is not clear that this had any reference at all to Hitler, but Erhard Wittek's *Durchbruch Anno Achtzehn: ein Fronterlebnis* ('Breakthrough AD 1918: A Frontline Experience'), published in the autumn of 1933 and announcing itself as a book about '*Führertum* and nothing else', though dedicated to the heroic battalion commander who had inspired and guided the author in 1918, was professedly written by way of penance for not having sooner embraced the irresistible greatness of Adolf Hitler and his National Socialist movement. Nor can there be any doubt as to where Otto Paust's exaggeratedly heroic novel *Volk im Feuer* (1935) stood: the four syllables of just the title ('Folk in the Fire' or perhaps rather 'A People in the Flames') are a miracle of compressed Nazi rhetoric. The novel is a hymn to comradeship:

> Comradeship is stronger than dying
> Comradeship is bigger than death
> Comradeship is something supernatural
> In it glows the spark of eternity.

It is also a hymn to collectivity:

> We are all only trustees of our blood, the Fatherland has us at its disposal. We are all merely tools, means to an end. But this end is so holy, that dying ennobles each and every one of us. In our death lies the fulfilment of an Idea called Freedom.

The one thing needed to pull all this together, the one thing lacking in 1918, was someone like Adolf Hitler: 'The Fatherland lacked a Führer, who stands above all, to whom the military and civil authorities are subordinated'.[11]

Next year, 1936, there appeared Sigmund Graff's *Unvergesslicher Krieg*, another popular history of the war which, like Beumelburg's *Sperrfeuer um Deutschland*, attempted to present the People as a single protagonist:

---

[11] Fritz Baur, *Vom Sterben . . ., 1914–1918* (Vienna, 1930), p. 60. Erhard Wittek *Durchbruch anno achtzehn* (Stuttgart, [1935]), pp. 189–90, end note; Otto Paust, *Volk im Feuer* (Dresden, 1935), p. 31; ibid., p. 39; ibid., p. 153.

One of the peculiarities of English is that we use a relatively bland term, 'the country', 'my country' where our neighbours use a much more evocative, resonant word, *la patrie, la patria, das Vaterland* – though to be fair they don't use these words very often in normal conversation.

Out of a people whose every member had believed himself entitled to something different, there grows – in the tattered garb of the fighter of the front in storms and battles – an idea that now all are under obligation to each other. This is the new thing, the overwhelming experience. The world changes and is transformed. From this new spiritual viewpoint, gained in the mud of the shell hole and at the bottom of the deepest dugout, a new order of things results, determined by necessity. The discovery of the Great War, the only discovery which made the war worth while for us, was the German human being [*der deutsche Mensch*]. Within the German community he and he alone must be in all the future the goal and starting point of all truly German politics, the object and centre of all internal struggles and discussions. This is the new achievement, overwhelming, unforgettable, and ever secure. For the sake of this one new thing two millions have died. And not one too many.

Another work which appeared in 1936 was the first part of an anthology entitled *Die Mannschaft: Frontsoldaten erzählen vom Front-Alltag* ('The men: frontline soldiers tell of everyday life at the front'). The editor, Jürgen Hahn-Butry, used his introduction to stress the importance of comradeship:

> The comradeship of men!
> That was our most abiding memory of this frightful yet beautiful war: that we had learnt to live together!
> Thus this holy comradeship forged something whole out of single men.
> One of the old force, Adolf Hitler . . .

It was of course Hitler's share in 'this frightful yet beautiful war' which qualified him, a man who was not even a German citizen by birth, to lead this nation of ex-soldiers. And not only ex-soldiers. Both Graff's *Unvergesslicher Krieg* and Hahn-Butry's *Die Mannschaft* were aimed at a popular readership, but 1936 also saw the appearance of a Greifswald university doctoral dissertation by Günther Lutz, one of the post-war generation that had grown up in the shadow of the Treaty of Versailles and saw in the Nazi regime an escape from the communal frustrations and contracted horizons that had hemmed in their adolescence. Lutz's dissertation, which was dedicated to Reinhard Heydrich, Himmler's second-in-command in the SS, was entitled *Die Front-Gemeinschaft: das Gemeinschaftserlebnis in der Kriegsliteratur*. This word

Gemeinschaft means an organic as distinct from an artificial collectivity or community, a distinction originating with the nineteenth-century social theorist Ferdinand Tönnies but much favoured by the Nazis. Lutz wrote that comradeship was the fulfilment of a Community of Sacrifice (*Opfergemeinschaft*). He adopted Volkmann's pairing of *Führer* and *Gefolgschaft*, discussing their mutual effect on one another and asserted that '*Gemeinschaft* is not equality but unity in spite of and through difference'. In his section on *Frontgemeinschaft* and *Volksgemeinschaft* he claimed that 'in the trenches and scattered holes, in filth and need [*in Dreck und Not*], there arose a new nucleus of true *Volksgemeinschaft*'. It was these new spiritual factors, he wrote, that Adolf Hitler had used as the basis for the Nazi movement:

> Thus the sacrifice and the legacy of the front and its two million dead is fulfilled, and an unshakable foundation laid for all political, social and spiritual life in future centuries and millennia.[12]

No doubt his 1936-vintage political correctness was regarded by the examiners of Lutz's dissertation as making up for a certain tendency towards over-simplification:

> Leadership is directly connected to the trust, love and loyalty of the followers [*Gefolgschaft*], yes, ultimately can only stem from community [*Gemeinschaft*] . . . In this double relationship of comradeship amongst the men, of trust and loyalty of the followers for the Führer, as in the solidarity of the Führer with his followers, lies the ultimate unity and wholeness [and] reciprocal solidarity.

Since Lutz says nothing of inspiration or exhortation or of officers setting a good example to their men, it all seems pretty mystical, and the ordinary structures of military hierarchy, backed up by courts-martial, seem rather to have become lost from view. Nor is this merely the verdict of hindsight. Till Kalkschmidt, author of an equally abstract thesis presented at Marburg University, *Der deutsche Frontsoldat: Mythos*

---

[12] Sigmund Graff, *Unvergesslicher Krieg: ein Buch vom deutschen Schicksal* (Leipzig, 1936), pp. 125–26; Jürgen Hahn-Butry, *Die Mannschaft: Frontsoldaten erzählen vom Front-Alltag* (4 vols, Berlin, 1936–38), i, p. 7; Günther Lutz, *Die Front-Gemeinschaft: das Gemeinschaftserlebnis in der Kriegsliteratur* (Greifswald, 1936), section 3 and also p. 54; ibid., p. 90; ibid., p. 92; ibid., p. 92.

und Gestalt (1938), reviewed Lutz's opus dismissively in *Dichtung und Volkstum*, mentioning the crudity of Lutz's ideas and his failure to recognize the Führer's creative role and his essential superiority to his followers, and assessing the 'literary-historical level' as 'lower than that of Cysarz, Pongs and Linden'.[13]

In his Marburg Ph.D. dissertation Kalkschmidt had suggested that a distinction should be made between the literature of comradeship, exemplified by Beumelburg's *Die Gruppe Bosemüller* and the literature of the *Führergestalt*, represented by Jünger's *In Stahlgewittern*, and also a distinction between the 'more human-natural action of the comrade-experience and the more spiritual-moral action of the follower experience'. Jünger himself, who, of course, unlike Lutz and Kalkschmidt, had actually lived through the worst awfulness of the frontline experience, was less concerned with abstract formula, and was still open to reconsidering the implications of what he had gone through. In 1925 he had written:

> To have to crouch under fire without cover, belaboured without a pause by shells of a calibre sufficient each one to lay a fair-sized village in ruins, without any distraction beyond counting the hits mechanically in a half-dazed condition, is an experience that almost passes the limits of human endurance. For this reason the men who issued the order, and threw hundreds of thousands naked and defenceless into the fire, took on themselves one of the heaviest responsibilities the mind can conceive. And yet, even though I may be one of the victims, I can but admit they were right. Time works with heavy tools, and in the battle for some slag-heap of horror, over whose wreathed smoke rival conceptions of the world's future are locked in demoniac strife, it is not a question of the few thousand men who may perhaps be rescued from destruction, but of the dozen or two survivors who are there in the nick of time to turn the scales with their machine-guns or their bombs. That is a view of the world's destiny which few have the iron nerve and masculine force to bear, and yet one may be proud to live in a time when such a spirit has shaped events to its mould of tempered steel. Though few may emerge from these flaming plains that offer no shelter but the mettle in a man's own heart, and though these few, resolute in aim and act, may still find fate turn against them

---

[13] Lutz, *Front-Gemeinschaft*, pp. 62–63; ibid., p. 64; *Dichtung und Volkstum*, 39 (1938), pp. 247–29. Another academic treatise was *Der Soldat in der deutschen Dichtung* (Stuttgart 1938) by Arno Mulot, 'Dozent an der Hochschule für Lehrerbildung, in Darmstadt'.

and deny them their goal, yet I feel as surely as I feel anything at all that a gain will be scored that can never be scored out. For they who can come through this – and, as I say, there can only be a few – what can there be that they could not come through? And so I see in old Europe a new and commanding breed rising up, fearless and fabulous, unsparing of blood and sparing of pity, inured to suffering the worst and to inflicting it and ready to stake all to attain their ends – a race that builds machines and trusts to machines, to whom machines are not soulless iron, but engines of might which it controls with cold reason and hot blood.

In 1929, in the Preface he wrote for the English edition of *In Stahlgewittern*, Jünger announced, 'Time only strengthens my conviction that it was a good and strenuous life, and that war, for all its destructiveness, was an incomparable schooling of the heart'. But as another war approached he began to turn things round in his mind and to have increasing reservations about the new Germany which had grounded itself, in part, on his rhetoric. Mobilized at the outbreak of the Second World War, and awarded the Iron Cross Second Class for rescuing a man under fire on the Siegfried Line early in 1940, by 1943 he was on the fringes of the military conspiracy to overthrow Hitler: but his failure to capitalize on his status as the leading ideologue of military enthusiasm during the mid-1930s suggests that his essential disenchantment dated from much earlier in the regime. By the mid-1930s however German literature was well on the way to becoming simply a component of an integrated political culture and so long as Jünger wished to stay in Germany he could not recant.[14]

Another contribution to the science of war literature by Günther Lutz was an article in *Dichtung und Volkstum* analysing non-German accounts of the war. Lutz decided that a characteristic of French writing about the war was that the war itself was not conceived as something

---

[14] Till Kalkschmidt, *Der deutsche Frontsoldat: Mythos und Gestalt* (Berlin, 1938), pp. 48–49; Ernst Jünger, *Copse 125: A Chronicle from the Trench Warfare of 1918* (1930), pp. 20–21 – originally published as *Das Wäldchen 125: eine Chronik aus dem Grabenkämpfen, 1918* (Berlin, 1925); Jünger, *Storm of Steel*, p. xii.

The distinction between the comradeliness of Beumelburg and the leaderishness of Jünger is somewhat spurious. Jünger does not become a company commander till halfway through *In Stahlgewittern*; Beumelburg's protagonist Bosemüller is a sergeant, promoted to staff sergeant (*Vizefeldwebel*) at the end of the book so that, though not commissioned, he is also in charge of other men.

experienced corporately, but only as something affecting individuals. 'In the foreground . . . stands not the crisis of the *Gemeinschaft*, not the crisis of the whole race, but the quite personal fate of the individual'. *Führer-Gefolgschaft* relationships were depicted, he claimed, simply as logical, intellectual, coloured by the ever-present fear of one's individuality being crushed in the military machine. As for English war literature, 'it was defined not by the War but by the *Zeitgeist*, and concerned not war as an inner experience . . . but as a literary "Destiny" of Mankind . . . as merely a *leit-motiv* or chance topic . . . War appeared only as an episode, through which the participant in the war passed as through one period of a lifetime'. Only the Italians, Lutz thought, recognized the *Führer-Gefolgschaft* issue and showed an 'emphasis on the Will as the source of power to overcome Fate'.[15]

This of course misrepresented just about everybody, even the Italians. There were in fact relatively fewer personal memoirs of the war published in Italy than elsewhere, as if the establishment of Mussolini's dictatorship had obviated the psychological need for such books, or else shifted people's attention from the past to the future: writing in exile in 1937 Emilio Lussu even claimed 'There do not exist in Italy, as in France, in Germany, or in England, books about the war'. What books there were represented, according to one officially-sponsored critic, 'the discovery of the people, of the mass, with its virtues and its blemishes . . . a precious experience which was to enter into the political action of the party which took power in 1922'. Even while the war was still in progress Michele Campana had written:

> The war has taught that in the gravest hour of communal life, the collective replaces the middlemen, abolishes the social classes, destroys the concept of property, provides directly for the life and work of millions and millions of men.

A little later, after the final victory over the Austrians at Vittorio Veneto, Enrico Corradini claimed:

[15] Günther Lutz, 'Europas Kriegserlebnis: ein Überblick über das ausserdeutsche Kriegsschrifttum', *Dichtung und Volkstum*, 38 (1938), pp. 133–68, at pp. 141–45; ibid., pp. 148–151; ibid., pp. 161–62. The Italian authors he cited were Mussolini, Marcipati (a leading Fascist intellectual) and Cornali: the appropriateness of the last two authors was demonstrated by the fact that their war books had been translated into German since Hitler's accession to power.

Our race which is in every one of us, in our flesh and in our soul, identified with our soil and our sky, with our language and with the structure
of our cities, in each one of us from the least citizen to the head of state,
from the obscurest private to General Diaz, from the factory worker to
the boss, from the humblest pleb to His Majesty the King, our race, so
ancient and always renewed and inexhaustibly everlasting, our race, without
which we have no awareness, is already working in its depths on the victory of Vittorio Veneto in order to transform it into new life force, new
power of will and capacity, new strength to do and suffer, to transmit and
distribute to the generations that will come. Rivers of blood from the
mountains and the plains, five million soldiers holding out in the trenches
for three and a half years, three and a half years of national unity and
solidarity and effort by every arm and every mind, three and a half years
of fervour and passion in every heart, fourteen battles, every miracle of
ancient times surpassed on land, at sea and in the air, an immense weep-
ing in every city, village and hovel, and the hymn to victory sung by forty
million Italians, that's what our generation offers to the race, to future
generations, to the Fatherland.

Of course, if one thinks about it, the winning side had much better
reason to be conscious of itself as a successful community than those
who, like the Germans, had been defeated and had thereupon col-
lapsed into revolution and civil strife. Again, soldiers in the French
and British armies were as fully aware of comradeship as their German counterparts:

> There is a very fine feeling of comradeship out here, both amongst the
> men and officers, and one really feels quite a little touch of pride every
> time one slides round these bally old trenches. Damn funny thing, patriot-
> ism, isn't it! Did I tell you of that most pathetic and touching incident of
> the aged French woman who strewed the road with flowers and sweet herbs
> for our fellows to march on when we had that long trek?

Cyril McNeile wrote of wartime comradeship in almost Germanic terms:
'One hoped so much that it would endure: that out of the furnace a
permanent welding might emerge'. He concluded sadly that it had
not: but one reason why the British did not need to insist upon it so
much was that, whereas in Britain's 1926 General Strike strikers played
football with the police, the more serious-minded Germans, seven

years earlier, fresh from fighting the enemy shoulder to shoulder, started shooting each other in the streets of their cities.[16]

One aspect of the new sense of national community based on frontline comradeship was the mingling of individuals from different social classes and different geographical regions, and this was something which received relatively less emphasis in German writing than in the literature of other countries. Most Italian regiments were composed of men from different regions. In the French and British armies, for reasons relating to class structure and social geography, the officers did not usually come from the same area as the rank and file. In the German army the strong regional basis of regimental organization meant that the officers usually came from the same district as their men, had mostly gone to the same schools (as was certainly not the case in the British army) and, in a culture which tolerated regional variations of language even amongst the educated classes, usually spoke, or at least understood, the same dialect. The use of sub-Kiplingesque soldier-cockney in, for example, Vernon Bartlett's *Mud and Khaki* (1917) or Cyril McNeile's *Shorty Bill* (1926), though well-intended seems condescending and inauthentic whereas the use of dialect by Jahier in *Con me e con gli alpini* (1919) and Paolo Monelli in *Le scarpe al sole* (1921) seems to refer to a personal discovery and also appears researched, the dialects in question being recognizably parallel derivatives of Latin, to which Jahier and Monelli attempt to give the orthographically correct form. Other than a few poems written entirely in dialect, published for strictly local consumption, this sort of thing had no counterpart in German war literature.

The different social backgrounds of men in the same section is referred to in Remarque's *Im Westen Nichts Neues* and in Johannsen's *Vier von der Infanterie*, and the theme of Benno von Mechow's *Das*

---

[16] Emilio Lussu, *Un anno sull'Altipiano* (Paris, 1938), Preface (dated from a Swiss sanatorium, April 1937: Lussu had contracted a lung complaint in one of Mussolini's gaols); Francesco Formigari, *La letteratura della guerra in Italia, 1915–1935* (Rome, 1935), p. 51: this book was published by the Istituto Nazionale Fascista di Cultura; Michele Campana, *Perchè ho ucciso?* (Florence, [1918]), p. 137; Enrico Corradini, 'Commemorazione' [18 December 1918], in Gualtiero Castellini, *Tre anni di guerra* (Milan, 1919), p. xviii: the word translated here as 'race' is *stirpe*, which has the sense of lineage or stock; Michael Moynihan, ed., *A Place Called Armageddon: Letters from the Great War* (1975), p. 128, letter by Lieutenant Robert Charles Case, July 1916; Cyril McNeile, *Sapper's War Stories: Collected in One Volume* [1930], p. 10, Foreword.

Abenteuer: ein Reiterroman aus dem grossen Krieg (1930) is the student-protagonist's difficulties in fitting in with his plebeian fellow soldiers, but there is nothing in German as self-consciously elaborate as the pop sociology which Barbusse established as the tradition amongst French and Anglo-American writers of war novels:

> what were we? Sons of the soil and artisans mostly. Lamuse was a farm-servant, Paradis a carter. Cadilhac, whose helmet rides loosely on his pointed head, though it is a juvenile size – like a dome on a steeple, says Tirette – owns land. Papa Blaire was a small farmer in La Brie. Barque, porter and messenger, performed acrobatic tricks with his carrier-tricycle among the trams and taxis of Paris, with solemn abuse (so they say) for the pedestrians, fleeing like bewildered hens across the big streets and squares. Corporal Bertrand, who keeps himself always a little aloof, correct, erect, and silent, with a strong and handsome face and forthright gaze, was foreman in a case-factory. Tirloir daubed carts with paint – and without grumbling, they say. Tulacque was barman at the Throne Tavern in the suburbs; and Eudore of the pale and pleasant face kept a roadside café not very far from the front lines. It has been ill-used by the shells – naturally, for we all know that Eudore has no luck. Mesnil André, who still retains a trace of well-kept distinction, sold bicarbonate and infallible remedies at his pharmacy in a *Grande Place*. His brother Joseph was selling papers and illustrated story-books in a station on the State Railways at the same time that, in far-off Lyons, Cocon, the man of spectacles and statistics, dressed in a black smock, busied himself behind the counters of an ironmongery, his hands glittering with plumbago; while the lamps of Bécuwe Adolphe and Poterloo, risen with the dawn, trailed about the coal-pits of the North like weakling will-o'-th'-wisps.
>
> And there are others amongst us whose occupations one can never recall, whom one confuses with one another; and the rural nondescripts who peddled ten trades at once in their packs, without counting the dubious Pepin, who can have had none at all.

An early imitator of this was Patrick MacGill in *Red Horizon*:

> Who were we? Why were we there? Goliath, the junior clerk, who loved Tennyson; Pryor, the draughtsman, who doted on Omar; Kore, who read Fanny Eden's penny stories, and never disclosed his profession; Mervin, the traveller, educated for the Church but schooled in romance; Stoner, the clerk, who reads my books and says he never read better; and Bill, newsboy, street-arab, and Lord knows what, who reads *The Police News*, plays innumerable tricks with cards, and gambles and never wins.

The British in any case had Fluellen, Macmorris and Jamy in Shakespeare's *Henry V,* plus all those there-was-an-Englishman-an-Irishman-and-a-Scotsman jokes:

> Grouped some few paces off three men are conversing. The first by his black hair, thick and hatchet face is Irish, the second red-headed, thick necked, with twisted smile a Lowland Scot, the third extraordinarily weedy, alert, a consumer of many cigarettes, a master of nick-names bestowed in a moment, is probably a Cockney.

In *Return of the Brute* (1929) Liam O'Flaherty (founder of the Irish Communist Party) devoted a whole chapter to describing his nine protagonists and their original civilian employments, which were:

> grocer's assistant
> labourer in a chocolate factory
> policeman
> officer in the Army Service Corps (cashiered)
> farm labourer
> drunken good-for-nothing 'a tout for a street book-maker . . . chucker
>   out in an illicit bookmaker': enlisted prior to 1914
> general labourer
> student [named, by coincidence (?), Louis Lamont]
> excise officer, but enlisted before 1914

Similarly, at the beginning of his novel *Squad* the American writer James B. Wharton listed the squad's members as:

> a Swedish-American rancher from Texas
> an American 'high school youth' from San Francisco
> a Serb coal-miner from Pennsylvania
> an American from Oklahoma
> a Jewish proprietor of a shoe store in the Bronx
> an Italian from Philadelphia
> an 'itinerant Irish-American worker'
> a high-school graduate from Ohio

Even non-fiction writers insisted on the varied backgrounds of the men in some units of the American Expeditionary Force:

> In the big war companies, 250 strong, you could find every sort of man, from every sort of calling. There were Northwesterners with straw-colored hair that looked white against their tanned skins, and delicately

spoken chaps with the stamp of the Eastern universities on them. There were large-boned fellows from Pacific-coast lumber camps, and tall, lean Southerners who swore amazingly in gentle, drawling voices. There were husky farmers from the corn-belt, and youngsters who had sprung, as it were, to arms from the necktie counter. And there were also a number of diverse people who ran curiously to type, with drilled shoulders and a bone-deep sunburn, and a tolerant scorn of nearly everything on earth.[17]

Regional differences were perhaps less striking, in the long run, than differences of social class which, in the French and Italian armies especially, came as a moral as well as a political revelation. The artist Fernand Léger recalled, nearly forty years later:

> It's in the war that I got my feet on the ground . . . I found myself on the same level as the entire French people; as I was assigned to the Engineering Corps my new comrades were miners, ditch-diggers, artisans who worked wood or iron . . . The coarseness, variety, humour, perfection of certain types of men around me, their concrete understanding of practical things and of their practical applications to this drama of life and death into which we had been thrown . . . Even more, they were poets, inventors of everyday poetic images – I mean of slang, so mobile and colourful . . .

During the war itself an anonymous contributor to a French soldiers' newspaper wrote:

> The lesson to be learnt by us thinking men from this war is a lesson in humility. Our brethren in glory and pain are unsophisticated . . . Our comrades of the great war surround us with ignorance and intellectual tranquillity . . . When our exhausted nerves and painful muscles let the pick fall, their strong arms continue to dig the trench with the same strong, regular rhythm; because our jerky efforts were slower and less skilled they had to do part of our work for us. Often during night fatigues they helped us carry the beam under which we would march at first, bending painfully down into the mud, and under which we soon staggered; they took our place and, still carrying their own burden, they helped us at the same time. It was they who pitied us, and our souls which were full of gratitude

[17] Henri Barbusse, *Under Fire* (1917), p. 16; Patrick MacGill, *Red Horizon* (1916), pp. 86–87; Public Record Office, FO 395/222/46969, draft by Robert Nichols; Liam O'Flaherty, *Return of the Brute* (1929), pp. 47–53; John W. Thomason, Jr, *Fix Bayonets! With the US Marine Corps in France, 1917–1918* (1925), pp. ix-x

and prayer, humility and shame; for we were ashamed of our white hands and our feeble arms. And we were ashamed sometimes of our excessive sensitivity. On days when the prolonged and violent bombardment brought our poor nerves to their limit, their calm and balanced temperament endured without impatience, without restiveness, all the emotions of the pounding, of that waiting below ground, in the shadow where death hovers, in the face of the terrible unknown . . . When we had to brave the open ground swept by shot they faced the fire with a broader and stronger breast, with stronger arms, with more skilful movements, more simple and more sure. Better than us at labouring, they were often better at fighting too, better shots, better runners, more dextrous with their bayonets. At rest, they slept more easily than those of us whose brains persisted in thinking. They soon forgot their weariness. And, although sometimes they would admire us in turn when our knowledge was apparent, although we would then feel their slightly superstitious schoolboy respect for us as for a schoolmaster, we remained humble before them because we felt keenly how much we lacked their strength and physical skills, how much our over-sensitive nervous system was something inferior, almost a handicap. We understood that there is no need to be a philosopher to be great when faced with the greatest of all things, to face up to danger despite the shrinking back of the flesh, to understand and perform all one's duty, to approach death proudly, 'stoically' – that death before whom we are all equal and which lays side by side these bodies of ours, similar and equal in value when the unequal flame of intelligence leaves them.[18]

The soldiers of other belligerent nations were also at least as conscious as the Germans that the trenches in some indefinable way strengthened those who were able to survive. Even in his anti-war tirade *Death of a Hero* Richard Aldington could write of the faces of veterans returning to the Front after leave in Britain:

They were lean and still curiously drawn although the men had been out of the line for a fortnight; the eyes had a peculiar look. They seemed strangely worn and mature, but filled with energy, a kind of slow, enduring energy. In comparison the fresh faces of the new drafts seemed babyish – rounded and rather feminine.

[18] *Fernand Léger, 1881–1955* (Catalogue of Exhibition at Palais de Beaux-Arts, Brussels October-November 1956), p. 30; Stephane Audoin-Rouzeau, *Men at War, 1914–1918: National Sentiment and Trench Journalism in France during the First World War* (Providence, Rhode Island, 1992), p. 49, quoting *L'horizon*, November 1917.

Frederic Manning saw something similar:

> It may have been a merely subjective impression, but it seemed that once they were in the front line, men lost a great deal of their individuality; their characters, even their faces, seemed to become more uniform; they worked better, the work seeming to take some of the strain off their minds, the strain of waiting. It was, perhaps, that they withdrew more into themselves, and became a little more diffident in the matter of showing their feelings. Actually, though the pressure of external circumstances seemed to wipe out individuality, leaving little if any distinction between man and man, in himself each man became conscious of his own personality as of something very hard, and sharply defined against a background of other men, who remained merely generalised as 'the others'. The mystery of his own being increased for him enormously; and he had to explore that doubtful darkness alone . . . If a man could not be certain of himself, he could be certain of nothing. The problem which confronted them all equally, though some were unable or unwilling to define it, did not concern death so much as the affirmation of their own will in the face of death; and once the nature of the problem was clearly stated, they realized that its solution was continuous, and could never be final. Death set a limit to the continuance of one factor in the problem, and peace to that of another; but neither of them really affected the nature of the problem itself.[19]

As in the German army, head-gear provided an outward symbol of inward militancy. The French were the first to introduce shrapnel-proof steel helmets – or almost shrapnel-proof, for Apollinaire was wearing one when wounded in the head – and their generals were regularly photographed wearing these medieval-looking casques, as was King Ferdinand of Rumania, who, commanding his army in the field though in little personal danger of being brained by shrapnel, evidently recognized that a helmet concealed the unusual prominence of his ears. There is also a famous photo of King Albert of the Belgians in a helmet but this appears to have been a studio portrait. As a symbol the helmet was much easier to depict in drawings or photographs than key concepts like the Front, the Trenches, *Führertum.* The English pudding-basin/shaving-bowl helmet was less photogenic than either the French or the German model but prior to its introduction frontline

---

[19] Richard Aldington, *Death of a Hero* (1965 edn), p. 253; Frederic Manning, *Her Privates We* (1930), p. 203.

troops had adopted the habit of removing the stiffeners in the caps worn by both officers and men, altering the angular flat-topped appearance to one of unkempt bagginess; this was known as a 'Gorblimey Hat' and was important as distinguishing frontline troops from staff and base personnel.

There were also numerous non-German writers who rivalled Ernst Jünger's dizzy pass-me-another-hand-grenade enthusiasm for the war: the problem was they were not generally such good writers as Jünger:

> A moment only – and we were right up against the enemy . . .
>
> I turn a corner quickly – two grey Germans stand straight in front of me . . . Two red flashes straight into my face – done for already! – but they haven't hit me, so now it is my turn. A snap-shot at one of the two, and the other disappears round a corner. The road is free! 'Come on boys, give them hell!' At the next corner a shower of rifle-bullets and 'sticks' whizz past my head from a machine-gun post . . . I fire away madly till my magazine is empty; then I fling down the rifle and hurl my bombs at them – the trench is chockfull of dust and smoke. Mac has come up close behind me, his shots thunder right into my ears . . . From behind they are throwing bombs by the dozen, without minding in the least who and what they are hitting. They shout and yell: 'Give them hell, boys!' The German dynamite-bombs are bursting everywhere around Mac and I; in the trench and on the parapet. We throw ourselves flat at the bottom of the trench and are not even hit by an explosion three yards away, though a cartload of rubbish descends on our backs. Jack comes up from behind with a fresh supply of Mills bombs. . . . 'Here you are, Fritzie boy, damn you! . . . and here is another!' Ah, they have had enough, they are done for, the bastards! A couple of survivors dash off from the post, and we rush after them, tear our hands and kilts on the wire, jumping across the overturned machine-gun and the dead or dying gunners, running panting and perspiring along the dry, hard trench, corner by corner . . . and then we reach the next machine-gun post and throw ourselves against it, yelling and roaring, with bombs and bayonets, battle-mad – regardless of everything in the world, our whole being intent on one thing alone: to force our way ahead and kill!

The writer just quoted also tried to find socio-cultural reasons to explain how men could persist and endure under such awful conditions:

> What is it that gives them their courage? Is it their religious faith, their trust in God's Will and Providence, their belief in a life after death? I

myself do not believe in or take count of another life after this, and death has therefore no fear or hope for me; but nearly all of the others believe certainly in eternal life – many of them even feel sure that he who gives up his life on the battlefield will be admitted at once into paradise. Or is it confidence they have in their righteous cause, their love for their country, their hatred of the Huns? I don't think so.

Such acquired dogmas and theoretical reflections may certainly help people to do their duty, to go voluntarily to their death if need be, but they do not free them from fear.

But for hundreds of years the spirit of the British race has striven towards one ideal, has valued one thing above everything else in the world: to be men – strong, inflexible, fearless. They have reached their goal: the old curse, the dread of death, has been defeated; they have learned to meet suffering and death with open, steady eyes – and they have gained the mastery of the world.

This reads like a fairly routine piece of patriotic tub-thumping but is worth quoting because it is not the author's own words but a paraphrase. What he actually wrote was:

Var vi bange? Mange af os ville ikke opleve næste solnedgang, – havde angsten for døden tag i os i de par stille nattetimer? Jeg så på kammeraterne omkring mig, de hviskede et par bemærkninger til hinanden med rolige stemmer og lo daempet. Her var hverken nervøsitet eller frygt at spore

. . .

Jeg tror, det er den britiske nations århundredgamle, klippefaste vilje til, fremfor alt andet i verden, at være mænd, stærke, ubøjelige, frygtløse mænd, som har undrettet vidunderet, har hævet den ældgamle forbandelse, dødsfrygten, lært dem at gå mod lidelser og død med åbne, rolige øjne, – og gjort deres race til verdens herre.

The author was Thomas Dinesen VC, one of several Danes who volunteered – and overcame various obstacles – to fight in a war in which their own country was neutral.[20]

---

[20] Thomas Dinesen, *Merry Hell! A Dane with the Canadians* [1930], p. 238–39. (The jeer 'Here you are, Fritzie boy, damn you!' isn't in the Danish text); ibid., p. 216; Thomas Dinesen, *No Man's Land: en Dansker med Canadierne ved Vestfronten* (Copenhagen, 1965 edn), pp. 160–61.

Dinesen explained (*Merry Hell!*, pp. 13–14) that he attempted to enter France and Britain to enlist and finally went to Canada to join up not out of 'hatred of the

Jünger himself fully recognized that even in Germany his attitude to the war had not been shared by every soldier:

> We, too, have no lack of those who, like the Frenchman, Barbusse, regard war as a material affair and, turning its negative side outwards, endeavour to run up on the other a temple of peace and happiness. They give as their reasons devastated towns and frightful sufferings – as though our highest duty was the avoidance of pain. They have no mind to accept the responsibilities that demand sacrifice of such corruptible treasures as life and property when a nation's greatness and its ideas are at stake.

On the other hand he was pretty sure which attitude he himself wished to be identified with:

> One man has a mind for adventure and is thrown like a modern Sindbad from one danger to another. Another sees only the sanguinary glare on the face of events and is petrified as by the sight of a Gorgon's head. Another goes with the stream because he feels that fate is stronger than he is. He takes his quarters as they come; trusts to his star in battle; and even in the drear monotony finds his little pleasures growing like the bright lichens on a bare stone. Others again are soldiers first and last. Their eyes are hard and cold beneath the rim of the helmet. They are centres of energy about whom the wavering lines rally in the battle. In them the will-power of a nation at war seems to be most clearly and terribly expressed.[21]

In his Introduction to the English edition of *In Stahlgewittern* R.H. Mottram wrote that Jünger 'seems to imagine that a sort of Nietzschean-Wagnerian atmosphere of heroics translated into terms of gas and tanks can be re-created out of the wreckage of empire', and it is worth asking how far is it true that only a German writer could have mixed violence and philosophizing in the way Jünger did. It seems obvious that people

---

continued
Prussians . . . enthusiasm for the cause of Liberty in danger; nor indignation at the sight of justice outraged . . . [but because] Everything at home seemed insufferably void, trivial and insignificant: Ypres, Gallipoli, Verdun; those were the names that stood for life and reality!'

Other gung-ho writers in the armies of the British Empire include A.O. Pollard VC, author of *Memoirs of a Fire-Eater* (1932), and Joseph Maxwell VC, author of *Hell's Bells and Mademoiselles*. For other Danish volunteeers see J. Ravn-Jonsen, ed., *Danske Frivillige I Verdenskrigen: Soldaterbreve frå Fronterne* (Copenhagen, [1917]).

[21] Jünger, *Copse 125*, p. ix; ibid., p. 3.

living in a different culture, reading different books, educated at schools organized according to different principles, governed according to different political traditions *must* to a large extent think differently. The following can only have been written by a Briton because it refers to a uniquely British institution and assumes that the reader shares prejudices that are specifically bred in such an institution:

> Bedwell had just left a public school sixth form and carried the *Iliad* about with him. What a magnificent type of man compared with the officers we got later from secondary schools or from the ranks. Nor was he the only example of the superiority of the public school boy – and of the public school boys the quiet scholarly type were the best. The smart young men and the athletes would throw their weight about behind the lines but they were not chosen for a nasty job and after a few months' real war they were likely to crack up. The middle-aged married men and the quiet young men were the war's heroes – and how much harder it was for them too.

The particular pitch and tone of British writers when they draw attention to the tinniness of tin gods is also hard to mistake:

> The Brigadier wore a mackintosh jacket over his uniform, a pair of mackintosh trousers over his breeches, and a steel helmet that tended to slide over his left ear. There was no visible mark of rank at first, but later he fixed on his helmet the crossed sword and baton. His real badge of office was a wooden staff exactly four feet six inches long, and with this he tested the height of the top layer of sandbags on the parapet over the fire-step. It was decreed that this height of four feet six inches must never be exceeded – there was little danger of any shortage, but a tall man standing on the fire-step felt acutely conscious of his upper eighteen inches. This mackintoshed figure, with boyish face and pouting expression, conscientiously measuring his staff against the trench wall, and finding a quiet satisfaction in the rare tallying of the two heights, commanded a force of three thousand men.

The different religious traditions of foreign countries might give a peculiarly alien quality to even their secular rhetoric:

> Men of my country, I learn to know you better each day, and it is from having contemplated your face in the depths of suffering that I have shaped a religious faith in the future of our race. Above all it is from having admired your resignation, your native goodness, your serene confidence in the best times, that I believe in the moral future of the world.

Even when the most natural instinct taught ferocity to the world, you retained on your beds of pain, a beauty, a purity of look which in themselves redeemed the great crime. Men of France, your naive greatness of soul exculpates all humanity of its greatest crime and its deepest fall.

The different historical mythology of different communities inevitably led to emphases that might seem strange and even disgraceful to readers educated in another country:

> Avant cette guerre on respirait un air impur . . .
> Dans l'histoire on ne parlera pas de nos pères vaincus, on dira
>   que nous fûmes des hommes neufs nés des pères obscurs . . .
> Nous engendrons dans la douleur de cette guerre notre joie.
> La joie de notre force, la joie de notre triomphe . . .
> Entre autres choses, nous avons fait La Marne and Verdun.
> Nos pères firent Sedan puis y pensèrent sans en parler
> Par delà des générations souillées nous réclamons comme
>   immédiats géniteurs ceux de 93 et tous ceux de nos ancêtres
>   qui furent vainquers

(Before this war we breathed impure air . . . In history they won't talk of our defeated fathers, they'll say we were new men born from unknown fathers . . . In the pain of this war we give birth to our joy, the joy of our strength, the joy of our triumph . . . Amongst other things, we achieved the Marne and Verdun, our fathers achieved Sedan so they think about it without saying anything. By-passing the dishonoured generations we claim as our immediate forebears the men of 1793 and all those of our ancestors who were conquerors.) But of course both the vaingloriousness of the last passage and the mawkishness of the extract preceding came out of the same national culture: however uniform and monochrome a national culture may appear to foreigners, the writers who partly embody it are nonetheless individuals speaking with their own personal voices even though obliged to use the idiom of their community. This of course was as true of Jünger as of anyone else. His philosophizing has its parallels in books by writers who served in the armies opposed to Germany, as do his scenes of violence and horror: it is the combination of disparate elements that is perhaps the most distinctive feature of *In Stahlgewittern* but this combination surely has less to do with German-ness than with the fact that a man who was at the forefront of so many battles survived to write it all down.[22]

Nevertheless the mere fact of Jünger's survival had an important influence on German literature in the inter-war years. There was a psychological need in Germany for someone like Ernst Jünger that did not exist in France or Britain because, quite simply, they had not lost the war. *In Stahlgewittern* was not a phenomenon that, if it had not existed, would have had to have been invented. It was something that could only have been produced by a gifted author like Ernst Jünger, and if he had not been born, or had been killed in the war like so many others, no conceivable substitute or replacement could have had the same impact. Beumelburg, despite his subsequent huge sales, or Otto Paust were not in the same league as writers. (This is a good illustration of the way in which the quality of a piece of literature is as much a factor in its impact on society as its timeliness or subject-matter; the writings of Paust and Schauwecker grew out of the war just as much as those of Jünger, but their growth was simply of a different, and much smaller, order. One may wonder what might have happened in Britain if Rupert Brooke had emerged from four years in the trenches as a lieutenant-colonel with a Victoria Cross: or Charles Sorley; or even Edward Mannock, a man of distinctly fascistic leanings remembered by his fellow officers as an electrifying public speaker.) There were however two peculiarly German factors which reinforced Jünger's influence. One was the particular conditions of German academe; a number of British writers on the war found at least temporary refuge in university literature departments – Blunden, Graves, Nichols, Lamont – though only Blunden, appointed a Fellow of Merton College, Oxford in 1931, attained a position of much eminence – but their teaching duties required them to turn their backs on the twentieth century. There were also fewer so-called scholarly journals in Britain and France than in Germany (though perhaps after

---

[22] Jünger, *Storm of Steel* (1930 edn), p. vi; Richard Devonald-Lewis, ed., *From the Somme to the Armistice: The Memoirs of Captain Stormont Gibbs MC* (1986), p. 68. After the war Gibbs ran a prep school; Llewelyn Wyn Griffith, *Up to Mametz* (1931), pp. 149–50; Georges Duhamel, *Vie des martyres* (1966 edn), pp. 187–88 first published 1917; Pierre Drieu la Rochelle, 'Chante de guerre des hommes d'aujourd'hui', in *Interrogation: poèmes* (Paris, 1917), pp. 169–71.

all they were more scholarly than *Dichtung und Volkstum*); thesis writing was much less established in Britain, whereas in France university *thèses* needed to be much longer than in German Ph.D.s and necessarily took much longer to appear. Neither Britain nor France had the kind of regime in 1936 which made it a smart move to dedicate one's Ph.D. thesis to the No. 2 in the SS/Secret Police organization. The scholarly debate in Germany on 1914–18 literature was thus a phenomenon without real parallel in other countries. Secondly, and more importantly, was the way that the Nazi regime simply eliminated half of the discordant voices amongst the chorus of war writers. The reason why Beumelburg replaced Remarque as the author of Germany's best-selling war novel, and the reason why Jünger's sales finally overtook those of the German translation of Barbusse's *Le feu*, was that the Nazi regime, as well as creating a climate favourable to the works of Beumelburg and Jünger, banned those of Remarque and Barbusse. If the Communists had gained power instead of the Nazis (not that there was ever much possibility of this) it would have been Ludwig Renn and perhaps Arnold Zweig who would have benefited from official controls and official sponsorship.[23]

Germany of course was not the only country to be defeated in the First World War. The lack of any considerable body of writing in Turkish dealing with the war may have less to do with the backwardness of Turkish literature than with the radical restructuring of public life in Turkey in the early 1920s. Parallel developments seem also to have cut off the flow of writing about the war in Italy and Portugal, which suggests that the important factor was not victory or defeat in the actual fighting but rather what happened afterwards. In Austria, defeated and dismembered, the most striking work inspired by the war was an extravaganza on the theme of its monstrous, destructive stupidity: Karl Kraus's satirical, apocalyptic and (as it unfortunately transpired) prophetic drama *Die letzten Tage der Menschheit* (1922: 'The Last Days of Mankind'). Kraus, a journalist, had been exempted from call-up on health grounds in 1915 and the two most notable works

---

[23] For Mannock as a public speaker, see Ira Jones *King of Air Fighters: Biography of Major 'Mick' Mannock VC, DSO, MC* (1934), pp. 101–2, 160, 165, 203, 205. For an amplification of some of the ideas in this paragraph see A.D. Harvey, *Literature into History* (Basingstoke, 1988), pp. 69, 76–84.

inspired by the war by Austrians who had served in the firing line, Joseph Roth's *Radetzkymarsch* (1932) and Robert Musil's *Der Mann ohne Eigenschaften* (1930–43; translated eventually as *The Man without Qualities*), both deal with the period before hostilities, and end more or less when the shelling starts, an idea possibly borrowed from Zola's *La bête humaine* of 1890. (Roth's Polish friend Józef Wittlin unintentionally managed the same effect with *Sol Ziemi*, 1935 – translated into English as *Salt of the Earth*, 1939 – which was the first part of a planned trilogy, of which the final third was never written and the middle section was lost when the author fled for his life during the German invasion of France in 1940; the published text ends as the recruits are given uniforms and sworn in.) In his Introduction to the first volume of the official history of the Austro-Hungarian army's part in the First World War, Carl Vaugoin, vice-chancellor and army minister in the Austrian government, announced the book as 'a last memorial of the gigantic battle of heroes which for more than four years the Austro-Hungarian army fought till, still everywhere on enemy soil, it fell victim to an inexorable fate . . .', but the prevailing attitude in post-1918 Austria to the war and the old Habsburg Empire seems to have been one of cynical bemusement.[24]

Hungary had officially enjoyed equal status with Austria within the Habsburg Empire in 1914 and was thus in theory equally responsible for the Empire's participation in the war. There was certainly not the same undercurrent of resentment at being dragged into Vienna's war that was evident in the Slav territories. The most widely-read anti-Empire text by a soldier in a 'Hungarian' unit, Miroslav Krleža's *Hrvatski Bog Mars* (1922: 'The Croatian God Mars') was by a Croat; a harsh and sombrely ironic treatment of the theme of Slavs dying for the Habsburgs; it reads like a sourer-toned continuation of Hašek's unfinished *Šveik* or Wittlin's truncated *Sol Ziemi*. (It was probably no coincidence that Krleža, Hašek and Wittlin all chose to write about fictional protagonists much less well-educated than themselves, as if

---

[24] For Kraus's exemption from military service, see Heinrich Fischer, Michael Lazarus, eds, *Karl Kraus: Briefe an Sidonie Nadherny von Borutin, 1913–1936* (2 vols, Munich 1974), i, p. 204, letter 302, 24 September 1915, and ii, p. 161 and 175, notes to letters 235 and 290. For Wittlin see Walter Jens, ed., *Kindlers neues Literatur Lexikon* (20 vols, Munich, 1988–92), xvii, p. 765; *Österreich-Ungarns letzter Krieg, 1914–18* (5 vols only, published Vienna 1930–34), i, p. v, 'Zum Geleite'.

to emphasize the distance between the Habsburg Empire's privileged
clases and its Slav subjects.) In 1917 Andreas Latzko produced a collection of anti-war, though not specifically anti-Habsburg, stories which
became an international best-seller during the last months of the
conflict. In English it may be found both under the title *Men in Battle*
and as *Men in War*, and there were also wartime translations into French,
Swedish and Dutch; but though Latzko had written in Hungarian at
the outset of his career, this particular book was composed in German, and was only published in Hungarian after the Austro-
Hungarian capitulation.

The characteristic Magyar literature of the war – Géza Gyóni's collection of poems *Levelek a Kálváriáról* (1916: 'Letters from Calvary'),
Lajos Zilahy's novel *Két fogoly* (1927: translated into English as *Two
Prisoners*, 1931) and Rodion Markovits *Szibériai garnizon* (1929: translated
as *Siberian Garrison* in the same year) — dealt with the experience of
being a prisoner of war in Siberia; Aladár Kuncz's *Fekete kolostor* (1931:
The Black Monastery, 1934) was based on the author's experiences as a
civilian internee in France. Hungary had obtained complete independ-
ence after the Habsburg collapse, so that the Hungarians, though
defeated on the battlefield, had come out of the war as a kind of win-
ner. The theme of military imprisonment – embracing defeat, suffering, survival and self-vindication – could not have been more
appropriate; though it was perhaps not entirely a coincidence that a
generation later the greatest Hungarian writer of the Second World
War, Miklós Radnóti, also a prisoner, ended up being shot by guards
who were just as Hungarian as he was.[25]

[25] Another Hungarian novel about the First World War – published in Russian
translation in 1937 but in Hungarian not till 1947 – was *Doberdo* by Máté Zalka (real
name Béla Frankl, but best known, in the final stages of his career, as General Lukács).
Doberdo describes how an enthusiastic, politically liberal officer in a Hungarian unit
is converted to communism and pacifism by his experiences on the Italian front.
Frankl, having been taken prisoner by the Russians, distinguished himself as a Red
Army officer in the Crimea during the Russian Civil War, served in the *Cheka* and
was killed in action, aged forty-one, while commanding the XIIth International Brigade
in Spain in 1937: Ludwig Renn commanded a battalion under him.

Amongst other novels about camp life in Siberia by Austro-Hungarian prisoners
of war perhaps the most notable is *Prameny* ('Rivulets') (1934), by the Czech writer
Jaroslav Kratochvíl, who died in a German concentration camp in 1945.

The history that we struggle to understand can only be seen through the distorting lens of hindsight. A generation of young men who had read Jünger as schoolboys became officers in an army that overran practically the whole of Europe. France, psychologically prepared, one might say, by the mawkishness of Duhamel and the hysterical rant of Drieu la Rochelle, was one of Germany's earlier victims; the Italians, coming into the war on Germany's side, staggered from blunder to blunder. One question to be answered here is whether any of this had to do with the books about the 1914–18 war published in the inter-war period: and the answer has to be *no*.

A neat formulation would be that for the French the First World War was something they survived, for the British something they handled, for the Italians something they proved themselves at, for the Austrians something they lost, for the Hungarians something the Austrians lost, for the Germans something that taught them to be stronger. Yet there seem to have been no gradations of difference in the lack of enthusiasm with which the general population of the belligerent nations entered the war in September 1939. After the collapse of France in June 1940 stories multiplied about French defeatism: in reality of course defeated armies always do appear defeated, and there were no convincing signs of French defeatism before the Germans attacked, other than those recalled after the event. It is true that Alan Brooke, later Chief of the Imperial General Staff and Britain's senior army officer, was astonished by the appearance of French troops at a parade he attended two months after the declaration of war:

> Seldom have I seen anything more slovenly and badly turned out. Men unshaven, horses ungroomed, clothes and saddlery that did not fit, vehicles dirty, and complete lack of pride in themselves and their units. What shook me most, however, was the look in the men's faces, disgruntled and insubordinate looks, and, although ordered to give 'Eyes left', hardly a man bothered to do so.

But Brooke, like most British officers of his generation, was a spit and polish man, out of sympathy with the casualness of continental armies. Most scholars who have examined the evidence agree that the true explanation for the French defeat is to be found in the strategic and tactical rather than the psychological sphere. They had more and better tanks than the Germans, though an inferior doctrine of employment, as many and almost as good fighter planes, good bombers even if too few of them owing to units being in the throes of re-equipment (though lack of numbers was less crucial than the poor use made of what was available): they were defeated quite simply because the Germans struck where least expected and having broken through pushed forward their armoured spear-heads with a boldness that made even Hitler nervous. The French High Command's inability to respond effectively was not owing to the senility of senior generals, the rigidity of command structures or the defeatism of majors, but owing to the way the army had been deployed. The Belgians had seen they were done for by 28 May, the nineteenth day of the German offensive: the French struggled on gallantly for almost another three weeks. The army that most disappointed expectations in the Second World War was the Italian one, trained up and equipped under the ostentatiously invigorating influence of Fascism: but the cause of the failure of the Italians could not have been Fascism as such, since it was the newer Fascist regime in Greece that first defeated it. The likeliest explanation lies in the emphasis on cosmetic appearances at the expense of underlying realities which characterized almost every part of Mussolini's administration but which cannot be regarded as altogether the inevitable consequence of Fascism. Meanwhile the British army, led by officers who in the 1914–18 war had been repeatedly decorated for gallantry and had risen to the command of battalions and even brigades, was consistently wrong-footed by German generals who in many cases had only had office jobs in the First World War.[26]

Nothing in pre-1939 literature caused or foreshadowed or represented tendencies parallel to any of this: for all that the achievement of authors like Ernst Jünger and Siegfried Sassoon continues

[26] Marlis G. Steinert, *Hitlers Krieg und die Deutschen: Stimmung und Haltung der deutschen Bevölkerung im zweiten Weltkrieg* (Düsseldorf, 1970), pp. 91ff. Arthur Bryant, *The Turn of the Tide, 1939–1943: A Study Based on the Diaries and Autobiographical Notes of Field Marshal the Viscount Alanbrooke* (1957), p. 71; R.H.S. Stolfi, 'Equipment for Victory in France in 1940', *History,* 55 (1970), pp. 1–20; A.D. Harvey, 'The French Armée de l'Air in May-June 1940: A Failure of Conception', *Journal of Contemporary History,* 25 (1990), pp. 447–65; MacGregor Knox, *Mussolini Unleashed, 1939–1941: Politics and Strategy in Fascist Italy's Last War* (Cambridge, 1982), especially pp. 232–72, and Stephen Harvey, 'The Italian War Effort and the Strategic Bombing of Italy', *History,* 70 (1985), pp. 32–45

to loom large in the imagination of readers born three or four decades later, the work of frontline writers was only a part of the story of how different societies attempted to come to terms with the experience of the First World War and, in particular, had only the smallest impact on the way the military establishments in different countries responded to the lessons of victory and defeat. In the end it was not the course of the Second World War but its literature which was most influenced by the writers of the 1914–18 generation.

Part Three

The Second World War

CHAPTER 10

Tired Accents

During the middle part of the Second World War, RAF bomber crews stationed in Norfolk were paying up to £5 – nearly ten times the original shop price – for copies of *Winged Victory*, Victor Yeates's novel of the air war on the Western Front in 1918; they told Henry Williamson, 'it was the only book about war flying which "wasn't flannel".' At about the same time Robert Graves began an article in *The Listener*. 'I have been asked to explain as a "war poet of the last war" why so little poetry has so far been produced by this one'. The inferiority of Second World War literature seems to have been taken for granted right from the start, and might be explained in terms of the different shape, so to speak, of the war: the idealistic young men of 1914 sucked into the holocaust of the Western Front and recording their disillusion in deathless verse, as compared to the chaps who hadn't expected very much in the first place spending most of the war in barracks and training grounds in Britain. Alun Lewis – killed by a bullet from his own gun before he ever saw action – explained of his stories about army life, 'Death in battle, death on a large scale, and all the attendant finalities and terrors – these are outside . . . the main motif is the rootless life of soldiers having no enemy, and always, somehow, under a shadow'. That shadow cast itself wider than ever before: in Britain even young women without dependants became liable to conscription: 'I wonder what you will do when you get home?' a character in a Graham Greene novel says to a survivor from a torpedoed ship: 'I supposed they'll conscript me', she replies:

> He thought: If my child had lived, she too would have been conscriptable, flung into some grim dormitory, to find her own way. After the Atlantic,

the ATS or the WAAF, the blustering sergeant with the big bust, the cook-house and the potato peelings, the Lesbian officer with the thin lips and the tidy gold hair, and the men waiting on the Common outside the camp. among the gorse bushes . . . compared to that surely even the Atlantic was more a home.

Part of the dreariness of it all was that, though the public rhetoric and the politicians' ranting was in the same ultra-black-and-ultra-white terms as in 1914–18, those who could not accept the crudity of official over-simplifications were denied the solitary satisfaction of private indigna-tion and self-righteousness, because this time the black bits of the truth really were blacker, and even the most dissenting had to admit that much of what the official tub-thumpers said was both justified and necessary. C. Day Lewis even suggested, in a poem entitled 'Where Are the War Poets?' that this was the reason why there weren't any:

> They who in folly or mere greed
> Enslaved religion, markets, laws
> Borrow our language now and bid
> Us to speak up in freedom's cause.
>
> It is the logic of our times,
> No subject for immortal verse –
> That we who lived by honest dreams
> Defend the bad against the worse.[1]

No doubt related, even if not exactly parallel, considerations af-fected poets living in Nazi Germany: yet in many respects the shape of the Second World War was not so very different from the First – the long slog on the Western Front replaced on an even larger scale by the long slog on the Eastern Front, the fervours of nationalism

---

[1] V.M. Yeates, *Winged Victory* (1961 edn), p. 8: Henry Williamson's 'Preface to the New Edition'; Robert Graves, 'War Poetry in this War', *The Listener*, 23 October 1941, reprinted as 'The Poets of World War II', in Robert Graves, *The Common Asphodel: Collected Essays on Poetry, 1922–1949* (1949), pp. 307–11; Alun Lewis, *The Last Inspec-tion* (1942), p. 5, Author's Note: for Lewis's death, officially judged to be an accident but suspiciously like suicide, see John Pikoulis, *Alun Lewis: A Life* (Bridgend, 1984), pp. 265–66; Graham Greene, *The Heart of the Matter* (1971 edn), pp. 181–82 – first published 1948; C. Day Lewis, 'Where Are the War Poets?', in *Collected Poems* (1954), p. 228, first published in *Word Over All* (1943).

replaced by the no less intense ardours of Fascism or of anti-Fascism. In any case it is a perniciously limited view of modern war to suppose that the depressingness and sense of dislocation and disorientation was confined to people who were obliged to don uniforms. Some of the finest literature produced by the Second World War arose from the French experience of German occupation: not just Vercors's *Le silence de la mer* (1942) about the relationship of a German officer, an anti-Nazi, with the French family on whom he is billeted, but also Albert Camus's *La peste*, which doesn't mention the war at all, and Sartre's play *Huis clos*, which was originally conceived as taking place in a cellar during an air-raid, though in its final version the hopelessly trapped characters are situated simply in unlocated space. Bohdan Czeszko's novel *Pokolenie* (1951), which provided the basis for Andrzej Wajda's classic film of the same title ('A Generation', 1954), also stemmed from the experience of occupation: in the film version at least the foreignness of the occupying soldiers seems incidental, as if they primarily represent a universal principle of totalitarian oppression and class exploitation.

Even neutral countries felt obliged to mobilize their armed forces and existed for four years in a state of siege: the situation in Sweden is evoked by Ivar Lo-Johansson's sardonic *Soldaten* ('The Soldier', 1959). The most detailed accounts of air-raids to be printed during the war appeared in the Swiss press in the aftermath of the accidental bombing of Basel and Zurich on 4 March 1945 by American bombers flying from bases in England. Elsewhere bombing raids brought the pyrotechnics of modern warfare home to the civilian front on a much larger scale than in 1914–18:

> Daylight again! The old cathedral stands
> Against the eastern sky, without a scar.
> Many who lived, with skill in brain and hands,
> Many who looked last night upon the star,
> Orion's Dog, and called him winter's hope,
> Are lying blinded underneath the rubble.
> The rescue parties call to them, and grope
> For them in vain. They are at peace. Their trouble
> And bewilderment are done. The tumbled city
> Becomes their garden. From street to street the fire
> Still rages.

In 1940 and 1941 it was often – not always – possible to be detached
about the experience of being bombed:

> Towards the far side of the town – the direction of the harbour – thin
> greenish rays of searchlight beams rapidly described wide intersecting arcs
> backwards and forwards against the eastern horizon, their range ever reduc-
> ing, ever extending, as they sliced purposefully across each other's tracks.
> Then, all at once, these several zigzagging angles of light would form an
> apex on the same patch of sky, creating a small elliptical compartment
> through which, once in a way, rapidly darted a tiny object, moving like an
> angry insect confined in a bottle. As if reacting in deliberately regulated
> unison to the searchlights' methodical fluctuations, shifting masses of
> cloudbank alternately glowed and faded, constantly redesigning by that
> means half-a-dozen intricately pastelled compositions of black and lilac,
> grey and saffron, pink and gold . . . All the world was dipped in a livid,
> unearthly refulgence, theatrical yet sinister, a light neither of night nor
> day, the penumbra of Pluto's frontiers.

One might perhaps see the bombing in terms of its resemblance to,
or parallel with, something else:

> At the nadir of the night
> When the ancient evil prowls,
> Lifts up its head, bares its fangs,
> And mad with fear and blood-thirst, howls
> Through the tangled human mind;
> In that crisis came the flight
> Of murder on its metal wing.

One might even manage to look upon the bombing as a kind of appropriate stage setting, a modern-day version perhaps of the dark forest where Dante met the ghost of Virgil:

> In the uncertain hour before the morning
>   Near the ending of interminable night
>   At the recurrent end of the unending
> After the dark dove with the flickering tongue
>   Had passed below the horizon of his homing
>   While the dead leaves still rattled on like tin
> Over the asphalt where no other sound was
>   Between three districts whence the smoke arose

I met one walking, loitering and hurried
As if blown towards me like the metal leaves
Before the urban dawn wind unresisting.

Or as a symbolic parallel to something else:

Waking from that racial dread
To these twentieth-century pangs,
I defied the planes to bring
Horror like that I left behind
In the comfort of my bed.

But as, with the advance of technology, the bombing of civilian targets
grew in scale and intensity, its victims, like the men who had cowered
in the trenches under bombardment a generation earlier, began to
think that what they were experiencing could only be compared to
nightmare visions of the Apocalypse. Miklós Radnóti wrote of the bombing of Budapest:

fáklya a templom tornya, kemence a ház, a lakója
megsűl benne, a gyártelepek fölszállnak a füstben.
Égő néppel az utca rohan, majd búgva elájul,
s fortyan a bomba nagy agya, kiröppen a sulyos ereszték
s mint legelőkon a marhalepény, úgy megzsugorodva
szertehevernek a holtak a város térein . . .

(church towers are torches, the houses hearths, inhabitants baking
within, factory blocks fly up in smoke: the streets run with burning
citizens stupefied by the sirens, bombs boil up like great featherbeds,
heavy components shooting out and like cow-pats in a meadow the
shrivelled dead lie in city squares . . .)[2]

Even with regard to serving in the front line it should be recalled
that the best-known British writers of the First World War had all been
volunteers (Edward Thomas at thirty-seven, Ford Madox Hueffer at

---

[2] Richard Church, *Twentieth-Century Psalter* (1943), p. 6; Anthony Powell, *The Soldier's
Art* (1968, paperback edn), pp. 14–15 – first published 1966; Church, *Twentieth-
Century Psalter*, p. 31; T.S. Eliot, 'Little Gidding', in *Collected Poems, 1909–1962* (1963),
pp. 216–17: first published 1942; Church, *Twentieth-Century Psalter*, p. 31; Miklós Radnóti,
'Nyolcadik Ecloga' ('Eighth Eclogue'), in *Művei* (Budapest, 1976), p. 238, translated
with the assistance of Enikő Nagy. On 3 and 13 April 1944 Budapest was bombed by
the 15th USAAF.

forty-one, C.E. Montague at forty-seven) and that volunteering, even
though over age, was possible in 1939 too. In *Men at Arms* (1952) Evelyn
Waugh provides a vivid picture of the discouragement facing older
men trying to get in on the action.

> 'Can you seriously imagine yourself sprinting about at the head of a
> platoon?'
> 'Well, yes', said Guy, 'That's exactly what I did imagine.'
> 'I'm afraid you won't get much encouragement. All that sort of thing
> happened in 1914 – retired colonels dyeing their hair and enlisting in
> the ranks. I remember it. I was there. All very gallant of course but it won't
> happen this time.'

In his desperation Guy begins writing round to old acquaintances and
almost-acquaintances:

> 'Dear Colonel Glover, I am writing to you because I know you served
> with my brother Gervase and were a friend of his . . .'
> 'Dear Sam, Though we have not met since Downside . . .'
> Always there was the same polite discouragement . . .
> 'We don't want cannon-fodder this time' – from the Services – 'we
> learned our lesson in 1914 when we threw away the pick of the nation.
> That's what we've suffered from ever since.'
> 'But I'm not the pick of the nation,' said Guy. 'I'm natural fodder. I've
> no dependants. I've no special skill in anything. What's more I'm getting
> old. I'm ready for immediate consumption . . .'

And of course Waugh did get in eventually, as did Matabele War veteran
L.F.W. 'Sos' Cohen DSO, MC, who won the Distinguished Flying Cross
as a rear-gunner in Coastal Command at the age of seventy, and Sir
Walter Cowan, a retired admiral re-employed with the rank of commander as a liaison officer, who in 1944 won a bar to the Distinguished
Service Order he had earnt for his part in the Sudan campaign in
1898.[3]
    After the war John Verney reflected on his own experience of fix-
ing things:

---

[3] Evelyn Waugh, *Sword of Honour* (1963 edn of Waugh's war trilogy, of which *Men
at Arms* is the first part), p. 23; ibid., pp. 25–29.

'Everyone gets the war he wants', Amos once said to a guilt-ridden Staff Officer in the bar of Shepheard's, who was telling us how much he would rather be up in the Desert, fighting.

Add 'if he's an officer' and 'if he's lucky', and the remark has as much truth as most generalisations. In war, with those two reservations, you have free will to this extent; you can make a paper boat of your hopes and launch it on one of perhaps half a dozen available currents in the main stream. After that it will be carried along by events.

Perhaps the most remarkable instance of an officer making his own war was Vladimir Peniakoff, a Belgian of Russian extraction who had been invalided out of the French army at the end of the First World War with an 80 per cent disability 'and a distaste for the French people which increased considerably in later years'; within thirty months of joining the British army he became a major commanding an independent unit with insignia of his own design, won the DSO and the MC, indulging his taste for 'bloodshed and violence . . . cunning and deceit and high spirits and the pleasant cudgelling of brains', and survived (minus one hand) to write memoirs that suggest a T.E. Lawrence high on champagne cocktails. For those who couldn't find a satisfactory billet in the services there was always the possibility of getting oneself killed as a war correspondent, for there were far larger numbers of reporters employed in the war zone during the Second World War than during the First. Of the four best-known Russian novelists of the war, three, Alexander Chakovski, Vasili Grossman and Konstantin Simonov, were reporters, and only Viktor Nekrasov a combatant officer. The work might be equally risky. Nordahl Grieg for example, one of the outstanding Norwegian poets of this century, went down in flames in a Royal Australian Air Force Avro Lancaster during a raid on Berlin, having pulled strings to accompany the attack as a correspondent: it was he who coined the image, later made famous by the American broadcaster Ed Murrow, of British bombers en route for Germany sounding like 'a giant factory in the sky':

> Vi ligger imørket og lytter til bombemaskinenes gang.
> Fra spinnerier i himlen sommer turbinenes sang.

(We lie in the dark and listen to the bombers' going

From factories in the sky drones the turbines' song)[4]

It was no coincidence that an image written down in private moments by a poet should be popularized by a broadcaster over the radio,
for in the Second World War it was the broadcasters rather than the
poets who made the biggest impact on the imaginations of their audi-
ences.

There is a paradox here. In 1914 there was no radio broadcasting:
in 1939 it was part of people's lives, though it never did, either then
or later, produce any distinctive art, never did reach beyond Wooden-O
drama and ex-music hall comedy; nevertheless one wonders if the
would-be writers of the radio generation were not already
subconsciously looking over their shoulders, already beginning to
suspect that the printed page was losing its status as the most powerful form of communication. But of course the greatest radio broadcaster
of them all, Winston Churchill, belonged solidly to the pre-radio era.

During the First World War Churchill's cocksure ambition, and the
stigma – not entirely deserved – of having been the architect of the
failure at Gallipoli, had made him one of the most loathed persons
in public life:

> I had not realised what a horrid little fellow he was – like some sort of
> *maggot.* His head is big, he stoops. He has thin nervous limp sort of hands.
> He looks like a drug-taker, or at least as if there was something wrong to
> be ashamed of. He went off in great high polished hat. I happened to be
> next him also in the lavatory and I hated the way he washed. He seemed
> self-conscious even there and on edge – indeed as if he were on fire within.

[4] John Verney, *Going to the Wars: A Journey in Various Directions* (1955), p. 127; Vladimir
Peniakoff, *Private Army* (1950), pp. 9–10, 32, 241–42; Nordahl Grieg, 'London', in *Friheten*
(Oslo, 1946), p. 225 – first published in English translation in Nordahl Grieg, *War Poems*
(1944), and cf. Edmund J. Bliss, Jr, ed., *In Search of Light: The Broadcasts of Edward R.
Murrow* (New York, 1967), p. 81, broadcast 6 June 1944. For Grieg's efforts to arrange
his flight on a bombing mission, see, Public Record Office, FO 371/36886, N 2976 and
N 3370; for the record of the mission itself, see AIR 27/1908, p. 570.

Alexander Chakovski was the author of *Eto bylo v Leningrade* ('It was in Leningrad')
(1945); Vasili Grossman wrote *Narod bessmerten* (1942: translated into English as *The
People Immortal,* 1943); Konstantin Simonov's *Dni i nochi* (1944) appeared in English
as *Days and Nights* in 1945 and his *Zhivye i mertvye* (1959), the first part of a trilogy,
was translated as *Victims and Heroes* in 1963: the Russian title actually means 'The
Living and the Dead'. Viktor Nekrasov's *V okopach Stalingrada* (1946) was translated
as *Frontline Stalingrad* in 1962.

But in 1940, as spokesman and embodiment of his country's defiance of the Nazis, he achieved heights of popularity never equalled before or afterwards. His wartime speeches were regarded as literary classics for twenty years, though they owed a considerable amount to his extraordinary rasping, lisping baritone which gave total conviction to rhetoric which might otherwise have sounded more than a little glib:

> What General Weygand called the Battle of France is over. I expect that the Battle of Britain is about to begin. Upon this battle depends the survival of Christian civilization. Upon it depends our own British life, and the long continuity of our institutions and our Empire. The whole fury and might of the enemy must very soon be turned on us. Hitler knows that he will have to break us in this Island or lose the war. If we can stand up to him, all Europe may be free and the life of the world may move forward into broad, sunlit uplands. But if we fail, then the whole world, including the United States, including all that we have known and cared for, will sink into the abyss of a new Dark Age made more sinister, and perhaps more protracted, by the lights of perverted science. Let us therefore brace ourselves to our duties, and so bear ourselves that, if the British Empire and its Commonwealth last for a thousand years, men will still say, 'This was their finest hour'.

Earlier war leaders, the younger Pitt and Lloyd George, had never spoken directly to more than a few hundred listeners at a time: their largest audience was reached through newspaper transcripts. Churchill's voice penetrated via the radio into every home, and was part of the news they commented upon:

> These cruel, wanton, indiscriminate bombings of London are, of course, a part of Hitler's invasion plans ... This wicked man, the repository and embodiment of many forms of soul-destroying hatred, this monstrous product of former wrongs and shame, has now resolved to try to break our famous Island race by a process of indiscriminate slaughter and destruction. What he has done is to kindle a fire in British hearts, here and all over the world, which will glow long after all traces of the conflagration he has caused in London have been removed. He has lighted a fire which will burn with a steady and consuming flame until the last vestiges of Nazi tyranny have been burnt out of Europe, and until the Old World – and the New – can join hands to rebuild the temples of man's freedom and man's honour, upon foundations which will not soon or easily be overthrown.

And it was not simply his delivery, or the self-conscious rhythms of
his sentences, or his deft choice of simple words capable of bearing
powerful emphasis, that mesmerized his listeners but the fact he said
it for real, *then*, with the Nazi hordes jostling on the French coast ready
to spring across the Channel – no one doubted this at the time – and
Nazi bombers, their twin engines synchronized to fire on an alternate
beat so that they sounded distinctively and sinisterly different from
RAF bombers, throbbing in the skies over Britain's blacked-out cities. What an opportunity for an old trouper! Churchill rose to it
triumphantly: but it was the meeting of the man with the moment
that created the poetry.[5]

As regards language Churchill's speeches were by no means up to
date. He was, and sounded like, a Victorian. That was what the moment required and, if the idea had ever occurred to him, it is very
unlikely he could have been able to make the same effect in a more
current idiom. Yet the incongruous position Churchill enjoyed, voic-
ing the determination of his fellow-countrymen in the language of
their grandfathers, was reserved for him alone. Evelyn Waugh's
somewhat overaged protagonist in *Brideshead Revisited* acknowledged:

> Gallipoli, Balaclava, Quebec, Lepanto, Bannockburn, Roncesvales, and
> Marathon – these and the Battle in the West where Arthur fell, and a
> hundred such names whose trumpet-notes, even now, in my sere and law-
> less state, called to me irresistibly across the intervening years with all the
> clarity and strength of boyhood, sounded in vain to Hooper . . .

– Hooper being the personification of the new war generation. Despite
the example of Churchill, Waugh's own turn-of-the-century idiom was
not that of the war years: and the majority idiom of the times was
something Waugh himself reacted against. Before 1939 he had succeeded in being, as a writer, elegant: now he tried to be ornate, later
writing of his somewhat fly-blown orchid of a masterpiece, *Brideshead
Revisited*, 'it was the product . . . of spam, Nissen huts, black-out – but
it won't do for peace-time'. He was not the only one to react defensively.

---

[5] David Newsome, *On the Edge of Paradise: A.C. Benson the Diarist* (1980), p. 326,
quoting Benson's account of seeing Churchill at the Athenaeum; Winston Churchill's
House of Commons speech, repeated as a broadcast, 18 June 1940; Churchill's
broadcast 11 September 1940.

Cyril Connolly's mandarin compilation of extracts and reflections, *The Unquiet Grave*, was a considerable success when it was published in 1944, but as Connolly himself admitted:

> *The Unquiet Grave* is inevitably a war book. Although the author tried to extricate himself from the war and to escape from his time and place into the bright empyrean of European thought, he . . . was affected by the dirt and weariness, the gradual draining away under war conditions of light and colour from the former capital of the world.

But reactionaries such as Waugh and Connolly recognized themselves to be an embattled minority. With Britain organized for war as no other country was organized for war before or since, to a remarkable extent the social groups that were on top beforehand remained on top throughout the period of hostilities. Churchill of course was the grandson of a duke, and a larger proportion of his ministers had been – like himself – officers in the First World War than was the case amongst the Nazi leadership. But the ideology of wartime Britain was as levelling and as egalitarian – perhaps one should say, as spuriously egalitarian – as in Nazi Germany. Old Etonian Lieutenant-Colonel R.C. Bingham, DSO was dismissed from his command of an Officer Cadets Training Unit for daring to write to *The Times* that officers from the 'middle, lower middle, and working classes', having no experience in man management, 'have very largely fallen down in their capacity as Army officers'. The approved attitude was that of Richard Hillary who speculated:

> Was there perhaps a new race of Englishmen arising out of this war, a race of men bred by the war, a harmonious synthesis of the governing class and the great rest of England; that synthesis of disparate backgrounds and upbringings to be seen at its most obvious best in RAF Squadrons?[6]

To a large extent what was happening was merely a temporary acceleration of a much longer-term process (still, in an uncertain fashion,

---

[6] Evelyn Waugh, *Brideshead Revisited* (1962, paperback edn), p. 15 – first published 1945; Mark Amory, ed., *The Letters of Evelyn Waugh* (1980), p. 322, Waugh to Graham Greene, 27 March 1950; Cyril Connolly, *The Unquiet Grave* (1961, paperback edn), p. xi, Introduction dated December 1950; *The Times*, 15 January 1941, p. 5f-g; Richard Hillary, *The Last Enemy* (1942), pp. 151–52.

in progress) derived from economic change, the enlargement of the franchise, improved educational opportunities. These changes in structure inevitably involved, not so much a shift in the location of political and economic power, but a modification of the way in which power relations were articulated. This was especially true with regard to language. Up till the time of Dickens writers had often been struck by the colourfulness of everyday speech and in writing dialogue, while trying to remain faithful to the 'characters' they were portraying, tended to play up rather than play down the colourfulness, the object after all being to write something the public would want to read. There was certainly no idea of transcribing literally the speech-patterns of everyday conversation, with its mumblings, hesitations and elisions: Wordsworth for example in his Preface to the 1800 edition of *Lyrical Ballads* spoke of using 'a selection of language really used by men . . . purified indeed from what appeared to be its real defects', and insisted that 'triviality and meanness, both of thought and language' was 'more dishonourable to the Writer's own character than false refinement or arbitrary innovation'. But from about the middle of the nineteenth century onwards writers set themselves the task of reproducing speech exactly, thereby presenting fictional characters who were evidently less articulate than their authors (a piece of authorial condescension evidently to be excused by the characters also being assumed to be less able to express themselves than the readers). This was an international trend, with the French novelist Champfleury writing the first manifesto (*Le realisme*, 1857 – obviously inspired by the painter Courbet's one man show in the so-called 'Pavillon du Realisme' at the Paris World Fair in 1855) and with Gustave Flaubert as perhaps the most influential exponent; but the new fashion was evident even in Tolstoy's *Anna Karenina*, this being one of the respects in which that novel differs from his earlier *War and Peace*. Significantly the only resistance to this trend was by a few writers who made a speciality of using dialect, these being the only authors with a vested interest in the colourfulness rather than the boringness of everyday speech: the most notable of this group was J.M. Synge. The contrived reticence of the dialogue in the novels of Henry James and later E.M. Forster, where a deliberately muted language was used to convey more meaning than was intrinsically contained in the words, became the standard literary mode of the 1900s and increasingly overflowed into the narrative as a whole. In James and Forster one senses behind the restriction of language the suppression of an authorial personality that possibly wasn't very charismatic in any case, while in H.G. Wells's *The New Machiavelli* this clumsiness presented as a self-consciousness expressive of profundity is already beginning to ring hollow. In novels of more strictly limited ambition however, such as Wells's *The War of the Worlds*, this technique is exactly, even brilliantly, appropriate, and much of the prose writing that came out of the First World War shows the benefit of a similar approach. Unfortunately the tradition continued to develop even after the point where a reaction might have been expected to set in. Because of the post-Tennysonian ambitions of the Georgian poets – perhaps because of a suspicion that deliberate impoverishment of language might not be poetry – linguistic pseudo-realism did not immediately manifest itself in verse, though there are already hints of it in the 'ordinariness' of the poetry of John Masefield, and more than mere hints in the poetry of the Imagists. It was not till the 1950s, with 'The Movement' (a school of Oxbridge-educated poets with oft-adverted to 'lower-middle-class' backgrounds, most of whom were – or were soon to be – university lecturers in Eng. Lit.) that writing drably became a self-conscious literary practice amongst poets, but to a considerable extent writing down had been acceptable procedure since the 1930s, though partly disguised by poetry's spokesmen using terms like 'colloquial' and 'intimate' and 'personal', when they actually meant 'flat' and 'banal' and 'colourless'; C. Day Lewis for example wrote:

> It will have become apparent by now, I expect, that in spite of my initial warnings against taking sides, I have betrayed a soft spot for poetry in which the colloquial element is strong. I would not deny it. There is a time for pure poetry, and a place for the undiluted grand manner, but I doubt if they are here and now, when the press of events, the crowding novelties, the so rapidly changing features of the world in which we live seem to demand of the poet that he should more than ever be responsive, fluid, adaptable; that his utterance should be human rather than hierophantic . . . I must freely own my preference for the intimate, personal idiom. Great as is my veneration for Tennyson, when I read lines like 'Come into the garden, Maud, for the black bat,

night, has flown', I am irresistibly reminded of the operatic tenor bawl-
ing endearments, at point-blank range, into the ear of his mountain-
ous *vis-à-vis*.

Thus it was that the Second World War, as the War of the Common
Man, came to be described in the Language of Ordinary Persons – as
if the Ordinary Person was someone who not merely sold insurance,
but was designed by God for no other function.[7]

Amongst those who celebrated the Ordinary Person was H.E. Bates
who, as 'Flying Officer X', specialized in stories about quiet, modest
(and usually below average height) bomber pilots who only very
exceptionally possessed anything resembling intellectual tastes:

> Pilots are often interested in nothing but popsies, kites, and beer. E.G.
> was interested in many things: so many that I never found out about them
> all. He raced motor-cars and collected stamps; he was interested in ships,
> had served in the Navy, and was a good radiographer. He had surprising
> tastes in advanced music; he was a good revolver shot and he was fond of
> flowers.

No doubt there *were* people compared to whom even E.G. seemed a
Renaissance man, though they certainly never carried out low-level
attacks on German tankers while flying four-engined bombers in the
way Bates describes. And no doubt there were heroes who didn't say
much:

> After a long, hard trip he would come into the mess quite quietly; drink
> a small light ale; warm his hands by the fire and talk for a few minutes;
> say that the trip was good or bad, in about as many words, and then go to
> bed . . .

But the inarticulacy of the ordinary fellow-countryman of Shakespeare
and Milton was a fiction that seems to have been revamped to suit
the notions of people who were themselves by no means bereft of
words. The language of Ordinary Persons was a mannered ordinariness created by an intelligentsia to deny the living principle of language

---

[7] C. Day Lewis, *The Colloquial Element in English Poetry* (Newcastle, 1947 – lecture
at Newcastle Literary and Philosophical Society, 24 March 1947), p. 31; C. Day Lewis's
response to the apostrophe to Maud may have been the one Tennyson intended
anyway.

as used by the classes which the intelligentsia regarded as less cultivated than itself. Real-life ordinary persons such as artisans or technicians, who might be as intelligent and as reflective as F.R. Leavis or Richard Hoggart (even if less expensively educated) and, though perhaps clumsy stylists with a pen in their hand, orally capable of the eloquence, verve, originality and flexibility in speech that Wordsworth and Dickens had recognized in their forefathers, did not get to become literary editors of the *New Statesman*. Latterly, with the intermixture of social classes having proceeded several stages further, the supposedly sub-articulate have found occasional champions, such as Steven Berkoff, author of *East*, a play in which (to quote Berkoff himself) 'the unveneered blast off at each other in their own compounded argot as if the ordinary language of polite communication was as dead as the people who uttered it'. Berkoff was born in 1937: the process just described, which can only be characterized as a kind of abdication of the scope of expression, was in its most energetic phase during and immediately after the Second World War when, as Cyril Connolly complained, 'Many war poets . . . are like boys playing about on a billiard table who wonder what the cues and pockets are for'.[8]

But it was not simply changing fashions in language and diction that gave the literature of 1939–45 its distinctive colour (or lack of colour): these changes in fashion, like the phenomenon of radio – like the paradox of Winston Churchill, product of the era of Trollope and Henty, leading his nation to the brink of the Welfare State – remind one of the important fact that the Second World War was not fought by the same society, at the same moment of historical development, as had engaged in the First World War: everything, individuals, institutions, influences, expectations, agendas, had travelled onwards willy-nilly during the twenty-one years that separated the two conflicts. The Second World War happened in different historical conditions from the First.

Yet perhaps the most important factor shaping Second World War art and literature was the simple, dreadful, non-coincidence that it was the *second* great war within the space of a generation.

[8] H.E. Bates, *The Greatest People in the World and Other Stories* (1942), p. 43; Steven Berkoff, *East: Agamemnon. The Fall of the House of Usher* (1977), p. 9, Introduction; Connolly, *The Unquiet Grave*, p. 21. For 'The Movement', see Blake Morrison, *The Movement: English Poetry and Fiction of the 1950s* (Oxford, 1980), especially pp. 56–57.

From the point of view of military technique and the individual skills required to use it the 1939–45 war's character as the second in a series was a clear advantage. The conditions of war in western Europe gave no opportunity for anyone to better Lance-Corporal Henry Norwest's record of 115 sniping kills 1917–18, though the Russians claimed scores of over 300 on the Eastern Front, and during the Finno-Soviet 'Winter War' of 1939–1940 Lance-Sergeant Simo Häyhä is believed to have killed 219 Red Army soldiers with a standard carbine, without special sights, and as many again with a sub-machine-gun. The improvement of anti-submarine technology prevented Kapitänleutnant Lothar Arnauld de la Perière's First World War record of 194 ships (448,024 tons) sunk by a single submarine commander being exceeded (the Second World War record is forty-four ships of 266,629 tons, by Otto Kretschmer), but the exploits of Richthofen and Bishop in the First World War pale besides Hans-Ulrich Rudel's destruction of 519 Soviet tanks, numerous bridges and artillery emplacements and the 23,000 ton battleship *Marat* as a ground-attack pilot on the Eastern Front, Erich Hartmann's destruction of 352 enemy aircraft in aerial combat, Gunther Scheel's seventy-one aerial victories in seventy missions (compare Guynemer's fifty-four victories in 600 combats), Emil Lang's eighteen enemy aircraft shot down in one day, and Erich Rudorffer's thirteen aircraft shot down in seventeen minutes. On the ground, Obersturmführer Michael Wittmann of 501 SS Heavy Tank Battalion knocked out 119 Soviet tanks before his transfer to Normandy, where on 13 June 1944, in his Pz Kw VI Tiger, he destroyed twenty-seven tanks and other tracked vehicles of the British 22nd Armoured Brigade in a few hours. In the First World War the only tank-to-tank combat ended with one of the German vehicles falling over on its side as it traversed a steep slope, but even Michael Wittmann had probably had an idea, when he joined the SS, of the kind of prospects mechanized warfare held out. Fighter pilots certainly did, because they had Richthofen's and Bishop's memoirs to tell them what was on offer:

> The war solved all problems of a career, and promised a chance of self-realization that would normally take years to achieve. As a fighter pilot I hoped for a concentration of amusement, fear and exultation which it would be impossible to experience in any other form of existence.

So wrote Richard Hillary, who shot down five Messerschmitts in his first – and last – week in action. Richthofen and Bishop had only discovered the possibility of being fighter pilots after they had become officers in the cavalry: Hillary and his generation had had the advantage of growing up with the idea.[9]

The second-time-round syndrome was less obviously an advantage in art and literature. Capitalizing on experience gained in the 1914–18 war, the British authorities rapidly set up a War Artists scheme, employing a number of important artists from the First World War including Paul Nash and Eric Kennington. The results were numerous but disappointing: the processes of bureaucratization which had created the opportunities Nevinson and Nash had had in the First World War had somehow, in progressing further, removed the element of urgency. Nash's First World War reputation did not protect him from accusations of being 'a bit leftish', or from the wish expressed by the acting Chief of Air Staff that an additional artist should be assigned to the Royal Air Force to 'cater for those – like myself – who are simple minded enough to like things as they really appear', and the work he produced had neither the appearance of being interestingly abreast of the latest artistic trends nor the emotiveness of horrified personal testimony that characterized his 1918 paintings. There was something hollow and poster-like about his later works, and his lack of attention to the precise detail of the war-machines he painted had come to look less like abstractizing, more like lack of interest in what were, after all, some of the most strikingly beautiful examples of functional design ever to be manufactured. Henry Moore's drawings of Londoners sheltering from German bombing on the Underground were not substantially more interesting, except in relation to his development as a sculptor. *Avant garde*, which had provided a striking pictorial vocabulary for the delineation of modern war in 1915, had moved

---

[9] Olavi Antila, *Suomi Suursodassa/Finland i Storkriget* (Jyväskylässä, 1984), p. 56; Günther Just, *Hans-Ulrich Rudel: Adler der Ostfront* (Hanover, 1971), p. 120; Raymond F. Toliver and Trevor J. Constable, *The Blond Knight of Germany* (Blue Ridge Summit, Pennsylvania, 1985), p. 297; Matthew Cooper and James Lucas, *Panzer: The Armoured Force of the Third Reich* (1976), pp. 143–46: and see Ernst Volckheim, *Deutsche Kampfwagen greifen an! Erlebnisse eines Kampfwagenführers an der Westfront 1918* (Berlin, 1937), for the kind of book Wittmann may have read as a boy; Hillary, *The Last Enemy*, p. 29, and cf. Hillary's combat reports in Public Record Office, AIR 50/167.

on by 1940 and left war behind: the best work of the 1940s fell back
on the representational *Neue Sachlichkeit* formula which, partly inspired
by the experiences of the First World War, had a disconcerting
resemblance to the kind of ideologically-conscious painting which Hitler
liked and which Nazi-sponsored painters, perhaps because they took
it more seriously, did better than anyone else. Perhaps the best of the
realist painters working in Britain was Laura Knight, whose often
unexpected female point of view added a quirky but appropriate
humour to her work; but taking into account the different style of
democratic/populist government in the twentieth century, her
emblematic realism ultimately seems just as much in the tradition of
Government Art as the neo-classicism of Louis David and Benjamin
West in the Napoleonic era.[10]

Second World War painting also suffered by comparison with
photography. The latter provided nearly all the most memorable visual
images of the 1939–45 era. The cameras of the earlier conflict had
only really been adequate for static images: there are some unforgettable photos of the harrowed, haggard of soldiers at rest, or of shell-
shattered groups of trees, but with the exception of one or two fuzzy
snapshots taken from too far away or at the wrong angle all the best
action shots seem to have been staged: there were very few suitable
cameras in the front line in any case. By 1939 cameras were smaller,
lighter, had more rapid exposure-times and more sophisticated lenses,
and there were more of them, so they were better able to penetrate
into the deeper intimacies of the war or to capture its most poignant
moments of drama: the teenage infantryman with the face of a child
at a Christmas party, standing amongst hard-mouthed veterans as they
watch the Stukas dive-bomb the entrenchments which they are to assault in a few minutes' time; the Stars and Stripes being raised on
Mount Suribachi on Iwo Jima; the Hammer and Sickle being raised
over the Reichstag; Hitler patting the cheek of a boy soldier in a parade
of last-ditch defenders of his Reich; the wardresses at Belsen being led
away. The much more powerful aircraft of the 1939–45 war were also

---

[10] W.P. Hildred to Principal Executive Officer, Artists Advisory Committee, quoted
in Alan Ross, *Colours of War: War Art, 1939–45* (1983), p. 28; Public Record Office,
AIR 2/6140, minute by acting Chief of Air Staff, 8 February 1940: I owe this reference to A.V. Beedell.

able, not merely to penetrate a thousand kilometres into enemy territory, but to take movie-cameras with them: film taken over Germany, with searchlight beams looping and snaking and entangling across the screen like electrified spaghetti, the sudden blips of *Flak* guns firing far below, slashing lines of tracer, shell bursts, the spreading fires suddenly convulsed by the detonation of 4000 lb bombs, does more than merely prefigure post-war Action Painting: it surpasses anything conceived in a studio.

As already suggested the aeroplanes that carried the cameras were themselves no mean works of art. Contrary to what is often supposed, the 1914–18 war did not accelerate the development of the aeroplane: most of the latest models in service in November 1918 were incapable of exceeding by any significant margin the speed and altitude records established by Prévost and Legagnaux five years earlier, and none of these end-of-war designs remained in production anything like as long as the Avro 504 series, first flown in September 1913 and still being built for government contracts more than eighteen years later. It can even be argued that the First World War actually retarded the development of the aeroplane, by consolidating the pre-eminence of the biplane at the expense of the monoplane, which in those days was regarded as too unstable in flight and too structurally fragile to be suitable for military purposes. Though the greater complexity of aircraft in the Second World War era meant that new designs took longer to develop than twenty years earlier, great effort was invested in speeding up the process, and though such standard types as the Supermarine Spitfire and the Messerschmitt Bf109 remained in service from beginning to end of hostilities, some of the most effective – and aesthetically exciting – designs originated on the drawing board after September 1939 and were in service by 1944: notably the Arado Ar 234, the world's first jet bomber, and the Boeing B-29 Superfortress, the plane used in the strategic bombing offensive against Japan in 1944 and 1945. When one examines the sleek art deco lines of such machines one might well wonder if the comparative banality of Second World War painting does not have something to do with the best talent having been creamed off by industrial design.[11]

---

[11] A.D. Harvey, 'Air Records and War Flying', *Despatches*, March 1994, p. 10–11; A.J. Jackson, *Avro Aircraft since 1908* (1990 edn), pp. 53, 117; William Green, *Famous Bombers of the Second World War: Second Series* (1960), pp. 109, 116, 128.

More than a generation seems to separate the linen and piano-wire contraptions in which Richthofen and Bishop flew from the streamlined, stress-skinned aircraft of the 1940s, with their radio telephones, oxygen supply, self-sealing petrol tanks and cockpits crammed with dials and levers; but with regard to writing the First World War was still recent enough in the 1930s to loom in people's minds as a real (even if subsequently somewhat mythologized) event rather than as a background tradition. An autobiographical story written by Keith Douglas in 1932 when he was twelve captures the war's combined status as recent fact and myth: 'As a child he was a militarist . . . "My father", said Billy "shot a German point blank . . ." in return he explained how his own father was shot by a Turk. "*My* father wouldn't have let a measly old Turk shoot him", said Billy . . .' John Mortimer recalled from his prep school 'shell-shocked masters who either confused us with the Huns or fell embarrassingly in love with us', and Evelyn Waugh's verdict on his tutor at Hertford College Oxford was, 'His conspectus of history was narrowed to a few miles of the Low Countries where he had fought, and the ultimate unattainable frontier towards which he had gazed through his periscope over the barbed wire'.[12]

So recent was the 1914–18 war that the best of its poetry had still to establish its reputation and the most famous of soldier poets remained Rupert Brooke – though what he was famed for was, in many people's eyes, his irrelevance. According to Keith Douglas, for example, Brooke in 1914–15 'appeared superannuated in a moment and wandered away fittingly, from a literary point of view, to die in a region of dead heroes'. Though full of the weariness of war, Second World War poetry has little of the passionate resentment expressed by Sassoon and Sitwell: everyone was so self-conscious about pulling together that only the occasional disgruntled Australian could perpetrate a subversive

continued

The Morane 'Parasol' monoplane was used by both French and British air squadrons in 1915: its flying characteristics are described in Cecil Lewis, *Sagittarius Rising* (1942 edn), pp. 49–50: see also, Public Record Office, AIR 1/2386/228/11/1, C.F.A. Portal, 'War Experiences', September 1922, pp. 2, 4, 9. Immelmann and Boelcke both became aces in the Fokker E.1 monoplane but this was a type introduced as an emergency measure, and was soon replaced by biplanes.

[12] Desmond Graham, ed., *Keith Douglas: A Prose Miscellany* (Manchester, 1985), pp. 12–13; John Mortimer, *Clinging to the Wreckage: A Part of Life* (1982), p. 18; Evelyn Waugh, *A Little Learning* (1983 edn), p. 174 – first published 1964.

gem like the following – inspired by General Sir Thomas Blamey's ordering an inscription commemorating the 1st Australian Corps's capture of Damour, in Syria, to be added to those left by the Assyrian, Babylonian and Roman armies that had passed the same way:

> Our general was the greatest and bravest of generals.
> For his deeds, look around you on this coast –
> Here is his name cut next to Ashur-Bani-Pal's,
> Nebuchadnezzar's and the Roman host;
> And we, though our identities have been lost,
> Lacking the validity of stone or metal,
> We, too, are part of his memorial,
> Having been put in for the cost,
>
> Having bestowed on him all we had to give
> In battles few can recollect,
> Our strength, obedience and endurance,
> Our wits, our bodies, our existence,
> Even our descendants' right to live –
> Having given him everything, in fact,
> Except respect.[13]

What was chiefly remembered about the First World War was not the best poetry but the sheer bulk of the poetry: the years 1914–18 had obviously been a good time to get one's verse into print and in 1939 hundreds of young men decided that the good times had come again: hence C. Day Lewis's question 'Where Are the War Poets?' The First World War had so consecrated the idea of the soldier poet that there did not seem anything ludicrous or uninviting in a title like *Poems from the Forces* (an anthology edited by Keidrych Rhys and published in 1941) or *Air Force Poetry* (edited by John Pudney and

[13] Graham, ed., *Keith Douglas: A Prose Miscellany*, p. 117: Douglas's essay 'Poets in this War' was written in the early summer of 1943; Kenneth Slessor, 'An Inscription for Dog River', in Dennis Haskell ed., *Kenneth Slessor: Poetry, Essays, War Despatches, War Diaries, Journalism, Autobiographical Material and Letters* (St Lucia, Queensland, 1991), p. 48: it is not clear when these verses were written but they may post-date Slessor's resignation in 1944 as Official War Correspondent and author-designate of Australia's Official History of the war. Slessor resigned because of army objections to some of his reports, and Blamey was by then Commander-in-Chief of the Australian army.

Henry Treece, 1944). According to Catherine W. Reilly's *English Poetry of the Second World War: A Bibliography* (1986), twenty-five out of forty-nine wartime poetry anthologies specifically related to the armed services. In fact there was so much frantic interest in the new poetry that it became difficult to make out what was actually being achieved. A generation earlier Siegfried Sassoon had known of Charles Sorley's work, had been in the same regiment as Robert Graves, knew Rupert Brooke and Robert Nichols, and graduated from the trenches to the same hospital as Wilfred Owen, whom he took with him the first time he called on Osbert Sitwell. To a large extent he was aware of, and assisted by, a substantial proportion of the most important contemporary writing. Even Isaac Rosenberg, serving in the ranks, had met T.E. Hulme and Ezra Pound before the war, corresponded with Laurence Binyon and was in close touch with Edward Marsh, editor of the *Georgian Poetry* anthologies: one of his poems appeared in the third volume of *Georgian Poetry* with work by Nichols, Graves and Sassoon, though Rosenberg does not seem to have been impressed by his company; his verdict on this volume was 'There is some good stuff in it but very little'. In the Second World War there was so much mutual back-scratching and log-rolling that it became compartmentalized, making it difficult to be sure anything was really happening. Evelyn Waugh remarked in 1948, 'England was no nest of singing-birds in that decade; lamas scanned the snows in vain for a reincarnation of Rupert Brooke', but G.S. Fraser, on the editorial staff of the forces' paper *Parade* in Cairo during the war, and later a lecturer in English at Leicester University, claimed in a memo written long afterwards:

> The Middle East in World War Two produced far more – and at times even finer – poetry than all the years of attrition on the Western Front in World War One. The poetry came from a more literate and aware generation. They had read more and employed a wider range of style and techniques.

Yet in 1949 Robert Graves seemed quite unaware of the existence of Keith Douglas, writing 'No poets seem to have assisted in the Eighth Army's eccentric Libyan campaign', and Kenneth Allott, in compiling *The Penguin Book of Contemporary Verse* (1950), seemed equally oblivious, concluding that Sidney Keyes, killed in action at the age of twenty-one while serving with the First Army in Tunisia, was 'the most promising of the younger war poets'. Allott also however gave favourable mention to the claims of Alun Lewis, who was Robert Graves's candidate for the topmost niche.[14]

In the event it was Keith Douglas who finally emerged as the critics' consensual choice, though indeed Donald Hall's claim that he left 'the finest poems written in our language by a soldier of the Second World War' does not necessarily mean very much. Douglas seems to have had a natural affinity for the understated 'ordinary bloke' idiom of his day and even at his best he showed a poor ear for the sound of words and a positively Wordsworthian knack for wandering around the margins of anti-climax:

> Three weeks gone and the combatants gone
> returning over the nightmare ground
> we found the place again, and found
> the soldier sprawling in the sun.
>
> The frowning barrel of his gun
> overshadowing. As we came on
> that day, he hit my tank with one
> like the entry of a demon.
>
> Look. Here in the gunpit spoil
> the dishonoured picture of his girl
> who has put: *Steffi. Vergissmeinnicht*
> in a copybook gothic script.
>
> We see him almost with content,
> abased, and seeming to have paid

---

[14] Rupert Hart Davis, ed., *Siegfried Sassoon Diaries, 1920–1922* (1981), p. 255, 25 September 1922; Ian Parsons, *The Collected Works of Isaac Rosenberg* (1979), prints more than fifty letters from Rosenberg to Marsh, 1913–18, and, on p. 248, a letter from Rosenberg to Binyon, 1916, which indicates their friendly relations; Evelyn Waugh, *The Loved One: An Anglo-American Tragedy* (1951, Penguin edn), p. 22: first published 1948; Victor Selwyn et al., eds, *Return to Oasis: War Poems and Recollections from the Middle East, 1940–1946* (1980), p. xix, and see also Andrew Sinclair, *War Like a Wasp: The Lost Decade of the Forties* (1989), pp. 93–99; Robert Graves, 'Additional Comment' (1949), *Common Asphodel*, pp. 311–12; Donald Hall quoted by Bernard Bergonzi, *The Turn of the Century: Essays on Victorian and Modern English Literature* (1973), p. 207.

and mocked at by his own equipment
that's hard and good when he's decayed.

But she would weep to see today
how on his skin the swart flies move;
the dust upon the paper eye
and the burst stomach like a cave.

For here the lover and killer are mingled
who had one body and one heart.
And death who had the soldier singled
has done the lover mortal hurt.[15]

Douglas was perhaps the outstanding example of a Second World War poet with a literary heritage that had advanced a stage beyond what the First World War poets had inherited or themselves developed. He himself did not regard the experience of the earlier generation as either an assistance or an inspiration, noting of his fellow soldiers in North Africa:

> They do not write because there is nothing new, from a soldier's point of view, about this war except its mobile character . . . hell cannot be let loose twice: it was let loose in the Great War and it is the same old hell now. The hardships, pain and boredom; the behaviour of the living and the appearance of the dead, were so accurately described by the poets of the Great War that every day on the battlefields of the western desert – and no doubt on the Russian battlefields too – their poems are illustrated.

The poet who had the greatest influence on him was T.S. Eliot, an essentially post-1918 construct, and behind Eliot, John Donne. Eliot provided Douglas with a model for a cool, ironical, ambiguous presentation, though it was precisely the Eliotesque note that makes Douglas now seem unappealing and perhaps even dated. Whereas Wilfred Owen had insisted that 'The Poetry is in the pity', for Douglas it was as if the poetry was in the lack of pity:

---

[15] Keith Douglas, 'Vergissmeinnicht', in Desmond Graham, ed., *Keith Douglas: Complete Poems* (Oxford, 1978), p. 111.

Perched on a great fall of air
a pilot or angel looking down
on some eccentric chart, the plain
dotted with the useless furniture
discerns crouching on the sand vehicles
squashed dead or still entire, stunned
like beetles: scattered wingcases and
legs, heads, show when the haze settles.
But you who like Thomas come
to poke fingers in the wounds
find monuments, and metal posies:
on each disordered tomb
the steel is torn into fronds
by the lunatic explosive.[16]

The paradox that combatants in a hi-tec war should concern themselves so much with verse-making was only partly resolved by making the technology a poetic theme:

I have been fighting in a dressing-gown
Most of the night; I cannot see the guns,
The sweating gun-detachments or the planes;
I sweat down here before a symbol thrown
Upon a screen, sift facts, initiate
Swift calculations and swift orders; wait
For the precise split-second to order fire.

We chant our ritual words; beyond the phones
A ghost repeats the orders to the guns:
One Fire . . . Two Fire . . . ghosts answer: the guns roar . . .

So wrote an officer in an anti-aircraft battery who later went on to teach the present author about Romanticism. Another AA gunner, who had 'entered the war as a refugee from Tacitus and de Musset . . . Present interests Shakespeare [and] Karl Marx', took a very similar view:

---

[16] Graham, *Keith Douglas: A Prose Miscellany*, pp. 119–20; Douglas, 'Landscape with Figures', in *Keith Douglas: Complete Poems*, p. 103.

Death is a matter of mathematics.
It screeches down at you from dirtywhite nothingness
And your life is a question of velocity and altitude,
With allowances for wind and the quick, relentless pull
Of gravity . . .

Or perhaps you walk oblivious in a wood,
Or crawl flat-bellied over pockmarked earth,
And Death awaits you in a field-gray tunic.
Sights upright and aligned. Range estimated
And set in. A lightning, subconscious calculation
Of trajectory and deflection. With you the focal point,
The centre of the problem. The A and B
Or Smith and Jones of schoolboy textbooks.

Ten out of ten means you are dead.

The same cold glaucous eye of the post-Eliot generation was also applied to the men who manned the machines and to their claustrophobic existence during off-duty hours:

The bulkhead sweating, and under naked bulbs
Men writing letters, playing ludo. The light
Cuts their arms off at the wrist, only the dice
Lives . . .
The air soupy, yet still cold; a beam sea rattles
Cups smelling of stale tea, knocks over a broom.
The light is watery, like the light of the sea-bed.
Marooned in it, stealthy as fishes, we may even be dead.

This is like a transcription of something painted like Fernand Léger in 1917. It might be wondered though if 'poetry' is quite the right term for writing which so resolutely insists on dimunition and deflation.[17]

---

[17] R.N. Currey, 'Unseen Fire', in *This Other Planet* (1945), p. 35; Barry Amiel, 'Death is a Matter of Mathematics', in R.N. Currey and R.V. Gibson, ed., *Poems from India: By Members of the Forces* (1946), p. 138 and cf. p. 159. Amiel's subsequent career is obscure: 'Soon after the war I twice used his poem on the BBC in the hope of getting in touch with him, but without any success' – R.N. Currey to A.D. Harvey, 15 February 1995; see too E. Hilton Young's 'In a Turret', in *A Muse at Sea* (1919), pp. 25–28, which also features long-distance killing with control wheels and gauges; Alan Ross, 'Mess Deck', in *Something of the Sea* (1954), p. 11.

A rather different approach was taken by F.T. Prince, in 'Soldiers Bathing', which according to one critic 'is generally considered to be the greatest poem in English to come out of World War Two':

> Yet as I drink the dusky air,
> I feel a strange delight that fills me full,
> A gratitude, as if evil itsclf was beautiful;
> And kiss the wound in thought, while in the west
> I watch a streak of red that might have issued from Christ's breast

It is difficult to account for the vogue once enjoyed by this infinite dilution of Gerard Manley Hopkins, though it may be something to do with the future provincial university professor already evident in

> And reading in the shadows of his pallid flesh, I see
> The idea of Michelangelo's cartoon
> Of soldiers bathing, breaking off before they were half done
> At some sortie of the enemy, an episode
> Of the Pisan wars with Florence . . .

It seems to be one of those literary confections where the message is more important than the medium, and which cannot be properly evaluated because the message has been addressed to people who have gone away. F.T. Prince, incidentally, like Alun Lewis, never saw action; after training he was assigned to Bletchley Park, where intercepted German radio traffic was decrypted. He also spent some months in Egypt, though only after the expulsion of the German Army from North Africa. Not his fault of course: but it is part of the explanation of the diffcrence between 'Soldiers Bathing' and any war poem by Wilfred Owen.[18]

---

[18] Stephen Spender's British Council pamphlet *Poetry Since 1939* (1946) quoted Prince's 'magnificent' poem *in extenso*, pp. 52–54. When Prince published it in book form in 1954, E.M. Forster hailed it as one of the three most outstanding books to be published that year: Donald E. Stanford *British Poets, 1914–1945* (Detroit, 1983), p. 284; *F.T. Prince: Interviewed by Stephen Devereux* (Grahamstown, 1988), pp. 11–12.

CHAPTER 11

Second Time Around

THOUGH THE poets of 1939–45 may not have got the poets of 1914–18 properly in focus, the novelists of the 1939–45 war, working at greater leisure, showed themselves all too aware that they were following close in the tracks of earlier writers.

In part it was simply a matter of apeing the mannerisms of the novelists of the previous generation as in *Signed With Their Honour* (1942) by Australian war correspondent James Aldridge, which begins *à la* Hemingway: 'All summer had been filled with dust. It had been so bad at times that everybody had gone around wearing gas-masks'. In Herman Wouk's *Youngblood Hawke* (1962) a character who is obviously intended to represent Norman Mailer is asked by an English novelist 'If Mr Dos Passos had not done his work – if you had not had him to imitate – how would you have known where to begin?' Norman Mailer later admitted,

> *The Naked and the Dead* had been written out of what I could learn from James T. Farrell and John Dos Passos with good doses of Thomas Wolfe and Tolstoy, plus homeopathic tinctures from Hemingway, Fitzgerald, Faulkner, Melville and Dostoyevsky.

Wouk's *Youngblood Hawke* (itself a kind of vulgarization of Thomas Wolfe's *You Can't Go Home Again* of 1940) concerns a writer who is at one stage busy with a Second World War novel entitled *Chain of Command*. 'What made the book more than anything else was a grand panorama of the invasion of Iwo Jima, almost on the scale of Tolstoy's treatment of the battle of Borodino, which Hawke had intently studied.' In an earlier novel Wouk has a character named Tom Keefer who is

writing a thick war novel in the time he can spare from his duties as
an officer on board a destroyer. According to another character it
was 'sort of a jumble of Dos Passos and Joyce and Hemingway and
Faulkner . . . It takes place on a carrier, but there are a lot of flashbacks
to the beach, with some of the most hair-raising sex scenes I have ever
read'; yet another character takes it for granted that

> it exposes this war in all its grim futility and waste, and shows up the military
> men for the stupid, Fascist-minded sadists they are. Bitching up all the
> campaigns and throwing away the lives of fatalistic, humorous, lovable
> citizen-soldiers. Lots of sex scenes where the prose becomes rhythmic and
> beautiful while the girl gets her pants pulled down.

It seems that for Wouk, who didn't himself go in for sex scenes and
slagging off senior officers, the worst trauma of the Second World
War was seeing Norman Mailer emerge, three years after the fighting was over, as 'the Hemingway of World War II that they'd all been
waiting for'.[1]

One might, it seems, even be traumatized by not actually getting
shot at, despite one's overwhelming desire to write a red-hot, first-
hand war novel. In Irwin Shaw's best-seller *The Young Lions* (1948),
authoritatively described as 'the finest novel of the European theatre'
(in contradistinction to Mailer's *The Naked and the Dead*, which was
already acknowledged to be the finest novel of the war in the Pacific),
there is a passage involving 'a Lieutenant and two Sergeants from a
Communications Zone Signal Corps message centre, who had somehow
arrived here [at the front line] in a jeep on a tourist visit'. The lieutenant explains, 'We heard we could pick up some pretty good souvenirs
in this neck of the woods. I go into Paris twice a month, and there's a
good market for Luegers and cameras and binoculars, stuff like that'.
They have descended on a frontline unit whose sergeant is trying to
locate the position of a dangerous German machine-gun nest. He

---

[1] Herman Wouk, *Youngblood Hawke* (1962 edn), p. 254: cf. pp. 246–49, 252–54 for
the Mailer-like character, though he is described as having served in Europe rather
than, as in Mailer's case, in the Pacific; Norman Mailer *Pieces and Pontifications* (Boston,
1982), p. 6 (Preface, 'An Advertisement Advertised', to 1976 edition of *Advertisement
for Myself*). Wouk, *Youngblood Hawke*, p. 271; Herman Wouk, *The Caine Mutiny* (London
1951 edn), pp. 464, 353; Wouk, *Youngblood Hawke*, p. 422, and cf. p. 240.

encourages the lieutenant and the 'two Sergeants with the bright stars in the circles on their shoulders' to go forward to look for saleable souvenirs: when the German machine-gun mows them down it gives its position away to the American frontline troops, who have the additional satisfaction as they advance of being able to snigger at the bullet-riddled corpses of the war-profiteers from the Communications Zone. One would have little doubt where the sympathies lie of the man who wrote this telling vignette, if it were not for the fact that at the period described he had been a warrant officer (complete with bright stars in a circle on his shoulder) in a Communication Zone Signal Corps unit assigned to taking photographs of newly liberated French towns. Afterwards Irwin Shaw was proud to recall that on one occasion a bullet – possibly even a German one – passed right behind his neck and under the chin of the man sitting in the jeep behind him: it was the sort of thing on his *curriculum vitae* that equipped him, when writing *The Young Lions*, to understand the mentality of the frontline soldier, and the reader can only admire the way in which his personal experiences seem to have been transposed in his book. Before the war Irwin Shaw had been a successful writer for the Andy Gump and Dick Tracy radio shows and author of the successful anti-war play *Bury the Dead*; he understood that what a mass audience wanted was the expected, not the unexpected. His evocation in *The Young Lions* of London in the winter of 1943–44 is sheer Hollywood. 'Overhead there was the steady drone of a thousand engines, as the Lancasters crossed the Thames on the way home from Berlin' – Berlin of course being considerably to the north of London, as were the RAF airbases from which it was attacked. A bar near St James's Palace (referred to familiarly as 'the Palace', a designation used by most people in Britain to mean Buckingham Palace) is described as 'three small basement rooms decked with dusty bunting, with a long plank nailed on a couple of barrels that did service for a bar . . .' The staff and clientele were almost as eccentric as the decor:

> Almost everyone could get credit if they needed it and no one was ever pressed for repayment . . . a huge dark Frenchman, who it was reputed, dropped by a parachute into France two or three times a month for British Intelligence, was eating martini glasses, something he did when he got drunk and felt moody.

Perhaps the martini glasses, in the fourth winter of the war, had strayed across from the next set, where they were filming *Pancho Villa Meets Ginger Rogers*. In later life Irwin Shaw, like Norman Mailer, is said to have become something of an expert in getting drunk and feeling moody; one notes that in the author's photo on the back inside cover of the *Young Lions* he is already doing his best to look like the author of *The Naked and the Dead*.[2]

Yet even authors like Irwin Shaw – perhaps one should say, *especially* authors like Irwin Shaw – benefited from the fact that as the second generation in thirty years to be faced with the challenge of writing a Great War Novel they had plenty of technical expertise to fall back on.

The novel portraying the shared experiences of a small group of combatants, for example, was as much a characteristic of 1939–45 war as of the 1914–18 war. Perhaps the earliest, Yves Dautun's *La batterie errante* ('The Wandering Battery'), completed in a German prison camp in January 1941, seemed to owe as much to the Barbusse and Dorgelès generation as to the author's own experiences in the campaign of May-June 1940:

> I found in our stable Gascony and the Limousin, Brittany, Provence or Flanders, a savoury mixture of dialects, of sonorous *patois*, faces sculpted by the sun and by the wind, bearing the stamp of the French earth, rich and various like France herself, at once strong and soft, and like France, eternal.

Other notable examples of the 'group' novel are John Prebble's *The Edge of Darkness* (1947), Alexander's Baron's *From the City, From the Plough* (1948), 'Zeno's' *The Cauldron* (1966), Willi Heinrich's *Das geduldige Fleisch* (1955, published in English translation as *The Willing Flesh* 1956), Norman Mailer's *The Naked and the Dead* (1948), Leon Uris's *Battle Cry* (1953), James Jones's *The Thin Red Line* (1962, dealing with 'C-for-Charlie Company' of the 'Umth Infantry Regiment') and Väinö Linna's *Tuntematon Sotilas* (1954 – an all-time record best-seller in Finland, published in English as *The Unknown*

---

[2] Ann Avory, ed., *Contemporary Authors: New Revision Series* (Detroit, 1981-), vol. 21, p. 407; Irwin Shaw, *The Young Lions* (1949), pp. 625, 629–35; James R. Giles, *Irwin Shaw* (Boston, 1983), p. 5; Shaw, *The Young Lions*, p. 365; ibid., pp. 380–81.

Soldier in 1957: despite its title it deals not with a single soldier but with a machine-gun company). The group approach had been applied to air warfare in Joseph Kessel's *L'équipage* ('The Crew') of 1923 (with the pilot in love with the observer's wife) but was obviously more appropriate for a later era when air-crew were provided with intercom devices that actually enabled them to speak to each other in the air. Second World War examples of air-crew novels include Edwin Morzfeld's *Er flog an meiner Seite* (1957: as *He Flew By My Side*, 1959); Gerd Gaiser's *Die sterbende Jagd* (1953: Paul Findlay's English translation appeared under the title *The Falling Leaf* in 1956 and, in paperback, as *The Last Squadron* in 1960); Victor Schuller's *Mit Eichenlaub und Schwerten . . . ging eine Welt zugrunde* (1958; as *The Sky Ablaze* 1958); and from the United States, Ward Taylor's *Roll Back the Sky* (1956), David Camerer's *The Damned Wear Wings* (1958) and John Hersey's *The War Lover* (1959).[3]

Oddly enough, though focus on a defined group lent itself readily to the depiction of life on board a small ship, this strategy seems not to have been applied to the fictionalizing of naval warfare in the 1914–18 war, whereas the 1939–45 war produced at least five classics: C.S. Forester's *The Ship* (1943), Herman Wouk's *The Caine Mutiny* (1951), Nicholas Monsarrat's *The Cruel Sea* (1951), Alistair Maclean's *HMS Ulysses* (1955) and Lothar-Gunther Buchheim's *Das Boot* (1974: 'The Boat'), which was the basis for a memorable television series. Also deserving mention is Thomas Heggen's *Mister Roberts* (1946; filmed by John Ford in 1955) in which a group of US Navy officers on a cargo ship experience not so much the war but the wartime navy in the shape of an 'irrefutably and unbelievably incompetent' captain; the officers are characterized as representing 'the miscellany of pre-war America', and include an insurance salesman, an assistant in a shoe store, a school teacher and two college boys. Perhaps significantly the writer who got in first with the

---

[3] Yves Dautun, *La batterie errante: récit de guerre* (Paris, 1942), p. 26.

The literal translation of Gerd Gaiser's novel is 'The Dying Hunt'; of Victor Schuller's novel 'With Oakleaf and Swords . . . Went a World to Ruin'. Oakleaf and Swords were equivalent to a first and second bar to the Knight's Cross. During the Second World War 1330 Luftwaffe aircrew were awarded the Knight's Cross, of whom forty-four subsequently received Oakleaf and Swords: Erwin Feuerstein *Mit und ohne Ritterkreuz: die Erfolgreichsten der deutschen Luftwaffe* (Stuttgart, 1974), pp. 62–63.

idea of a ship's company as group-protagonist, C.S. Forester, was a
civilian, observing at second-hand, but as a practised author well
aware of issues of organizational format: he may have derived the
idea for *The Ship* from Noel Coward's 1942 film *In Which We Serve*,
based on the exploits of Lord Louis Mountbatten in HMS *Kelly*,
with John Mills as Shorty Blake and Richard Attenborough providing plebian foils to Noel Coward's well-connected flotilla captain.

Other writers however seem to have perceived that the portrayal
of a group had, as a structural expedient, become banal and predict-
able, and they attempted to look not for an organizational principle
but for some sort of key symbol around which to arrange their narratives. Even in Norman Mailer's *The Naked and the Dead* the platoon
which functions as group-protagonist is involved in an increasingly
futile attempt to climb a mountain in order to reconnoitre a route
round the Japanese flank, and this attempt on the mountain, including its ultimate defeat by a swarm of hornets, is clearly intended as
some sort of allegory.

Several novelists of the 1939–45 war managed to hit on situations
in which the symbolic element seemed to follow naturally from the
flow of events. Herbert Zand's *Letzte Ausfahrt* (1953; translated into
English as *The Last Sortie*, 1955) took a not unusual military scenario
– a town in eastern Germany cut off by the advancing Red Army – as
an allegory of the human predicament. Shohei Ōoka's *Nobi* (1951;
translated as *Fires on the Plain*, 1957) portrayed a Japanese soldier
wandering sick, alone, starving and desperate through the Philip-
pine countryside. Jens Rehn's *Nichts in Sicht* ('Nothing in Sight', 1954)
depicted a German submariner and an American airman drifting and
dying in a rubber dinghy in mid-Atlantic – a situation reminiscent of
Alfred Hitchcock's 1944 film *Lifeboat* (based on a story by John
Steinbeck), in which the survivors of a torpedoed ship rescue the U-boat
captain who torpedoed them. One may also see symbolic pretensions in Eric Williams's thinly fictionalized accounts of prisoners of
war escaping from German camps, *The Tunnel* and *The Wooden Horse*,
as when the protagonists discuss the tunnel they are digging:

> 'It's funny,' Peter said, 'it's almost like going to a woman.' He laughed,
> conscious of a slight embarrassment. 'I get a sort of peace down there –
> the peace you get from a woman.'
> 'Sort of symbolism?' John said.

'I don't know, it may be. It's certainly not entirely because we're getting out – it's the tunnel itself. It's a sort of retreat, almost like burrowing
back into the womb. Sounds silly, I expect . . .'

Such pretensions often did not add up to very much. Gore Vidal's
first novel *Williwaw* (1946) seems to be only incidentally about the
American army (in one of its more unusual avatars, operating
transport ships in the North Pacific) and is essentially just another
storm-at-sea novel like Joseph Conrad's *Typhoon* or Richard Hughes's
In Hazard. John Horne Burns's *The Gallery* (1948) uses the Galleria
Umberto in Naples to link stories about various protagonists –
'Everybody in Naples came to the Galleria Umberto' – but the result
is scarcely more symbolic than the use of adventitious topographical points in Mottram's First World War trilogy *The Spanish Farm*
trilogy or Giono's *Le grand troupeau*: though one may detect the
influence of Thornton Wilder's 1927 Pulitzer Prize-winning novel
about early eighteenth-century Peru, *The Bridge of San Luis Rey*, which
also uses a place (and an event) to bring together otherwise uncon-
nected characters.[4]

In other instances the symbol seems forced, and the symbolic
nexus uninteresting. Howard Clewes, a major in the Green Jackets,
subsequently best-known for his script for the Trevor Howard, Marlon
Brando *Mutiny on the Bounty* of 1962, possibly intended a self-
portrait in his company commander in *Dead Ground* (1947), a worthy
moral parable with John Cowper Powys-like ambitions about troops
stationed in a small English port at a time when the German invasion was expected imminently, and about the old merchant navy
captain who sails his derelict steamer, detailed as a blockship for
the harbour, into a minefield. In John Hersey's *A Bell for Adano* (1944)
an idealistic Italian-American major, placed in charge of a newly-
occupied Italian town, attempts to procure a bell for the church: a
prophetic allegory if seen in terms of yuppies moving into communities where they are not wanted, and making themselves
responsible for the maintenance of whichever local traditions appeal most to their misconceptions about communal life, but thin
stuff in so far as it has anything to say about regeneration and cross-
cultural co-operation, and a whole universe distant from the Italy

---

[4] Eric Williams, *The Tunnel* (1951), p. 185.

evoked in the novels of Italo Calvino and Beppe Fenoglio about partisan bands operating against the Germans in the north of the country. Not much more convincing is Pierre Boulle's *Le pont de la rivière Kwaï* (1952) where British prisoners of war build a railway bridge for their Japanese captors, necessitating a commando attack by other Britons to destroy it. After the attack has been thwarted by the prisoner of war in charge of the construction project – a stiff-upper-lip colonel who rises to heroism 'in his insistence on a proper code of conduct' – one of the raiders explains to his superior the reason for his comrade's failure to blow up the bridge:

> 'More insight, that's what he needed; then he would have known who his enemy really was, realized it was that old bull-shitter who couldn't stand the idea of his fine work being destroyed. A really perceptive mind would have deduced that from the way he strode along the platform. I had my glasses trained on him, sir; if only it had been a rifle! He had the sanctimonious smile of a conqueror on his lips, I remember. A splendid example of the man of action, sir, as we say in Force 316. He never let misfortune get him down; always made a last effort. It was he who shouted to the Japs for help!
>
> 'That old brute with his blue eyes had probably spent his whole life dreaming of constructing something which would last. In the absence of a town or a cathedral, he plumped for this bridge . . .
>
> 'He had a highly developed sense of duty and admired a job well done. He was also fond of action – just as you are, sir, just as we all are. This idiotic worship of action, to which our little typists subscribe as much as our great generals! . . . Perhaps he really had a genuine ideal? An ideal as sacred as our own? Perhaps the same ideal as ours?'[5]

Perhaps the most durable symbolic treatments of the war turned out to be the ones that did not mention it: Rex Warner's *The Aerodrome* (1941), depicting the relationship between the benighted inhabitants of a village and the personnel of the neighbouring aerodrome,

---

[5] See Italo Calvino, *Il sentiero dei nidi di ragno* (1947; English translation published under the title *The Path to the Nest of Spiders*, 1956), and Beppe Fenoglio, *Primavera di bellezza* (1959; 'Springtime of Beauty', a phrase from the Fascist anthem *La giovinezza*) and *Il partigiano Johnny* (1968 'Johnny the guerilla'); Pierre Boulle, *The Bridge on the River Kwai* (1954), p. 166 – first published in French two years previously.

which represents some sort of principle of modernity with totalitarian overtones, and Albert Camus's *La peste* (1947; English translation, *The Plague*, published 1948), describing an epidemic of bubonic plague in wartime Oran, the latter evidently a city of mythic stature as it also figures in Howard Clewes's *Dead Ground* as the port the old captain says he is heading for with his ship: 'Finest woman I ever knew was a whore in Oran, in a brothel . . . Oran was a stinking hole. Always remember the way it stank'. Camus's account of the plague outbreak provides an allegory of war not as an absolute and autonomous phenomenon but as a distillation or concentration – perhaps even in itself a symbol – of human malaise. At the end of the book Dr Rieux decides to write an account of the epidemic:

> But he knew that this chronicle could not tell of final victory. It could only be the record of what had had to be done and what, no doubt, remained to be done against terror and its tireless weapons, by all those who, despite personal anguish, unable to be saints, refusing to scourge themselves, strive nevertheless to be doctors.
>
> Listening to the cries of gaiety which rose from the town, Rieux remembered that this gaiety was forever under threat. He knew what the celebrating crowd did not know, though it could be read in books, that the germs of the plague never died or disappeared, but could remain dormant for decades in furniture and linen, waiting patiently in rooms and cellars and suitcases and handkerchiefs and waste paper, and that perhaps the day would come when the plague would again summon its rats and send them out to die in a happy city, for the misery and instruction of mankind.[6]

Despite their deliberately wooden style – part of the Language of Ordinary Persons, it seems, of the 1940s – *The Aerodrome* and *La peste* will endure as authentic and deeply-considered testimonies of what it was like to live through the war – the war seen as a social crisis on the home front rather than as a series of military campaigns. In any discussion of the twentieth century it is impossible to leave the 1914–18 and 1939–45 wars out of the agenda: consequently *The Aerodrome* and *La peste* must be acknowledged as major works of twentieth-century

---

[6] Albert Camus, *La peste* (Paris, 1947), final paragraphs.

literature. But their objective status as great works of literature, separate from their stature within the twentieth-century canon, seems disputable.

The first writer to elaborate a symbolic nexus in his work may claim to have achieved something of major significance in literature, but subsequent writers who do the same thing are only as creative as their choice of symbols. Pestilence is a wonderful symbol for social crisis but had been used as far back as 1799 by Charles Brockden Brown in *Arthur Mervyn*. The aerodrome is a more original symbol – one that was hardly available before the invention of the aeroplane – but an aerodrome is after all only a matter of Nissen huts, control towers and acres of concrete, and represents no fundamental symbolic advance on other human violations of the natural order. The use of such symbols was not the invention of Warner's and Camus's generation. If one looks at the career of many nineteenth-century novelists one perceives that, as they got into their stride, became more confident of their audience and of their own skill, more engaged with artistic ambitions, they often became more self-conscious in their use of symbolism. One sees this with Dickens in *Dombey and Son* (1848) and especially *Bleak House* (1852–53) with its famous opening evocation of fog; with Thomas Hardy one recognizes the same process in *The Laodicean* (1881), with its ruined castle owned by a *nouveau riche* woman who wants to restore it, and *Two on a Tower* (1882), with its tower observatory and discourses on astronomy. In both Dickens's and Hardy's case there seems to have been a subsequent retreat from symbolism for symbolism's sake, and in the later works of both authors – *Great Expectations*, say, and *Tess of the D'Urbervilles* – the symbols appear less obtrusive elements within a more powerfully integrated whole.

In the 1940s symbolism was enjoying something of a vogue because of the discovery of Kafka. In his introduction to the 1930 English translation of *Das Schloss* – *The Castle* – Edwin Muir described Kafka's novel as 'a sort of modern *Pilgrim's Progress* . . . like *The Pilgrim's Progress* a religious allegory'. Muir was no doubt justified in the emphasis he placed on the superior refinement and complexity of Kafka's allegory as compared to Bunyan's but the comparison with the latter's seventeenth-century classic serves to remind us that any attempt to organize novels around symbols is bound to have an academic, derivative element. (The first book about symbolism and art was by a university professor, G.F. Creuzer of Heidelberg, back in 1810.) The earnestness of Kafka's own engagement with symbolism may be illustrated by a letter he wrote to Max Brod following the diagnosis of the tuberculosis that finally killed him:

> However there is still the wound of which the lesions in the lungs are only the symbol. You misunderstand it, Max, to judge by your final words in the hallway, but perhaps I also misunderstand it and there is no understanding these things (the same would be true of your inner affairs) because there is no seeing it whole, so turbulent and ever-moving is the gigantic mass which yet at the same time never ceases to grow . . . I am constantly seeking an explanation for this disease, for I did not seek it. Sometimes it seems to me that my brain and lungs came to an agreement without my knowledge. 'Things can't go on this way', said the brain, and after five years the lungs said they were ready to help.

One suspects though that many of Kafka's imitators operated nearer to the surface. As G.S. Fraser later boasted, the writers of the 1939–45 war 'came from a more literate and aware generation' than the men of 1914–18: 'They had read more and employed a wider range of style and technique'. An analysis of books published in Britain in 1911 and 1938 shows almost no change in overall numbers or the proportion that are novels but a large rise in the number of books relating to education (from one in twenty-one to one in nine of the whole) and an almost fivefold increase in the number of books reprinted or reissued in new editions, largely, it seems, to satisfy the demand for school and university editions or for popular editions of works that an increasingly university-orientated critical establishment had made voguish. The 1939–45 war itself, in Britain at least, saw a significant increase in what can only be described as the professionalization of reading, with the establishment of the Army Education Corps, the Army Bureau of Current Affairs (which produced a regular flow of pamphlets for the soldiers to talk over in discussion groups under the supervision of their subalterns) and, in 1944, R.A. Butler's Education Act which, in effect, guaranteed that any ex-serviceman who wanted to be a schoolmaster after demobilization would be able to find a job in the rapidly growing secondary-education sector. This was the intellectual climate in which a more sophisticatedly literate poetry-and-novel-writing officer class wrote its more sophisticatedly literate poetry and novels.[7]

Of course not every writer took his ideas of symbolism from Kafka. Evelyn Waugh, already a successful humorous novelist before Kafka became known in western Europe, was one of those who looked to older sources of inspiration. Nothing in Waugh's sharp, sour, elegant pre-war novels suggested he would ever write a great war novel, not even the ending of *Vile Bodies*:

> The scene all round him was one of unrelieved desolation; a great expanse of mud in which every visible object was burnt or broken. Sounds of firing thundered from beyond the horizon, and somewhere above the grey clouds there were aeroplanes. He had had no sleep for thirty-six hours. It was growing dark.
>
> Presently he became aware of a figure approaching, painfully picking his way among the strands of barbed wire which strayed across the ground like drifting cobweb; a soldier clearly. As he came nearer Adam saw that he was levelling towards him a liquid fire projector. Adam tightened his fingers about his Huxdane-Halley bomb (for the dissemination of leprosy germs), and in this posture of mutual suspicion they met. Through the dusk Adam recognised the uniform of an English staff officer. He put the bomb back in his pocket and saluted.
>
> The newcomer lowered his liquid-fire projector and raised his gas mask. 'You're English, are you?' he said. 'Can't see a thing. Broken my damned monocle.'
>
> 'Why', said Adam. 'You're the drunk Major.'
>
> 'I'm not drunk, damn you, sir', said the drunk Major, 'and, what's more, I'm a General. What the deuce are *you* doing here?'
>
> 'Well,' said Adam. 'I've lost my platoon.'
>
> 'Lost your platoon . . . I've lost my whole bloody division!'

---

[7] Richard and Clara Winston, eds, *Franz Kafka: Letters to Friends. Family and Editors* (1978), pp. 137–38, Kafka to Max Brod, September 1917; Selwyn, ed., *Return to Oasis*, p. xix; *Whitaker's Almanack* (1913), p. 764, (1940), p. 1115.

Georg Friedrich Creuzer's *Symbolik und Mythologie der alten Völker, besonders der Griechen* was published in six vols, Leipzig and Darmstadt, 1810–23.

Nor, though he changed enormously as a writer during the 1940s, did he ever succeed in writing a great war novel: but he made several interesting dry runs.[8]

His first attempt, or gesture that might be seen as some sort of attempt, was *Put Out More Flags* (1942) which was stylistically and conceptually the last of his 1930s novels. Waugh himself explained in his 1966 Preface:

> This is the only book I have written purely for pleasure . . . After the fall of Crete the Commandos in the Middle East were disbanded, and officers and men returned to their regiments. I found myself in a comfortable liner, full below decks with Italian prisoners, returning to the United Kingdom by the long route round the Cape . . . I had comfort and leisure and negligible duties, a large cabin with a table and a pile of army stationery. I wrote all day, and the book was finished in a month.
>
> The characters about whom I had written in the previous decade came to life for me. I was anxious to know how they had been doing since I last heard of them . . .

Basil Seal's racket of extorting money in exchange for not billeting the three horrible Connolly evacuees is pure civilian humour. Alastair Trumpington, the baronet who insists on serving as a private, and Cedric Lyne, the unsoldierly re-employed regular officer, are weak early sketches for *The Sword of Honour* trilogy. Perhaps the best thing in the book is Ambrose Silk, 'sole representative of Atheism in the religious department' at the Ministry of Information and author of 'Monument to a Spartan', a paean to gay Nazi youth which sends Silk into exile and his publisher to Brixton Prison; but as Waugh admitted in his 1966 Preface, 'I had no personal knowledge of the Ministry of Information and relied on gossip for my caricature'. The novel is a very adequate evocation of the Phoney War, but the Phoney War had after all soon given way to the real shooting war, in which Waugh had been involved. In fact he had been thoroughly traumatized by his experiences in the Battle of Crete, and *Put Out More Flags* was written as a therapy, an exercise in escapism rather than in exorcism.

Next came *Brideshead Revisited* (1945), with its brilliant introductory vignette of Britain's civilian army in its campsite life in England.

---

[8] Evelyn Waugh, *Vile Bodies* (1932 edn), pp. 248–49 – first published 1930.

One's sense of its brilliance is by no means reduced by the recollection that Waugh had not been a junior officer in the army, but in the Royal Marines (a very different set up in Britain) and that when he did transfer to the army it was not to a third-rate county regiment such as Charles Ryder's, but to the ultra-exclusive Royal Horse Guards. In any case the army parts of the novel are simply the frame for what appears to be the main business, the wallowing in nostalgia for the era before 'spam, Nissen huts, black-out'. At the time of writing Waugh was feeling particularly negative about the way the world was going and *Brideshead Revisited* is in some ways reminiscent of Joseph Roth's *Radetzkymarsch* (1932) and Robert Musil's *Der Mann ohne Eigenschaften* (1930–43) in that all three novels look back to the period before hostilities commence. In *Brideshead Revisited* one tends to be so dazzled by the Oxford sequences with Lord Sebastian Flyte that it is difficult to focus on what the book is about: but when one recognizes what that is one sees that this isn't just another book that is about the war while pretending not to be, it is about something even more important than the war, something so important that even world war might fall into place as simply a link in a destined chain. *Brideshead Revisited* is a book about discovering Faith. Perhaps it would have been more convincing if this process had been signposted earlier, or if the Faith in question hadn't been Roman Catholicism, or if the Roman Catholic in question hadn't been Evelyn Waugh, or, even less plausibly, his protagonist Charles Ryder: nevertheless, turn it which way you will, that's what *Brideshead Revisited* is about, not about the war or nostalgia for before the war.[9]

Waugh's attempt to tackle the war head-on was *The Sword of Honour* trilogy: *War and Peace* in modern dress by an author who has lost hope in everything save the Catholic liturgy. Not inappropriately, in view of the comprehensive depressingness of world war, there is a waste of spirit at the middle of this work. It's the author of *Decline and Fall* failing to achieve maturity as a more serious type of novelist. The protagonist is a bore: Charles Ryder in *Brideshead Revisited* isn't quite such a bore and is adequate for his off-centre narrator role, but Crouchback is a failure. One sees that he is a kind of fictionalizing of

[9] Roth's and Musil's novels were both translated into English: Joseph Roth, *The Radetzky March* (1933); Robert Musil *The Man without Qualities* (1953).

Waugh's own situation and preoccupations, but one is constantly aware that Waugh himself was a more complex and far more striking personality, and apart from some of the minor threads – the career, for example, of Brigadier Ritchie Hook (apparently a conflation of Albert Clarence St Clair Morford, CO of the Royal Marine Brigade, and Lieutenant-General Sir Adrian Carton De Wiart, VC, who had one hand, one eye, and allegedly one testicle) – the whole thing reads as if it could have been done much better as a non-fiction memoir. Waugh himself was aware of his trilogy's shortcomings, writing of the first volume, 'It has some excellent farce, but only for a few pages. The rest is very dull. Well, the war was like that'. This is no more satisfying than the generality of excuses.[10]

The three most successful novels of the war – even if only *faute de mieux* – succeed largely, it seems, because they do not succumb to the kind of allegorical ambitions that tempted both Waugh and the disciples of Kafka. Graham Greene's *The Heart of the Matter* (1948) is perhaps his finest book, but one of his own least favourite. In his edition to the 1971 edition Greene claimed 'my writing had become rusty with disuse and misuse . . . The real fault . . . lay in the rustiness of my long inaction'. He recalled problems with the movements between one scene and another, and with narrative viewpoint. 'A dozen such technical questions tormented me as they had never done before the war . . . The scales to me seem too heavily weighted, the plot overloaded, the religious scruples of Scobie too extreme.' But the portrait given of individuals accelerated into their own personal catastrophes by the cruel logic of world war, with the comprehensible tragedies occurring only off stage, *was* the war for most people. The novel is set in Sierra Leone. At one point the protagonist, Scobie, the deputy commissioner of police at Freetown, is near the border with Vichy-controlled French Guinea:

> They stood on the verandah of the DC's bungalow at Pende and watched the torches move on the other side of the wide passive river. 'So that's France', Druce said, using the native term for it.
> Mrs Perrot said, 'Before the war we used to picnic in France'.

[10] *The Letters of Evelyn Waugh*, p. 370, Waugh to Graham Greene, 27 February 1952.

Survivors from a torpedoed ship are brought ashore. Mrs Perrot asks

> 'Does one ever get over a shock like that? Forty days in open boats.'
> 'If you survive at all,' the doctor said, 'you get over it. It's failure people don't get over, and this you see is a kind of success.'

Scobie, searching a Portuguese ship, finds a letter from Germany concealed in the cistern of the captain's WC.

> 'Oh, this war,' the captain burst out, 'how I hate this war.'
> 'We've got cause to hate it too, you know', said Scobie.

It is with such economical brush strokes, with references to air raid alarms and black-outs every month or so, and Helen Rolt's boasting of her school netball team, 'In 1940 we beat Roedean and tied with Cheltenham', that a conflagration spreading across three continents is sketched in. For a novel about people in wartime one doesn't really need very much more: and of course it would be difficult to imagine Scobie, or any other Graham Greene character, leading a platoon in an assault on the Siegfried Line or thumbing the gun-button on the joystick of a Spitfire.[11]

In Joseph Heller's *Catch-22* (1961: probably the most durable American novel of the 1939–45 conflict) there is much more of the sharp edge of war, but during the novel's comparatively long gestation period both the details and the sensibility that had first observed them had gone out of chronological focus. 'There was no debris', Heller writes of a crash at sea. 'Helicopters circled the white cloud till sunset.' Heller really had been an American bomber crewman in the Mediterranean, but he would have seen no rescue helicopters, for though the first helicopters had entered service with the USAAF by the end of the war, they were employed in other roles. Again, in a mode which Heller probably helped make fashionable, his American airmen make no secret of being scared shitless by German ground fire, whereas during the 1940s it was regarded as normal to pretend one wasn't in the least afraid. And the novel is so redolent of what was soon to be established as the characteristic humour of

---

[11] Graham Greene, *The Heart of the Matter* (1971 edn), pp. vii, xii, xiii; ibid., p. 123; ibid., p. 130; ibid., p. 49.

the 1960s that it seems irretrievably inserted into its period of publication. 'Don't walk on the grass – what would happen if everyone walked on the grass?' 'If everyone walked on the grass, I'd be a fool not to.' Whoever invented this form of wit, Heller was one of the first to exploit it. An oft-repeated exchange runs: 'Suppose everyone felt that way?' 'Then I'd certainly be a damned fool to feel any other way.' The Catch-22 of the title is founded on an analogous principle. 'Orr was crazy and could be grounded. All he had to do was ask; and as soon as he did, he would be no longer crazy and would have to fly more missions.' The same notion is transferred to private life: 'You won't marry me because I'm crazy, and you say I'm crazy because I want to marry you'.[12]

In *Catch-22* only an inconvenient few have any positive interest in the war: Nately, Appelby, Havermeyer, Captain Piltchard and Captain Wren. 'Nothing so wonderful as war had ever happened to them before, and they were afraid it might never happen to them again.' The main preoccupation of the senior officers is competition for power and promotion. The actual function of these senior officers often has little to do with defeating the enemy: 'General Peckem from Special Services, the man who gives us all our soft ball bats, comic books and USO shows'. Irrelevance of function is no obstacle to empire-building: when General Peckem's staff is joined by an extra colonel, Peckem realises that he can now ask for 'two additional majors, four additional captains, sixteen additional lieutenants and untold quantities of additional enlisted men, typewriters, desks, filing cabinets, automobiles . . .' Internecine strife amongst the senior officers is complicated by the inexplicable workings of the system of promotion: Scheisskopf, a colonel who has neither seen action nor filled a key post, is unexplainedly promoted to lieutenant-general; and a young man surnamed Major, whose father had sadistically had him christened Major Major, finds himself with the Air Force rank of major, and in command of a bomber squadron. Real power is in any case held elsewhere, by mythic figures such as ex-Private First Class Wintergreen, and the administration of the Air Force proceeds with a systematic disregard for reality that is impossible to check. Mudd, 'the dead man in Yossarian's tent', had

[12] Joseph Heller, *Catch-22* (London, 1962 edn), p. 103; ibid., p. 46; ibid., p. 158.

flown on a mission before he had officially reported for duty and
had been shot down, but not having officially reported for duty could
not be reported dead; Doc Daneeka is on the crew list of McWatt's
plane when it crashes, and though Doc Daneeka is actually standing on the ground amongst his fellow officers when the crash occurs, everyone regards him as dead, actually as well as officially. Within
this monolithically unresponsive bureaucracy certain forms of initiative are, paradoxically, welcomed: Milo Minderbender, who, in pursuit
of the goals of Free Enterprise, uses American planes and crews to
bomb American bases in fulfilment of a profitable contract with
the Germans, is greatly admired.[13]

Much of this is merely a more extreme formulation of what had
been written about by earlier writers: here for example is an account
of the empire building in the RAF in 1918:

> There was great elation when we learnt that a big scheme of expansion
> was going through and that we would all move up in the hierarchy . . .
> Every head of department wanted to out do his neighbour. Happy indeed
> was he who had three GSOs under him while his rival had only two!

The notion that the real enemy in war is not the opposing army but
one's own military system had been a theme of American fiction
especially, ever since John Dos Passos's *Three Soldiers* of 1922. One of
the most harrowing novels of the war era, James Jones's *From Here to
Eternity*, about life in the American army just before the Japanese attack on Pearl Harbor, dispenses with foreign belligerents for the first
forty-nine of its fifty-seven chapters. (The notion also appears in one
of the few Japanese war novels to have been rendered into English,
Hiroshi Noma's *Shinku chitai* – Tokyo, 1955; translated as *Zone of Empti-
ness*, Cleveland, 1956 – which ends with the protagonist shipped off
to the war zone after months of being ground down by the military
machine at home.) The vainglorious commanders who give orders
that are impossible to carry out had already had the appearance of a
cliché in Andreas Latzko's *Menschen in Kriege* (1917), where 'His Excellency, the Victor of –' asks, 'Since when is the commander instructed

[13] Ibid., p. 144; ibid., pp. 322–23; ibid., p. 312; ibid., p. 382; ibid., p. 106–7; ibid.,
p. 333–35.

by the officers under him as to what is possible . . .?' Again, the subordination of the national objectives of the war to business opportunism had been a theme of peace campaigners in the 1930s, and, apparently, occurred even in Nazi Germany:

> 'From Soeft's point of view,' said Asch 'the whole war is just one big business deal . . . Sometimes I think that in his eyes there are no fronts, and no enemies, only good opportunities and different people to do business with.'

The paradox of ex-Pfc Wintergreen, combining the minimum of rank with the maximum of influence, is reminiscent of the *aides de camp* in *War and Peace* who behave so superciliously to mere generals, and has a parallel in the War Office clerk in Anthony Powell's *The Military Philosophers* (1968):

> His rank . . . usually so manifest in every civil servant, seemed in Blackhead's case to have become blurred by time and attrition. To whom was he responsible? Whom – if anyone – did he transcend? Obviously in the last resort he was subservient to the Permanent Under-Secretary of State for War, and Blackhead himself would speak of Assistant Under Secretaries – even of Principals – as if their ranks represented unthinkable heights of official attainment. On the other hand, none of these people seemed to have the will, even the power, to control him. It was as if Blackhead, relatively humble though his grading might be, had become an anonymous immanence of all their kind, a fetish, the Voodoo deity of the whole Civil Service to be venerated and placated, even if better – safer – hidden away out of sight: the mystic holy essence incarnate of arguing, encumbering, delaying, hair-splitting, all for the best of reasons.

Even the oft-repeated threat in *Catch-22* that recalcitrant officers would be posted to the Pacific theatre seems merely an imitation of the supposedly standard threat in the German armed forces, that if one didn't toe the line one would be sent to the Russian Front. (An early version of this is in Jaroslav Hašek's *The Good Soldier Schweik* where Major-General von Schwarzburg 'had a mania for transferring officers to the most unpleasant places'; but in the Second World War the crews of multi-engined bombers might actually have preferred the Pacific to the Mediterranean since they would be equally safe from enemy ground troops, and Japanese Anti-Aircraft fire was far less formidable than German *Flak*.) But *Catch-22* is likely to survive as the classic presentation of these and other myths. If it is not an entirely satisfactory book – comic novels about unfunny subjects rarely are entirely satisfactory – as an attempt to explore some of the issues of the combatant's life, written by a combatant, it is an unusual achievement. Yet its anachronism in both tone and detail do suggest that an easy way – perhaps the easiest practical way – of handling such themes is to remove oneself as far as possible from the framework of reference within which the issues were originally encountered, as if one could see the more clearly the further off one stood from the subject.[14]

Authorial strategies of this kind depend on opportunity and the peculiarity of individual personality. In *Kaputt* (1944), the first of Curzio Malaparte's two internationally celebrated war novels, the author's unsurprised tone and his cast of eminent but marginal characters in picturesque but tangential places – Swedish princes, Spanish diplomats, Romanians, Finns, future Nuremberg defendant Hans Frank holding court in Cracow with boxer Max Schmeling in attendance – suggest that such wars have been recurring since the beginning of time, and that the only novelty is in the new refinements of human degradation: and though Malaparte does perhaps overdo the world-weariness he had after all fought in a previous world war, enjoyed a reputation as a trouble-maker during the Fascist era, experienced imprisonment, and been on hand when both other countries and his own were bombed and invaded. His masterpiece *La pelle* (1949; English translation published as *The Skin*, 1952 – a memorable Franco-Italian film, 1980) describes the American occupation of Naples, with disillusioned American GIs queuing up to look at the last virgin left in the city, and wig-makers enjoying a roaring trade in blonde pubic wigs ('Your negroes like blondes,

---

[14] John Evelyn Wrench, *Struggle: 1914–1920* (1935), p. 244; Andreas Latzko, *Men in Battle* (1918), p. 140; Hans Hellmut Kirst, *Gunner Asch Goes to War* (1978 edn), p. 66 – originally published as *Null-acht funfzehn: die seltsamen Kriegserlebnisse des Soldaten Asch* (Munich, 1954) but generally known in German as *08/15 Im Krieg*, and cf. Fenner Brockway, *The Bloody Traffic* (1933), pp. 14–18, 60ff; Leo Tolstoy, *War and Peace*, iii, ch. ix; Anthony Powell, *The Military Philosophers* (1968), pp. 38, 40; Jaroslav Hašek, *The Good Soldier Schweik* (1951 edn), p. 204, first published as *Osudy Dobrého Vojáka Švejka za Světové Války* (Prague, 1921–23).

and Neapolitan girls are dark'). Most if not all of his stories are fabrication, yet none more nightmarish or bizarre than what really happened:

> Thousands and thousands of unfortunate people, dripping with burning phosphorus, had thrown themselves into the canals which cross Hamburg in every direction, into the river, the harbour, into ponds, even into the basins in public gardens, hoping thereby to extinguish the flames that were devouring them ... Clinging to the banks and to boats and immersed in the water up to their mouths, or buried in the earth up to their necks, they waited for the authorities to find some antidote to those treacherous flames. For the nature of phosphorus is such that it adheres to the skin like a sticky leprous crust, and burns only when it comes in contact with the air ...
>
> For a few days Hamburg presented the appearance of Dis, the infernal city. Here and there in the squares, in the streets, in the canals, in the Elbe, thousands and thousands of heads projected from the water and from the ground, looking as though they had been lopped off by the headsman's axe. Livid with terror and pain, they moved their eyes, opened their mouths and spoke. Those horrible heads, wedged between the paving-stones of the streets or floating on the surface of the water, were visited night and day by their doomed owners' relatives, an emaciated, ragged throng, who spoke in low voices, as if to avoid intensifying their excruciating agony ... Packs of dogs ran hither and thither, barking and licking the faces of their interred masters, or jumping into the water and swimming out to help them ...
>
> The bravest and the most patient were the children. They did not cry or call out, but looked about them with serene eyes, gazing at the fearful spectacle, and smiled at their relatives, with that wonderful resignation so characteristic of children, who forgive the impotence of their seniors, and pity those who cannot help them. As soon as night fell a whispering arose on all sides, a murmuring, as of the wind in the grass, and those thousands and thousands of heads watched the sky with eyes that were bright with terror ...

Malaparte's exaggerations achieve an almost surreal effect; but that surely is the objective of fiction: to show the essence of reality, in a way that would not be quite possible from a careful transcription of ascertainable facts:

'Dance with my friend', said Gerda, pushing Lanza into the arms of the girl who looked like Diana, and with innocent grace pulling the fat, slow-moving Ridomi towards her by the hand. The other four girls had split up into couples and were dancing languidly, each pressing her bosom and hips close against her partner's. Lanza's partner clung tightly to him and gazed into his eyes, smiling and constantly fluttering her eyelids . . .

Suddenly the music stopped . . . and a hoarse, breathless voice announced: 'Before we read the proclamation by Marshal Badoglio here is a summary of the latest news. At about six o'clock this evening the Head of the Government, Mussolini, was arrested by order of His Majesty the King. The new Head of the Government, Marshal Badoglio, has addressed the following proclamation to the Italian people . . .'

At the sound of that voice, of those words, Lanza's partner broke away from him, repelling him with a shove that seemed to Lanza like a blow of the fist . . . As Lanza and Ridomi stood face to face with the young women they were conscious of the same bewilderment and terror as had seized Apollo when Daphne was transformed from a young girl into a laurel before his eyes. In the space of a few seconds those fair-haired, gentle girls turned into men. They *were* men.

'Ach, so!' said the one who a moment before had looked like Diana, in a harsh voice, staring at the two Italian diplomats with a menacing expression. 'Ach, so! Do you think you can get away with it? Do you think the Führer will let you arrest Mussolini without bashing your heads in?' And turning to his companions, 'Let's go to the camp at once', he went on. 'I've no doubt our squadron has already received orders to start. In a few hours we shall be bombing Rome.'

'Jawohl, mein Hauptmann', answered the four Air Force officers, clicking their heels loudly.[15]

It may seem perverse however to accord any high place to fiction relating to a war in which unpalatable realities were brought home to more people, with more detail, precision and rapidity, than in any previous conflict: and after all it had been the memoirs (including the slightly fictionalized ones) rather than the deliberately fictive novels that constituted the most important part of the prose writing about the previous world war. Moreover, though there were some memorable First World War accounts of unusual experiences (*Seven*

---

[15] Curzio Malaparte, *The Skin* (1952), pp. 126–29, referring to the aftermath of the bombing of Hamburg in July 1943; ibid., pp. 134–35.

Pillars of Wisdom, for example, or Plüschow's *Das Abenteuer des Fliegers von Tsingtau*), the emphasis in First World War writing was on experiences that were widely – too widely – shared, whereas amongst the most striking personal testimonies of the Second World War are those that by their very nature must be almost unique: *The Diary of Anne Frank*, Rudolf Höss's *Commandant in Auschwitz*, Primo Levi's *If This Is a Man*, Ryuji Nagatsuka's *I Was a Kamikaze*, the poems written by Miklós Radnóti while guarded by the Hungarian soldiers who were soon to kill him, and recovered from his sodden pockets when his remains were exhumed more than a year and a half later:

> Kilenc kilométerre innen égnek
> a kazlak és a házak,
> s a rétek szélein megülve némán
> riadt pórok pipáznak.
> Itt még vizet fodroz a tóra lépő
> apró pásztorleány
> s felhőt iszik a vízre ráhajolva
> a fodros birkanyáj.

(Nine kilometres from here the haystacks and the houses are burning and at the edges of the fields scared peasants sit in silence smoking their pipes. Here a little shepherdess crinkles the water as she steps on the lake and her crinkly flock bending over the water drink clouds.) Amongst these personal testimonies is one that is unusual in that, of all the first-hand memoirs by men who distinguished themselves by their aptitude for killing other people, it has a freshness and a vividness and a gracefulness that make it one of the finest books ever written about war. It is much less well-known in university circles than Ernst Jünger's *In Stahlgewittern*, which by comparison is ponderous and self-conscious, but it has been translated into thirty-four languages and, according to one commentator, 'will remain the classic book of the 1939–45 war'. Pierre Clostermann's *Le grand cirque* (Paris 1948; translated as *The Big Show*, 1951), based on letters written while winning the Distinguished Service Order and the Distinguished Flying Cross with bar as a pilot with the Royal Air Force, has essentially the same origin as a number of books by RAF personnel published during the war itself, with titles like *Fighter Pilot* or *Bomber Pilot* or *Spitfire Pilot* or, by way of variety, *Tail Gunner*: but these, by comparison with Clostermann's account, are grey and stodgy:

> 'Focke-Wulfs eleven o'clock, Yellow!'
> Led by a magnificent Fw 190 A-6 painted yellow all over and polished and gleaming like a jewel, the first were already passing on our left, less than a hundred yards away, and turning towards us. I could see, quite distinctly, outlined on their long transparent cockpits, the German pilots crouching forward.
> 'Come on, Turban Yellow, attack!'
> Martell had already dived straight into the enemy formation. Yellow 3 and Yellow 4 immediately lost contact and left us in the middle of a whirlpool of yellow noses and black crosses. This time I did not even have time to feel really frightened. Although my stomach contracted, I could feel a frantic excitement rising within me. This was the real thing, and I lost my head slightly. Without realizing it I was giving vent to incoherent Redskin war-whoops and throwing my Spitfire about.
> A Focke-Wulf was already breaking away, dragging after him a spiral of black smoke, and Martell, who was not wasting any time, was after the scalp of another. I did my best to play my part and back him up and give him cover, but he was far ahead and I had some difficulty in following his rolls and Immelmann turns.
> Two Huns converged insidiously on his tail. I opened fire on them, although they were out of range. I missed them, but made them break off and make for me. Here was my opportunity!
> I climbed steeply, did a half-roll and, before they could complete the 180° of their turn, there I was – within easy range this time – behind the second one. A slight pressure on the rudder and I had him in my sights. I could scarcely believe my eyes, only a simple deflection necessary, at less than 200 yards range. Quickly I squeezed the firing-button. Whoopee! Flashes all over his fuselage. My first burst had struck home and no mistake.
> The Focke-Wulf caught alight at once. Tongues of flame escaped intermittently from his punctured tanks, licking the fuselage. Here and there incandescent gleams showed through the heavy black smoke surrounding the machine. The German pilot threw his plane into a desperate turn. Two slender white trails formed in the air.
> Suddenly, the Focke-Wulf exploded like a grenade. A blinding flash, a black cloud, then debris fluttered round my aircraft. The engine dropped like a ball of fire. One of the wings, torn off in the flames, dropped more slowly, like a dead leaf, showing its pale yellow under-surface and its olive green upper-surface alternately.

I bellowed my joy into the radio, just like a kid:
'Hullo, Yellow One, Turban Yellow Two, I got one, I got one! Jesus, I got one of them!'

Clostermann's first 'kill' provides a fitting note on which to conclude, for it was *The Big Show* which, more than any other book, first interested the author of this study in the literature of war.[16]

---

[16] Miklós Radnóti, short poem which he called a *Razglednica* (Croatian word for picture postcard), written 6 October 1944 at Cservenka, in *Művei* (Budapest, 1976), p. 241, translated with the assistance of Enikő Nagy; *Pierre Clostermann: une sacrée guerre! Daniel Costelle questionne et enregistre les réponses de l'auteur sur sa vie, sa guerre et ses aventures, 1921–1945* (Paris, 1990), p. 17; Pierre Clostermann *The Big Show* (1958 paperback edn), pp. 40–41: Clostermann was officially credited with shooting down thirty-three German aircraft, with twelve probables.

Fighter Pilot, by Paul Richey, was published in 1941; *Bomber Pilot*, by Leonard Cheshire – later Group Captain Leonard Cheshire VC, DSO and two bars, DFC – was published in 1943; D.M. Crook's *Spitfire Pilot* came out in 1942 and R.C. Rivaz's *Tail Gunner* in 1943.

APPENDIX

Charles Napier at La Coruña

Written in 1810, first published in William Napier's *The Life and Opinions of General Sir C.J. Napier* (4 vols, 1857), i, pp. 94–95, 97–104. See page 19 above.

THE IMPERIAL TROOPS, on higher ground, hung over us like threatening clouds, and about one o'clock the storm burst. Our line was under arms, silent, motionless, yet all were anxious for the appearance of Sir John Moore. There was a feeling that under him we could not be beaten, and this was so strong at all times as to be a great cause of discontent during the retreat wherever he was not. Where is the general? was now heard along that part of the line where I was, for only of what my eyes saw, and my ears heard, do I speak. This agitation augmented as the cries of men stricken by cannon-shot arose. I stood in front of my left wing, on a knoll, from whence the greatest part of the field could be seen, and my picquets were fifty yards below, disputing the ground with the French skirmishers: but a heavy French column, which had descended the mountain at a run, was coming on behind with great rapidity, and shouting *En avant, tue, tue, en avant tue!* their cannon at the same time, plunging from above, ploughed the ground and tore our ranks. Suddenly I heard the gallop of horses, and turning saw Moore. He came at speed, and pulled up so sharp and close he seemed to have alighted from the air; man and horse looking at the approaching foe with an intenseness that seemed to concentrate all feeling in their eyes. The sudden stop of the animal, a cream-coloured one with black tail and mane, had cast the latter streaming forward, its ears were pushed out like horns, while its eyes flashed fire, and it snorted loudly with expanded nostrils, expressing terror, astonishment and muscular exertion. My first thought was, it will be away like the wind! but then I looked at the rider and the horse was forgotten. Thrown on its haunches the animal came, sliding and dashing the dirt up with its fore feet, thus bending the general forward almost to its neck; but his head was thrown back and his look more keenly piercing than I ever before saw it. He glanced to the right and the left, and then fixed his eyes intently on the enemy's advancing column, at the same time grasping the reins with both his hands, and pressing the horse firmly with his knees: his body thus seemed to deal with the animal while his mind was intent on the enemy, and his aspect was one of searching intenseness beyond the power of words to describe: for a while he looked, and then galloped to the left, without uttering a word . . .

I walked up and down before the regiment, and made the men shoulder and order arms twice to occupy their attention, for they were falling fast and seemed uneasy at standing under fire. The colours also were lowered, because they were a mark for the enemy's great guns: this was by the advice of old John Montgomery, a brave soldier who had risen from the ranks. Soon the 42nd advanced in line, but no orders came for me. Good God! Montgomery, I said, are we not to advance? I think we ought he answered. But said I, no orders have come. I would not wait he said. The 4th did not move, the 42nd seemed likely to want our aid, it was not a moment for hesitation, and John Montgomery, a Scotchman, said laughingly You cannot be wrong to follow the 42nd. I gave the word but forbad any firing, and to prevent and occupy the men's attention, made them slope and carry arms by word of command. Many of them cried out, Major let us fire! Not yet was my answer, for having advanced without orders, I thought to have them more under command if we were wrong, whereas, firing once begun, we could not change. At that moment the 42nd checked a short distance from a wall and commenced firing, and though a loud cry arose of Forward! forward! no man, as I afterwards heard, passed the wall. This check seemed to prove that my advance was right, and we passed the 42nd. Then I said to my men, Do you see your enemies plain enough to hit them? Many voices shouted By Jesus we do! Then blaze away! and such a rolling fire broke out as I have hardly ever heard since.

After passing the 42nd we came to the wall, which was breast high and my line checked, but several officers, Stanhope one, leaped over, calling on the men to follow. At first about a hundred did at a low part, no more, and therefore, leaping back, I took a halberd and holding it horizontally pushed many over the low part; and again getting over myself, run along, followed by my orderly sergeant, Keene, with his pike. As we passed, four or five soldiers levelled together from the other side, but Keene threw up their muskets with a force and quickness which saved me from being blown to atoms, as it was my face was much burned: then all got over, yet it required the example of officers and the bravest men to get all over.

Now the line was formed beyond the wall, and I, recollecting Voltaire's story of the guards' officers laying their swords over the men's firelocks to keep their level low, did so with the halberd to show coolness, and being cool, though the check at the wall had excited me and made me swear horribly. We then got to marshy ground close to a village, where the fire from the houses was terrible, the howitzers from the hills pelting us also. Still I led the men on, followed closely by Ensigns Moore and Stewart with the colours until both fell, and the colours were caught up by Sergeant Magee and another sergeant. My sword-belt was shot off, scabbard and all, but not being hit I pushed rapidly into the street, exactly at the spot where, soon after, I was taken prisoner. Many Frenchmen lay there, apparently dead, but the soldiers cried out bayonet them, they are pretending. The idea was to me terrible, and made me call out No! No! Leave those cowards, there are plenty who bear arms to kill, come on!

At this place stood the church and towards the enemy a rocky mound, behind which, and on it, were the grenadiers; but no officer met my sight, except Captain Harrison, Lieutenant Patterson, and Lieutenant Turner, and my efforts were vain to form a strong body; the men would not leave the rocks, from which they kept up a heavy fire. No time was to be lost, we could not see what passed on our flanks, we had been broken in carrying the village of Elviña, and as a lane went up straight towards the enemy, I run forward calling out to follow: about thirty privates and the above-named officers did so, but the fire was then terrible, many shells burst among us, and the crack of these things deafened me, making my ears ring. Half way up the lane I fell, without knowing why, but was much hurt, though at the moment unconscious of it; a soldier cried out the major is killed. Not yet, come on.

We reached the end of this murderous lane, but a dozen of those who entered with me fell ere we got through it. However some shelter was found beyond the lane; for Brooks of the 4th had occupied the spot with his picquet the day before, and had made a breastwork of loose stones, which was known to me, having been there, and nearly killed the evening before, when visiting the picquet as officer of the day. The heap remained and about a dozen of us lodged ourselves behind this breastwork, and then it appeared to me that by a rush forward we could carry the battery above; and it was evident we must go on or go back, we could not last long where we were. Three or four men were killed at my side, for the breastwork was but a slender protection, and two were killed by the fire of our own men from the village behind. The poor fellows kept crying out as they died, Oh God! Major, our own men are killing us! Oh Christ God I'm shot in the back of the head! The last man was so, for he fell against me, and the ball had entered just above the poll. Remembering then that my father had told me he saved a man's life, at the siege of Charleston, by pulling a ball out with his finger before inflammation swelled the parts, I thought to do the same, but could not find it, and feared to do harm by putting my finger far in. It made me feel sick, and the poor fellow being laid down, continued crying out that our men had killed him, and there he soon died.

This misery shook us all a good deal, and made me so wild as to cry and stamp with rage, feeling a sort of despair at seeing the soldiers did not come on. I sent Turner, Harrison and Patterson, the three officers with me, to bring them on, and they found Stanhope animating the men, but not knowing what to do, and calling out Good God where is Napier? When Turner told him I was in front and raging for them to come on for an attack on the battery, he gave a shout and called on the men to follow him, but ere taking a dozen strides cried out Oh my God! and fell dead, shot through the heart. Turner, and a sergeant who had been also sent back, then returned to me, saying they could not get a man to follow them up the lane. Hearing this, I got on the wall, waving my sword and my hat at the same time, and calling out to the men behind among the rocks; but the fire was so loud none heard me, though the lane was scarcely a hundred yards long. No fire was drawn upon me by this, for a French captain afterwards told me he, and others, prevented their men firing at me; he did not know, nor was he told by me, who it was, but he said, instead of firing at him I longed to run forwards and embrace that brave officer. My own companions called out to jump down or I should be killed: I thought so too, but was so mad as to care little what happencd to me.

Looking then along the field, from the height of the wall, our smoke appeared to be everywhere retiring; but the French smoke was not advancing, which gave me comfort. However it was useless to stay there, and jumping down I said to Harrison, Stay here as long as you can, I will go to the left and try to make out how the 42nd get on. No one was to be seen near our left from my standing place near the wall; but there was some brushwood, and a ridge with a hedge on the top which debarred further sight, and the thought came to me that instead of being foremost, we might be in line with some of the 42nd – and though the 4th had not advanced, if fifty men of the 42nd and 50th could be gathered, we might still charge the battery above us; if we failed there was a house near, into which we could force our way, and as it was conspicuous from the English position Moore would send me support.

Telling this to Captain Harrison, I went off along a lane running at right angles from the one we were in, and parallel to our position; this exposed me to the English not to the French fire, but being armed with only a short sabre, useless against a musket and bayonet, and being quite alone, shortsighted, and without spectacles, I felt very cowardly and anxious. Pursuing my course however for about a hundred yards, I came near a French officer lying on his back wounded, and being myself covered with blood and my face smeared, for two of the killed men had fallen in my arms, my look was no doubt fierce; and though I approached him out of pity, he thought it was to kill him: His feet were towards me and as he raised his head he cried out to some comrades above him, pointing with a quick convulsive motion towards me. Those whom he addressed could not be seen, for the ridge was about six feet high, nearly perpendicular, with the thick hedge at top; but my danger was soon announced through the roots of the hedge by a blaze of fire poured so close as to fill the lane with smoke. All went over my head, being evidently fired without seeing me, or my body must have been blown to pieces.

Giving myself up for lost, the temptation to run back was great, but the thought that our own line might see me, made me walk leisurely, in more danger indeed yet less alarmed than when going forward without knowing what would happen. The whole excursion along the lane was the most nervous affair I ever experienced in battle; nor was my alarm lessened on getting back, for Harrison and the others were gone! They could not stand the fire. I felt very miserable then, thinking the 50th had behaved ill; that my not getting the battery had been a cause of the battle being lost, and that Moore would attribute all to me. The English smoke had gone back, and my only comfort was that the French smoke had not gone forward. The battle seemed nearly over, I thought myself the last man alive belonging to our side who had got so far in front, and felt certain of death, and that my general would think I had hidden myself, and would not believe me to have done my best. I thought also my little party had been taken. Lord William Bentinck afterwards told me that he had ordered my regiment back, in direct contradiction of Moore's design, who had, he admitted, told him not to recall me, but send men to my assistance!!!

In this state of distraction, and still under a heavy fire, I turned down the lane to rejoin the regiment and soon came on a wounded man, who shrieked out, Oh praised be God major! my dear major! God help you my darling, one of your own 50th. I cannot carry you, was my reply; can you walk with my help? Oh no major I am too badly wounded. You must lie there then till help can be found. Oh Christ God, my jewel, my own dear major sure you won't leave me! The agony with which he screamed was great, it roused all my feelings, and strange to say alarmed me about my own danger, which had been forgot in my misery at finding Harrison was gone from the corner, and thinking the battle lost. Stooping down, I raised the poor fellow, but a musket-ball just then broke the small bone of my leg some inches above the ankle; the pain was acute and though the flesh was not torn, the dent made in my flesh remains to this day and is tender to the touch! Telling the man of my own wound, my course was resumed; his piteous cries were then terrible, and fell bitterly as reproaches for my want of fortitude and courage. Yet what could be done by a man hardly able to walk, and in great pain, with other duties to perform? I felt it horrible to leave him, but selfishness and pain got the better, and with the help of my sword, limping and with much suffering, I arrived at a spot where two other lanes met at the corner of a church: there were three privates of the 50th, and one of the 42nd, an Irishman, there, who said we were cut off, and indeed Frenchmen were then coming up both lanes, one party from the position of the 50th and the other from that of the 4th. The last appeared the least numerous and the nearest, they were not thirty yards from us, and forgetting my leg then, though I had not pluck to do so for the poor wounded man left behind, I said to the four soldiers, follow me and we'll cut through them: then with a shout I rushed forward.

The Frenchmen had halted, but now run on to us, and just as my spring and shout was made the wounded leg failed and I felt a stab in the back: it gave me no pain, but felt cold and threw me on my face. Turning to rise I saw the man who had stabbed me making a second thrust; whereupon letting go my sabre I caught his bayonet by the socket, turned the thrust and raising myself by the exertion grasped his firelock with both hands, thus in mortal struggle regaining my feet. His companions had now come up and I heard the dying cries of the four men with me, who were all bayoneted instantly. We had been attacked from behind by men not before seen, as we stood with our backs to a doorway, out of which must have rushed several men, for we were all stabbed in an instant, before the two parties coming up the road reached us: they did so however just as my struggle with the man who had wounded me was begun. That was a contest for life, and being the strongest, I forced him between myself and his comrades, who appeared to be the men whose lives I had saved when they pretended to be dead in our advance through the village. They struck me with their muskets clubbed, and bruised me much; whereupon, seeing no help near, and being overpowered by numbers, and in great pain from my wounded leg, I called out *Je me rend.*

Index of Personal Names

Adam, Albrecht (1786–1862), 16
Adams, Bernard (1890–1917), 99, 166
Addison, Joseph (1672–1719), 8, 9
Addison, Rev. William Robert Fountaine (1883–1962), 138
Adler, Rev. Michael (1868–1944), 138
Alain-Fournier, Henri: *nom de plume* of Henri-Alban Fournier (1886–1914), 103, 104
Aldington, May (fl. 1892–1917), 195
Aldington, Richard (1892–1962), 81, 90, 101, 102, 126, 150, 166, 171–72, 182, 194–95, 240
Aldridge, James (1918–   ), 285
Allott, Kenneth (1912–1973), 278–79
Altdorfer, Albrecht (*c.* 1486–1538), 4, 111
Amiel, Barry (fl. 1940–46), 282
Andersen, Lale: stage name of Lise-Lotte Helene Berta Bunnenberg (1905–1972), 78
Angiviller, Charles-Claude de la Billarderie, *Comte* d' (1730–1809), 12
Apollinaire, Guillaume: pseudonym of Wilhelm Apollinaris de Kostrowitzki, (1880–1918), 103, 107, 161–62, 241
Arnauld de la Perière, Lothar, *Kapitänleutnant*, afterwards *Vizeadmiral* (1886–1941), 272
Auden, Wystan Hugh (1907–1973), 41
Austen, Jane (1775–1817), 22, 23

Bacler d'Albe Louis Albert Guillain, *Baron*, *Général de Brigade* (1761–1824), 15, 16
Bainbrigge, Phillip (d. 1918), 175
Baldwin, William Charles (fl. 1852–63), 203, 204
Ball, Albert (1896–1917), 192, 205, 210–11
Baracca, Franco, *Maggiore* (1888–1918), 213
Barbauld, Anna Laetitia (1743–1825), 40

Barbusse, Henri (1873–1935), 86, 87, 169, 183–84, 185, 221, 222, 224, 237, 244, 248, 288
Barker, William George, Lieutenant-Colonel (1894–1930), 211, 213
Baron, Alexander (1917–   ), 288
Bartlett, Vernon (1894–1983), 130–31, 187, 236
Bates, Herbert Ernest (1905–1974), 270
Baur, Fritz (fl. 1914–29), 228
Beaverbrook, William Maxwell Aitken, 1st Baron (1879–1964), 126
Beers, Ethel Lynn (1827–1879), 52, 53
Beresford, Rev. William, Lieutenant-Colonel (1875–1917), 138
Berkoff, Steven (1937–   ), 271
Beumelburg, Werner (1899–1963), viii, 169–70, 186, 223, 225, 229, 232, 247, 248
Bierce, Ambrose (1842–1914), 52
Bingham, Ralph Charles, Lieutenant-Colonel (1885–1977), 267
Binyon, Laurence (1869–1943), 77, 278
Birkin, Henry Ralph Stanley ('Tim') (1896–1933), 196
Bishop, William Avery, Lieutenant-Colonel, afterwards Air Marshal (1894–1956), 122, 204–5, 209, 211, 272, 273, 276
Blackburne, Rev. Harry William (1878–1963), 138
Blake, William (1757–1827), 178
Blamey, Sir Thomas, General, afterwards Field Marshal (1884–1951), 277
Blixen, Karen (1885–1962), 170
Bloem, Walter (1868–1951), 54, 59
Blok, Alexander (1880–1921), 100
Bloomfield, Robert (1766–1823), 34
Blunden, Edmund (1896–1974), 84, 86, 126, 127, 130, 134, 141, 180, 247

140 n. 16, 141, 172–73, 184, 193, 252, 276, 278, also quoted 73
Scharf, Georg (1788–1860), 16
Schauwecker, Franz (1890–1964), 223–24, 225, 247
Scheel, Gunther (d. 1943), 272
Schlemmer, Oskar (1888–1943), 108
Schnack, Anton (1892–1973), 126
Schramm, Wilhelm von, quoted 198
Schreuer, Wilhelm (1866–1933), 112
Schuller, Victor (fl. 1939–58), 289
Scott, Michael (1789–1835), 48, 49
Scott, Walter (1771–1832), 26–27, 28, 41
Seeger, Alan (1888–1916), 173, 174
Seldte, Franz (1882–1947), 185
Serres, Dominic (1722–1793), 12
Shakespeare, William (1564–1616), i, 4–5, 85, 184, 270, 281
Sharpe, Charles Kirkpatrick (1781?–1851), 22
Shaw, Irwin (1913–1984), 286–88
Shelley, Percy Bysshe (1792–1822), 40, 48
Sherriff, Robert Cedric (1896–1975), 95, 126, 137
Simms, William Gilmore (1806–1870), 51
Simonov, Konstantin Mikhailovich (1915–), 263
Sitwell, Osbert (1892–1969), 84–85, 101–2, 117, 118, 276, 278, also quoted 97
Slessor, Kenneth (1901–71), 277 and n. 13
Smith, Archibald William (fl. 1914–63), 96
Smith, Helen Zenna: pseudonym of Evadne Price (1901–1985), 140
Smylie, Gilbert Formby, Squadron Leader, afterwards Air Commodore (1895–1965), 205
Snook, J.F. (fl. 1914–30), 139–40, also quoted 167
Sorley, Charles Hamilton (1895–1915), 177, 247, 278, also quoted 167–68
South, John Flint (1797–1882), 24
Southey, Robert (1774–1843), 41–43, 164
Soy, Emmanuel (fl. 1914–18), 72
Springs, Elliott White (1896–1959), 129–30
Starrett, David (fl. 1914–18), 157
Steinbeck, John (1902–1968), 290
Stendhal: pseudonym of Henri Beyle (1783–1842), 30–31, 65–66
Stenner, Hermann (1891–1914), 107
Sterne, Laurence (1713–1768), 10–11, 84
Storck, Abraham (1644–1708), 11–12

Stramm, August (1874–1915), 82, 86, 164–65, 172
Strange, J.D. (fl. 1914–32), 166
Studdert Kennedy, Rev. G.A., *see* Kennedy, Rev. George Anketell Studdert
Synge, John Millington (1871–1909), 268

Tallents, Thomas Francis (1896–1947), 195
Tandey, Henry (1891–1977), 214–15
Tawney, Richard Henry (1880–1962), 89–90
Taylor, Ward (fl. 1941–56), 289
Tennyson, Alfred, 1st Baron (1809–92), 47–48, 62, 79, 85, 237, 269–70
Thomas, Edward (1878–1917), 97–98, 261
Tolstoy, Lev Nikolayevich, *Graf* (1828–1910), 19, 31, 64–66, 165, 181, 182, 268, 285
Tönnies, Ferdinand (1855–1936), 231
Toti, Enrico (1882–1916), 214
Toynbee, Arnold (1889–1975), 102
Trakl, Georg (1887–1914), 92, 226
Treece, Henry (1912–1966), 278
Trelawny, Edward John (1792–1881), 48
Trollope, Anthony (1815–1882), 81, 271
Twain, Mark: pseudonym of Samuel Langhorne Clemens (1835–1910), 52

Uccello, Paolo (1397–1475), 3, 115
Udet, Ernst (1896–1941), 228
Uhland, Ludwig (1787–1862), 179–80
Ungaretti, Giuseppe (1888–1970), 72, 81–82, 172
Unruh, Fritz von (1885–1970), 185
Uris, Leon (1924–), 288

Vachell, Horace Annesley (1861–1955), 60
Vallotton, Félix (1865–1925), 111
Vaughan, Edwin Campion (1897–1931), quoted 191–92
Vaugoin, Carl (1873–1949), 249
Vercors: pseudonym of Jean Marcel Bruller (1902–1991), 259
Vernet, Horace (1789–1863), 16
Verney, John (1913–1993), 262–63
Vic, Jean (1896–1925), 72
Vidal, Gore (1925–), 291
Villon, Jacques (1875–1963), 106
Volkmann, Ernst (1881–?), 226–27, 231
Voss, Julius von (1768–1832), 32
Vring, Georg von der (1889–1968), 127, 222
Vulovici, Nicolae (1877–1916), 100, 103, 104

Wadsworth, Edward (1889–1949), 111